# Dark Memories

## LIZ MISTRY

ONE PLACE. MANY STORIES

HQ
An imprint of HarperCollins*Publishers* Ltd
1 London Bridge Street
London SE1 9GF

www.harpercollins.co.uk

HarperCollins*Publishers*
1st Floor, Watermarque Building, Ringsend Road
Dublin 4, Ireland

This paperback edition 2021

This edition published in Great Britain by
HQ, an imprint of HarperCollins*Publishers* Ltd 2021

ISBN: 9780008358396

MIX
Paper from
responsible sources
FSC
www.fsc.org          FSC™ C007454

This book is produced from independently certified FSC™ paper
to ensure responsible forest management.

For more information visit: www.harpercollins.co.uk/green

Printed and bound in Great Britain by
CPI Group (UK) Ltd, Melksham, SN12 6TR

*To my family, you always have my back and you keep me strong even when the Black Dog bites xxx*

# Prologue

## December 1993

Layla sat at the dressing table applying a coat of red lip gloss. The light from the unshaded bulb exposed the room's shabbiness. She paused, looking at the reflection of her two children in the mirror. They were leaning against the wall, a duvet wrapped around their shoulders at the top of the grubby single mattress that lay on the floor. An episode of *Teenage Mutant Ninja Turtles* was playing on the crappy telly that she'd positioned on an upturned box at the end of their bed. Her oldest was speaking. 'I'll be Raphael; you can be Donatello.'

'You're *always* Raphael. I want to be Raphael.'

'But Donatello's the clever one. Don't you want to be the clever one?'

Head to one side, Layla's youngest acquiesced. 'Okay. But you got to call me Donatello or Don all night and I'll call you Raph.'

Layla smiled. They were so cute, so beautiful it made her heart bleed. Their skinny arms holding the duvet under their chins, their too-small Ninja pyjamas riding up their little bellies, their eyes flitting across the screen, enraptured by the antics of the Turtles, made her sad. Why should they be content with so little?

She looked round the room, hating it. The grubby wallpaper peeled from the walls and the threadbare carpet offered no warmth to their feet in the frozen winter. The single-glazed window rattled and let in a force-ten gale when the wind was high. It was a dive and she was ashamed of the life she'd brought her babies into. Next to the children, a single bed was positioned underneath a window, which was shrouded in a scrappy curtain. She'd left the drape open a few inches to allow the amber glow of the streetlamp to illuminate the room when she was gone. Positioned near the mattress was another upturned box with a plate of sandwiches and two yogurts on top.

She placed her lip gloss back on the dresser and started applying cheap make-up to cover her bruises. When she was ready for work, she jumped to her feet and walked over to the mattress, grabbing her little turtles, tickling them mercilessly for a few minutes until *he* yelled up the stairs. 'Shut the brats up, or I'll come up there and do it myself, Layla.'

All three of them froze. She forced herself to smile as she leaned over and kissed them before pulling them close to her chest. *I hate him, I hate him so much and I hate that bloody name – Layla. Why did I allow him to call me that? It's just another way for him to scrape away my identity.*

Who was she kidding though? She had no choice in anything. Her cheek rested on her eldest's shaved scalp, the barely growing bristles scraping her skin. Her lips thinned and she closed her eyes tightly to stop her tears from falling When the kids had come home from school the other day with a letter warning parents to be vigilant about head lice, he'd grabbed them and, ignoring their protests, had shaved all their hair off, saying, 'This will stop the brats catching nits.'

She ran her hands over their heads and whispered, 'It'll grow back soon.'

'We hate him, Mummy. Why is he so nasty to us? We try to be good.'

2

A voice came roaring up the stairs again. 'Get an effing move on – you've got money to earn.'

She inhaled and counted to three. One day she'd get away from this. One day the three of them would escape ... one day. But, for now, she had to get a wriggle on. Cupping her oldest child's face in her hands for a moment, before repeating the gesture with her younger child, she smiled. 'Now, you know what to do. No noise, only the little light and don't go near the window.'

They smiled up at her, their eyes filled with a love she didn't deserve. 'Don't worry, Mummy. We won't make a noise. No one will know we're home alone. We'll be good.'

She nodded once. 'Don't forget the bucket if you need to wee wee.' From her pocket she took out a key and placed it beside their food. 'Remember, don't open the door for anyone except me, unless ...'

Two small mouths opened and chanted in synchronicity: '... There's a 'mergency.'

'That's right.' She grinned and handed them a packet of Rolos. She rose. 'Don't forget to share.' Walking to the door, she flicked the main light switch off, leaving the room in a dull glow. 'Love you!'

As footsteps thundered up the steps, she slipped out of the room, locked the door and sneaked her key into her pocket before moving over to meet the grunting man who had now reached the top of the stairs. 'Thank God you're ready. Hope them brats are sorted.'

She nodded, avoiding his gaze. One of these days she'd kill him! No matter how long she had to wait, she'd kill him!

The children looked at the door after their mother left, Donatello's lips trembling. 'Why does she have to go? Why does he always make her go? He knows she doesn't like it, Raph.'

By the time the Ninja Turtles' episode had finished, the room had become colder. The creaking central heating had long since clicked off and the old radiators were making cooling-down sounds. Snow fell outside, illuminated by the orange streetlight. 'It's snowing. Shall we climb onto Mummy's bed to watch the snow?' Donatello's tone was hopeful. If they moved onto the big bed, the draught from the door wouldn't hit them and they'd be able to peek out the window. If they switched off the small lamp, no one would spot them.

Raphael grinned, and in a good imitation of the Teenage Turtle's New York accent said, 'All right, Don, but you'll have to invent a screen so no one can see us from outside.'

They peered through a gap in the curtains, enjoying watching the layer of snow build on the pavements and on the few cars that were parked in their street. Car lights driving up the road made the snow glisten, but as the snow got heavier, fewer cars chanced the shortcut offered by their street, which was on a steep slope. Only a few well-wrapped-up figures braved the weather and the pretend Ninjas watched as their footprints disappeared under the snow.

'Do you think Mummy's cold?'

Raphael didn't know exactly what Mummy did when she went out to work, though one of the lads at school had said their mummy was a slut. Not quite sure what a slut was, Raphael, in true Raphael Ninja style had punched the kid on the nose and had earned a beating from *him* afterwards for drawing attention to them. Mummy was probably cold, but there was nothing they could do. To distract Donatello, Raphael held out a fisted hand, then grinning, opened it up. 'I love you enough to give you my last Rolo, Don.'

Cuddling together, they continued to watch the snow until a figure walking up the hill drew their attention as it weaved from side to side, slipping a few times in the slush and getting back to its feet again. As it got closer, Raphael saw that the person carried a bottle, which surprisingly hadn't broken despite its owner's frequent falls. 'Who's that, Raph? Do you think he's drunk?'

Raph did indeed think the figure was drunk, and noting worry in Don's voice said, 'Don't worry. Nobody can get in here. Remember we've got the key. And you activated the magic screen didn't you?'

Don, nose pressed to the cool glass, shuddered. 'Is it him, Raph? Is it him?'

Raph knew exactly who "him" was, but as the figure drew closer, Raph relaxed. 'No, it's too skinny to be him.'

The figure tottered closer to their house and then stood in the middle of the road waving the bottle in the air. 'Come out, you fucking pervert. Where are you? You're a dirty fucking old perv. A nonce and a pimp, that's what you are.'

The hood that was obscuring the man's face fell back, but they didn't need to see his face to recognise him.

'It's Dexy.' Don's tone was a weak gasp. 'What's wrong with Dexy?'

Raphael shrugged. Who knew, but whatever it was, it was bad. Without warning, Dexy made a staggering run towards the pavement in front of their house, arm raised as he propelled the bottle through the air and against their living-room window. The sound of glass shattering was loud. Dexy had fallen to the wet ground and was now trying to get on his knees, when Raphael noticed the door from the house opposite open and a man, pulling on a coat as he ran to help Dexy to his feet.

'What you doing here, Dexy? You'll get yourself in trouble. You can't go about smashing windows. You can see nobody's home. Look, the house is in darkness. Come on. Come in here with me and we'll get you dry.'

But as other doors opened, Dexy's voice rose in volume, and flinging a mis-aimed fist at his would-be helper, he ended up on the ground again. 'You're a pervert too. You dirty old git. I know what you did to me … and to my mates too.' Dexy half turned towards his initial target, now with a broken window. 'And *he* fucking organised it. You sick bastards need locking up. Every one of you.'

The erstwhile helper stood statue still, then glancing round at the other neighbours who had gathered and were watching him in silence, stammered, 'He's lying. The lad's drunk. Talking nonsense.'

Sirens in the distance seemed to bring him to his senses and he took a step away from Dexy and, as if afraid to turn his back on him, walked backwards till he reached his gate, before spinning round and hotfooting it into the house and slamming the door shut. Within seconds, his house too was in darkness and the other neighbours were sidling back into their homes, leaving Dexy on the road as a police car drove down the street and parked up.

Dropping the curtain into place, Raphael and Don crawled up to the top of their mum's bed. Pulling the duvet over their heads, they tried to block out the shouts from Dexy and the hammering of fists on their front door. If anyone found out they were home alone, they'd be taken from Mummy. Hands over their ears, they muffled their sobs underneath the duvet, wishing their mummy would soon come home.

# Present Day

## August

# Chapter 1

With a pint of real ale in front of me, I wait in The Sparrow till
night falls. I keep my head down; don't make eye contact with
nobody. Just another bloke having a quiet drink on his own.
There must have been a Bradford City home football match as
some of the other punters are wearing the amber and claret
scarves. By the sound of their laughter they must have won. I
don't betray my disbelief, but bloody hell, Bradford F.C. winning.
Must have been a right duff team they were up against.

I cup my pint in my hand, savouring it, and I think about why
I'm here. It's all for *her*. It's always been all for her. For as long
as I can remember all I've ever wanted to do was protect her –
look out for her – even if she doesn't realise it. She's too good
for that bastard, but she just doesn't seem to get it, so all I can
do is sit on the side-lines and make sure she's okay. He'd never
think of doing anything like this to protect her – never! Too
bloody soft. Too selfish to make sacrifices or too stupid to realise
that he needs to. I take a slurp and enjoy the malty flavour as it
trickles down my throat. Usually I'd be off partaking in my little
hobby. But that got hit on the head. Another reason I hate that
bastard. Another reason she needs looking after. Never mind, I'll
sort out Peggy Dyson and make sure the shit doesn't hit the fan.

The manager calls last orders and I watch as the city centre pubs throw out their last rowdy occupants and leave the streets of Bradford to the young clubbers, those intent on criminal activity, and the rough sleepers currently congregating under the arches near the Forster Square train station.

During the day, I'd sidled past, trying to spot Peggy ... although there were plenty to choose from, I wasn't one hundred per cent sure if she was one of the motley bunch of homeless people that laid their heads down in this little pocket of misery hidden from the mainstream Bradfordians. It would make my job easier if the old bint had OD'd – but knowing my luck she'd still be hanging around ... It doesn't matter either way; I've geared myself up for it now.

Pulling my hooded top more tightly round my head, I'm glad of the cooling breeze that accompanies the fall of darkness. It's important that I get this right – even more so now that Liam is causing trouble, stirring up shit, and that good-for-nothing tosser just sits and waits for it all to land. *Idiot!* Peering into the tunnel, I exhale and contemplate the problem. I could just yell out her name and hope for the best. On the other hand, last thing I want is any of the blokes to come forward and challenge my presence. Some of them look harmless enough, but there's a crowd in the far corner who look like they'd be up for trouble – probably coked up.

I'm not certain how Peggy'd found us, but I reckon that loser Liam had more than a little to do with it. Stirring things up, causing problems that were nothing to do with him. When the scratty note arrived, written in the clumsy hand of a child, I panicked. Peggy couldn't have reared her ugly head at a worse time and now she has to be dealt with – just like anyone else who poses a threat. It isn't ideal, but it's the only way. I'm not a killer – just protecting myself. No sin in that. Anybody would do the same – well anybody except *him* – especially with so much at stake.

Any other time, I'd be all over the skinny young girls, bundled into layers of clothes that still don't conceal their emaciated frames. Ripe for the plucking and probably still in their teens – just the right age for my tastes. Ignoring them, I focus on the four older women who seem to be in the right age range for the woman I'm looking for. Sixties, weather-beaten skin, lined with creases that could be filth or wrinkles – I'm not sure. I'd seen them earlier in the day. Followed each of them in turn as they begged for money in City Park, one eye always out ready to dodge the occasional police officer who strolled through the park. Most people gave them a wide berth, faces scrunched up in distaste; some were openly hostile and shouted verbal abuse, which the women shrugged off; a few even punched or shoved them; while some gave them a handful of coins or a sandwich that was scoffed down in almost one gulp. It was a sorry life for them.

What I planned for the target is actually a blessing – an end to her debasement, an end to this non-life that she'd sunk to. I owe her nothing. She's a parasite and if she gets her claws into me, she'll end up destroying the only good thing she *could* claim responsibility for – and I'm not about to let that happen. No bloody way!

It's midnight, and I still haven't managed to identify which, if any, of the women is Peggy Dyson. My nerves are frayed, but my resolve strong. I *have* to do this tonight. Can't come back another day. I've already taken a huge risk being here for so long. Anyone could notice me; take note of my interest in the inhabitants of the arches. No, to minimise any fallout landing on us, I have to do it tonight.

A skinny youth, backed up by a couple of equally skinny lads, arrives and struts towards the homeless and stands expectantly. His designer clothes set him apart from the inhumanity that lives rough under the arches. Even from the shadows on the periphery of the area, I can sense the change in the atmosphere. An eerie silence falls. Some of the rough sleepers, already huddled into

11

their chosen makeshift beds for the night, hunker deeper beneath their layers, their eyes closed, their bodies still. The group of loudmouths settle down, watching with wary eyes as the skinny lout grins round at them. Then one of the women I've been watching drops her coat to the floor and sidles up to the lad, her non-existent hips gyrating in macabre enticement, her dress riding up her backside as she stumbles her drunken way over to the three boys. Her face is fashioned into what she presumably thinks is a sultry siren look; her greasy hair falls in rats' tails to her shoulders. Embarrassed by her actions, I want to look away, but find my glance skewered on the scene.

'Asif baby, looking for some fun, are you?' Her voice, high and reedy, splinters the atmosphere. She reaches out a skinny arm with track scabs clearly visible and makes to grip the ringleader's arm.

He steps back, watching her miscalculate her balance and stumble onto the floor. 'Aw, fuck off, Peggy. You're old enough to be my grandma – no my fucking great-grandma. I've told you before to keep your minging hands off me.'

'Aw, Asif.' Her voice wobbles with tears. 'A lady's got to make a living somehow. You know I'm cheap and give good service.'

He sniggers and aims a kick to the prone woman's belly, eliciting a yelp. Lying there, her hair falling in front of her face, her entire body trembles. Asif looks at her, then round at the crowd who stand watching the scenario play out. He turns to one of his boys. 'Give her a bag – not the pure stuff though.'

As the lout strides over to the group of loudmouths, his lieutenant tosses a bag at Peggy's feet. After scrabbling for it, she jumps to her feet, scurries back to retrieve her coat, and limps away with a satisfied grin on her lips into the shadows.

Now I've got my target confirmed, it's only a matter of waiting till the drug dealers finish conducting their business and leave. That's when I'll strike. Not for the first time, I slide my hand into my pocket and touch the tool concealed there. Through the moonlit shadows I study my target. Watching as she snorts her load. Watching her body relax. Watching her sink back into oblivion. What a life. I'm about to do her the biggest favour ever. For once, she won't waken to continue her senseless existence.

A half-hour later, the skinny lout's business complete, the area settles down bar the few hacking coughs and snores that break the silence. I creep through the huddled bundles of inhumanity, none of whom so much as twitch as I pass. When I reach Peggy, her coat is huddled round her, head flung back. Her open mouth reveals blackened teeth stumps and her chest, rising and falling, is the only indication she's alive. Disgust floods me – not at what I'm about to do, but at what Peggy Dyson has become. Taking the tool from my pocket, I take a quick glance around to double-check nobody is watching.

Now the time is here, my heart speeds up, but I'm not scared. I'm excited and maybe after I'm done I will just visit one of those mangy girls. Coast clear, I allow my disgust and anger to drive the tool repeatedly into her body. I had expected her to scream – was prepared for it, but the only sound she makes is a quiet whoosh as the first hit penetrates her heart and begins to drain her life's blood.

Job done, I retreat the way I entered, a shadow dressed in black.

# Chapter 2

The drizzle made the crime scene more sordid somehow. Dingy and dark, with shadows hovering just outside the lit crime scene area, it had the appearance of an apocalyptic world – a lawless one. The very thought of that made DS Nikki Parekh shudder. Apart from that, the rain seemed to stir up a variety of eye-watering stenches, the origins of which were best left to the imagination. As Nikki looked at the blood-soaked body lying in a forlorn heap on the floor, an unexpected tear came to her eyes. She blinked it away and sniffed, heart heavy as the corpse was zipped into a body bag and transported away.

Her partner DC Sajid Malik placed a comforting hand on her shoulder. 'You okay, Nik?'

Nikki's shrug was less than convincing. She knew this woman – Peggy Dyson. Dyson had been a friend of her mother's from years ago and periodically she'd shown up at Trafalgar House, arrested for some misdemeanour or other. The woman hadn't stood a chance in Bradford's underworld. Getting older limited her options on how to make money, and no doubt she'd been stabbed by someone she was indebted to, or maybe even someone higher on drugs than Peggy herself had been – who knew?

Still, no matter how slim the chances were of finding the

perpetrator, Nikki had to try. For all her lifestyle was dire, Dyson was always cheerful, always funny and surprisingly loyal to Nikki's mum. Despite the fact that Lalita had escaped this world whilst Peggy had sunk deeper and deeper into it, Peggy had been pleased for her friend. It seemed to give her hope that perhaps one day she could escape too. Now, that hope had been snuffed out and Nikki didn't know how she was going to tell her mum. No doubt she'd admonish herself for not doing enough for her one-time friend. That wasn't true. Lalita Parekh had tried everything she could to help Peggy, but Peggy had lost too much, fallen too far and become too reliant on her various fixes to respond to Lalita's overtures.

Nikki looked round at the huddle of people watching the proceedings. She'd set up a team of uniformed officers to get statements from them, but the feedback had been that everyone in the area had become selectively mute and deaf. CCTV might throw up something, but Nikki wasn't optimistic. Under the arches here was a safe haven for dealers, pimps and prostitutes to ply their trades and little was recorded.

Walking back towards the car with Saj, Nikki was aware that no matter how hard she worked this case and no matter how many of Peggy's acquaintances she approached, she'd get no further. As for the official channels – a worn-out junkie wasn't on anyone's priority list.

'What can you tell us, Langley?' Nikki had thought that Peggy Dyson couldn't look any more forlorn, but here, lying naked and skinny on Langley Campbell's slab in the mortuary, she did just that.

Langley had finished his post-mortem and now, looking down at Peggy's emaciated frame, he shrugged. 'Not a lot to tell you, Nik. Malnourished, addicted, her tox screen was off the scale – but that was to be expected. The wounds speak of a frenzied attack.' He shrugged again and met Nikki's eye. 'But that's hardly unexpected – it could be drug-fuelled, it could just be frustration or anger – who knows. These sorts of attacks on the homeless and drug-addicted turn up too often for my liking.'

Sajid's ultra-professional stance – the one he always took around his boyfriend Langley when interacting in a professional capacity – made Nikki smile. *Who does he think he's kidding?*

'Any useful forensics?' Sajid's tone was hopeful rather than expectant.

Langley's snort told them all they needed to know. 'She was a hive of forensic clues – semen on all her garments as well as traces of rat, canine and human faeces, urine, cocktails of drugs and more. The only thing I can conclusively link to the attack or the attacker is some paint scraps that were in the wound. I've sent them off for analysis.' Feeling that they were getting nowhere very fast, Nikki and Sajid took their leave.

# Chapter 3

Nikki waited till dark before heading back down to the Forster Square arches. She had told Saj to dress down and was now looking on in amusement at her partner's idea of dressing down – Armani jeans and a Gucci leather jacket were not, in her humble opinion, dressing down for the occasion. *Serve him right if he gets something on himself.*

Trying to look unthreatening, Nikki made her way to a group of older women who crowded round a small fire they'd lit in a metal container. Indicating for Saj to hang back, Nikki extended her cold hands to the flames, without making eye contact with any of the women, whilst watching them from the corner of her eye. The woman she was hoping would talk to her glanced nervously in her direction and looked ready to run, so Nikki raised her head and, looking directly at the woman, flashed a twenty-pound note, so only she could see. The woman sniffed, her small nose scrunching up as she did so, and with a slight toss of her head, walked into a darker area under one of the columns.

Nikki gave her twenty seconds before following her. By the time she reached the woman, she was sniffing a line of coke from the back of her hand and Nikki wasn't sure if that would knock her out or clarify her thoughts. 'Jemmy, you know owt about Peggy's murder, eh?'

Jemmy wiggled her nose to make sure she inhaled every last grain of the powder. 'Murder? Humph. You call that murder, do ya? None of *us* do. Don't know why you're wasting your time – don't know at all.' She grinned, her few remaining teeth black, her breath putrid. She began singing tunelessly, arms out before her as if she was conducting an orchestra. 'It's the circle ... Bradford's circle of death.' And when she'd finished she cackled like a witch at her own humour.

Playing along, Nikki grinned too. 'I get you, Jem. I really do. But, you must know who had it in for Peggy. She was your friend ...'

All at once, Jemmy's smile disappeared and she drew closer to Nikki, who held her breath against the overwhelming stench that accompanied the woman. 'Peggy didn't owe anybody owt. You hear me? Nobody. Nobody had no reason to kill her – not Peggy.' Jem's hand wiped across her eyes as if scrubbing away a tear. 'She was going to move away. Move to be with her kids. That's what she was hoping for anyway. She was waiting for them to get back in touch.'

'Peggy had kids? Where are they and how did she get in touch with them?' Nikki was sceptical – she'd never heard tell of Peggy having any family at all, but Jemmy was insistent.

'She had kids – she told me so. She saw one of them in the paper – a grandson or summat and she tracked them down.'

'You have a name, Jemmy?'

'Na, no name – she was secretive about it all. Said she had to keep quiet about them or they could all get in bother. Now – where's my twenty?'

Sensing that she'd got her lot from Jemmy, Nikki handed the note to Jemmy and left, the woman stuffing it down her front, cackling to herself at her good fortune.

# Tuesday 1st September

# Chapter 4

'You reckon it's true, Nikki?'

Nikki frowned and looked up at Sajid. 'What are you on about? Can't you see I'm concentrating?' She pulled her ponytail tighter and started to jab her fingers repeatedly on the computer keys. 'Bloody thing. Why does everything have to be so damn hard in this shithole?'

Saj moved behind her and looked over her shoulder. 'Holiday request form? God, Nik, it's easy to fill in.'

'Damn thing keeps bouncing around.' She pushed her chair away from her desk, causing Sajid to jump out of the way to avoid being knocked over. She glanced up at him. 'Don't suppose …?'

'If I do this, I expect breakfast at Lazy Bites tomorrow.'

Nikki gave an exaggerated eye roll. 'Okay, you're on. I want to book Christmas Day off.'

Grinning, Sajid stepped forward, typed for a couple of seconds and then stood back. 'Done.'

Nikki's mouth fell open. 'You're kidding, right? For literally two seconds' work, I have to buy you breakfast?'

Grinning widely, eyes sparkling, Saj shrugged. 'You agreed. There'll be a confirmation email in your inbox shortly.'

She elbowed her colleague out of the way, muttering under her breath about how it used to be that colleagues helped each other out for nothing, instead of blackmailing them.

Sajid nudged her with his elbow. 'You still didn't reply.'

'What?' Nikki's face was screwed up in confusion. 'Reply to what?'

Elongating each word as if he was talking to a child, Sajid repeated his earlier question. 'Do you think the gossip about the boss having a girlfriend is true?'

Nikki's confused expression intensified. 'What are you on about?'

Shaking his head, Saj exhaled. 'Aw, Nik, don't you ever listen to the chat that goes on around you?'

'Eh, no. Should I? It's all a load of gossip, isn't it? Can't be bothered with that crap.'

'Yeah, but this is important, isn't it?'

Studying Saj's serious expression, Nikki considered his question. In all the years she'd worked for him, she'd never known her boss, DCI Archie Hegley, to have a love interest. Besides, who would be daft enough to take her stubborn old boss on? Whoever it was would need to be one stalwart of a woman. She smiled. That possibility seemed very unlikely. 'Still don't see what's prompted that gossip.'

Sajid groaned. 'Haven't you listened to what I've been telling you, Nik?'

'Eh ...'

'For goodness' sake – are you listening now?'

Resigned to having to endure this particular snippet of gossip, Nikki sat back, folded her arms over her chest and said, 'Shoot.'

Raising his hand, Sajid began counting off on his fingers 'One ... he's been different since he came back to work – less shouty – smiling more.'

'Yeah, a heart condition might make you reassess your life. He was a grumpy old bugger before, but his little brush with death is a reasonable catalyst.' Nikki knew this first-hand, as a near brush with death the previous year had helped her prioritise her own family more.

'Two … aftershave.'

Inclining her head, Nikki nodded. 'Yeah I'll give you that. He's been using a bit too much of the stuff. Between *your* eau de toilette and his, the place smells like a brothel.'

Ignoring her dig, Saj continued raising three fingers in the air. 'Three … new suits.'

'Aw, I can't give you that one – he's lost weight since his scare, so he had to buy new ones.'

'That's my point four … He's coming into work with a "healthy lunchbox" with salads and stuff in it – you telling me Archie's taking the time to make himself lunch every day?'

'Hmmm – yeah, that seems unlikely, but you never know. People change. Look at me – I'm more outgoing – more sociable now.'

As Saj's mouth fell open, Nikki narrowed her eyes. 'Don't even think about bursting my bubble, Malik. I *am* more sociable.'

Presumably choosing to be diplomatic, Sajid moved on. 'Five … all the mysterious phone calls that make him laugh and … the lunchtime meetings that go on for over an hour … You telling me that's not conclusive?'

'I've not noticed any of that.' Nikki scrunched up her forehead. 'Maybe you've got a point. I nominate *you* to ask him. Here he is now.' She raised her voice. 'Archie … Saj has something he'd like to ask you.'

Saj scrambled to his feet, face flushing, straightening his tie as he spun round only to see an empty office and hear Nikki laughing behind him.

'Got ya!'

'Cowbag!'

'Oh yeah … now piss off home, I've got to go through my mail and then I'm leaving too.'

Sajid grabbed his jacket and headed out with a cheery, 'See ya tomorrow, boss.'

Nikki still had some paperwork to do on the Peggy Dyson case. Not that they'd managed to find much in the way of evidence, and as for suspects – well that was a round zilch. It was so frustrating, but Nikki wasn't ready to give up on the case just yet, regardless of Archie's suggestion that she wind things down.

There was an A4 envelope sitting next to her computer, so before bringing up Peggy's file, Nikki ripped it open and shook the single sheet of paper onto her desk. Puzzled for a moment, she frowned, for this wasn't a letter. Instead, what Nikki was looking at was a photocopied newspaper article. She shook the envelope again, to dislodge anything else it might contain, but nothing came free. Stuffing her hand in the envelope, she wondered if an accompanying note had got stuck inside, but again found nothing. The headline of the copied article with its accompanying photo alerted her to its content. *Prostitute murdered in drug-related crime!* The photo accompanying the article that had been sensationalist enough to make the front page of the *Bradford Chronicle* the previous week, was Peggy Dyson's mugshot. In it she looked like a depraved psychopath, which was probably exactly what Lisa Kane, the journalist responsible for the article, had aimed for.

An annoyed tut escaped Nikki's lips. She was working the Peggy Dyson case, but despite her best efforts had got nowhere. Now here was some idiot taunting her for her failure.

Nikki's mum had been upset when she saw the photograph and read the uncharitable venom spewed onto the pages. Venom that would no doubt make some Bradfordians unsympathetic to the plight of rough sleepers and their associated problems. This was irresponsible journalism at its worst and it was what Nikki had come to expect of her long-standing adversary Lisa Kane.

In anger, Nikki crumpled the article up and tossed it in the bin, not wanting to look at it a moment longer, and instead focused on her other correspondence. However, whilst responding to each, the absence of an accompanying note with the article niggled her. Why would anyone send her that particular article? The more she thought about it, the more she realised that only someone who was aware of her tenuous personal link to Peggy Dyson would bother. More to the point, only someone with malicious intent would send it anonymously – but who?

Her first thought went to Lisa Kane, the reporter responsible for the article in the first place. She and Lisa were definitely not friends. Nikki had no doubt that Lisa Kane had dodgy friends she could get to find out stuff – her sort always did. She wondered if she'd somehow got wind of her family's links to Peggy Dyson and although she would rather keep her past where it belonged – well behind her – she was past the stage of allowing a low-life like Kane to intimidate her. As best she could, Nikki had pushed the somewhat unsympathetic article to the back of her mind and got on with her job.

Grabbing a pair of latex gloves – *snazzy lilac* ones according to Saj – she scooped the article out of the bin, and mindful of the fact that she'd probably contaminated any forensic evidence already, shrugged. *Probably won't send it off to the lab anyway. But best to keep it – just in case.*

Laying it on her desk, she smoothed it out, then photocopied both the sheet of paper and the envelope before securing the originals in evidence bags and shoving them in the bottom drawer of her desk with the copies. She then decided to put the matter to the back of her mind.

# Chapter 5

I expected to feel different – maybe guilty or something. I mean one day you're going about your business as usual, saying hi to people, doing your job, and then the next you're having to deal with shit and make decisions you shouldn't ever have to make. Finishing off the old skanky cow wasn't as bad as I'd thought it would be. I mean it *was* time-consuming – but that was because I had trouble identifying Peggy Dyson initially. The actual act was easy enough in the end – enjoyable even. The only downside was that I couldn't share it with *her*. Couldn't tell her what I'd done to protect her. Couldn't show her that I was the one that she should respect, the one she should love – not him. What the hell has he ever done for her? Drained her, made her sad, made her ill – that's all.

I slam my fist onto my thigh. That's enough isn't it? He's made her ill. She's so frail now and it's all his fault. If it wouldn't kill her, I'd finish him off completely. Instead I have to clear up all this crap. Makes me mad that she can't see what I'm doing. The sacrifices I'm making. Had to give up on a night with a pert little 14-year-old last week. I'm not complaining – not really. It'll all be worth it in the end. Still, I gave it a few days to make sure there was no fallout. No comeback on me.

This next one won't be as easy. It won't be a quick in and out like before. No, this time I need information and it's information that only he can give. He's the one who's been researching this shit. He's the one been mouthing off to all and sundry. Now, before I end it, I need to find out who else I should add to my list. I've got a couple of names already, but I want to make sure I get them all. Can't take any chances on this. Too much at stake. Glad I watched all those *CSI* programmes now. I took care of Dyson in a rush, but I've had time to think now. Time to work out all the precautions I need to take. I made a big mistake on the last one – hadn't realised there'd be so much blood. Good job it was dark.

This time I'll be prepared. Easy enough to buy one of them burner phones and leave my own phone switched on at home. No point in risking the police being able to trace it and link it to me. Changing the reg plate on my van will be easy too and I'll just swap it back when I get home. I'll snatch another plate from a scrapyard and when I get near to Cambridge I'll put that to good use too. I'll steal a van; change the plates and bongo. No point in leaving any forensic evidence in my own van. I smile. I'm well satisfied with my forensic measures. It takes time plus a lot of thinking time but it's worth it. Bet that tosser Liam couldn't have planned it any better, and now that I've had my trial run, I'm sure I've covered all my bases.

Slouched in the Costa coffee, I watch the passers-by through the smeared windows. I don't much like Cambridge. Seems a bit too snobby to me. Mind you, this area is definitely not. Already seen two beggars, one with a dog, sitting in the street – can't look after themselves, but they have a bloody dog, yapping at folk as they pass by. It's not right. Not when the rest of us poor fuckers have to do hard graft to get by. Bloody nuisances the lot of them – just like that Peggy Dyson. A waste of space, no loss to society, them lot.

I take a slurp of my vanilla latte and then grin as another

thought occurs to me. Maybe when this is all done and dusted, I'll do a bit of community service by getting rid of some of the parasites for free. Yeah, I won't even charge anybody – free and gratis – my service to humanity.

I'd expected to see a whole load of posers wearing them black university gowns with them stupid hats. Liam had told me not to be a twat – cheeky bastard. Just cause he's all up with the posh gits. Hobnobbing with the hoity-toities. Yeah, Liam Flynn could do with being taken down a notch or two. Mind you – that's exactly why I'm here.

A quick glance at my phone and I'm off. Need to intercept him at just the right place. I've already sorted it. Reconnaissance they call it. Well, I've reconnoitred the area and found the only freaking blind spot in the whole of Cambridge – okay, so that's a slight exaggeration, but it's the only blind spot on his regular route ... and I need to time it when a double-decker bus is parked up at the stop. I've already parked up the stolen van. Changed the plates and all – I'm not a fool. I'm not taking chances.

He'll come with me. I know he will. He's angry right now. Hell, maybe he has a right to be, but that doesn't mean he can go mouthing off, causing grief to everyone. Don't understand why he can't just keep his fat trap shut. If he did, none of this would have happened. It's all his own fault and I'm fucked if I'm going to feel guilty about sorting out the mess he created. No damn way!

Never thought you could feel the blood pumping through your veins like you're gonna pop a blood vessel. Not till now anyway. I'd decided that it was better to coax the details out of him, so that's what I did. Pretended to be on his side. Pretended to agree with him and bit by bit he spilled it all. Sucker! For all his brains he was bloody thick as shit. His fancy education didn't save him from the same fate as Peggy Dyson.

He struggled a bit at first. But I'm bigger than him. Said he works out at his poncey gym, but I reckon all he did was go there to eye up the other guys. I might need to research ways of drugging the next one – maybe chloroform or summat. The internet will tell me. The initial wound didn't slow him. Must have miscalculated that first blow – it were meant to give me the upper hand, but instead he turned and swung at me. He didn't have a weapon, but as I was all pumped up on adrenaline I just let loose. Each thrust made me harder. The taste of his blood as it spatters onto my lips is oddly erotic. Sweat drips from my forehead, and then with my last ounce of energy I send a final thrust through his chest and, with a judder, I come … Made a bit of a mess in the van, but what the hell – it's not mine, so who cares. The lay-by on the A605 was deserted. Well it would be, at three in the morning, so dumping him was easy. Didn't even have to bother about the mess in the van.

I drove back up North, dumped the stolen van where it wouldn't be found for a few days – why these posh golf clubs don't have CCTV covering the entire car park puzzles me – but I took advantage of it anyway.

Now all I need to do is wait and see what happens. Bet that dozy bloody partner of his will report him missing – aw well, nothing I can do about that. Just have to see where it all takes us.

# Chapter 6

Freddie Downey in his stained, faded T-shirt and worn blazer, wearing his baseball cap backwards, was given a wide berth by people around him. He merged in with Bradford City Park's great unseen and that suited him just fine. Blending in had been his aim today and he hadn't had to do much to his overall appearance to make it work. Greying stubble and scruffy clothes tended to be enough. He sat on a bench next to an elderly woman in an M&S matching outfit, who reeked of expensive perfume. He didn't bother to silence his satisfied chuckle when she screwed up her nose and edged further away from him before finally hefting her bags up and moving to the empty bench nearby. He could have chosen that bench himself, but there was something so satisfying about annoying silly old cows.

From his prime position he observed his surroundings. *Well, well, well. Bradford was coming up in the world – who'd have thought it?* Gone was the manky old Central Library building, replaced by a swanky new one right in the heart of this bustling little place they called City Park. All posh fountains with screaming kids playing in them, Wetherspoons filled to the ginnels with Bradford's all-day drinkers, quaint cafés nestled under the watchful gaze of City Hall, and tucked round the corner was Sunbridgewells – yep, things had changed in his absence.

But for all the changes, Bradford was still a city of contrasts – an architectural smorgasbord of modern concrete buildings juxtaposed with the Gothic-style town hall and Victorian builds, an ethnic melting pot representing a range of races and languages, an economic divide illustrated by the disparity between M&S lady, the rough sleepers hovering on the fringes and the cheap and cheery working-class families gathered round the Big Screen watching some crappy cartoon or other. Bradford: the lost city rising from the ashes like a crass, flamboyant phoenix. His meandering thoughts amused him. He was a people-watcher – always had been – and it was particularly satisfying to observe, from the distance of time, the city he once knew so well.

Today though, he had one particular focus, one special person to monitor. From his position in the warmth of the sun, he watched his prey inside the Starbucks, chatting to the barista, laughing and smiling. Little did she know that he'd be wiping that smile off her face before too damn long. For the first time in twenty-five years, he could see her – so close he could almost smell her perfume. He'd waited for this chance for a long time. Many years with only the thought of seeing her to keep him going. Hard years. Cold years. Years where the softness of a woman's body was all he craved. He'd sometimes wake up in the middle of the night, hard as wood, the scent of her in his nostrils, the feel of her on his body – only to have it drift away, replaced by the smell of stale farts, snoring and guards and screaming.

'Layla, Layla, Layla. What *am* I going to do with you?' He spoke the words under his breath. For what seemed like forever, he'd kept an eye on her from a distance. Reports and photos hadn't done her justice though. The years had been kind to her. Smartly dressed, she hadn't succumbed to that middle-aged spread many women of her age developed. Hair still black although shorter than he remembered. Bet she could still give a man a good time

31

– she was made for it. Ripe for the picking then and damn well still ripe for the picking now. Busy woman, she was – always off somewhere, always chatting to folk – popular, with the men too. Wonder if they knew that in the past she'd slide her mouth between their legs, those lush lips of hers all over their dicks for little more than a fiver? Or spread her legs in an alleyway off Thornton Road for a tenner. Bet they didn't. Bet the whore kept that secret. Trying to act all respectable now – her and her damn kids.

That had been his mistake – letting her keep the brats. He should've got rid of them soon as she told him she was up the duff, but she tricked him. *Bitch!* Promised she'd do anything for him – well that was a fucking lie, wasn't it? Mind you, he taught her a good lesson or two then. Didn't work though, she still managed to push those two little scrotes out, screaming and yelping like piglets ripe for the slaughter.

He should have punched her in the belly harder – till she bled the little fuckers out. He thought when she fell with the second one that they'd tie her to him. Didn't fucking give her credit for being a good mum. From the start, the bitch put them before him. He should have known after the first one came. The way she pandered over it – little fucking creature – smelly and snotty and loud. Then the second came along and again the witch convinced him to let her keep it.

'Go on. They'll be company for each other. Look after each other and then I won't be so distracted.'

He slammed his fist onto his thigh and lit up another cig. Well, she'd better laugh while she could, for when he finally made his move the last thing she'd be doing was laughing – her and those fucking sprogs of hers. They'd all pay. Especially the older one – yep, especially that one.

Thursday 17th September

Thursday 7th September

# Chapter 7

'*Early this morning the body of a young man, later identified as 25-year-old Liam Flynn, was discovered in the field behind me, not far from this lay-by on the A605 near Peterborough. It seems clear that the death is being deemed as suspicious although no one from the Cambridgeshire constabulary has yet made a statement. Flynn was first reported missing by his partner, Daniel Lammie, two weeks ago. Behind me the crime scene investigators comb the area for clues to the death of this young man; a Cambridge University researcher with a bright future ahead of him, which has been cut so very tragically short …*'

Nikki Parekh's attention was drawn to the large-screen wall-mounted TV, which was on mute, but with subtitles, when she saw the subheading from the corner of her eye. Now that the young lad's body had been discovered in suspicious-looking circumstances, she wondered if it was, perhaps, time to confide in her partner DC Sajid Malik. Not that she had anything to confide … not really. A couple of anonymous letters containing an online newspaper report from two weeks ago about Peggy Dyson's murder, the one with the clipping from a news report relating to the investigation into the murder of the Cambridge lad that was on the news right now and another missive this morning containing extracts from a diary. None of it necessarily directly related to her, as far as she could determine. Still, it made her nervous.

Ignoring the hubbub of Saj attempting to drum up support for the bet he was trying to set up for the detective inspector interviews that were finally being held today, much to their boss DCI Hegley's disappointment, Nikki continued to watch the news report. They were back in the BBC newsroom now with two news presenters talking about the case.

'... *whilst DCI Jones from Cambridge CID is keeping remarkably quiet, the discovery of a body will lead the investigation in a new direction.*'

'*Of course, that's inevitable. Already the media have been speculating about the involvement of Flynn's parents, from whom he was reportedly estranged and who have declined to comment. In such circumstances often the partner is scrutinised to eliminate him from the investigation ...*'

A series of images of Flynn's family and his partner made the background to the interview and Nikki was all too aware of the tension along her shoulders as the two reporters continued with their uninformed hypotheses. Gosh, the media truly were a nightmare.

'Hey, Nik, wakey-wakey. You gonna make a guess as to what sort of DI we'll end up with?' Sajid bounced in front of her. His turquoise shirt was completely crease-free with a tie that picked out the exact same shade of blue in its pattern.

The past few months had been hard for the team, dealing with the aftermath of the organised modern-day slavery ring they'd busted before Easter, so she was well aware that Saj deserved a bit of light relief. And the distraction of the detective inspector interviews for the entire squad, including her partner DC Sajid Malik, had provided it. However, for Nikki it was unbearable. Not only was she being teased for not going for the job, but Saj was running this damn sweepstake, guessing which candidate would get it: a high-flyer, fast-tracker fresh from university and green to the gills; an uppity git from some posh area who had no idea about Bradford; someone from another station in the district with a hard-on for tough policing and intent on setting their minions to be tough on their behalf; some upstart from inside the station full of good intentions, but with no balls. The list went on ad infinitum and was making Nikki more and more nervous.

She hated change and dreaded the necessary "getting to know you" conversations that were inevitable with a new team member. Unlike Saj, she clammed up when it came to other officers, and she'd more than likely put her foot in it and insult them in some way. She'd been acting DI on the chilling modern-day slavery operation, which had rescued hundreds of victims as well as having far-reaching consequences for the City of Bradford. The mere thought of it now deepened Nikki's frown. Her boss DCI Archie Hegley was annoyed with her for not taking the job on full-time, but Nikki hadn't wanted it. She had a family and although the extra money would have come in handy, she was too aware of how much her job already impacted on them. Besides, she was better with just the one partner. Heading up an entire team would force her to talk to other officers – be part of their lives – be approachable, and Nikki wasn't up for that. She didn't know how to be that person.

Agitated, the need for fresh air and space to think had Nikki grabbing her bag.

'You okay, Nik?'

Nikki's smile was tight, but she nodded. Saj was aware that things were tense between her and her mother at the moment and although he didn't know the reason behind that tension, he was worried about them. No way was Nikki about to confide that her mum had clammed up when she'd asked her about Peggy. She'd refused point-blank, in a way that was uncharacteristic of her mum, to discuss her past with Peggy. Even when Nikki had mentioned that Jemmy had suggested Peggy was waiting for her kids to contact her, Nikki's mum had tightened her lips and yelled at Nikki to quit interrogating her like a common criminal.

In response Nikki had stormed out of her mum's house and the two hadn't spoken since. Nikki's mum was like a second mother to Saj, particularly since he was recently estranged from his own family.

She waved a hand in Saj's direction, and made her escape.

38

# Chapter 8

Despite the late September sun beating down on her back as she walked from Trafalgar House police station to the Lazy Bites café, Nikki had a deep frown on her forehead. Although she wouldn't admit it to anyone, she kept a more than usual alertness about her as she walked. The anonymity of the letters unsettled her, whether or not that had been their intention. Every passing stranger could be her letter writer and the thought made Nikki more vigilant than ever.

It wasn't only Sajid's banter that had driven her from the station. It was the letter she'd received that morning. It was the third of its kind and she'd been reluctant to discuss it with her partner until she'd had a chance to make some sense of it. Until today she'd seen no reason to – with only an online newspaper article from the local rag in an envelope, followed by a completely unrelated one about a national investigation, it seemed irrelevant. However, the news report she'd just heard, combined with the strange mail that arrived today, made it more imperative that she share it with Saj. So, she'd vacated the open-plan office on pretence of visiting the loo and hotfooted it over to the café.

Lazy Bites had only been open a few months but was fast becoming popular with the locals and the employees of Trafalgar

House alike. It was run by a charitable trust and its main aim was to provide apprenticeship-type experiences for young adults with learning disabilities to help them into employment in the hospitality industry. One of the trainee chefs, a lad called Thasavar, who rarely spoke but was a dab hand at making curries, had already been snapped up by the Trafalgar House canteen.

Nikki loved the relaxed atmosphere, the variety of tables with hard-back chairs, comfy corners and some more private booths. A few tasteful paintings of cobbled Bradford streets and old tramlines were interspersed with vividly coloured paintings of chameleons and butterflies. As she entered the café, the jaunty bell tinkled, and before she'd even closed the door, Elaine the waitress hurried back over to the serving counter, leaving her cleaning spray and cloth on the table she'd been cleaning. Dressed all in pink down to the two bobbles that held her hair in pigtails, Elaine was a breath of fresh air, always ready with a smile. Nikki's frown faded as she grinned in response to Elaine's enthusiastic greeting.

'Usual is it, Nikki?'

Nikki grinned. Grayson, one of the tutors, had warned her that Elaine used this phrase in lieu of a greeting whether she knew your "usual" or not. 'Yeah. A large cappuccino and ...' Nikki moved along the counter, studying the array of scones, brownies and cakes displayed behind a glass case. 'Ooh, who made the scones?'

A voice from near the cooker, which could be seen beyond the counter area, chimed up. 'Me. It was me. I learned today; Grayson showed me. They're good. Have two.'

Nikki nodded. 'They do look good, Billy. Tell you what, since you made them, I'll have one now and four to go. Marcus and the kids will love these.'

Billy's round face lit up and he turned to Grayson and high-fived him. 'Best scones in Bradford, eh, Gray?'

Grayson grinned and winked at Nikki. 'Better than mine, Billy,

40

better than mine. I'll have to keep an eye on you or you'll be the next one being poached to Trafalgar House.'

Billy sniggered, clearly pleased with himself as Elaine rang up Nikki's order and counted out her change precisely, checking it twice. 'I'll bring it over to you, Nikki. Have a seat. But not at that table – I'm still wiping it.'

Looking round, Nikki settled on the furthermost corner booth, where she could slide close to the window and hopefully not be seen by anyone coming into the café. She waited till her coffee and scone arrived and chatted with Elaine for a few minutes before being left alone. Sighing, she took the A4 envelope from her bag and pulled the first photocopied item out.

Then, the following week, another envelope arrived. This time it contained an online newspaper article with a photograph, again without a note. The envelope, a bog-standard white A5-size one, carried a Manchester postmark, and was addressed to DS Nikita Parekh at Trafalgar House. Nikki photocopied it and placed the original and the envelope it came in into an evidence bag, which she then placed in her desk with the first note and pushed it to the back of her mind, still convinced it was just the work of somebody trying to yank her chain … until today.

She reread the article. It was about the disappearance of the Cambridge student Liam Flynn originally from Ashton-under-Lyne near Manchester, whose body had been discovered in Cambridgeshire that morning. It was short and to the point:

*"The brother of Manchester man Liam Flynn, who has been doing ground-breaking research in genetics at Cambridge University, makes an impassioned plea for anyone who has seen his brother or knows of his whereabouts to contact Cambridgeshire police. Flynn left the flat he shared with his partner Daniel Lammie to go into university at his usual time and was last seen getting into a black van with covered number plates. Reports that Liam was estranged from his parents, pictured above, are being fuelled by their refusal to comment. According to our source, both parents were interviewed*

*by Cambridgeshire police in Manchester. The police have declined to comment on whether they suspect foul play, but the lengthy interview with Liam's parents indicates they are no further forward in their investigation."*

Nikki scrutinised the photo. A man and a woman had been caught on camera exiting the police station. The couple, who looked to be in their forties, had startled expressions. They were dark-haired, the man a foot or so taller than the woman, of average weight and height, and both looked nondescript.

Nikki's curiosity was piqued because now, it seemed, Liam Flynn had been murdered. So why would anyone anonymously send *her* a newspaper article with no note or indication of its significance? At the time she received the communication, she had racked her brain to see if she recognised either of them. She was sure she didn't. Of course, she'd gone online and checked it out, but had come up empty. There was nothing – just nothing – to indicate why she'd received it. The family themselves seemed to be private people.

Over the next few days, Nikki had followed the reports in the local Cambridgeshire online paper, the *Cambridge Independent*, as well as those of the national papers, and whilst the local and national newspapers had stuck to the investigation, the *Manchester Gazette* had focused on the parents. With seemingly little of note to report, the papers had concentrated their efforts into digging for filth and seeking out interviews with neighbours who described the parents as "secretive and rude", or who cited their son's sexuality as the cause of their estrangement between Mr and Mrs Flynn.

The article itself carried no further information, so Nikki put it away and pulled out the contents of the letter that had arrived that morning. As with the newspaper article, Nikki had again copied the sheets of paper and both envelopes. She'd bagged the originals, but hadn't yet decided what to do with them. It seemed too coincidental for her to receive three anonymous missives so closely together from two separate senders, and particularly on the day they found Liam Flynn's body. This morning's letter had been especially intriguing by its difference from the previous two. In all her time in the police, Nikki had never received an anonymous letter or email. She'd been threatened plenty of times, but these letters weren't overt threats – were they? They seemed more like clues to Nikki – but clues to what? Besides, the envelopes were similar and the handwriting on the front was to Nikki's unpractised eye a match. She might have put it down to coincidence if the postmark on the second envelope hadn't been Cambridgeshire. The Cambridge/Manchester link plus the content of the first letter were too pointed to be arbitrary.

However, the contents of the third anonymous letter were somehow more insidious – or at least strange – depending on who the sender was. The pages were diary entries written in what Nikki considered to be a young person's handwriting, on lined paper and photocopied. Each entry looked like it had been ripped from a book, as clearly visible in the copy were a tattered edge down one side and a raggedy edge where the page had been ripped crossways, as if only allowing Nikki access to part of the content.

The account seemed to indicate a younger teenager and the format of the diary entries was too similar to be from different hands. Although in the latter two extracts, the paper, judging by the shadows around the copy, was from a slightly wider book:

*Wednesday 8th December*
    *When I see him it's like I can't even breathe. He's ugly – ugly and mean and fat and I hate him – hate him so much. Hate what he does to me. Hate his smell, his filth, the way he touches me. Hate hate hate hate hate hate hate him!!!!!!*

Each of the "hates" was in a slightly darker colour, as if the author had pressed harder on each subsequent one. Nikki traced a finger over the words. Initially, she'd wondered if they'd been written the previous year – but when she'd checked, 8th December 2019 had been a Sunday, not a Wednesday. So, when had the diary entry been written and by whom? Was it the anonymous sender? Although she was inclined to think the writing belonged to a girl, she knew she couldn't count on it. Was it some sort of cry for help – from a young person being abused? She turned the page to the next entry:

*Thursday 24th June*

*It was so sore … couldn't have done it without D. Was like I was being split in two. Don't know what I think when I look at him. Sometimes I hate him so much I want to suffocate him and then that breathing thing starts again and I can't breathe. I never can. All the time I'm barely breathing … barely living. When will he let me go outside again? When will I escape? I hate it. I hate all of them. Hate hate hate hate hate!*

Again, when she checked, the dates didn't make sense. The 24th of June this year had landed on a Wednesday and in 2019 the 24th had been a Monday, so she'd no idea when this last entry had been written either. Still, it was ominous. All of Nikki's instincts made her almost a hundred per cent sure that the diary writer was a girl and that that poor girl was describing childbirth. Nikki's stomach clenched. The writing looked so young – loose-looped and – just young. A bit like Charlie or Ruby's writing. Thinking of her daughters made Nikki want to connect with them, so she took a sip of her cappuccino and fired off an *I love you* text to both of them, complete with teddy bear hugging GIFs. Who said she was too damn old to keep up with new technology, eh?

*Monday 14th February*

*Valentine's Day! What a load of old crock! He noticed. Knew he would. That old bastard opposite said something – I know he did. Now I've got a black eye to thank him for and I'm grounded. D put his window through and that serves him right. Interfering old git.*

*Thing is, I'm scared. Really scared. Scared of what he'll do if he can't make money from me. I hate hate hate hate hate all them fuckers.*

Nikki took a deep breath. She'd no real idea of the order of these entries. The lack of a year made it possible they were decades old. But then again, they could be recent … and what was the link to that murdered geneticist and his family?

Draining the last of her coffee, she got to her feet and thrust everything back in her bag. Time to spill the beans to Saj and take a trip down to Cambridge.

With a cheerful wave at the workers in the kitchen and Elaine, who had, seeing her leave, scuttled over to clear her table, Nikki opened the door and almost bumped straight into a mother carrying a baby. At once she was transported out of her puzzled mood and straight into grabbing the baby from the mother's hands. 'Hi, Stevie, what brings you over to this neck of the woods?'

Turning her attention to the baby who grinned at her from a drooling mouth, Nikki spoke in a baby voice, making faces at the 6-month-old as she did so. 'Are you teething, Amy? Yes, you are. You're all rosy-cheeked and drooly, but you're still the most beautiful baby I know.'

Stevie grinned. 'It's Amy-Nikita, Nik. Don't forget.'

Nikki groaned. 'You have to just ignore my mum – she can't help herself.' Six months earlier, Nikki had saved both Stevie and her baby from certain death and since then Nikki's mother had insisted on hyphenating the baby's name to Amy-Nikita … much to the annoyance of Stevie's partner and Nikki's colleague DS Felicity Springer.

Nikki was glad Springer wasn't here. Much as Nikki liked Stevie, she was less fond of her partner, and was always on guard to make sure she didn't betray her feelings.

'I'm just dropping Fliss off. She's got an interview this afternoon.'

*Interview?* The only one Nikki was aware of was the DI one. How the hell would she cope with Springer as her boss? Whilst Stevie ordered a drink to go, Nikki schooled her face not to betray her dismay. She hadn't been aware that Stevie's partner, DS Felicity Springer, was going for the inspector job. She reckoned that Sajid was probably unaware of that fact too or it would have been all over the office by now.

With a sinking heart, Nikki said her goodbyes and trooped back to Trafalgar House with the feeling that everything was conspiring against her.

46

# Chapter 9

Lalita Parekh walked out of Tyersal Library anticipating an enjoyable afternoon spent with a good thriller – despite the fact that her detective daughter Nikita told her they were totally unrealistic. Lalita smiled. Nikita always looked so cross when she argued her case: 'Yeah, I'd like to see some of those detectives you read doing the job I do. None of them know what it's like on the streets.'

Lalita partly agreed with Nikki; on the other hand she enjoyed the escapism of a good detective thriller as did the majority of library borrowers, or so it seemed by the lending figures at the library where she worked, and Nikki wasn't going to make her change her mind.

She loved her job. Loved the community feel of it. This morning they'd had a visiting local author in for coffee and a chat with the library's reading groups. It was a huge success and Lalita was kept busy.

Now on her half-day, she was happy to anticipate an afternoon of lapping up the late summer sun whilst she still could and watching the kids play on the street in front of her house. Not that many of them were allowed out on the street these days. Things had changed since her two daughters were kids. In those days, the kids ran free on the streets playing football or cricket or whatever and the cars just had to accommodate that. Nowadays it was far too risky with cars zooming up and down the street – even kids on quad bikes. Only last year one of the local kids had revved down the street, hit a bit of black ice and landed up with permanent brain damage because he hadn't worn a helmet. Those things were a hazard. She was always telling Nikki they should be banned – still, they tore up and down the street at all hours of the day and night.

Thinking about her eldest daughter cast a cloud over Lalita. She and Nikki had had a spat and now they weren't speaking. Peggy Dyson's death had been hard for Lalita to cope with, but the added pressure of her daughter wanting her to relive her and Peggy's shared past was intolerable. Then, when Nikki had asked about Peggy's children, Lalita had frozen. She couldn't go there – not now. She couldn't let all of that poison her current life. So, she'd yelled. She wasn't proud of it, but she'd had no option. Since Peggy's funeral she and Nikita had been circling each other at a watchful distance that tore at Lalita's heart. She wanted to reach out to Nikita, but she was aware that her daughter needed time to process what she'd learned.

For a long time now, Lalita had wanted to open up to her girls about their childhood, but at the back of her mind she'd always wondered if her desire to get things off her chest was more for her benefit than theirs. Now, she wished she'd bitten the bullet and worked it through. When she looked at Nikita, so strong, so responsible, so serious, she wondered if she'd burdened her too much, treated her more like a support system than a vulnerable child who needed protection. Anika, on the other hand, had been spoiled. Both Nikita and Lalita herself had been at great pains to shield her from everything that went on and, again, Lalita wondered if that had been a mistake for her youngest daughter was quite selfish, far too dependent on Nikita to sort her life out for her, and very prone to make bad choices where men were concerned. She sighed. Approaching her fiftieth birthday, Lalita could no longer use the excuse that she'd been a mere child herself. She had to sort things out like an adult.

With a wave to a couple of library visitors, Lalita skirted the building – one of the lucky libraries that had been refurbished before austerity kicked in – to the car park. Her Mini was parked as far away from the library as she could manage – *got to get my daily steps in whilst the weather's good.* Only a few vehicles were lined up near the back of the building. One, she noticed, had parked right in front of the "Keep Clear" notice. She was on the point of taking a photo of it to report it, then shook her head. She wasn't on library duty now. Someone else could deal with it; besides they weren't expecting a book delivery that afternoon.

Stepping off the pavement, she crossed the concrete car park and then stopped sharply. Something was on her windscreen. A flyer – it certainly couldn't be a parking ticket because she had her library employee badge stuck on her windscreen. She hated people meddling with her car. As far as she was concerned, she wasn't likely to employ a plumber, builder or gardener who stuck leaflets under her windscreen wiper. Bloody nuisances. No, Lalita was far more likely to ask Marcus to recommend someone. Anyway, who was to say that someone was in need of one of those services at that precise time – stupid and ineffective advertising.

Lalita approached and tugged the paper from the wiper, snagging it slightly so it tore. It wasn't a leaflet or advert – well at least not a glossy professional one. It was a scrap of lined A4 paper folded into four. After glancing round to see if the person who had left it was hanging about nearby, Lalita opened it. There were only four words scrawled there in red biro:

*I Am Watching You.*

Each word started with a capital letter.

Lalita's heart flipped. Was that a threat? A joke? She spun round and scrutinised the area, expecting to see a group of kids huddled in a corner watching her, giggling at their joke – but the car park was empty and the people walking about on the street beyond paid her no heed. She scrunched the note up, shoved it in her trouser pocket and walked back to the vehicles parked in the front car park spaces. She hadn't noticed anything on their windscreens as she'd passed – but then again, she wasn't actually paying particular attention to them. She'd been too busy scowling at the illegally parked car – which was no longer there.

None of the other cars had anything tucked under their windscreens. A sudden chill made her shiver and again she looked round. The idea that someone was watching her, no matter how unlikely that might be, unsettled her. Scanning the shops opposite the car park and the windows of the flats behind them, she felt exposed. Anyone could be watching her right now. Right this minute. They could have binoculars watching her every move.

Lalita was tempted to return to the library and access the CCTV. Then she remembered that the community officer had been in earlier in the week informing them that a gang of vandals were targeting CCTV cameras in the Tyersal area – spraying them with black paint or throwing bricks at them till they were damaged beyond repair. One of the cameras vandalised was the library's car park one and, money being tight, it was yet to be repaired. The CCTV footage that had captured the little scrotes in action had only caught kids in hoodies and balaclavas. Unless they were caught in the act, they would get away with it.

Wishing she'd chosen a light-hearted comedy for a change, instead of her usual thrillers, Lalita straightened her back and strode back to her car. If the prankster was watching her right now, she wasn't about to give them the satisfaction of seeing just how affected she was. Once sitting in the driver's seat, Lalita clicked the locks shut and turned the ignition. It irritated her that her hands were shaking as she placed them on the steering wheel and drove out of the car park. It was the red ink that made it even more threatening. If it had been your normal blue or black pen, it wouldn't have seemed half as malevolent.

Never mind, she'd soon be home. Still, she wished she was on better terms with Nikita so she could get her take on it. Nikita's no-nonsense attitude was just what she needed to set her mind at ease.

*Bloody kids! Nothing better to do with their time.*

# Chapter 10

A buzz of speculative whispers greeted Nikki when she returned to the office. Catching Sajid's eye, she made her way over to their desks that sat opposite each other near the front of the room. As expected, Nikki's was just as she'd left it: overflowing with empty coffee cups, Post-it pads and pieces of paper with her scrawl all over them, whilst Sajid's was pristine. She scowled. How the hell could he work and not make a mess? In his hand Sajid held the paper with all the bets on it and, judging by his wide grin, he was excited to be finally hearing the results first-hand.

'You'd have been better employed cleaning my desk than carrying on with your stupid wager, Saj!'

'I'm not your damn skivvy. You're more than able to clean up your own mess. Besides which, I could never be one hundred per cent sure what dead creatures I might find under those wrappers.'

'Cheeky!' She glanced round and saw that most of the Major Incident Team were present and accounted for. 'Archie making an announcement soon?'

'Yeah, we were all told to present ourselves here for the big revelation.' He took a sideways glance at Nikki. 'You regretting not going for it now, Nik?'

Nikki slid into her seat and turned it to face the front of the room. 'Well, I'll wait and see who gets it first, but my money might be on an outsider you didn't even consider.'

'You know something I don't, Parekh?'

Nikki tapped her index finger to the side of her nose. 'That's for me to know and you to wait and see.'

Leaning back, with his chair at such an angle, Nikki was sure Saj would topple over. He folded his arms. 'Where did you disappear off to?' He wiggled his eyebrows. 'Something you're not telling us? A secret DI interview perhaps?'

For a second Nikki was tempted to kick the chair with her foot, just to see his reaction, but she took pity on him. Instead she clicked her tongue and shook her head. 'Nah, not me who's the wild card in this one …'

'But where did you go then?'

The volume of noise in the room went down a notch and Nikki turned her head to see her boss DCI Archie Hegley enter the room. Since his heart scare a few months ago, Archie had lost weight and now his trousers and shirt hung off him, making him look more like Columbo than his own previous self – although that wasn't strictly true, for unlike his past self, Archie seemed to have either invested in an iron or Saj was right and he had got a female friend to impress. She turned back to Sajid. 'Later – hang around after this carry-on and I'll update you.'

Archie reached the front of the room and turned to his staff. His hair stood in two horns at either side of his near-bald pate. His face was pale and his lips drawn into a straight line. Uh-oh, looked like the interviews hadn't gone as planned. And Nikki had a sneaking suspicion she knew why. Archie must have been forced to employ Springer as the DI and, although they'd had a thaw in relations since Springer had been kidnapped and nearly lost her life, she was no more Archie's Earl Grey than she was Nikki's. A random thought that perhaps she should apply for a transfer ran through her mind, but deep down inside she knew she couldn't. How could she leave the best boss she'd ever worked under, to say nothing of Sajid, her partner. The two of them worked well together, anticipating each other's moves, and she couldn't imagine having that relationship with anyone else.

Archie cleared his throat, raked his fingers over his head once more and began. 'Well, ye've all been waiting to find out who the new DI is.' He glared at Sajid, with a slight shake of the head. 'Some of you have even been betting on it, I believe.'

There were guffaws around the room and Sajid had the grace to look mortified at being caught out. Despite the knot in her stomach, Nikki grinned. Sajid should have known there was no way he could keep a secret from Archie. The boss knew everything that went on in the office.

Archie raised a hand again for silence and bit his lip. 'Well, it's with regret I have to …'

Nikki's mouth fell open. Surely he wasn't going to tell everyone that he disapproved of Springer as the new DI – not in front of the detectives she would be leading?

A voice from the back of the room made Nikki turn round as Detective Chief Superintendent Eva Clark, trailed by none other than Felicity Springer, made her way to join Archie at the front of the room. 'I think, if you don't mind, DCI Hegley, that I'll do the honours.'

A low hum went round the room as the DCS smiled around at them. Saj turned to Nikki with a raised brow. 'Did you know about this?'

Nikki shook her head. 'Just twenty minutes ago. I'll explain later.'

DCS Clark, smiling widely, waited till Felicity Springer had joined her at the front. Springer, although a little gaunt around the cheeks, looked much better. Which may have been accentuated by her new short haircut. The last six months had put her through the mill, both physically and emotionally and she still had many trials ahead of her as her testimony would be required in not one, but two separate but very high profile cases. That aside, she looked well and even carried the hint of a smile on her lips too. Something Nikki wasn't used to seeing on the other woman's face. Nikki moved her gaze from Springer, unwilling to watch her as she was announced as the new DI and instead focused on Archie. Archie had taken a step back and was studiously looking into the space as if to distance himself from whatever was about to happen.

'Well, DCI Hegley was about to make an announcement before I so rudely interrupted, but I thought it might be better coming from me. Today, as you all know, we conducted the interviews for the vacant detective inspector position, which DS Parekh filled so efficiently during an incredibly stressful investigation and at very short notice, on a temporary basis earlier in the year. The competition was fierce as you'd expect. Applicants ranged from those in the district, in our station and, in fact, throughout the country. In the end, the decision was unanimous. The person appointed has all the people skills necessary to work with an established team of detectives ...'

Nikki turned to Saj and shook her head. *Really? Springer a people person?*

'... this officer's experience is far reaching and I have yet to find anyone with a bad word to say with regard to their commitment to the job, their staff and the public. It is my greatest pleasure to announce that the new detective inspector who will join DCI Hegley's team in January will be Detective Inspector Ahad who moves from Greater Manchester to join us ...'

For a moment there was stunned silence. Everyone, like Nikki, had assumed that Springer's presence at the front had heralded her promotion to DI. Like a Mexican wave, relief rippled across the room and a delayed clapping began.

Bringing the room back to order again, DCS Clark continued. 'You're probably all wondering why I have DS Springer here with me today and I am pleased to say that, now that she is signed fit to work after her traumatic experience before Easter, she has requested a transfer from the CCU to the MIT. I am pleased to say that DS Springer will be joining the team as a liaison between DCI Hegley and myself, working from this office and coordinating the employment of civilian staff and uniformed officers attached to the team as necessary. I hope you will all make her very welcome.'

Springer's face broke into a wide smile. Her cheeks were flushed as both Archie and the DCS stepped forward to shake her hand.

'Well,' Saj echoed Nikki's own thoughts. 'That's a turn-up for the books. Never saw that one coming, but rather that than have her lording over us as DI, yeah?'

Nikki inclined her head. She was glad that Springer wasn't her superior, however, she was aware that the newly created role offered Springer a degree of power that the other woman would relish. As long as she stayed out of Nikki's way and didn't act like a damn jobsworth, Nikki would just have to deal with it.

# Chapter 11

It's strange watching the news in the pub. Everyone yapping on about it and me sitting here keeping schtum. Inside I'm grinning like one of them cats they go on about. But not outside. No, I'm smart enough to keep my real feelings under wraps. I really want to blurt out what I've done, so instead, I drink up, wave to the lads and head off back home.

My room's the only place to get a bit of quiet so I head straight upstairs and shove my headphones in. Time for a bit of Eminem as I go over the news report in my head. They still haven't got a Scooby. Lot of damn incompetents. Not that I'm complaining like, it's just when you pay your taxes you expect a bit better. They've not even found the van yet – how bloody dumb is that?

I didn't think I'd find it so hard to cover up my real feelings. Thought I'd be bricking it all the time, but it's not been like that. After Dyson, I realised I was made for this sort of stuff. Clandestine operations they call it in the military. Well, that's what I'm doing. I'm waging my own sort of war – a war of self-protection.

Can't wait though till things have died down a bit and I can come clean. Tell her what I've done to protect her whilst he's sat on his fat arse panicking and offering stupid platitudes. Then she'll see. Then she'll realise who's got her best interests at heart.

Nearly gave it away today at work. Old biddy kept blabbing on and on about it. What a waste his death had been. Such a nice young boy, so clever – a genius, she'd heard. I just about managed to stomach that, but then she started on about the killer being a pervert and a sociopath and all. I almost blurted out right there and then, 'What, you dozy old cow? Do you think I look like an effing sociopath or pervert, do you?'

I laugh, imagining her face if I'd let rip with that. She'd have shit her bloomers that one. Anyway, I reined it in and got out of there pronto like. No point in tempting fate. She's just a dopey old bitch anyway. What does her opinion matter? I know what's important and the likes of her aren't.

After Liam, despite all of my careful planning, I half expected them to come knocking on the door, their handcuffs at the ready, but they haven't looked at me askance. It never occurred to anyone that I was capable of that. They haven't put the two deaths together either. Well, that's because of the distance between them. There's no real reason for them to put them together – not the police nor anybody else.

Glancing over at the door to make sure it's locked, I shut my eyes and relive the sensations of my weapon slicing through flesh and muscle and fat, and then I take care of myself. Seems like I don't always need my little hobby to get my rocks off.

# Chapter 12

'Hey, Mongol boy, got my money yet?'

Isaac Khan lowered his head, and kept walking. Maybe they'd leave him alone this time. Maybe he'd reach the bus stop before they got to him.

'Hey, you? Retard boy – get your ass over here and tell me where my money is!'

Calum Jefferson frightened Isaac. Last time he'd gone near him and his friends, they'd pushed him over, stole his best Dr Who badge and all his money. Isaac shuffled faster, wishing he could outrun him, but he had a heart condition and he wasn't allowed to run – not really fast – not really, really fast. He wished he had a TARDIS, like Dr Who. Or a sonic screwdriver. Then he'd sort them out. He'd pretend they were Cybermen or Zygons and he'd zap them or send them into space, somewhere where they couldn't find him.

A hand landed on his shoulders, the fingers digging right into his skin as Calum forced him to stop and turn round. He was with his mates and Isaac's heart began to race. How had they found him? He'd thought that he'd be safe from them once he moved into the shared accommodation that his social worker sorted out for him. Now they were here, right outside, waiting for him.

'Hear you got a job, retard. Who the hell would give you a job? You're ugly with your big head and bulgy eyes. What sicko would want to employ you?'

Tears ran down Isaac's cheeks and his lower lip trembled. He kept his head down. Through his tears all he could see were three pairs of trainers. He'd left most of his precious stuff in his room – his TARDIS model, his Dr Who figures, his sonic screwdriver – so at least they couldn't take those. But he did have something in his bag that he didn't want them to take. It was a gift – a gift for Sunni. He gripped the strap of his rucksack tight, hoping they wouldn't take it from him like they did last time.

Calum let his shoulder go and moved his fingers to Isaac's scalp. He pressed them tight and Isaac flinched. Then the bully gripped his hair and pulled Isaac's head till it was close to his face. Whispering in Isaac's ear he said, 'We heard you've got a house. Property, up Listerhills way.'

Isaac said nothing and Calum shook his head, making Isaac's teeth rattle together. 'You answer me, Isaac. You got a house up Listerhills way or not?'

Isaac nodded. He did have a house in Listerhills. He hadn't been back since they took him away from Mrs Parekh after his mother died. He missed Mrs Parekh – and Nikki and Marcus and Sunni and Charlie and Ruby and Haqib. He even missed Anika, but most of all he missed Mrs Parekh and then Sunni.

'You want us to leave you alone, Isaac? Leave you alone for good, eh?'

Calum let him go and pushed him into one of his mates, who pushed him against the other mate – on and on, Isaac was getting dizzy. His nose was running and he was crying and begging for them to stop – but still they went on, pushing him this way and pushing him that way. Until he fell in a heap on the floor. Calum kicked him in the ribs. 'You want us to leave you alone, then you gotta do something. Will you do it?'

Curled up in a ball, Isaac nodded. 'Yes.'

'You'll sell that house on Listerhills and you'll give us the money. If you've got a job then you won't need it.'

The young lad shook his head. 'I can't do that. I don't know how to.'

'Don't worry about that, Isaac boy. We'll sort it out for you – see, we like to help our friends.' Calum leaned over and hefted Isaac to his feet, brushing him down as if they were besties. 'So, you'll sell the house and give us the money and we'll leave you alone. Is that a deal?'

Isaac nodded.

'Oh, one more thing. You don't tell a soul about our deal – yeah?'

Again he nodded.

Calum looked at him for a long time then. 'You gotta promise properly. You gotta make it mean summat. Your mum's dead in't she?'

'Yes.' Fresh tears flowed down Isaac's cheeks. He didn't want to think about his mum, not here, not with them about.

'Okay, so we can trust you. You'll need to promise on her grave.'

Isaac frowned. 'Why?'

'Because if you don't, your mum will go to hell – you know what hell is, don't you? It's where all the fires are. She'll go to hell and all her flesh will melt off her bones and her eyes will fall out and she'll be in pain forever and ever. You gotta swear on her grave and then you gotta keep your promise or that's what'll happen to her.'

Isaac couldn't let that happen to his mum. She was the best. He didn't want her in pain again. She'd been in so much pain before she died, he couldn't let that happen to her. He held out his little finger and Calum looked at it. 'What's this?'

'Pinkie promise on my mum's grave. I won't tell anyone.'

Calum grinned and looked at his friends, raising one finger to his head and twirling it round and round, before linking his pinkie with Isaac's. 'Say it again now.'

Isaac repeated his promise.

Soon as he'd finished, Calum shoved him on the ground once more and began kicking him. 'That's just so's you'll remember.'

'Hey, you boys – leave him alone – leave that poor boy alone, you monsters. I'll get the police on you.'

Laughing and whooping, Calum and his mates ran off, and seconds later Isaac was helped to his feet by an old man who had his phone out ready to phone the police. Isaac shook his head. If he phoned the police, then Nikki would know – and Nikki had a way of getting him to say stuff even if he didn't want to. 'No, no police.'

Isaac retraced his steps back into the room that he'd just moved into and packed all his precious belongings into his rucksack. He couldn't stay there anymore.

# Chapter 13

Nikki pulled into her street and scoured the road for a parking place. Unfortunately, with none close to her house, she was forced to park a good five blocks away. Before leaving Trafalgar House she'd brought Sajid up to speed with the three anonymous letters and after the customary sulk because she hadn't told him when the first one arrived, Saj had been mollified to learn he was the first one she'd shared them with. They'd batted the reason for the letters around and guessed at the possible identity of the sender, but Saj agreed that other than the coincidence of the postmarks there was little to report to DCI Hegley that couldn't wait till the next day. After warning her to be vigilant – 'you never know what folk who send this anonymous stuff are really thinking, Nik,' he had rushed off to meet his partner Langley for a meal.

With her earlier unease, combined with Sajid's warning, Nikki wished she'd been able to park closer to her house. Not that it was far and, although the nights "were fair drawing in" as Archie would say, it was still light. Yet, for some reason she was antsy. Probably just the pent-up emotions of thinking she was going to have Springer as her boss, followed by the release of said emotions when she realised she wasn't. Nikki got out of her car, glad that it was Marcus's turn to cook, and rolled her shoulders back a couple of times to relieve the tension before locking her car with a smart chirrup and heading down the path.

She'd only passed about five of the ten houses she needed to, when she heard hurried footsteps approach from a gate behind her and before she had a chance to turn round to see who it was, a gun was poked into her right kidney. Her heart sped up, pumping adrenaline through her and in an instant she rose onto the balls of her feet, her hand gripping her car keys inside her pocket, the ignition one between her middle and index fingers, her body tensed. Almost simultaneously, she lifted her right leg and spun to her left ready to kick her assailant where it hurt, only to be faced by a familiar figure whose first words spoken in a robotic tone were: 'You are a Dalek, Parekh.'

The words Dalek and Parekh were rhymed together and Nikki grinned and launched herself at the lad who still pointed his finger at her. 'Where the hell have you been, Isaac? So much for keeping in touch, yeah? We've not seen you for over a year.'

Laughing, Isaac's eyes crinkled. 'Got you, Nik Nik, didn't I?' The lad returned Nikki's hug with a huge one of his own, which left her breathless. 'Been in Bradford Five with my foster carers. But, I'm 18 now, so I left. I'm moving home now. We'll be neighbours again.' He puffed up his chest. 'Got a job and everything.'

Nikki frowned. Isaac and his mum had lived next door to Nikki's mum for as long as they'd lived in this street. Isaac was just a little older than Nikki's eldest daughter, Charlie and, when his mum died two years ago, Nikki's mum hadn't thought twice about taking the young lad in. However, social services reared their ugly heads and because no will had been left registering Lalita Parekh as the proposed carer for Isaac if anything happened to his mum, they'd decided to put him in the care of foster parents and Nikki hadn't seen him since.

She linked arms with him and together they started to walk towards Nikki's home, him lugging an overfilled rucksack.

'Thought you had a room in one of the new flats over near where I work?'

Isaac's eyes flitted towards her and then he shrugged, his head bowed. Nikki was familiar with that look. It was his "I don't want to talk about this" look.

'Marcus at home, Nik? And Charlie and Ruby and Sunni? Has Sunni been watching the new *Dr Who*? Love Jodie Whittaker, do you?'

Nikki stopped walking. 'Isaac, why are you not living in your flat? Are you being bullied? Is that it?'

Isaac shook his head rapidly from side to side as if the ferociousness of his denial would stop Nikki asking any more awkward questions.

But Nikki wasn't to be put off. 'You come clean to me, Isaac. Why do you want to move into your old house?'

'It's mine, Nik. Lally Mum told me so. I can do what I like, now I'm 18.'

'But what about all the bills and stuff, Isaac? You thought about that?'

For the first time since they'd started discussing his moving back home, Isaac's frown disappeared and his usual smile was back in place. 'Got a job, Nik. Doing a prentice ship at Lazy Bites. I'm gonna be Gordon Ramsay.'

His enthusiasm was irresistible and Nikki, despite her concern, grinned widely. 'As long as you don't start all that swearing. I prefer Gino D'Acampo – he's my favourite.' The change of subject seemed to have reassured Isaac as the furtive expression she'd noticed earlier had gone, replaced by a flushed grin that told her he was excited by the prospect of cooking all day long. He'd always loved working in the kitchen. 'You know the Lazy Bites café is opposite where I work at Trafalgar House. I was in there today. I think you'll be a cracking chef, Isaac.'

As they walked on, Nikki sighed. Getting to the bottom of his desire to move home wasn't a conversation they could have out on the street. Clearly Isaac had his reasons, but Nikki was aware that she'd have to tease them from him and probably with her mum's help, which of course brought with it its own problems. Now, she'd be forced to invite her mum over, but they wouldn't have the space to talk in private. Not with her house full of kids. Besides, she still hadn't worked out what she wanted to say to her mum or how she wanted to handle things. She decided to put that problem to the back of her mind for now and, re-linking her arm in Isaac's, they started walking again. *Hope Marcus has made enough tea to feed a few extra mouths.*

As they walked the last few yards, Nikki became aware that Isaac kept looking around him. Peering behind them and in front of them. Every time a car passed he peered into it as if expecting it to be someone he knew. 'You okay, Isaac?'

Again, the closed-off look spread over his face as they walked through the gate leading to her front door. 'Yeah. I'm fine, Nik Nik.'

Nikki thrust the door open and, stepping inside, she raised her voice so she would be heard at all corners of her spacious terraced home. 'Hey, guys, get yourselves downstairs; I've got a surprise visitor who's dying to see you all.'

She turned to help Isaac off with his rucksack and found him peering up and down the street before pulling his head back inside, closing the door, turning the lock and fastening the safety chain. Nikki's partner Marcus, a large bloke with broad shoulders, and an all-year tan that came courtesy of his job as a landscape gardener, strolled out from the kitchen and having witnessed Isaac's strange behaviour, exchanged a raised eyebrow with Nikki before stepping forward to pull the lad into a one-armed hug.

'You okay, mate? Staying for tea, are you?'

Before Isaac had a chance to respond, there came the sounds of feet hurtling down stairs followed by squeals of delight by Sunni: 'It's Isaac! Yeah. Come and see my new TARDIS.'

Not long after followed by a 'Hey, Isaac, long time no see, how's it going?' from Ruby and a quieter but more heartfelt:

'God, I've missed you, Isaac. You stopping for tea?' from Charlie.

'Yeah, Nik says I can. I'm a chef now, Marcus.'

Marcus grinned. 'Well maybe you can come and make us all a meal one day.'

Isaac put his head to one side. 'I can make buns. Chocolate ones.'

Sunni, never one to say no to a baking activity, wrapped himself round Isaac's stomach and looked at Marcus. 'Can we, Dad? Can Isaac and me make buns?'

Charlie, stepping back into her usual role as Isaac's wingman, jumped in. 'Yeah, you and Dad have a sit-down before tea. I'll help with the bun making.'

Nikki mouthed a "thank you" to her daughter and went into the living room, pulling her phone out to call Isaac's social worker, whilst Marcus said, 'I'll get the wine.'

Nikki stared into space wondering just what had spooked Isaac so much. Whatever it was, she'd have to get to the bottom of it, but with Isaac, she'd have to tread very carefully.

# Chapter 14

Lalita wished she could shake off the malaise that had settled on her like a dark malignant cover since she'd discovered the note beneath her windscreen wiper at the library car park. She should have shown it to Nikita, but her daughter was always so busy juggling her kids and her job. Besides, they hadn't really spoken since their tiff and Lalita didn't want to burden her with this. For once she would be the responsible adult. For once she'd deal with it on her own. Anyway, it hadn't been overtly threatening or anything – *I Am Watching You* – scrawled on a scratty bit of paper. Not very imaginative as threatening notes went; still, she didn't like to think that someone was watching them from the shadows. It had probably just been kids messing around, but it had unsettled her.

Peggy's death had raked up old memories. Memories that she had managed to suppress for a long time now. If she didn't feel so guilty about how their childhood must have affected her kids, she could have shared her concerns with Nikita. She'd never seen such disgust on her eldest daughter's face and she was really scared that by refusing to talk about their past, she might have irreparably damaged their relationship.

Maybe she'd have a word with Marcus. He was always so

sensible – so calm and reassuring. She was happy that he'd come into their lives. He made Nikita happy and for such a long time, Lalita had wondered if that would ever be possible – especially after Charlie's dad had disappeared. She sighed and wished her younger daughter was as happy as Nikita. Anika was going through the mill at the moment and there was no way Lalita could add to her burden. She let out a puff of air. Who was she kidding? Anika didn't take on anyone else's burden unless it directly affected her. Besides, she suspected that for Nikita's sake she'd have to examine their past and try to undo some of the damage; however, Anika would want to keep the past firmly buried.

It wasn't that she didn't have friends. Lalita had plenty of friends. People at her book club, people at her Pilates class, co-workers – but there was no way she could ever share the secrets from her past with them. As for her family – well, her brothers and sisters just wanted to pretend that none of it had ever happened. With both her parents dead now, she didn't want to rock the boat. She loved being part of the extended family, yet wondered how precarious her position in the family would be if any of her past life became more public. No, she'd just have to deal with this on her own.

When she got home, rather than sit in the patch of garden at the front of the house as she'd planned, Lalita had locked her doors and secured the safety chain, feeling a little bit silly as she did so. However, as the evening progressed, she found she still couldn't settle. Startled by the sound of kids yelling on the street outside and rattled by the sound of bottles being tipped into a recycling bin at the back of the house, she flicked off the TV and for the umpteenth time, peeked through her kitchen blinds into her backyard. Was that movement, over by Mr Mahmood's wheelie bin?

She held her breath, peering through the dusk, annoyed with herself for being so foolish. When a fox sleeked out, bushy tail at half mast, hungry eyes seemingly catching hers mockingly, she exhaled in relief. A fox – only a damn fox. Not a monster, or a stalker or a serial killer. Perhaps Nikki was right: maybe she did need to extend her reading repertoire – maybe she should read a good old chick lit novel. Maybe she could borrow the copy of *Fifty Shades of Grey* that Nikita had confiscated from Charlie. That would get them all talking. Maybe she could even suggest it as next month's read for the book club. Smiling, a little more relaxed now, she opened the fridge and contemplated pouring a glass from the half-full bottle of white wine.

Her phone rang and she rushed through to the living room and found it slipped down the side of the couch. Grabbing it as if it was a lifeline, she saw it was Nikita and her heart sped up. This was the first time Nikita had phoned her since the funeral. Maybe she was ready to talk. Calming herself so her daughter wouldn't realise how tightly wound she was, Lalita answered.

'Mum, can you come round? We've got a surprise visitor you might like to see.'

Pleased to have a distraction, despite the blandness of her daughter's tone, Lalita ran out the door, locked it behind her and scurried along to her eldest daughter's house. She had nothing to worry about – not with her daughters living nearby. Her past was behind her and she was an idiot to let a stupid note upset her so much. She was safe and happy; her daughters were safe and happy, as were her beautiful grandchildren. Life was good for Lalita Parekh.

# Chapter 15

Downey had expected more of a reaction from her when she found the note and had been disappointed when she hadn't freaked out. Seemed like she'd developed a bit more spine since he'd last seen her. He couldn't wait to reacquaint himself with her, but that was a secondary aim. He'd other, more important things to sort out here in Bradford. Putting the note on her windscreen had been juvenile – he could have been caught and that would have scuppered everything. He hadn't been able to resist though.

Still, he needed to dial things back a notch. He shouldn't even be here. It was too risky. She hadn't been one to keep herself out of the limelight over the years and now he was going to use her for his own ends.

Bradford wasn't the safe haven it used to be for him and yet, for now, his presence in this godforsaken city was essential. He needed her to do the deed. Sort it out. She had her father's brains, that one, so she should be able to work it all out. By the time she'd got to the bottom of it, he'd be on a flight to Thailand under an assumed name – no way was he going back inside, and he'd heard that the law wasn't so strict in Thailand about the sorts of things he wanted to get up to.

Flicking the butt of his cigarette down a nearby drain, he dug his hands in his pockets and walked off down the road. Good job Freddie Downey had friends in Bradford. Loads of places to lie low till things were a bit safer for him. But for now, he had other things to do. Things to sort out, people to see, places to go, scores to settle. Oh, it was good to be back in his old stomping ground.

Then, one last detail to deal with, before he headed off to where the sun always shone. Payback. He could almost smell it and he grinned and sang under his breath, changing the lyrics to suit himself as he walked. 'I got you on your knees … dah dah dah dah dah … all you gotta do is please, please, please, please … me. Dah dah dah dah da. Get on your knees. Laylaaaaa!' You gotta love Derek and the Dominos.

# Chapter 16

Nikita had hugged her mum when she arrived at her house and Lalita had never needed a hug more. Yes, their embrace had been a little awkward – not as tight, a bit fleeting compared to their usual hugs – but it marked a slight thaw between her and her daughter. There was still a long way to go, but the promise of things turning out all right was strong. Tonight had been all about Isaac. Lalita had been so pleased to see the boy that she'd hugged him and kissed his cheeks until he'd finally pushed her away giggling. 'Stop it, Lalita mum. You're breaking my bones.'

She, Nikki and Marcus had discussed the situation. Isaac's social worker had told them he hadn't returned to his flat in the shared accommodation and that they would need to work out what was best for Isaac. Isaac was unaware that the house he considered his home in actual fact belonged to the father who had deserted him and his mother when he'd been born. According to the social worker, although he'd been letting it out for the past few months, Sharukh Khan was putting it on the market now and had refused to make any provision for his son. Thankfully Isaac had agreed to stay at Lalita's for now.

Lalita had been incensed on the boy's behalf. Sharukh hadn't stepped up to the plate when Gillian, his ex-wife, had died, insisting that the fact he'd let her live rent-free in his property had paid his debt to her. Now, it looked very much like she and Nikita would have to be the ones to explain the situation to Isaac.

When they'd walked back to her house, Isaac had all but run, his head bobbing from side to side as if scared of someone. This of course made Lalita jittery too and she found herself doing the same thing. She'd been relieved to get indoors, slam the door behind them and engage the lock.

Footsteps on the stairs announced that Isaac had finished his shower and was heading down for his promised hot chocolate. Lalita exhaled, pasted on a smile and poured the steaming drink into two mugs. When she put them on the table, Isaac was standing by the door in a pair of stripy pyjamas that he'd left behind the previous year. His cheeks were scrubbed to a glowing pink and his damp hair was flattened across his scalp. A surge of love swept over Lalita as she quirked an eyebrow at him. 'Suppose you'll be wanting some more cake?'

Grinning, Isaac sat down at the table with a nod. Then, he jumped up again and hugged Lalita as if he'd never let her go. 'You kept my TARDIS mug, Lally Mum.'

Extricating herself, Lalita ruffled his hair. ''Course I did. Knew you'd be back.'

They sat blowing on their hot drinks, munching on what was left of the cake Isaac had made with the kids in Nikita's house earlier. Isaac kept glancing round the kitchen and Lalita suspected he was reacclimatising himself.

'You know, you can stay here as long as you want, Isaac.'

The boy nodded, intent on fishing out the marshmallows Lalita had added to the spray cream on top of the hot chocolate.

'You'll need to make up your mind soon, love. They need to know if you're going back to your flat.'

Isaac shrugged. 'I'm gonna sell the house. Want to make sure Mum stays in heaven.'

Taking a moment to try to work out the link between selling the house and Gillian remaining in heaven, Lalita paused. Then, hesitantly: 'Your mum's in heaven, Isaac. You know that, don't you? She was such a good person, where else would she be?'

Still not meeting her eyes, he shrugged. 'Glad Sunni still likes *Dr Who*. We're gonna binge-watch all the Jodie ones together on Saturday. Nik Nik said that was fine. Marcus said he'd make popcorn.'

Well used to Isaac's diversionary tactics, Lalita decided to let things lie for now. It had been a busy day and it was getting late. 'Drink up, Isaac, then off to bed. You've got work in the morning, I hear.'

In companionable silence they finished their drinks. Lalita, happy to have company, savoured the moment.

'Lally Mum?'

'Hmm?'

'If you break a pinkie promise, bad things happen, don't they?'

Lalita studied the boy. His head was bowed, his fingers wrapped round his mug, eyes flitting sideways towards Lalita and then just as quickly away. Something was troubling him. Taking her time to respond, she chose her words carefully. 'Pinkie promises are just like any other promise. If you make one, then you should try your best to keep it. But, if you were scared, or not sure, or you were made to make a promise you didn't want to make, then you don't need to keep it.'

Isaac nodded. 'But sometimes you can't risk it, can you? Cos if you do, something bad might happen and I don't want her to go to hell.' With that he jumped to his feet, dropped a hurried kiss on Lalita's cheek and rushed upstairs.

Picking up the empty cups, Lalita put them in the dishwasher and decided to talk to Nikita about this before speaking to Isaac again. Moving round the house, Lalita's unease returned with Isaac's obvious anxiety. She checked the locks and through a slight gap in the front-room curtain, she scoured the street outside, then repeated the process with the kitchen curtains. All the while she chided herself that she was being melodramatic.

Heading upstairs, she poked her head into Isaac's room and saw his shape under the TARDIS duvet cover. With a smile, she switched on the night light in the hallway and left his door open a crack. It was good to have him back. Now all she needed to do was work out what was troubling him.

Isaac loved being back in Lally Mum's house and seeing Nik Nik and everyone again. Especially Sunni. But he was still scared. He had to sell the house and that Calum had said he'd show him how. He didn't want to sell it. He didn't want to live there anymore, but he didn't want to sell it either. Isaac snuggled under his duvet, inhaling the familiar smell of Lalita's house. He loved it here. He felt safe here, especially with kick-ass Nik Nik just down the road. But he didn't want Calum and his friends to hurt Lally Mum … or Sunni. Maybe he should have stayed at the home. Maybe he shouldn't have come back.

He waited till Lalita had checked on him. She always did. He smiled when he heard the click of the night light going on. She looked after him, did Lally Mum. He loved her almost as much as his real mum.

Unable to sleep, Isaac listened to the sounds of Lalita getting ready for bed in the next room. When there was silence, he got up, bare feet sinking into the carpet, and padded over to the window. Pulling the curtain to the side, he peered out, craning his head to see as far along the street as he could. He couldn't see anyone and, reassured, he went back to bed, pulled the cover over him and went to sleep, dreaming of Daleks zapping Calum and his mates.

# Friday 18th September

# Chapter 17

Parked outside Nikki's house, Sajid was leaning on the bonnet of his Jaguar, scrolling through his phone when she joined him. He scrutinised her as if she was a specimen in a lab before speaking. 'You okay?'

Her partner was referring to more than the anonymous mail she'd received. Saj was well aware that there was tension between Nikki and her mum and, after a brief phone call the previous evening telling him of Isaac's mysterious return, he was aware that she and her mum had met up. After she'd shown him the contents of the letters, Saj had advocated bringing Archie into the loop, but Nikki had expected that. Sajid was nothing if not predictable when it came to playing by the book. However, he was also loyal to a fault and Nikki was lucky enough to have his complete allegiance.

Although he'd initially balked at her plan to do a bit of investigation into Liam Flynn's abduction and subsequent murder without informing Archie, she'd soon won him round to her way of thinking. As things stood, other than the anonymous communications, there was no clear link between Peggy's death and the one in Cambridge. Neither missive had contained even the hint of a threat to Nikki other than the one evoked by their anonymity. But the clincher had been her desire not to overburden Archie with unnecessary hassle after his hospitalisation a few months earlier for a heart condition.

"Course, I am. I'm always okay, aren't I?' And with a reassuring smile, Nikki updated him on the Isaac situation and skimmed over her slightly uncomfortable interaction with her mum. Nikki loved her mum and, although hugging her had been awkward, there was no way she could maintain her distance indefinitely. Besides, her mum's face had been drawn with tension lines spreading out from her mouth and her smile had been forced. *Why was she punishing her mum with her distance?* It made no sense. Nikki had long since accepted that her mother was a child victim who had fallen through the cracks and, despite being subjected to the utmost cruelty and exploitation, had somehow managed to come out the other side. Okay, she'd leaned on her eldest daughter more than she should have and that had meant Nikki took on more responsibility than any child should have to. Still, her mum did the best she could and the bottom line was that Nikki loved her.

She gave Saj the Parkside police station postcode for the sat nav. Despite keeping Archie out of the loop, Nikki had already reached out to the investigating officer in Cambridge and he was expecting them by lunchtime. Sliding into the car seat beside her, Saj gave a last-ditch attempt to change Nikki's mind about them flying solo, well in tandem – but not in any official capacity. 'I think we really need to bring Archie in on this. He'll be livid when he finds out.'

Sajid was right, of course he was, but Nikki wanted to be sure there was something to report before she wasted anyone's time. She turned her laser gaze on him and remained silent.

Tapping his hand on the steering wheel, Saj tutted and looked out the windscreen. Engaging the clutch, he set off. 'You win, Nikki. Since you've already set up those meetings in Cambridge we'll go down there. But, everything we find out gets reported right back to Archie on our return, okay?'

If he hadn't been driving, Nikki would have kissed him.

# Chapter 18

Decided to take some time out after they found Flynn's body. Shit, I thought they were never going to find it. Thought maybe he'd end up being just another missing person. Suppose it's better he got found. It's what I'd thought would happen and now it's like closure, innit? The police don't seem to have much to go on, which is a relief. All my plans and the measures I took seem to have paid off. Last thing I want is to have left a big clue pointing straight in my direction.

I'm trying to act normal. Working as usual, going to the pub and all, but it's like I'm in a dream. Like I'm looking down from above and it's creepy. I keep wondering what they'd all think if they knew the truth – that I'm a killer. That I've got blood on my hands. Sometimes I drift off mid-conversation and they take the piss about that. I'll be careful though. Will make sure I don't do that again. Don't want anyone to notice anything out of the ordinary.

I regret having to kill Liam, but there was no other option. Shame really. He wasn't a waste of space like Dyson was or like most of them on my list are. But, he was a threat and there was no way I could risk him mouthing off. It had to be done – for the greater good. Weird though – I was all excited when I offed the Dyson whore, but with Flynn it was different. I still got a buzz, like. But I didn't come. Just shows I'm not a poofter like he was. Not a pervert. Not that I'd have had a go with that Dyson thing. God no. Bet she had the clap. Dirty bitch.

It's easy to choose who's next from my list. He should have been the first really. Hmm or maybe number two … Nah definitely him first. He's behind all of this. He's got the most to pay back. He's the one I'll least regret killing. As I look at his name, an idea forms in my head and I smile. I'm going to enjoy disposing of this one and I'm going to enjoy seeing him squirm. I'll not let him off lightly like I did with Dyson. No. He's going to pay big time.

I've got rid of the burner phone I took to Cambridge, so first up, I need to buy another. Got to be sure I don't leave a trail. I had wondered about stealing a van – just for the night, but decided it was too risky. Best to just go with the anonymous look.

I decide to do a bit of surveillance. I take the train, pay cash, keep my head down and blend in. Nobody notices me and there's no reason why anyone would bother checking CCTV around the train station. Nothing to say I made a recce and even if they considered it, they'd have no idea when I made it or how I arrived. Also, they'd not see me returning by train on the actual day I dispose of him. Hell, for all they know, I might live in Bradford.

It's weird seeing where he's lived all these years. Knowing the sorts of things he's done – the risk he could pose if he blabbed. If anyone gets wind of what I'm covering up, they'll rake every-thing up. What I need to do is make sure that there's only dead bodies to rake up. Protecting those you love has its price, but in this particular instance payback is a major motivator.

If it was anyone else, I'd feel sorry for them, living on their own, in a crappy house that's falling to bits. No visitors, only that care worker. His house stands out like a sore thumb – an eyesore. Decrepit, filthy and decaying. Just like him. Through his grimy window I see him, eyeing the people who pass. My stomach clenches as I see him lift something to his face when a mother and child step out into their garden opposite. Bastard's got binoculars. I want to storm over and smash his window in, yell at the mother to take her kid indoors till I've dealt with this old pervert.

Instead, I continue to walk down the hill, my heart hammering against my chest, my hands clenched into fists by my sides. Yes, this is one person I'll have no regrets for. None at all.

# Chapter 19

'Still don't get why you won't let me share the driving. It's a long journey, you know? Over three hours *and* we're driving back tonight too. You'll be knackered.' Nikki glared out the side window, seeing fields, and buildings and whatnot zoom past. Saj was making good progress and, with luck, they'd arrive in Cambridge in time for a late lunch. Nikki hated being a passenger on long journeys – hated not being in control. It wasn't just that she wanted another go at driving the Jag, it was that driving helped her think – and she had loads to think about. Perhaps she should have insisted they use her car. But deep down, she realised that that idea would have been totally impractical. There was no guarantee her increasingly temperamental Zafira would make it to their destination and back.

Saj laughed, his deep brown eyes sparkling. 'Not this again, Nik. You know fine and well that last time I let you drive my baby, you sped – not just a little bit – a huge, massive well-over-the-speed-limit amount. In fact, I'm surprised you weren't caught. So, if you think I'm risking Parekh's answer to Lewis Hamilton on the damn motorway with my car, you've got another thing coming.'

Nikki huffed and popped a piece of chocolate into her mouth.

'Well don't even *think* about asking if you can drive my Zafira either, Sajid Malik – two can play that game, you know!'

'Your old wreck – as if?' A combination of a snort and a belly laugh made Nikki smile. She loved it when Saj laughed that deep rolling thunder right from the depths of his belly. It always made her heart sing and right now her heart could do with a rousing chorus of something upbeat.

DCI Davy Jones was a stocky Welshman with a gruff warm smile and bits of loo roll stuck to his face where he'd apparently cut himself shaving. He and Archie, so he told them, had come up the ranks together before Jones moved down to Cambridge. Thankfully, he didn't appear to have been in contact with DCI Hegley, accepting Nikki at her word when she'd explained they were looking into a possible, but extremely unlikely, link between Peggy Dyson's murder and that of Liam Flynn. Nikki could understand why the two men would get along so well together. She winked at Saj and extended her hand to greet Jones. His grip was a little too tight, but not one of those handshakes made by smarmy gits out to prove a point and Nikki flinched as her finger bones squished together. It was just his way and from Saj's reaction, he'd suffered the same fate.

'Come on, come on. I'll take you back to the incident room. I got a load of sandwiches in and told Irna to make the decent coffee – can't have you reporting back to Archie that we didn't treat you right.' Jones set up a pace, flinging his arms out in different directions to introduce staff or show them the facilities – none of which Nikki took in as it was all delivered at breakneck speed and she had to focus on keeping up with him.

'Archie all right? Heard he had a bit of a heart scare a while back. Me too. It's the damn job, you know. Takes it out of you.'

'Yes, he's fine. Back at work and he's lost a bit of weight. Still doing too much though.' Nikki shrugged in a what-can-you-do sort of way and Jones laughed.

'And he's got himself a lady friend, I hear. Nothing like love to mend a broken heart!'

Nikki stopped dead in her tracks. *Lady friend? Looks like Saj was on the ball with that bit of gossip. But who was the mystery lady?* She looked at her partner, whose lips carried a smug grin that Nikki found quite annoying. Trying for non-committal in the hope Jones would reveal more, Nikki said, 'Yes, nothing like the influence of a girlfriend to make you slow down.'

Davy turned, tongue lodged in his cheek and looked from Saj to Nikki. 'I've put my foot in it, haven't I? You two had no idea he was seeing …' He stopped and waggled his finger in the air. 'Oh, no – I'm not giving you any details about the old mucker's love life. You'll have to ask him yourself.'

Laughing, Nikki began to walk on. 'You caught us out there, Davy. Can't believe he managed to keep it a secret.' *Actually, I can't believe anyone in their right mind would be able to put up with him.*

'I'm more surprised he's managed to find someone patient enough to put up with him,' Sajid said, then yelped and rubbed his shoulder when Nikki punched him. He glowered at her. 'What was that for?'

Jones laughed. 'Malik's right. Archie's not the easiest man to put up with. You know he was a different person in the company of his wife. Still gruff, but in a more loving sort of way. He'd have done anything for her – anything. Let's move on. This reminiscing isn't getting you lot closer to working out if there's a link between what's going on in Bradford and Liam Flynn's murder down here.'

He thrust open a door and ushered them into a spacious incident room with whiteboards filled with intel at the front, a large conference table with chairs spaced around it and a spread of sandwiches and coffee Thermoses on top. Round the edge of the room a few detectives worked on computers and in the background Radio One played softly. 'I'm not convinced there is a link, you know. It all seems a bit thin: a newspaper cutting about the murder and then diary excerpts from the same sender. Not sure it links up. Maybe someone's just yanking your chain.'

Before Nikki had the chance to tell him they'd considered that possibility – in fact still were considering it, Jones raised a hand. 'I know, I know you'll have considered it. Truth is, if it was my investigation I'd be down here too looking at this case. Coincidences do happen – but not very often. Either way, if you link Liam's murder with your one then well and good. If not, at least you've eradicated a line of enquiry. Now sit and eat. We'll chat whilst you're eating and then I'll let you loose on the files. That suit you?'

Saj's stomach chose that moment to rumble and that settled the matter. As promised the coffee was good – full-bodied and flavoursome – and it was enough to wipe away the lethargy from the long drive. Trafalgar House needed to up its game when catering for external visitors and Nikki made a mental note to suggest they use Lazy Bites. She grabbed a ham roll, reminding herself to make room for a vanilla slice … and a jam doughnut. In between bites she asked Jones all about Liam Flynn's murder. 'Did you have anyone in mind for it? Any clear suspects?'

'It was one of those tragic cases where you start off hoping for the best, but as time passes you realise the chances of a happy ending are practically non-existent.' Pouring himself another coffee, Jones, eyes narrowed, appeared to put his thoughts in order before continuing. 'Liam was reported missing by his partner, Daniel Lammie. According to him, Liam left to go to his research job at the university – but he never arrived – even missed a couple of lectures he was supposed to deliver. So we looked at Lammie for it first – but he was alibied. CCTV showed Liam leaving the flat and making his way into town at the time Lammie said. Lammie headed in the opposite direction of the university and arrived at his place of work at eight forty-five, from which time he was alibied right through till he left at five-thirty. When he got back to the flat, there were messages on the answer phone from his university colleagues asking where Liam was. He waited till eightish, and when Liam didn't return and didn't respond to his phone calls, he phoned us. My feeling early on was that he wasn't our guy – but you gotta look at everyone.'

'Any other suspects? Had he had beef with work colleagues, family?'

'He was estranged from his parents. According to Lammie that had been a fairly recent thing; although Liam refused to confide in Lammie, he said Liam had been devastated by whatever had caused the rift.'

'Was it to do with his sexuality, do you think?' Saj's mouth was set in a thin line as he asked the question. His own family's response to his sexuality had been traumatic for him and he was now estranged from his entire family, extended and immediate, apart from his sister.

'Apparently not. Liam and Daniel had been together for a couple of years and had met each other's families. There was no problem of that sort.'

'Hmm.' Nikki was thoughtful. 'Did the parents tell you what had caused the rift?'

'Now, that's where things got a bit weird. The parents were really tight-lipped – grieving – definitely grieving, mind, but they refused point-blank to explain why they and their youngest son had argued.'

'Brothers, sisters? Any of them know anything?'

'The eldest brother, Johnny Flynn, has become the family spokesperson – says his parents are too distraught, so he did the media appeals and such. He and the other siblings …' Jones reached for and consulted his notes. 'Josie, Maria and Tommy know something – mark my words – but they're keeping schtum.' He tapped his fingers on the table. 'Thing is, who knows if this rift is relevant anyway? We've got it down now as some sort of stranger abduction. Maybe a homophobic attack – maybe he was having an affair?'

Saj joined in again. 'You've got a lot of maybes going on, sir; does that mean you're no further forward?'

Heaving his broad shoulders back in a stretch that made his chair scrape across the lino, DCI Jones exhaled. 'You've got it. We ran all the CCTV, interviewed every bugger and his mother who had anything at all, no matter how vague, to do with Liam Flynn and all we're coming up with is a big fat ZERO!'

The last word came out on a burst of frustration and caused the other officers in the room to look in their direction for a moment before continuing their work. Nikki sympathised. They'd all been there working a case that seemed to be going nowhere fast and she hoped that they'd soon catch their killer. The letters sent to her made it all too close to home and she needed to find out who had killed Peggy Dyson. 'So did you manage to track Flynn at all after he headed into town?'

'Yeah, last footage we got of him was him hanging about outside the bus station then he got into a black van. CCTV showed the number plates were covered, and the driver wore a cap.'

With a grim smile Nikki tutted. 'Don't tell me: a baseball cap pulled down over his or her eyes?'

'You got it. Couldn't even be sure whether it was male or female. We found the car two days ago parked up in Maxstoke Golf Club car park, west of Nuneaton. It had initially been reported missing from a small town called Bedworth near Nuneaton.' He held up a hand again. 'And, before you ask – no CCTV – they wipe their cameras every forty-eight hours. And nobody could say for certain when they first noticed it parked there. They initially thought it belonged to a dog walker, or one of their members who'd had a bit too much in the club house and got a lift home.' He slammed his fist on the table. 'If only they'd got their putters out of their arses and phoned it in sooner, we'd maybe have an idea – now we've hit a bit of a dead end.'

Nikki and Sajid spent another hour looking at the files and studying the crime boards, and, although there was nothing concrete to link the cases, Nikki was still unable to dismiss the possibility. After thanking their host and promising to take the bottle of whisky he proffered back to Archie, Nikki and Saj left the station to keep their appointment with Liam Flynn's grieving partner.

Lips turned down, Saj said, 'Maybe the whisky will be enough to stop Archie ripping us apart when he finds out we've gone off on our own, keeping stuff from him.'

# Chapter 20

The man in the baseball cap had enjoyed catching up with the gang. Amazing what twenty-odd years could do to a man. Some of his old muckers were hardly recognisable. A few had succumbed to disease and left this mortal coil, but he was still going strong – at least for now. He prided himself on always taking care of himself, not getting too fat like some of them – big lumps of lard, with builder's bums and man boobs – disgusting.

Today, though, was the day he'd been waiting for. The day when he reacquainted himself with someone he'd not seen in a long time. He'd something to give the old fucker and, although he could have posted it, he preferred to see his face when he delivered it. He'd heard on the grapevine that Hudson was still in the old place. Heard he was in a wheelchair – nearing the end anyway. Still, he wanted to make one last visit to him before he left for good. After all, he and Hudson had shared a lot all those years ago. Boy had they shared a lot. Some of those things had been delectable nubile little arses ripe for the plucking – and pluck them they did.

He wanted to be in and out quickly. No point in drawing attention to himself, no point in making a meal of it. Do what he had to do – straight in and out and then that was another little job ticked off his to-do list.

When he stepped off the bus, the first thing he noticed was the smell of curry in the air. He breathed in deep and promised himself that when he was done he'd head to the Kashmir restaurant on the other side of Bradford. It was still there after all this time and he wanted to see if it had changed at all. Bringing his attention back to the present, he walked down from the huge McDonald's on the Thornbury roundabout. That was all new too. Big difference from the run-down grey area he remembered.

Gaynor Street had transformed, but he walked sprightly, kept his head down and didn't take much notice of the changes. Other things on his mind. He reached number 83 near the top of the hill, paused and glanced round quickly before slipping through the gate, reasonably sure no one had spotted him. Even if they had, what did it matter? He was just another bloke in a T-shirt wearing a baseball hat, wasn't he?

The door was easy enough to jimmy, although he didn't really need to, for by the time he'd opened it and stepped into the hallway, Hudson was leaning on a Zimmer frame by the living-room door. 'Saw you from the window. I'd have let you in if you'd waited, you know? No need to break in.'

The man grinned. 'Where's the fun in that, Gerry, eh?' He looked around and screwed up his nose. 'Fucking stinks in here.'

Gerry Hudson laughed, a brittle crackly sound that spoke of clogged lungs and breathlessness. 'You never did mince your words did you, Freddie? Come away in. I can't stand for too long and this damn contraption is useless.'

Freddie nodded and followed him through to a cluttered living room. Hudson's chair was angled towards the window. *The dirty old perv was still getting his jollies where he could.* Well, maybe by the time Freddie had finished with him, the old cripple would be in no mood for window stalking.

# Chapter 21

The flat that Liam Flynn had shared with Daniel Lammie was in a row of houses in a quiet avenue near a cemetery, with a church at the top of the road. Behind the flat, the River Cam flowed gently by, a few punters and kayakers taking advantage of the sun. Nikki turned from the window and looked at the young man who sat on the edge of a couch, next to his sister. He was in his early twenties, skinny, short-haired and totally distraught. His swollen eyes were surrounded by dry flaking skin, as was his red nose. A pile of tissues in the bin beside him told their own story. 'I'm really sorry to have to intrude at a time like this, but we really want to try to find out who did this to Liam.'

Daniel straightened and looked straight at Nikki. 'I just don't get it. I really don't. Everyone loved him – he'd no enemies.'

Nikki sat in the chair opposite him, and nodded towards Saj. 'DC Malik will record this, so we don't miss anything out. What I particularly want to ask is about Liam's estrangement from his parents. DCI Jones informs me that's a recent thing. Have you any idea what could be behind it?'

Wiping a tissue across his eyes, Daniel shook his head. 'No – I can't think what caused it. I mean they were never super close, but they got on well enough until a couple of months ago. It just happened all of a sudden. He came home one Friday night, and said he was heading off to Manchester as he had to sort something out with his parents. I offered to go with him, but he said it was family business.'

'Family business? Was that usual – did he often have family business to deal with?'

'No – never before that I know of. He came back late on the Saturday and he was in bits. He curled up in bed and cried like a baby and then when he got up all he said was that he was finished with his parents and he never wanted them mentioned again.'

'Did you try to find out more?'

''Course I did, but he was adamant he wouldn't talk about them. Said they were an abomination – that was the word he used. Said he was glad we, me and him, wouldn't have kids, cause he wouldn't want them to inherit his parents' warped genes.'

'That's quite strong isn't it – abomination and warped genes?'

'That's what I thought, but he refused point-blank to say any more.' Daniel sniffed again and pulled a cushion onto his knee, hugging it tightly. 'You say you're from Bradford? What has Liam's murder got to do with Bradford police?'

Sajid looked up. 'We know Liam's got no links with Bradford, we already looked at that angle, but something's come up and we're just checking it out.'

'Liam's never been to Bradford, but I think his parents might have.' He paused, head angled to one side as he thought about it. 'Yes, I'm almost sure his dad told me one night at the pub that he grew up there. Mind you, it might have been Birmingham. Definitely somewhere beginning with a B.'

This was news to Nikki and Saj. They'd checked Liam and his family for links to Bradford, but he'd lived in Manchester his entire life until he moved to Cambridge and they could find nothing linking the rest of the family to Bradford either. If this was true and Liam's parents were brought up in Bradford, maybe they'd found their link.

Liam Flynn's office was small and cramped and although the Cambridge police had already been over it, Nikki wanted to get a feel for Liam's place of work. He had been neat and organised. Everything was filed and his desk had only a photo of Daniel, a pen pot and his laptop. Nikki opened the top drawer and looked in. There was a photo frame face down lying atop a few shards of glass. She turned it round and saw that it was a photo of Liam's family – parents and siblings – but the glass had been broken and his parents' faces scribbled out in black permanent marker. What had made this previously devoted son turn his back on his parents like this? What had they done and why wouldn't they share the information with the police?

Nikki showed the smashed photo frame to Sajid before she replaced it and then, with a smile, accepted Professor Downford's offer of coffee next door in his much more spacious office. Nikki and Saj sat on what Sajid whispered to her was a Chesterfield settee, whatever that was, and sipped their drinks. Professor Downford needed no prompting to chat about Liam.

'He was a lovely man – had so much potential, liked by students and staff alike and I'm not just saying that because he's dead. I don't hold with all this speaking no ill of the dead – if they deserved to be spoken badly of, then so be it.' He leaned back in his chair, elbows resting on the arms, fingers steepled across his nose in what Nikki thought of as a typical professor-style pose.

'What was his research about? Could he have made enemies in his area of research?'

'Oh no. Liam's research was all about familial DNA and how it could be traced back over history to perhaps solve cold cases where the perpetrator's DNA wasn't held on file – or to iden-tify and reunite long-dead people with their families. Quite a fascinating area of work, although he had become a little distracted recently and had taken off on a sub-strand of research.'

'Oh?'

'Yes, he was looking at gene pools and the effects of narrowing them – fascinating stuff, but not directly linked to the work he was doing for me. However, I let him go with it. I'm all for letting researchers develop their own ideas for research strands and Liam was particularly talented.'

As Nikki and Saj left the bustling campus, Nikki wondered if Liam's research had been at the root of his murder. If this was the case, it seemed even less likely that there was a link to Peggy Dyson. Although the possibility that Liam's parents, or at least his dad, had perhaps been born in Bradford opened up new avenues to explore. However, Daniel hadn't seemed one hundred per cent sure about his facts and Nikki couldn't base an entire investigation on a half-remembered conversation in a pub.

# Chapter 22

By 7 p.m. Nikki and Sajid were on their way home.

'You sure you don't want me to take a turn with the driving? You must be knackered and it's still another two and a half hours' drive.'

'Good try, Nik, but I'm good.'

Hunched up in the passenger seat, enjoying their cushioned comfort, Nikki was less bothered about exerting her right to drive than she had been on the way down to Cambridge. She hadn't slept well the previous night and was beginning to fade. It had been a long day. Forcing a yawn back, Nikki made an effort to stay awake. 'What do you reckon – was the newspaper clipping just a red herring – something to put us off the trail?'

Saj indicated and overtook a caravan before replying. 'I don't think it was, Nik. I don't know how it all ties together, but Liam Flynn's murder, although we can't see it yet, must relate to Peggy Dyson's murder. Why else would your anonymous admirer send the clippings?'

Nikki sighed and, eyes on the passing countryside, allowed her mind to wander. All this talk in Cambridge about genes and such like had got her thinking about her own gene pool. She'd always been of the mind that genes and DNA did not a father make –

but what if her father's meanness was inside her – rotting and spreading its own unique brand of sadism like a tumour transmitting its malignant, destructive spores throughout her, just looking for a weak area to attach itself to, so it could grow and grow until it engulfed her?

A sharp twang of her wristband calmed her a little – it always did. It was her coping mechanism and one she only relied on in times of stress. Still, she couldn't get the thought out of her head. What if she'd passed that gene on to her kids? What if, despite the good genes passed down by their respective fathers, she'd managed to give them that one rogue gene? The gene that would turn her precious, beautiful, thoughtful children into monsters as they grew up? Studiously looking out the window so Saj wouldn't see her face, she asked, 'What's your thoughts on nature versus nurture, Saj?'

The silence stretched out and, heart pummelling her chest harder than Tyson Fury's fists, her head snapped round, dreading what she'd see on her partner's face. Perhaps Saj had seen something in one of her kids that neither she nor Marcus had.

'Aw, Nik.' His voice, raw and anguished, tore at her and a tear rolled down her cheek. She rubbed it away with the back of her hand and turned her head away from him again. Her partner knew her too well and the look on his face told her he'd understood where her question had come from.

Something soft was pushed into her hand and she looked down at it – a handkerchief. A reluctant smile tugged at her lips. 'Seriously, Saj – a proper hankie? Do you keep a stock of these, or what? Tissues not good enough for you?'

'Aw shut up, Parekh – some of us have standards. I want that back freshly laundered and ironed.'

'Eh, do people really iron hankies? I knew there was a really good reason why I stick to tissues.'

Shaking his head, Saj looked sideways at her as he drove and, seemingly satisfied with whatever he saw there, he nodded once and then spoke. 'Look, Nik. This case must be really difficult for you. I get that, but you can't give in to these stupid thoughts. You asked about nature versus nurture – well here's my take on things. I think you inherited a lot from your dad.'

Her stomach contracted – she hadn't realised Saj thought that she was like her dad. She opened her mouth but Saj lifted one hand from the steering wheel. 'No, Nik. Let me finish. What I think you inherited from your dad was a greater understanding of evil and *that* has made you the best detective I know. What you endured growing up – and I suspect you only told Langley and me the bare minimum – has shaped you. It's made you empathetic to victims. It's given you a moral compass that makes you able to swerve a little to make sure we get justice. Yes, you're hard to get to know, rough round the edges, prickly and down-right rude on occasion – but those who know you well, understand that *all* of that comes from a good place. So, in answer to your question – my money goes on the nurture side every time. That's the reason you're not like your dad. Although …' his grin took the sting out of his next words '… let's face it, you *do* have issues.'

He glanced at her wristband. 'And so does Anika – but the reason you're not like him is that throughout all that you endured, your mum tried to nurture you, to shield you – to teach you right from wrong, and ultimately tried to put you first.'

Saj indicated to overtake a truck and Nikki used that as cover to wipe another errant tear from her eye. *Come on, Nikki, get a damn grip. You don't do tears.*

'As for your brood – well, Charlie has inherited her mother's prickliness, Ruby, her mother's sarcasm and Sunni, Marcus's sunny disposition – they're normal happy kids – they're *not*, in any way, shape or form like Downey. So, I'm telling you right now, Parekh, you put that damn thought right out of your head, so we can crack on with working out what these messages are all about.'

Nikki pouted for a bit, mulling over Saj's words. Then:

'Soooo ... I'm prickly and sarcastic – which my daughters have inherited from me, yet Sunni's "joyful temperament" you attribute to Marcus? Wow.'

'Just saying it like it is, Nik. Just saying it like it is.'

Laughing, Nikki punched his arm. 'I can do joyful ...' she pursed her lips and thought about what she'd just said and added '... well, at the very least I can manage slight enthusiasm. Got to balance out Marcus's overenthusiastic personality somehow.'

A belly laugh filled the car and Nikki, smiling, rested her head on the doorframe and snoozed all the way back to Bradford.

Saturday 19th September

# Chapter 23

A rainbow over the M62 raised Nikki's spirits. Despite all the evil and nastiness in the world, there was also beauty and it was well worth her time to notice it and savour it – even if it was a Saturday and the kids had moaned about her taking off for the morning. Only promises of a trip to Temple Newsam farm in the afternoon had pacified them. She crossed her arms over her chest and sneaked a glance at her partner. 'Can't you make this heap go any faster? My Zafira would be quicker.'

With that, Saj increased his speed, overtook a caravan and then glared at her in mock annoyance. 'You see that manoeuvre I just did? Well, in your Zafira we'd end up with the exhaust in the middle of the motorway and our arses on the concrete.'

Throwing her head back, Nikki laughed and enjoyed the rest of the drive.

Ten minutes later when they reached the street where Liam Flynn's parents lived in Ashton-under-Lyne, just outside Manchester, they parked up and took a few minutes to study the area. A row of three-bedroom Lancashire terraced houses, similar to the ones in Bradford, sat right on the pavement with no front gardens. Most of the doors were painted blues and reds; a few were plain wood, but the one Nikki and Saj were looking for was green. Unlike the other houses, which all had net curtains or blinds for privacy, the Flynns' living-room curtains were closed tight. Nikki wasn't sure if that was their habit for extra privacy from passers-by or a result of being hounded by journalists since Liam's death.

A few cars and a van with a comic logo of two men fighting over a stepladder, with a pot of paint ready to tip onto their heads, lined either side of the road. Nikki wasn't entirely sure the image would encourage her to employ "Paint for U". Small wheelie bins stood neatly next to each of the doors. Nikki looked for a bell, but unable to find one, resorted to slamming the knocker a few times. Sajid had phoned the son Johnny Flynn earlier and despite his obvious reluctance, Saj had insisted on this visit. When there were no immediate signs of activity inside, Nikki wondered if they'd elected to go out to avoid this interview. She grabbed the knocker and again rapped hard. After a few seconds there was movement from indoors and Nikki exhaled a breath of relief. She would have been well pissed off if their trip into Lancashire had been a wasted journey.

Nikki recognised the figure who opened the door. It was Liam Flynn's eldest brother Johnny – the one who had taken over the role of family spokesperson for the public media appeal the Cambridgeshire police had instigated. Having watched the appeal and seen the online news report photo that she'd been sent, Nikki was surprised by his appearance. Gone were the suit, shirt and tie, replaced by paint-stained overalls open to the waist, an equally stained T-shirt and a faint whiff of sweat. Since the public appeal, Johnny had allowed rough stubble to grow over his chin and had clearly neglected to wash his hair, since a greasy fringe flopped listlessly over his forehead. His eyes were red-rimmed, whether from grief or drink, Nikki was unsure. However, when he spoke, his alcohol-tinged breath confirmed the second option – or perhaps a combination of both.

The man had just lost his younger brother and alcohol was

an easy self-medication. After her daughter Charlie's dad disappeared, Nikki had had a week of drowning her sorrows, before the reality of her pregnancy with her eldest daughter sunk in and she got control of herself.

'Yeah?'

*Okay so it's going to be like that, is it?* Nikki and Saj showed him their IDs as she introduced them, making sure to keep her voice pleasant – for now. 'We have an appointment to meet with your parents, Mr Flynn – or can I call you Johnny?'

With his hand still protectively holding the door half shut, Johnny Flynn glowered at them. 'They're not in.'

Despite her irritation at the dance she felt obliged to partake in with Johnny-obstructive-Flynn, Nikki forced a smile to her lips. 'We'll just come in and wait for them, thanks.' And she took a step towards the door, which Johnny immediately closed another few inches.

'No point. They're away.'

Sajid now stepped forward in line with Nikki. 'I made the appointment with you to meet with your parents this morning and you agreed.' He too kept his voice pleasant, but his brown eyes had darkened and there was an edge to his smile.

'You didn't.' Johnny glared at Sajid, shaking his head to emphasise his denial.

'I most certainly did, Mr Flynn, and you agreed.'

'Nope. *You* said you wanted to speak to my parents and the rest of the family and could you come this morning and I said yes.'

Nikki, sensing Saj's frustration, jumped in. 'And here we are – on your doorstep, as arranged, to meet with you, your parents and the rest of the family.'

He shrugged, and shuffled forward, so that he stood on the doorstep, the door behind him, sliding to only a couple of inches ajar. 'I said yes you could come this morning. Didn't say anything about you meeting anyone – just that it's a free country and you coppers do what you like anyway. Lucky to have caught me – just stopped back to change into clean overalls.'

Catching another whiff of sweat, Nikki thought that a shower seemed more of a priority than a change of clothes. She studied him. Why was he so reluctant to let them into his home? According to Cambridgeshire police, the Flynns cooperated fully with them, although Davy had said the parents were a bit vague – a bit reserved – so what had changed? Why the barriers now? Realising that Johnny was playing semantics with them, Nikki, smile still in place, said, 'Well, it's fortunate that we caught you then, isn't it? We'll just come in and ...' As she reached out her hand to push the door open, Johnny grabbed her wrist.

Saj stepped forward, but Nikki flashed him an "I'll deal with this" look. She looked pointedly from her wrist with his nicotine-stained fingers gripping it, to his face. Eyebrows pulled together, and at closer proximity to him, the speckles of pale blue paint that dappled his brows and fringe were apparent. The body odour stronger. 'Do you *really* want to go down the road of assaulting a police officer, Mr Flynn?'

His mouth worked, but his grip on her wrist loosened before finally falling to his side. 'I've got five minutes, that's all.' And he turned through the door, allowing them access to a hallway with two rooms leading off it and a staircase to the left. Blocking the staircase, he motioned for them to head straight through to the kitchen at the end.

Glancing round the room, Nikki pulled out one of the dining room chairs that were positioned round a wooden table. The room was clean and fresh – dishes all washed, dried and put away – not really what she'd expected judging by Johnny's appearance if he was home alone. 'Only you at home then?'

Leaning against the sink, no offer of tea or coffee forthcoming, Johnny glared at her. 'I live with my mum and dad.'

'Yes, but you told us they were away just now. That right?'

'Yeah. Mum's been upset since Liam – you know – crying and

stuff, depressed, not sleeping and she's had to see the doctor and he's given her pills. So Dad took her away for a few days – cheer her up, like – somewhere sunny.' All the time he spoke, his fingers tapped the unit behind him, and he kept glancing everywhere except right at Nikki.

'Oh, abroad then?' Johnny's newfound chattiness combined with the replacement of his earlier insolent behaviour had Nikki's senses tingling. For all that Johnny Flynn was now attempting to appear accommodating, he was ill at ease at having them in his home.

He shrugged, glanced to the side, bit his lip. 'Not sure. They didn't say. Dad wanted to get her right away from it all – no phones or internet – somewhere where she could just switch right off.'

Nikki kicked Saj under the table and, catching her unspoken instruction, he stood up. 'Just need to use your loo – too much coffee and then a long drive. Upstairs is it?'

Flynn pushed his frame away from the sink, a flash of something – fear? worry? – darted across his face and he pushed past Sajid, into the hallway, his voice louder than strictly necessary in the confined space. 'Yes, the toilet's upstairs, DC Malik, first on the right.'

Nikki smiled, sure that like herself Sajid would have noticed the increased volume in Flynn's voice and suspect the reason why. Johnny walked back into the kitchen, leaving the door open, casting anxious glances down the hallway.

'Bit strange though, them just heading off – leaving no contact details?'

'They wanted privacy.' Again his eyes darted along the hallway, then when the toilet flushed, he relaxed a little. 'Been through too much, have Mum and Dad. It's been a bad time for them. Losing their youngest son, like that.'

'Heard they were estranged though – Liam and your folks. Heard they didn't get on. Had a bust-up?'

Johnny's face reddened and he took a step forward, making Nikki wonder if he was going to grab her again, but the sound of voices from upstairs had him changing direction as he ran back out of the hallway yelling at Sajid who was coming downstairs followed by Mr Flynn senior. 'You've no right to be prying about our home – no fucking right. You need a warrant.'

'Actually, I think a warrant is the least of your worries right now, Johnny. Why don't you try obstructing the police in the line of their duty or obstructing a murder inquiry as well as the earlier assault on a police officer that we've not quite sorted out yet.'

William Flynn stepped off the last step, his arm round his wife, baseball cap pulled down over his eyes. 'Let's all go into the kitchen, eh? I'm sure we'll be able to sort this out over a cup of tea.'

# Chapter 24

Sitting round the Flynns' kitchen table, cups of tea in front of them, Nikki was in no rush to start the interview. She was intrigued that the parents had tried to avoid speaking with them, so she was happy to take the time to observe the three Flynns. The whole charade of the parents going away had piqued her curiosity and she wondered what exactly they were trying to hide. Maybe they were just grieving and nearly at the end of their tether. It was true that Sarah Flynn looked gaunt and haunted – nothing strange there – you'd expect her to be grieving. No parent expects to see any of their children die before they do and for Liam to have been killed in such a violent way must make it worse.

Sarah Flynn had made the tea, her movements uncoordinated, her hands shaking. Milk had been spilled, water from the kettle sloshed over the work surface. She was a woman operating on zero juice. The image Nikki had been sent showed a thin woman, with long black hair, but now the description "emaciated" suited Sarah better. But what really made Nikki question the entire bereavement act was the fact that sometime in the couple of weeks since her son's murder, Sarah Flynn had found the time to not only change her hair colour to a stark blonde but also to change the style. The two images – that of a woman thinking about her looks and the worn-out, bedraggled creature sitting opposite just did not add up.

William Flynn sat next to his wife, but his chair was angled away from his wife, although he clasped her hand tightly on the tabletop. He wore the baseball cap, covering his bald head – another bereaved parent with a need for a change in haircut., Mind you the image had been so unclear that she couldn't be one hundred per cent sure she'd have recognised him as the same man even without the shaved head. He had grown a beard since she'd seen him on TV. Despite the late summer warmth and the dapples of sweat across his forehead, he wore a long-sleeved polo neck. Every time Nikki looked away, she sensed him watching her, yet when she turned her attention to him, he averted his eyes.

Johnny, now that his parents were here, seemed content to take a back seat. Slumped in a chair on the other side of his mum, he drank his tea, slurping it loudly, head bowed and eyes focused on the tabletop. Probably wondering just how serious Nikki had been about arresting him.

Nikki gestured to Saj, who put his tea down and got out a notebook. She started the interview. 'This is just an informal chat, you know. Nothing to get aerated about. So, that being the case, would one of you like to tell me what all that hiding upstairs was about?'

Johnny's head dipped even lower, making it clear that he was not going to respond to that one. Sarah began to weep, her shoulders heaving, and Saj and his never-ending supply of linen handkerchiefs jumped to the rescue. It was as if he was just waiting for the opportunity to give the damn things away.

Nikki turned her gaze to William. 'Mr Flynn, care to explain?'

'It were stupid … really daft …'

Nikki started, she hadn't expected Flynn to have a Bradford accent, but then remembered Liam's partner telling her that William was from Bradford originally.

'Don't know what we were thinking. Well, we weren't really. We can't get our heads round our Liam being gone, like.'

Sarah's weeping increased and William wrapped an arm round her and hugged her to him. 'It's just hard … that's all.'

Nikki could see that – it was etched in every crease in their faces, in their sunken cheeks and in the way their bodies slumped as if the weight of holding them up was too much. Nikki had witnessed grief before and she was sure this was the real deal. However, she still had questions and she was sure this family were keeping secrets. Whether the secrets had anything to do with her investigation remained to be seen.

'I can see you're distressed, so I'll be as quick as I can. The reason we're here is that we believe there may be a link between Liam's murder and one that happened in Bradford earlier this week. I'd like to show you a photo to see if you recognise the victim, and if you could take your time and really think about it, we'd appreciate it.' Watching both Flynns closely, focusing on their faces, she placed the enlarged photo of Peggy Dyson before them.

She thought William Flynn flinched, but she couldn't be certain. However, the small gasp that Sarah made was indisputable. Nikki looked at her. 'You recognise this woman, Sarah?'

Holding Saj's hankie, now wrapped around her index finger, up to her mouth, she shook her head and looked away. 'No, never seen her before.'

Nikki pressed her. 'You sure? You gasped as if you did.'

'She said no, didn't she?' Johnny glared at Nikki, his eyes flashing with the same anger that had caused him to grab Nikki's wrist earlier. 'Leave her alone – she's had enough.'

Nikki ignored him and turned to William. 'What about you, Mr Flynn? Do you recognise her?'

Lips pursed, William too shook his head. 'Nope.'

'Just take your time. Maybe you came across her when you lived in Bradford?'

Gaze unflinching, William looked straight into Nikki's eyes. 'Never lived in Bradford, love. I'm a Lancashire man, born and bred.'

'Oh.' Sajid's open smile was designed to reassure. 'Funny that, I was sure that was a Bradford accent you have.'

William shrugged. 'Work with a couple of Bradford lads in the factory – probably picked it up from them.' He stood up, pulled his hat lower over his eyes and scratched his beard. 'Now if you're done …'

Picking up the photo, Nikki got to her feet and extended her hand to the older Flynns, ignoring Johnny's sullen expression as he remained seated. 'Well, that's us for now. I'm sorry for your loss and thanks for your help.'

Mr Flynn got to his feet and Nikki headed towards the door, swivelling at the last moment. 'Oh, nearly forgot. What was it that you and Liam argued about before his death?'

A crash from behind him had Mr Flynn spinning round. Sarah had dropped her teacup and tea was spreading over the table and onto the floor.

'Now look what you've done. Have you coppers no decency?' William Flynn backed into the kitchen. 'What happened between us and our lad was summat and nowt. Private business. Let yourself out … I've got my wife to look after.'

Back on the pavement, the Flynns' door shut behind them, Nikki looked at Saj. 'Well?'

'Exactly … I think there's a lot more to this than meets the eye.'

Nikki agreed. 'Tell you what, whilst I drive, you phone in a request to get as much background info on the Flynns as you can – right back to birth certificates et cetera. There's something iffy going on.'

'Ha bloody ha – nearly got me then, Parekh. I'll do the driving and you do the phoning, okay?'

'Well, it was worth a try, wasn't it?'

Saj unlocked the Jag and when they'd both slid in, he shook his head. 'Bloody Bradford born that one – did you hear the "summat and nowt"?'

Nikki laughed. Saj had read her thoughts. 'Maybe when we talk to the sisters and the younger brother, they'll let something slip. Yes. Let's get those interviews over with so I can get back to Bradford and take the yelling brats to the farm.'

In direct contrast to their parents and their elder brother, Liam's other siblings were a complete delight – eager to talk, to do anything that might help to find the bastard who had killed their younger brother. Josie, the next oldest after Johnny, was married, but a severe heart condition prevented her from working. Desperate for company, she'd agreed to meet with Nikki and Sajid in her home and had arranged for her other sister to be present too. Josie was devastated about Liam's death. 'He was the bright one in the family. The rest of us are just sort of normal like. Except for poor old Tommy who's as simple as they come. He works as a cleaner, but that's all he's able to do.'

Clearly keen to talk, Josie had made them tea and settled down. 'We often say that Liam inherited all our brains because apart from him and Maria, the rest of us haven't a GCSE between us.' She shrugged. 'Just the way it is really. Liam was lovely though. A beautiful kid. He doted on Tommy.' She sipped her tea. 'I reckon Tommy's condition and my heart condition was what made him interested in all that genetic stuff. Can't get my head round it meself.'

'Did you know Liam and your parents had fallen out?'

Wafting her hand dismissively, Josie snorted. 'They were always falling out. Dad thought Liam was getting uppity, him being so brainy and all. We kept out of it.'

Nikki realised they wouldn't get any more information from Josie about the estrangement between Liam and their folks. Her impression was that Josie was being truthful and really didn't know what was going on.

They were onto their second cup of tea when Maria Flynn walked in. Tall and striking, like the other Flynn siblings, she bore a strong resemblance to her dead brother. Maria was a career woman in Media City in Manchester and although amenable, she could contribute nothing that Nikki and Sajid hadn't already learned. So, Saj and Nikki returned to Bradford convinced that whatever secret the Flynns were keeping was confined to the elder three.

# Chapter 25

I didn't expect to be back in this dump so soon, but you've got to do what you've got to do. Now I've got my list, it's easy to prioritise. I'll get round to them all in the end. Any of them who threaten me, will wish they'd never been born. There's too much at stake to let them live. But this one, I'll particularly enjoy doing. The others on the list are more of a necessity. This one will give me great satisfaction. He deserves what's coming to him – no argument about that. I scoped the area out a couple of days ago. Nobody paid any attention to me and my recce was quick.

I get myself a McDonald's Drive Thru – Big Mac extra-large with a milkshake. Hungry work all of this: planning and covering my tracks. Making sure nobody realises I'm missing – not that anybody keeps too many tabs on me, but best to be sure anyway. I'm getting good at the whole swapping reg plates business. Didn't know there was so many scrappies around – not surprising really – all those boy racers pratting around, being chased by the coppers and ending up wrapped round a tree.

The lights from Maccie D's go out, cloaking me in semi-darkness. The only light comes from the streetlights. I deliberately park in a far-off corner and none of the staff even glance my way as they make their exit. Still, I shuffle down in the seat so the car

I've borrowed looks empty. Don't want to have to explain myself here, do I? I wait till the car park's empty and then give it another ten minutes before exiting the van. I have all I need with me in my bag and with my hat pulled down over my eyes, nobody could describe me.

This area of Bradford's full of young Paki lads, smoking weed and mouthing off, all big talk, but as I draw nearer to the street I need, it quietens off. The takeaway at the top of the road's shut now and there's nobody around on the street either.

Standing for a few minutes, just to be sure, I take in the surroundings. The lights are off in most of the houses; only a few are still on, but all the curtains are shut. It looks like the owners have put a bit of effort into their homes – all except his, that is. The one I'm heading for is a decrepit, filthy-looking atrocity amid the other well-cared-for homes. The neighbours will thank me for this. Maybe now they'll get someone who gives a shit living here instead of him. His lights are off downstairs and I reckon he's gone up to bed. He was in bed by half ten the last time I came and it's nearly one o'clock now. There's no move-ment from inside – no sound.

I pull on gloves and move forward. The gate's hanging off its hinges, so I squeeze past – no point in risking it creaking. I grab the crowbar from my bag and insert it between the rotten doorframe and the door. I barely need to use any muscle as the thing's so rotten it gives straight away, and I'm in, closing the door behind me.

I'm curious about how he lives, so I do a quick tour of the downstairs. I see the photos on the dressing table and I want to trash the whole room, but when I look closer, I realise I'll have to take these ones with me. No point in leaving any clues behind – no point at all.

The old bastard lives like the piece of crap he is. Whilst I might have had a pang of regret for Peggy and maybe for Liam too, I have no such pangs for this monster. The world will be well rid of him. I push the photos in my pockets, put on the overall I'd brought with me – no point in spoiling any more of my clothes – deposit my bag at the bottom of the stairs and take out my weapon. For a second, I listen. The only sound I hear is my own breathing, loud in the silence. I creep upstairs, adrenaline making my heart beat faster, and I steady myself, before gently pushing the bedroom door open. He's lying on his back, mouth open, a gentle puff of air leaving his lips as he sleeps. I want him to know who I am and why I'm doing it, so I put on the bedside light and put my hand on his shoulder and shake him awake.

'Wakey-wakey, you old bastard.'

He wakes, his rheumy eyes blinking in protest against the light, his lower jaw falling open. Waves of stale sweat and urine roll off him and I flinch. Disgusting old pervert.

His voice rasps over me, deathly and sour. 'Who are you? What are you doing here?'

Well, he asked, didn't he? So, I tell him. I tell him exactly who I am and exactly what I'm about to do to him and exactly why I'm doing it. I relish his fear. I celebrate the fact that he knew he'd pissed and crapped himself, before I finish him off. I make sure I tell him that he'd be found like this – a soiled piece of worthless crap gone for good, making the world a better place.

And then I leave.

Monday 21st September

# Chapter 26

*Gaynor Street!* The address jumped from DS Nikki Parekh's phone like a neon beacon, taking her by surprise. Unbidden, a tune sprung into her mind and the words: *We are strong. We three survived.* It took her back to another place ... another time. Hearing Gloria Gaynor's 'I Will Survive' had always made her blood run cold. The association between the singer and Gaynor Street evoked hateful memories, memories Nikki wanted to suppress.

One day, not long after they'd escaped Gaynor Street, the song came on the radio. Nikki, the familiar cold sweat instantly forming on her brow, jumped up to switch it off, but her sister Anika grabbed her arm to stop her. 'Don't, Nik. Leave it.'

And before Nikki could respond, Anika was jumping about their sparsely furnished living room, among the boxes they had yet to unpack, singing at the top of her voice. 'We are strong. We three survived.'

Hesitating briefly, Nikki watched her sister's flushed face, listened to her determined voice and then she too was on her feet prancing around, singing the lyrics Anika had created. Within seconds, their mum, alerted by the racket downstairs, had thrust open the living-room door. The look of momentary panic disappeared from her face when she registered her daughters dancing and singing and she joined them till they were breathless and sweaty, repeating the words over and over like their own personal mantra: 'We are strong, We three survived.' At the end they collapsed together onto the sofa, hugging each other.

The memory always made Nikki happy. Her mum and had been so brave … a loving constant throughout their childhood, their protector – well, when she could be. Sometimes she hadn't been strong enough, but in the end she'd managed. In the end she'd come through for them.

Nikki exhaled. Seeing the address she'd been called to as a probable murder scene had thrown her. Of course, it had always been a possibility that at some point she'd be called to an incident at this address, but as the years passed, the worry of that happening had been buried in the back of her mind.

Glad that her partner Marcus, and Charlie, Ruby and Sunni had already left for work and school, she placed her phone on the table with trembling hands. Last thing she needed was for them to see her reaction to this. She'd always realised that this was a possibility albeit a slim one. She just wished it hadn't happened today of all days. Not when she had to deal with the letters too – Saj would have her guts for garters if she didn't inform Archie that she'd received them – plus she needed to get to the bottom of Isaac's stubborn, tight-lipped attitude.

Resigned to a busy and probably emotional day, Nikki texted Saj to let him know she'd meet him there. Finally, with a deep sigh, she prepared to step back into her past to go check out the murder that had been committed in her old street.

Driving from Listerhills estate past Jacobs Well and Broadway to head towards Thornbury, Nikki schooled herself to take slow breaths and to keep her shoulders loose. This was a crime scene like any other. Didn't matter what the address was. It wasn't her old house; she wasn't going to have to step into that. Not this time at any rate. She had a choice, whether to drive up Leeds Old Road and down Gaynor Street from the top end, or head up Leeds Road and enter the street from the bottom end.

Approaching the turning to Gaynor Street, Nikki's heart sped up. *This is it then.* However, as she indicated to pull in, she realised the road had been made into a one-way, with granite bollards blocking her entry. Ignoring the hoots from the cars behind, Nikki flicked her indicator right and rejoined the line of traffic. She'd go round the Thornbury roundabout and enter the street from Leeds Road instead.

As she drove into Gaynor Street, Nikki was struck by how much it had changed. The line of terraced houses had been sandblasted and were now a rich cream colour and most had double-glazed windows. The majority of dwellings had opted to increase space by adding attic rooms, which indicated a slight change in the wealth of the area. Although some of the front gardens were unkempt, with weeds and overgrown lawns or bin bags spewing rubbish onto the pavement near their rickety gates, many were well cared-for. A few owners had opted to get rid of the small square of grass at the front and had replaced it with concrete and flower pots.

In this area most of the population were Pakistani Muslim, with a few white British families and an increasing number of Eastern Europeans. Although there was a Bangladeshi mosque, the Bangladeshi community were situated closer towards town. Nikki drove slowly up the middle of the street, the lines of parked cars on either side making it impossible to do otherwise. The house she was looking for was at the top end and Nikki could already see three police cars and two CSI vans. As she looked for space to park and finally elected to block in one of the patrol cars, Nikki watched the lookie-loos who had gathered on the street behind a string of tape, which cordoned off the house and garden as well as the pavement in front of number 111. They were fascinated by what was going on, and among them she saw uniformed officers chatting with their tablets open, making notes of what was being said. Whoever had organised them had done a good job to date.

So far, Nikki had averted her eyes from the other side of the street. The one where her old house was. The one with the lamp post right in front of it. Before she got out of her car, she inhaled deeply, and trying to ignore the sweat that had gathered on her palms because she was gripping the steering wheel so tightly, she turned her head to look at it. It was just a house. Whoever owned it now had cleaned it up big time and, if the address hadn't been ingrained on Nikki's mind, she wouldn't have recognised it from the leaky, unkempt, unloved house she'd lived in for the first decade of her life.

The garden had a child's outdoor playhouse in one corner. Pastel-coloured, it was similar to the one all three of her kids had played in when they were younger. For a second, Nikki allowed herself to imagine what it would have been like for her and Anika to play in that house when they were kids. Or to ride those little bikes she could see on the pavement leading up to the front door. As she sat lost in thought, the front door opened and a heavily pregnant woman in a niqab helped a toddler down the steps into the small garden. As the child ran off to play in the house, the woman checked to make sure the gate was securely closed and went back, lowering herself onto the step as she kept one eye on her child and the other on the police activity opposite.

A rap on Nikki's window startled her and she looked up to see DC Anwar smiling in at her. Pulling herself together, Nikki got out of the Zafira, slammed the door shut and locked it. 'Sorry, Anwar – lost in my own thoughts then for a moment. Is DC Malik here yet?'

'No, not yet – oh, I tell a lie, he's just got out of that pool car behind us.'

As usual, Sajid was as smart as she was scruffy. His shirt freshly ironed. *How long does it take him to get dressed in the morning?*

That was a new tie he was wearing too. Light blue with flecks of a darker blue. Nikki looked down at her T-shirt. Somehow she'd managed to drop a dollop of egg on it this morning and there was a yellow splodge just where her right nipple was. She picked at the blob, succeeding only in making it larger, then gave up with a sigh. 'Bet it matches your socks.'

'What?' Saj's frown was dark, his shoulders slumped.

'Your tie. Bet it matches your socks.'

Sajid's cheeks coloured and he tutted. 'Just because you don't give a damn about how you look doesn't mean the rest of us shouldn't make an effort.'

Nikki's grin widened. Taking the piss out of Saj was just what she needed right now. 'They do, don't they? You matched your damn socks to your tie.' She shook her head, then as another thought occurred to her, her grin widened even more. 'And your boxers. Bet they match your boxers too.'

'Sod off, Parekh. You're never going to get the chance to find out now are you?'

Nikki studied her partner. Grumpy didn't cover it. He was dejected and there could only be one reason for that. For the past few months, since he'd been outed to his family and community Saj had been the victim of sustained sabotage against his most prized possession. 'Surely not again, Saj?'

Lips tight, Saj approached the two officers. 'Wouldn't bloody mind if they could spell – but spraying Paedo spelled P.E.E.D.O – over my windscreen really gets me. Somebody's letting them into the complex and not only that, they're also covering them-selves up so I can't recognise them on the CCTV.'

'That's crap. Have you logged it, Saj? It's a hate crime and it needs to be logged.'

But Saj was batting away her concern with an impatient hand. 'No damn point, Nik. Langley and I are seriously considering moving. This is crap we don't have to put up with.'

Nikki squeezed his arm, as Anwar handed them their crime

scene suits. 'Come on. Let's see if a good old crime scene will cheer us up. What do we have, Anwar?'

The other officer grimaced. 'Not sure that what you find in there will cheer you up, but it's a murder, definitely. A stabbing. Old bloke by the name of Gerry Hudson.'

The name tugged at Nikki's memory. Could it be the same old bloke who'd lived opposite her when they were kids? She'd vague memories of her mum warning her and Ani to stay clear of him. She made a mental note to slip it into the conversation with her mum that evening. Her mum didn't like talking about those days, but if it was relevant to Nikki's current investigation, then she'd just have to stiffen her spine. Despite her thoughts, Nikki was reluctant to upset her mother. Those days were part of their past and they'd all moved on. She didn't want to distress her mum, so she'd have to be gentle with her. Besides, they'd only just made up after their disagreement over Nikki's questions about Peggy Dyson. Pity things with Anika were still frosty or she'd be able to ask her. Mind you, with her sister being younger than Nikki, the chances of her remembering were slim to non-existent.

Pulling her mind back to the present, Nikki unpacked her crime suit. 'Who found him?'

'His carer …' Anwar looked at her notes for the name '… a woman called Kussum Lad, found him in his bedroom this morning.'

'She still here?'

'Nah, we had to get an ambulance for her. She had a panic attack and fainted and cracked her head on the kitchen table. Paramedics took her to Bradford Royal Infirmary. I sent a uniform with her and when she's been given the all-clear, the officer will take an initial statement. I've got her details so we can follow up when she's back at home. Maybe we'll get more from her in her home environment. All we were able to ascertain before it all got too much for her, was that Hudson had no living relatives that she knew of and no visitors that she'd ever seen.'

That was true: being away from the crime scene, and all the images that she wouldn't be able to un-see, might make the carer more ready to share anything that might elicit a possible motive for the attack on the old man. On the other hand, if she was the deceased's most frequent visitor, at some point they'd have to bring her back for a walk-through of the house. They'd need to see what, if anything, was missing or moved. Nikki pulled her crime suit on, yanked it up and pulled the hood round her head. 'Have you been able to establish an entry point?'

Anwar nodded. 'Straightforward, boss. Looks like the killer jimmied the lock.'

Nikki walked to the cordon, signed herself in and after ducking under the tape looked at the house. Unlike most of the other residences, this house was decrepit. The windows, although double-glazed, were in need of reglazing. The bay window at the front had many cracks and condensation had steamed up between the two layers of glass. The front door was wooden, but hadn't been cared for or varnished in a long time and there were clear areas where the frame was damp-ridden and soft. Around the lock were clear crowbar marks, which the CSIs had already given a yellow number. *Middle of the night, quick job to jimmy the lock, old bloke sound asleep, it'd be an easy entry from even an inexperienced burglar.* Though the fact that the old bloke was stabbed multiple times in his own bed made Nikki question the "burglary gone wrong" theory. At this stage, she'd keep all avenues of investigation open.

Walking up the uneven path, with weeds sprouting from the numerous cracks and a garden filled with debris fighting for dominance with the brambles, which attacked Nikki and Saj, they battled their way to the door. When she reached it, an unexpected reluctance to step over the threshold took hold of Nikki and she stumbled on the bottom step.

Saj grabbed her arm to steady her. 'You okay, Nik?'

Exhaling slowly, Nikki shook his hand off and threw him a

quick grin. ''Course I am. Just tripped on these fucking slabs.'
And forcing the weight that rested in her chest down to her
stomach, she climbed the few steps and entered the dingy hallway.

A yell from the stairs that went up from the left of the dimly
lit corridor grounded Nikki in the present – in her job. She looked
up and grinned as Gracie Fells the CSI manager pulled the mask
from her face. 'Can you just make do down there for now, Nikki?
We're a bit crowded up here right now. Give us ten minutes and
you can come up. We've just had death certified and we want to
crack on with the room before we focus on the victim. We won't
move him till you've seen him though.'

Nikki waved a hand to let Gracie know she was fine with that
and then, Sajid at her heels, made her way on the specially laid-
out tracks towards the living room, which led off to the right of
the lobby. The smell of stale nicotine hung like a layer of cloud,
but it was the underlying smell of mould that caught in Nikki's
throat. The wallpaper was so faded that it was impossible to tell
its original colour, far less what the pattern was. The skirting
board was black with grime. At the end of the hallway, a door
leading into the kitchen stood ajar, releasing a faint odour of bins
that needed emptying, old fried food aromas and general filth,
whilst another door revealed a rather disgusting toilet tucked
under the staircase. Wishing she hadn't opened the door, nor
witnessed the level of bacteria forming in the toilet pan, nor felt
the smart of ammonia that stung her eyes, she quickly slammed
it shut.

Sajid pinched his nose with two fingers. 'Whatever the carer
did, she clearly didn't have enough hours to make any sort of
indent into this cesspit. Not the most appealing environment to
work in.'

Breathing shallowly through her mouth, Nikki fastened a mask
around her neck and pulled it over her mouth. 'Got any Vicks?'

When Sajid shook his head, she rolled her eyes. 'Can't rely on
you for owt, can I? What about a scoosh of that very expensive

eau de toilette that you favour? Even that'd be an improvement on this.'

Sajid pushed past her, fastening his own mask over his mouth, and braved the living room. 'Philistine.'

Nikki braced herself and followed him in, only to be surprised at the contrast between the neglected hall and the equally neglected kitchen that she'd glimpsed a moment ago. 'Ah, looks like the carer chose her battles. She must have focused on this room, presumably because it's where our victim spent most of his time.'

'Looks like it,' said Saj walking over to inspect a dresser that was positioned in one corner of the room and hosted a range of photographs. Its drawers were pulled open and various things scattered across the carpet, which, although faded and threadbare, had once been of good quality and judging by its cleanliness, had been hoovered recently.

Before joining him, Nikki took the time to absorb the room. Focusing on the wider picture first often made her more perceptive to the little idiosyncrasies that could lend insight into a victim. This was their domain after all. The place where they could indulge any private interests, the room where they could tell her, even in their death, something about the real them – not the one that others saw. However, whether this room would give more insight into the old man who now lay dead upstairs or not, remained to be seen. If, as Sajid thought, it was more of a reflection of the carer's priorities than the victim himself, then perhaps this room would reveal little. Thinking of the old man growing cold upstairs, his life's blood draining from his body, Nikki wondered at the cowardice of the murderer to kill him in his bed. She put that thought to the side to consider later when she could view the body.

Instead, she did a mental inventory of the room. The dresser that Saj was examining was hefty and old, like the antique ones you would see at auction. It shone as if it had been buffed to within an inch of its life and the faint scent of furniture polish battled with the overriding cigarette smoke. A large recliner chair with a remote control to raise and lower it, stood sideways-on in the bay window. Nikki appreciated that the combination of sunlight filling the room, the heat from the old radiator that followed the lie of the bay round the alcove and the proximity to the window itself, would be motivation enough for a lonely old man to choose this area as his main space. Opposite the strangely positioned recliner, in the middle of the room, stood a large TV angled to give the chair's occupant a prime view. Beside the recliner was a table with an overflowing ashtray, a Thermos flask, a cup with only dregs remaining, a pile of crossword books, and copies of the *Bradford Chronicle*. The most recent one was dated the previous day – most likely either delivered or brought in by his carer.

An old-fashioned cottage suite with faded cushions was placed in a line against the back wall, as if the owner had no use for it, – which, if he had no visitors as they'd been told, he probably didn't. She wondered what Hudson's job had been, for although the house was a mess, the few contents, although old, seemed of good quality. She moved over to stand beside the recliner and saw that she'd been right about him having a bird's eye view of the goings-on in the street.

Perhaps he'd sat here watching Anika and herself playing in the street when they were little or maybe watching her mum taking them to and from school. She frowned. Something was niggling her, but she couldn't put a finger on it. If she left it alone it would probably come to her. She turned and joined Sajid who was rummaging through the items on the floor. Leaving him to it, Nikki studied the photographs. For such a reclusive old man, with no living relatives, he sure had a lot of snapshots. As Nikki's eyes drifted over the images, which were mainly of children, a few with adults and children, she realised that there was a clear space where two photos were missing. It seemed that the killer had taken them with him. She made a note to ask the carer if she could identify what those particular photos were of. Nikki looked closer. Some of the many photos were dated. She squinted her eyes at the small faces trying to see if she could identify any of them and then paused. *That's odd.* 'Saj …'

'Hmmm.'

'Look at this.'

Saj finished studying the utilities bill that he held in his hand before standing up and looking at the photo frame Nikki pointed out. He pursed his lips. 'Sorry, Nik. Don't get it. It's just a family photo. What do you see?'

'That's what I thought at first glance, but it's not, is it? Look closer.'

Saj leaned in and studied the image. 'Nope, still don't get it, Nik.'

'The image is the bog-standard one that comes with the frame – it's not a photo of anyone he knows, it's just a random image.' She lifted her hand and pointed to another. 'As is this … and this … and this.'

After studying them all again, he nodded. 'Shit, you're right … but what the hell does it mean? Why would the old bloke display snaps that aren't real? It's like he's creating false memories. Maybe he had dementia or something?'

Nikki shrugged. 'Maybe, but Anwar didn't mention that and I'm sure she would have, if she'd known. It might mean nothing, then again, it could mean something.'

She sighed. She really wanted to make sense of this crime scene and get ahead of things before the media started prying. Any time Nikki was heading up an investigation she could be pretty sure Lisa Kane would turn up, like dog turd on a shoe – unwelcome, stinking of crap and persistent. The journalist hadn't quite forgiven herself or Nikki for being duped by her photographer partner earlier in the year. 'Only a few of the photos are real – these ones and presumably the two that are missing from these spaces. Not much point in taking them otherwise,' and she pointed to seven different images that were proper photos.

The pair studied the images in silence. One drew Nikki's attention and she took a photograph of it on her phone, before deciding to snap all of them to show to her mother later. Hopefully she'd be able to recognise some of the kids in the photos. 'All the real photos are of kids ...'

Sajid took up her train of thought. 'And all of the false ones are of families ...'

'We need to look into this a bit more before we start jumping to conclusions.' Nikki's brows gathered together. 'But I don't bloody like this. Not one little bit, Saj.'

'Me neither ... it makes the hairs on the back of my neck stand on end.'

Reluctant to enter the kitchen, Nikki took a last glance at the photos and as a CSI photographer entered the room, said, 'Make sure you get photos of all of those images on the dresser ... and I want all of them bagged.'

The kitchen was everything Nikki had expected it to be apart from one small oasis of cleanliness at the sink, one of the work surfaces and the cooker. Kussum had clearly decided that if she had to supply some meals for Mr Hudson, she would do it in as clean an environment as she could. The cause of the pungent smell was mildew that was sprinkled in black over most of the wall surfaces and dampness coming from curtains, which were pooled at the bottom in a sodden pile of mucky water let in by the leaky windows and left to stagnate. Nikki wondered why social services hadn't insisted Mr Hudson move into a home and, more to the point, how poor Kussum had managed to work in such an environment. She was becoming more desperate to speak to the carer to find out what light she could shed on Hudson.

A yell from above in Gracie's less than dulcet tones had Saj and Nikki exchanging a grin. It seemed it was time for them to view Mr Hudson's body.

Before heading up the stairs, Nikki cleared her mind of any of the possibilities that were floating around there. She didn't want any of the assumptions gleaned from what she and Saj had seen downstairs to get in the way of bonding with Mr Hudson as a victim of an atrocious crime – not yet anyway.

The tread on the stairs was as threadbare as that of the living-room carpet, and the stair-lift, which was waiting at the top of the stairs for a man who would only ever go back downstairs in a body bag seemed poignant, as did the Zimmer frame discarded in readiness at the bottom of the stairs. The only discernible marks on the stairs were traces of blood, which got darker as Nikki and Saj climbed. The killer hadn't bothered to clean up before making his escape and by the last few faded marks on the hall carpet, it looked like after he'd done the deed he'd left the house pronto. Which meant he'd taken the time to go through the downstairs and take what he wanted, including those photos, before heading up to finish Gerry Hudson off.

Gerry Hudson's bedroom was cramped, filled with boxes piled up on every conceivable surface. For a second, an image of the boxes monitoring her father's whereabouts she kept in her own bedroom, flashed in Nikki's mind. What if in thirty years' time she too was found dead in a manky old bedroom like this, surrounded by boxes containing evidence that her father was miles away from her? She gave herself a mental shake. *What the hell am I thinking? I'm not a sad, lonely old geezer like Gerry Hudson. I've got Marcus and the kids. I'm not alone. I have my family.*

'I want all of those boxes taken over to Trafalgar House.' Some uniformed officer would thank her for the lovely little task of dredging through them and logging whatever they contained.

Ammonia and dirt were pushed into the background by the metallic stink of blood and Nikki moved closer to examine the body, wondering if some faded memory might tug loose. It was difficult to tell what Gerry Hudson had been like in life – or

133

when younger and fitter – because lying in his bed fully dressed, dirty duvet pulled neatly back from his shrivelled frame, he looked completely inanimate. Pale, bald, and emaciated. His cheeks were sunken and his pure white eyebrows neglected. The only splash of colour was the blood that had pooled on his sheets from the numerous stab wounds on his upper body and stomach.

Nikki looked at his hands, but lying by his side, they were covered in blood too. 'Any defensive wounds?'

Gracie shook her head. 'It's difficult to tell, but I don't think so.'

'Walk us through it then, Gracie – I won't hold you to it, but it'd be good to hear your thoughts on what played out here.'

Gracie and Nikki had worked together for a long time and, although she wouldn't do this with any other officer, Gracie would do it for Nikki. Maybe it was female solidarity or maybe she just really trusted Nikki.

'For you, Parekh, but don't take any of this as gospel, will you?'

As Nikki shook her head, Gracie inhaled and then began. 'I reckon the old bloke was asleep. The attacker came upstairs with the knife and just laid into him. It will be your Langley ...' she nodded to Sajid '... who will work out which of the wounds was fatal.'

It had been Gracie who had inadvertently outed Sajid and his partner, Langley Campbell the pathologist, to one of the immoral local journos during a particularly demanding investigation earlier in the year.

'There's so much overkill here though. I'd be surprised if this isn't a revenge kill.' She turned and grinned as two uniformed officers and a couple of her CSIs began to take the boxes downstairs ready to offload at the incident room at Trafalgar House. 'You might need a few more officers to help you with those – there's a whole other room full of them – all sealed and ready for you to take.'

Gracie turned back to Nikki and Saj and spoke to one of her

team who was processing the contents of the wardrobe, which was a similar style to the dresser downstairs. 'You got that bag, Jen? The loose pages?'

Nodding, Jen rummaged in the box next to her until she retrieved a sealed and bagged item and handed it over. Gracie handed it to Nikki. 'We found this under the deceased's pillow.'

The blood drained from Nikki's face as she looked at the top page.

The paper had been ripped from a book. Beside her, Saj inhaled then exhaled in a whoosh as he read.

*Thursday 3rd March*
*He hurt me again tonight. I don't want to do this anymore. When he put me to bed I was barely breathing … I hate hate hate hate hate doing this. I hate it.*

'Fuck's sake, Nik. This is bad.'

*Saturday 6th November*
*One of these days I'll do what DD says – I'll kill him. I'll take that great big kitchen knife and I'll stab it right in his gut – his big fat gut – and then I'll cut off his willy and stuff it in his big smelly slobbering mouth and make him eat it – see how he likes it. I hate him and one of these days I will do it. I swear I'll do it and then he'll be sorry – he'll be damn sorry. Maybe I'll even do the rest of them. Maybe I'll do every single one of them.*

'You can see a mark here – like a teardrop. This fucking sucks, big time.'

Before he could utter another word, Nikki spoke. 'We'll take this with us and get it processed quickly. Was there any sign that the pillow had been moved after death?'

Gracie was definite about that. 'No way. There would have

been blood on it, but as you see it's clean. It's a photocopy – not the original. You're wondering if the killer left it?' Gracie bit her lip as she considered this. 'To be honest, Parekh, I don't think so. Most times when the killer has left something behind on purpose, it's been visible from the start. Positioned where it can be easily found. On the chest, or near the body – sometimes on the floor or on a piece of furniture. Not often it's hidden away like this. We only discovered it because it rustled when the doc turned him over to check his back.'

That had been Nikki's thinking too, but she wanted to double-check. None of this made sense, but all of a sudden this whole case seemed too close for comfort.

With a gesture for Saj to follow her, Nikki completed her tour of the upstairs. Once out in the fresh air, she inhaled sharply. Her head was fuzzy and now that she was outside, she was aware of how tense her body was. 'You phone Langley to arrange an expedited post-mortem whilst I make sure everything's under control here.' She tossed him her keys. 'Looks like we're travelling Nikki style today.'

# Chapter 27

Although he hadn't returned to Bradford in order to catch up with old acquaintances, there was something satisfying about realising that, while the world had moved on for Freddie Downey, for some it had remained stagnant. Although the city had changed over the years and his friends had inevitably grown older, fatter and uglier, their basic outlook on life was pretty much the same as it had been twenty-five years ago. Pie, beer and wheeling and dealing were the extent of their vision. Paycheques and dodgy deals, living hand to mouth, no thought to the future. He wondered if he'd be the same had he remained in Bradford. However, his enforced exile had prompted him to think ahead. It had been difficult to forge out a new path for himself, to make the changes he needed to, but he'd done it. Out of prison now for fifteen years, he'd used the time wisely and now he was in a position to put the past behind him once and for all.

Well, that had been before his sources highlighted the little issue that he'd returned to Bradford to address. At first he'd thought the slut Peggy's murder might have been just a drug-related cluster fuck – but word on the street that had filtered back to him indicated it wasn't. Peggy had become a blabber-mouth and that had sealed her fate. As soon as he'd heard about the Cambridge lad's disappearance he'd known he was right, which was when he headed "home". Nowt like a bit of Yorkshire hospitality to set you up with a lasting memory of your old place before heading off to pastures new.

The pub wasn't the one he'd frequented in the old days. That one had long since shut down and was now a Chicken Cottage takeaway. *Bloody sacrilege, if you ask me.* It hadn't taken him long to find out where the old crew hung out nowadays and, downing a pint in the Duchess of York in Eccleshill, catching up with the gossip and stuffing Yorkshire pudding filled with beef and gravy, was a pleasant enough way to fill the time until he made his next countermove.

Jimbo Lane, one of his mates from way back, had given him the heads-up about the pig activity on the old street. 'Summat's gone down there, you know. Full of oinkers all over't place.' He'd laughed, swigged his beer, scratched his groin and continued. 'Mark my words, old friend, you'll notice a big difference there. Full of Pakis now, like. Nowt like it was in our day. Bloody mosque spewing gibberish on a Friday and bloody curry shops every-where.'

Little did Jimbo know that his friend had already reacquainted himself with Gaynor Street. A little walk down memory lane had been called for and there was no way he'd miss that area out. Besides, he'd had a job to do there. Fed up with Jimbo's drunken big talk, he vacated the pub and called a taxi. Some things you had to see for yourself and, if he was lucky, he might just catch a glimpse of her.

It was easy to merge in with the crowd. Baseball cap on front-ways today, pulled down, covering most of his face, he stood towards the back of the crowd watching the activity on Gaynor Street from Leeds Old Road. Jimbo had been right. The area had changed. The church and the old Victorian first school had been bulldozed and replaced by a row of new shops, as had the middle school on the opposite side of the road. A Morrisons, a B&Q and other shops were set back off the road and the area was thriving with folk desperate to find a way to spend their incapacity money. He coughed and spat the product onto the pavement. A woman holding a kid turned and glared at him, edging away from him as if he could infect her kid. He grinned, enjoying the buzz of power that small interaction had given him. Then, mindful of the need to keep a low profile, he skirted round to the back of the crowd and watched the activity from behind a group of young lads smoking weed.

They were out in force: police cars, CSI vans, uniforms, CID ... And there she was. His eyes narrowed as he saw her leaving old Hudson's house, a smart-looking lad following along behind her. DC Malik, he reckoned, if his sources were accurate. She'd clearly been inside doing her "police thang". He wondered how much she remembered of her time on Gaynor Street, what she made of all this. Had she managed to put things together yet?

He smiled. The diary entries were a streak of genius. But was DS Nikita Parekh smart enough to put it all together? He doubted it – not if she took after her stupid mother. His grin widened and a short bark of laughter escaped his mouth, making the lads in front of him look at him as if he was mad, before they edged away. Maybe the second-hand weed smoke was making him high. He watched her, looking to see who she took after. She had her mother's stature – no doubt about that – and her colouring – yes, she definitely looked half-caste. Not that you were supposed to use that term these days. He shrugged. He was old-school. What was it they said about old dogs and new tricks? He coughed again, but this time directed his phlegm into the gutter. He'd already been too visible, no point in pushing his luck.

It was strange watching Nikita, trying to second-guess her. The human element piqued her interest, no doubt. That's why the diaries were a stroke of genius. She'd always been the protector – protecting her mum and her sister even though she was just a

139

scrawny brat. Those diary entries would keep her focused – but would she make the link? It didn't really matter to him whether she did or not. For him it was all sport. He'd be all right. His escape route was infallible, but if she couldn't put things together, then he'd have underestimated her and she'd be the one to suffer the consequences.

He couldn't believe his luck when he found the books all those years ago. He hadn't known then how useful they would be now. Some of the things in those entries were harsh – very harsh. Good job he didn't find the diaries before she left or she'd have suffered. Mind you, he supposed in a way she was suffering now. Living a lie, hiding her past, pretending to be all respectable whilst anybody with a bit of sense would take one look at that family and see it for what it is – an abomination – a freak of nature.

Never mind, their time would come – no matter what they tried to do to cover up. They should have been more careful with Peggy Dyson and the lad in Cambridge – that's what started this whole thing. Now he could just sit back like a puppeteer and watch them run around trying to make sense of his directions and misdirection.

He walked away, satisfied with what he'd seen. Now, he had other business to conduct. Other messages to deliver and this one was personal. Whistling under his breath he checked his pocket and smiled. It was there. Ready and waiting – and then after that a curry to celebrate.

# Chapter 28

Sajid was still on his phone arranging the post-mortem with Langley when Nikki returned to the Zafira. She'd used the few minutes to calm herself in preparation for baring her soul to her partner. There was no doubt in her mind that she had to come clean. Sajid deserved the truth and she would have to face the consequences. Hudson's death and what they'd found in his bedroom made it a priority for her to come clean. Sliding into the driver's seat, she tried for distraction – as much to allow herself breathing space as to annoy Saj. Her partner, however, ignored her juvenile attempts to irritate him by making mock-kissing sounds on the back of her hand.

Hanging up, he turned to Nikki. 'He says he'll work late if you stop making stupid smoochy noises and will start this post-mortem at six.'

Despite her heavy heart, Nikki grinned. She had been teasing her partner in an attempt to lighten the atmosphere before she confided in him her connection to this street. After yesterday's revelations compounded by today's link to them, she suspected he wouldn't be too chuffed. Better to get it over with before it had time to come a big thing between them. She prodded him on the arm. 'Langley did *not* say that. He loves me. He appreciates my humour. He too thinks you should lighten up a little.'

Sajid shook his head slowly from side to side. 'Oh, Nikki, you should know by now that you can't get to me. I'm the master of cool.'

Nikki smothered a snort and then placing her hands on the steering wheel, looked straight out the windscreen. 'I've got to tell you something, Saj, and I'm telling you this now right at the start – so you don't go mad at me for not baring all. I didn't say anything inside the house because I was still processing it all myself, but I'm coming clean now, okay?'

As Saj swivelled in the seat, Nikki felt his eyes on her, but continued to stare straight ahead. 'I used to live in this street. When we were kids, before my mum managed to get us out. We lived over there in number 86.'

The silence before Saj replied was leaden and Nikki held her breath, dreading his response. Although she would at a later date fill Sajid in more fully, she was too drained – too fragile to do it right now.

As if sensing her need to process, Saj kept to the pertinent issues. 'Right … Well, did you recognise Hudson – or any of the kids in the photos?'

Nikki shook her head. 'I was only a kid. I thought I recognised the name, but …' She shrugged.

'Well, in light of those anonymous letters combined with what we discovered in old man Hudson's bedroom, it's safe to assume that it's all linked and someone is letting you know it is. We need to go to Archie with this, Nik.'

Nikki had expected this. It was the right thing to do. Archie needed to know the full picture and although she wasn't looking forward to revealing details from her childhood to her fellow officers and her boss, she was more concerned with how her mother would take all of this. Lalita Parekh had put her past well and truly behind her, refusing point-blank to discuss it with either

Nikki or Anika over the years until finally the sisters had just stopped probing.

'Couldn't have been easy for you, Nik. Not for any of you. But coming back now, seeing it again – well ...' He shook his head. 'I just can't imagine what that's dragged up.'

Nikki smiled. The way Sajid described it in the past, his childhood had been little short of idyllic. No fears for his safety, no money worries, no hunger ... but that had all changed for him when his family discovered he was gay. Okay, he was financially secure, happy with Langley, but the fear for his safety was very real. Both he and Langley had been physically threatened and their secure little bubble was no longer quite as safe. The baggage the pair of them carried was what made them such good detectives. Nikki reached out and squeezed his arm. They made a good team and there was no one she'd rather have in her corner when this shitstorm exploded around them.

In her side mirror, Nikki spotted Lisa Kane the journalist, pacing up and down just outside the crime scene tape. She exhaled. If that woman got a hold of this, Nikki and her family could wave bye-bye to any privacy. Her stomach churning as if a ball of maggots had hatched en masse and were eating their way through the lining, Nikki realised that she'd have to speak to her kids. She'd always meant to tell them. Thought she'd sit each of them down at 16 and tell them a watered-down version of her childhood, but now she was being forced to do it, she was sickened. The last thing she wanted to do was bring that poison into their lives.

She visualised her children – laughing, happy, full of joy – and then before her eyes Charlie, Ruby and Sunni's faces distorting, melting, their features transforming into pained gargoyle expressions. Twanging her elastic band didn't make the images disappear and it wasn't until Sajid pressed his fingers into her arm that she realised tears were pouring down her cheeks. As she blinked, the tortured images disappeared and Nikki was once more back in her battered old Zafira.

143

# Chapter 29

Isaac, headphones on, rucksack swung over one shoulder, got out of Lally Mum's car and walked up the road towards Lazy Bites café. He'd told her he didn't want his new boss, Grayson, to think he was a baby. But the truth was, he'd spotted Calum and his mates at the bus stop. He didn't want them to see him with Lally Mum. Didn't want them to know where he was living and didn't want them to hurt her, like they hurt him.

He'd no idea how they'd found him, and he was petrified. Would they kick him like they did last time? He remembered the pinkie promise he'd made with Calum and was sure they'd come to see what he'd done about that. Eyes on the pavement, Isaac shuffled forward, hoping that maybe they wouldn't notice him, but no such luck. A yell from behind made him stop.

'Hey, Reeetard, wait a minute. We've got business to sort out.'

Within seconds the three louts were next to Isaac, yanking his cap, and nudging him. Calum placed a heavy arm around his shoulders and pulled his head down, before repeating his usual greeting of rubbing his knuckles into Isaac's scalp.

'Ouch, Calum. That hurts.'

'Aw sorry, mate. Only playing, you know?' Calum, huge grin

144

spread over his acne-covered face, let go of Isaac and moved so that he was blocking Isaac's route to the café.

'You've not forgotten your promise, Mongol boy?'

Isaac shook his head. Course he hadn't forgotten it. It was all he could think about and he just wanted to get it sorted so Calum would leave him alone and his mum wouldn't go to hell.

'That's good cos I've arranged a meeting with you and a lawyer. You've to meet this bloke outside your house at six o'clock tonight.' Calum handed Isaac a slip of paper, then banged the heel of his hand against this forehead. 'What am I thinking? Bet you can't read.' He high-fived his mates as the three of them collapsed into raucous laughter. 'Or tell the time.' Again the raucous laughter.

Isaac hoisted his bag onto his back, and studied the piece of paper. 'Mr McIvor Law-yer. Six p.m.' He looked up at them triumphantly when he'd finished reading the name aloud, but the boys for some reason seemed to find it even funnier. Isaac wondered if they were on drugs – or drunk maybe.

'I can tell the time. Look, I've got a watch.' He held out his wrist, displaying the watch his mum had given him before she died. 'My mum taught me.'

One of Calum's mates grabbed his wrist and began to unbuckle the watch strap.

'Nooo!' Isaac yanked his arm back. 'Mum gave me that.'

The boy grabbed his arm again and elbowed Isaac in the ribs. 'Well, it's mine now.'

'Leave him alone, Gordy. The idiot will need that to make sure he keeps his appointment, won't he?'

Gordy let go of Isaac's hand and then elbowed him again. 'You got lucky, fat boy. Next time, it's mine. Got it?'

As the three boys headed back towards the bus stop, Isaac took his watch off and hid it in his pocket. He once more set off to work, wishing he could tell Nikki all about it. But he'd made a pinkie promise and there was nothing Nikki or Lally Mum could do about that.

145

# Chapter 30

A sharp rap at the half-open car window made Nikki jump. She angled her head away from DC Anwar whose smile was replaced by a concerned frown. Scrubbing her cheeks with the soft fabric handkerchief Sajid had thrust into her hands, for once not teasing him about the never-ending supply, she took a moment. Then, cursing her momentary weakness, Nikki pasted what Saj often described as "her battle-axe" face on and more abruptly than she intended said, 'Well, what is it?'

Anwar's concerned expression was immediately replaced by a blank look. The only sign that her superior officer's harshness had bothered her a slight flush on her cheeks. 'The carer has come back, boss. Kussum Lad. She wants to get the interview over and done with. Poor woman can't get her head round this, but is desperate to help.'

Adding a smile to her quick nod, Nikki followed up with a shrug. 'Sorry for snapping, Anwar. Things just got to me for a moment. I'll sort out the interview. Where is she?'

With a shake of her head to indicate Nikki's apology was unnecessary, Anwar pointed towards a battered Corsa parked up just beyond the cordoned-off street and then frowned. 'I better go, boss. The bloody hyenas have arrived and they're already

146

hassling Dobbs. It's his first day on the job, so I should rescue him.'

Nikki glanced in her side mirror and groaned. As expected, the press had caught wind of a juicy story and Lisa Kane, blonde hair like a beacon, was clearly visible leading the pack. *What a crap fest this is turning out to be.*

'You okay, Nik?'

Sajid had left her to her own thoughts until now – given her the space she needed to compose herself. He was another one of life's sound men, just like his partner Langley and Archie – and Nikki was glad to be surrounded by them. Hoping that he wouldn't hear, she exhaled in one long slow breath, shut her eyes and touched the dashboard to ground herself. 'I'm fine.'

'We can't interview the carer, Nik. We've got to report back to Archie and let someone else take over.'

'Springer? You think she's up to it, do you?'

Saj shook his head. "Course not. But you're too close to this. You can't be the SIO. You need to step back. You know that. We can't compromise the investigation.'

Slamming her fist onto the steering wheel, Nikki released a long slow measured breath. 'Okay. I promise. But can't we just interview this Kussum Lad? We're here now. Soon as we've spoken to her, we'll head back to Trafalgar House. I promise.'

Considering the situation, Saj finally sighed. 'Okay. But soon as we're done here, we go bring Archie up to speed.'

As they walked towards Kussum's vehicle the group of insistent journalists jostled each other in their attempts to get her attention. 'Bloody vultures are out in force.'

Glowering at Lisa Kane, Nikki avoided eye contact. Kane thrust her Dictaphone under Nikki's nose. 'Can you give us an update, DS Parekh? What progress have you made so far? Are you looking at any suspects?'

Nikki stopped, and rather than her usual "no comment" said, 'There will be a briefing at Trafalgar House later today. I can't say any more now. Thank you for giving us space to work.' And she marched over to the Corsa where Kussum waited for them.

'What have they done with the real DS Parekh?' Saj whispered in her ear.

'Gotta bloody be nice to them. Last thing I want is a whole load of angry reporters on my back when the crap does go viral. I'm playing nice to get them onside.' She nudged Saj. 'Not that I think it'll work. Particularly not with Kane. It'll take more than a few sucking-up type comments to get her off my back – she'd like nothing more than to string me up by my bollocks.'

Smiling, Nikki held her badge up for the woman in the car to see. Kussum wound down her window. In her mid-forties, she wore a worried frown and her lips were dry and cracked as if she'd been biting them. Smiling reassuringly, Nikki introduced herself and Saj.

It wasn't hard to work out the woman's reluctance to re-enter the house. What she'd witnessed earlier would haunt her for a long time to come. 'Hey, Mrs Lad. Can I call you Kussum?'

The woman nodded and Nikki continued. 'Look, we're really grateful to you for doing this. You appear to be the only person who ever had any personal contact with Mr Hudson, so whatever you can tell us could be really valuable in finding out who did this to him.'

Kussum exhaled, her eyes flitting around, not settling on either of the officers, her fingers tapping on the steering wheel. Nikki doubted she even realised that she was doing that. 'Tell you what. If it's okay with you, Kussum, myself and DC Malik will conduct the interview here in the car and then we won't have to spend so long in Mr Hudson's house. How does that sound?'

With a quick nod Kussum agreed and Nikki opened the front passenger door and slid in beside her whilst Sajid squeezed himself into the cramped back seat. 'What can you tell us about Mr Hudson?'

'Nothing really. He was always okay with me. I only came in

148

a couple of mornings a week. Brought him his shopping – mainly microwave meals. He was quite independent, despite needing to use the Zimmer frame. He made himself drinks, pinged his food in the micro and spent his days either watching TV – rubbish mainly – looking out his window and doing them Sudokus and crosswords and such. I had to buy him a new collection every other week.'

'What else did you do for him?'

Kussum relaxed a bit, her eyes meeting Nikki's now as she answered. That would change of course as soon as Nikki led her to describe how she'd found him, but for now, Nikki wanted to just get a general feel for life chez Hudson.

'Well, by the time I'd got his shopping, I didn't have much time so my jobs were to hoover the living room and hallway and dust and polish his furniture – heavy old-fashioned wooden stuff it was, but Gerry took pride in it.'

'So, you polished the surfaces where the photos were?'

'Yes, he made me lift one and polish under it and replace it exactly where it had been. I was due to do that today – only did the photos once a fortnight.'

'Did he ever talk about the photos – you know reminisce about who was in them? Their names, how he knew them?'

Kussum smiled and shook her head. 'Most of them were ones with fake photos in them. There were only a few real photos.' She caught Nikki's eye. 'He was a lonely old man, really, DS Parekh. Most of the time I spent with him we chatted. He loved to hear about my kids.'

*I bet he did!* Nikki exchanged a glance with Sajid. This was another nightmare this poor woman would have to face when the truth came out – that she'd shown her kids' photos to a suspected paedophile. It would change the way she interacted with her other clients. The seeds of doubt would begin to grow and she'd grow a prickliness – a distance that would make her less sociable. She'd do her job – no doubt she needed the money

– but she'd hate it. Every conversation would leave her wondering if the person could be trusted, every innocent question about her family would be shot down and she'd look at people differently for the rest of her life. Her children would be coddled and they'd rebel at her overprotectiveness. They'd not understand – how could they? They were too young to understand a mother's fear for her children – that fierce visceral love that would turn a frightened mother into one who saw danger on every corner. Nikki knew – she *was* that mother.

'... and what they were doing at school. I always brought photos to show him. He loved to hold them as we were talking. I brought my youngest a couple of times in the holidays – Gerry always slipped him a fiver and Dipesh was happy to sit chatting to the old man – on those days I was able to clean a bit more.'

The mere thought of a young lad entertaining Gerry Hudson, no matter how innocently, made Nikki want to scream. Her headache was moving up her skull and now pounded in time with her breathing. Realising that she had looped her index finger round her elastic band ready to twang, Nikki decided to move the conversation away from Kussum's children. 'So what other jobs did you do for Mr Hudson?'

'Well, I cleaned the kitchen table and the fridge and one of the worktops. He was very specific about that. Said he'd rather spend the time chatting than live in a palace.'

*Yeuch! Palace?* True the areas that Kussum cleaned were pristine, but the rest was an advert for salmonella in the making. Clearly Nikki's idea of how royalty lived was vastly different from Gerry Hudson's.

'I didn't like it.' Kussum shuddered. 'Truth is, it made my skin crawl, but he was adamant and ...' She splayed her hands towards Nikki. 'What can you do? A lot of the old dears are like that. Being a care worker is more than just cleaning and shopping. For some of them it's their only lifeline to the outside world – Gerry was one of those.'

'Other than yesterday, did you ever go upstairs, Kussum?'

Now that they were veering closer to her discovery of Gerry Hudson's body, Kussum tensed and her eyes filled with tears. From the back seat, Sajid offered her a handkerchief.

Nikki glanced at him, eyes wide in mock disbelief and decided to lighten the moment a little to allow Kussum to prepare herself. 'Really, a proper hankie – made of material? – a tissue not good enough for you?'

Saj's grin was wide as he shrugged. 'I like my little luxuries. Besides, it's not too good for Kussum here.'

And he turned his reassuring smile on their witness. Nikki could almost see the moment Kussum's heart melted. Saj had a way of making witnesses view him as their little brother or their son. Worked every time! As she'd hoped, the brief exchange between Nikki and Saj relaxed Kussum and despite her tears, the carer grinned. 'You remind me of my oldest son – charming and sensitive.'

Nikki rolled her eyes, there it was – the Malik Magic.

Kussum blew her nose long, loud and by the sounds of it very productively, giving Nikki the satisfaction of seeing Sajid's mouth turn down. He wouldn't be wanting *that* particular hankie back.

'Once a fortnight, I changed his sheets – supposed to be once a week as per regulations, but he insisted. Whilst I was up there I bunged some bleach down the loo – that was all I had time for on those days as I had to take his sheets and clothes hamper to the launderette.'

'When did you last change his sheets, Kussum?'

'I was due to change them again tomorrow.'

Nikki exchanged a look with Sajid. So, Hudson had put the diary excerpts under his pillow in the last two weeks. Did that mean he'd also received them sometime during that time or had he always had them and only just placed them there?

'Did Mr Hudson give you anything to post recently?'

Kussum shook her head and watched as a huge bin truck drove

up between the rows of parked cars, stopping every few yards so the bins could be emptied into its bottomless belly.

'What about any mail he received? Anything with a handwritten address in the last couple of weeks?'

Kussum started to shake her head and then stopped, her brow gathered together, then cleared. 'Yes, it was maybe the last week. When I arrived, there was an envelope on the table next to his chair, but it hadn't been posted.' She flushed. 'I had a good look at it – he didn't get any letters except bills and stuff. This was one of those big brown envelopes with his name written across the front.'

Keeping the excitement from her voice, Nikki said, 'Any idea what was in it?'

But this time Kussum was quite definite. 'No, he didn't show me and when I came in the next day, he asked me to bin the envelope, so I chucked it in the recycling.'

'Saj …' Nikki's gaze was on the bin lorry that was progressing up the street.

'On it …' Saj jumped out of the car, pulling on the latex gloves that most detectives carried somewhere about their person, and sprinted towards the bins that were lining the street. 'Stop, Police, stop, don't tip those bins in.'

The bin men, spun round, glaring at him. 'What you on about? Eh? We're on the clock here, mate. What's up?'

Saj flashed his badge at them. 'I need number 83's recycling bin.'

A young lad in boots that looked too big for him, marched up the street. 'This one, mate. Number 83?'

Nikki hadn't realised she was holding her breath until Saj turned with a thumbs up to her, before jogging up to the bin. The lad had already flipped the lid open and was just about to reach inside, when Saj grabbed his arm.

'What you looking for mate? I'll help.'

Saj shook his head. 'It's okay, son. I've got this.' He peered inside the bin, reached in and came out with an A4 envelope that he took back to his Jag and sealed in an evidence bag.

'So, the letter is important?' said Kussum, her voice filled with wonder.

'Just covering all our bases, that's all. Now, apart from his bedroom and the upstairs toilet did you go in any of the other rooms?'

Kussum shook her head. But her eyes flitted out the window and Nikki had the sense that she was lying.

Keeping her tone gentle, she reached out and touched the other woman. 'I don't care if you had a peek in any of the other rooms – it'd be human nature to do so.'

When Kussum hesitated, Nikki pressed a little harder. 'It could really help. You see, Kussum, we've got nothing to go on. Not really, anyway. By all accounts, Mr Hudson never went out and never had visitors, so you're our only hope. Anything, anything at all that you can tell us might be important. You want to find out who did this terrible thing to poor Mr Hudson, don't you?'

The word poor might have stuck slightly in Nikki's throat, but she needed something to go on. Something to blow the case wide open, something to point them in the right direction, maybe even give them some sort of link to the murdered Cambridge researcher.

Saj had returned to the Corsa before, at last, Kussum nodded. 'I did just glance in the room next door to his bedroom.'

'And ...?'

'Filled with box files, you know? Them sort of black and grey files.'

'Did you look in any of them?' Nikki knew the answer before the carer replied, because if Kussum had looked in any of those, she wouldn't be so sympathetic to Gerry bloody Hudson.

'No, 'course not.' Kussum's hand raised to her chest, emphasising the veracity of her denial.

'Kussum, it's time now for us to walk through the house. You've been such a great help so far and we just need you to do this one thing more. We'll be with you all the way. We need you to focus on anything out of the ordinary – anything that you notice that's different from the last time you were there, okay?'

Without a word, Kussum got out of her car and followed Nikki and Sajid towards Gerry Hudson's house. The crime scene tape was still in place and a uniformed officer stood outside the gate. Nikki nodded to him, signed his book, on behalf of herself and Kussum, and Sajid did too, then she walked up the path. Kussum's breathing became heavier as they approached the door, so Nikki took her arm in a gentle hold. 'We're with you. I know you've already told the other officers what you did, what you touched and where you went when you came in, so you don't need to tell us that. I just want you to look for things that are out of place, different or odd in some way, that's all.'

Nikki led Kussum first into the kitchen. Standing just inside the door Kussum took her time glancing round the room, then shook her head. 'Can't see anything out of place here.'

Nikki nodded and they retraced their steps back into the living room. Kussum gasped. 'Someone's tipped his drawers out all over the floor.'

'Would you know if anything was missing from the drawers?'

Kussum shook her head. 'Maybe some money? I don't know where he kept it because he always had the shopping money on the table next to his chair.' She took Sajid's hankie and gave her nose another blow. 'He was always here when I polished so I never opened the drawers.'

Saj smiled at the inference that, had she had the chance, she would have been tempted to have a peek.

Not wanting to lead her in any way, Nikki said. 'What about the rest of the room. Take your time. Is anything else out of place or strike you as unusual?'

Kussum stepped forward and then stopped, frowning. 'There's two pictures missing. Two of his photos – the real ones like, not the pretend ones.'

154

Nikki understood what she meant by not the pretend ones. 'Can you remember what or who was in the photos?'

A smile drifted over Kussum's face. 'Well of course I can. One of the photos had a boy and girl sitting on a chair – I think it was that one over there. They were huddled together. Gerry said they were his great-niece and nephew. Now what were their names? I should remember – he told me often enough.'

The urge to shake the memory out of the woman was almost too strong for Nikki. This could be their first real clue. That photo was obviously important to their killer and if Kussum could give them a name, then it might lead them somewhere.

'That's it, Dexy and Candice – that were their names. He loved that photo. Said he had precious memories of many happy times with the two of them. Pity they never visited the old man.'

*Maybe they did. Maybe one of them was the last one to visit Gerry Hudson.* Nikki's blood ran cold at the thought of just what type of memories Hudson had with those two kids. Were those kids' images in any of the box files they'd taken? She glanced at her watch. Time was flying by. They'd have to ask Kussum to come to the station to get a uniform to take as detailed a description of the two children in the photo as Kussum could give. At some point she was sure, Kussum would have to look at a series of carefully edited images of kids from the files who matched whatever description she gave. 'What about the second photograph? Can you remember it?'

'Oh that? It was of Gerry and his friend, Freddie. Gerry always said they shared a delightful hobby and that he missed his old friend.'

Nikki's mouth filled with bile as she pushed past Sajid and out the front door into the fresh air. She barely made it to the side of the road before vomiting.

# Chapter 31

Fuck's sake! You'd think the old perv's body would have been discovered by now. I mean, he must have a carer or somebody checking up on him. Then again, maybe not. The damn house was a bloody cesspit on Saturday night. Stank too.

I put the radio on a little louder. Nearly time for the news. Surely they'll have found him by now. I'd been a bit off my game over the weekend. *Him* having a go at me hadn't helped either. Bloody tosser. Makes me want to smash his bloody face in. I listen as Ed Sheeran fades away and the bong, bong, bong sound of the news announcement comes on. Still nothing. Not a damn thing.

Oh well, so what. I'll just work my way down my list and they'll catch up sooner or later – not with me, like. No they'll not make a connection to me, but at least I'll see the results of all my planning on the news. Gives me a buzz, that. A real buzz. The names are ingrained on my brain. The thing is, who shall I opt for next? I've located all but one of them, so it'll have to be one of those. Trouble is, it'll mean another trip to Bradford. Not sure whether to go for one of the bints or that old ice-cream guy. I'm tempted with the other old whore, but then again, that might be too obvious. Last thing I want is them closing in and offering protection for my targets, if they make the links. Not that they can. How could they? I've left no clues. I tap my steering wheel, waiting for the traffic lights to change. Maybe I should focus on finding the one person I've been unable to locate so far? Hold off on killing another till I've found him. But where would be the fun in that, eh?

I pull up outside the florist's. I know just what'll make her feel better. A huge bunch of flowers. That waste of space never thinks to bring her anything. I might splash out on a box of choccies too. Got paid on Friday and the money's burning a hole in my wallet. 'Sides. It's good to be kind and nobody can say I'm not kind. Always been kind I have, right from when I was a kid. Taking in stray pets and all. Used to do my mum's head in. Used to make her cranky. I know now that's because we didn't have much money when I was a kid. No spare cash for cat food or dog food. That's why she was always crying. No money made her worry. It wasn't my fault, I know that, but who else could she take it out on?

It got better though. Later we had more money – well I suppose we must have. Cos that's when we got a cat. It wasn't my cat. It belonged to my sister and she called it Graham. Bloody Graham? Who the hell calls a pet Graham? I laughed like billy-o when it had kittens though. Stupid cow thought it was a boy until it snuck under her bed and she ended up with five little kitties to deal with. Nobody knew what to do with them. She tried to give them away, but nobody wanted them. As usual it was left to me to sort it out. A trip down to the reservoir with a sack and it was done.

The bell rings as I walk into the shop. The old dear behind the counter smiles at me. I'm a regular here and she loves that I buy her flowers every payday. 'I'll have the biggest bunch you've got, darling.' I lean on the counter. 'You done something to your hair? You look gorgeous today – radiant.'

# Chapter 32

Bent double, hands on her knees, Nikki gulped in the fresh air, but the taste of bile still soured her mouth. The words "shared a delightful hobby" echoed through her mind. This was so sick – so twisted. Footsteps approached her, so Nikki sniffed, wiped the back of her hand over her mouth and straightened. The heavily pregnant woman who lived in the house Nikki had lived in as a child – the one with the toddler – stood there, a glass of water in her hand. Her eyes were the only part of her face that was visible, yet they were full of concern. 'Are you okay?'

Unable to speak, Nikki nodded and tried a smile. The woman offered her the water and Nikki took it, grateful for the chance to wash the bile from her mouth and hopefully steady her stomach. She took a long gulp and emptied the glass, before handing it back to her saviour.

'More?'

Nikki glanced down the street to where the journalists had congregated and was thankful that a police car obscured their vision of her throwing up. No way she'd be able to recover from that if it got out in the press. Nikki shook her head. 'No, thanks. You've been more than kind. Thank you.'

'Are you okay now? You were sick.' The woman's eyes smiled. 'Perhaps you're pregnant like me?'

Nikki, soothed by the woman's gentle tone, grinned. 'No, that's not it. It was just a bit stuffy inside. What's your name? I accepted your hospitality and didn't even bother to ask your name.'

The woman wafted her free hand in an "it doesn't matter" way. 'I'm Sabeekah.' She hesitated, then continued. 'I saw you earlier. You're a police officer?'

Extracting her badge from her jean pocket, Nikki showed it to Sabeekah. 'DS Nikita Parekh, but you can call me Nikki. I presume one of the uniformed officers asked you a few questions earlier?'

'Yes, two very polite young women officers asked me all sorts.' She looked straight into Nikki's eyes. 'I'll tell you what I told them – I didn't like that man. I never spoke to him, never even saw him outside the house, but he always seemed to be watching us from his window. I'm sure he had binoculars. Sure he spied on us. My husband said I was being silly. That he was just a frail, lonely old bloke, but I couldn't shake that feeling. He gave me the creeps, so I kept the curtains and blinds at the front of the house closed.'

Nikki remembered noticing that and thinking it was odd when she'd arrived at the scene. A quick glance told her that now Sabeekah had opened the blinds and curtains. Wishing she could tell the woman her instincts had been right, Nikki restricted herself to a smile and a nod. Sabeekah would find out soon enough when the media got wind of what the police knew. 'Don't suppose you've thought of anything else that might be important? Anything unusual?'

'Actually, that's part of the reason I came over. There was just one thing that was unusual. Probably nothing – Hamza told me to forget it, but your two officers were very clear about that. They said anything at all different that I thought of and I'd to call them. I might not have bothered if I hadn't seen you here just now.'

Not wanting to build her hopes that it was something important, Nikki kept her tone light. 'You just never know with these sorts of cases. Any little thing can help.'

'Well, I dismissed it at the time as someone who'd gone to the wrong house.' She backtracked. 'What I mean is, I was in the garden with the little one. Our backyard needs a complete overhaul and Hamza keeps his old Jaguar there.' She rolled her eyes. 'Collector's car, apparently – junk heap as far as I'm concerned. Anyway, that's why we have to play out front and with me being so big now, I couldn't face taking Zain to the park. Anyway, I was sitting on the step and Zain was calling out to everyone who passed by. This one person – a man, all bundled up with a baseball cap pulled down over his face, glanced at our house first and then went through number 83's gate. He went inside. He was only there a half-hour or so. That's all – not much, I know, but it was preying on my mind.'

'I'm glad you told me this. Can I just ask a few more questions about it?'

Sabeekah glanced back at her house. 'Look, if you come over I'll make you a cup of tea – you still look like you need it. Zain is asleep and I need to get off my feet.'

Nikki hesitated. The thought of entering the house she'd spent her childhood years in made her exhale. She bit her lip, glanced up and down the street, looking for an excuse to refuse. Then, as if compelled, she nodded. Her heart hammering, she sent off a quick text to Saj telling him where she was. Walking beside Sabeekah, her fists clenched by her sides, Nikki made her way across the street into her old house. Fearing that she'd freak out, Nikki focused on chitchat with her new friend. 'When are you due?'

'Three weeks, but I was early with Zain, so I'm expecting to go into labour anytime from now on. Hamza's working overtime – he's an anaesthetist at BRI – so he can have more time with me and the baby when the time comes.'

'Do you know the sex yet?'

Sabeekah laughed. 'No, I said I didn't want to know. Hamza wants a girl this time. One of each. Me? I'm not bothered as long as they're healthy.'

As they entered the house, Nikki untied her Doc Martens and slipped them off and when she looked up, Sabeekah had removed her face covering. 'Only wear this outside the house when I'm likely to be in mixed company.'

Nikki was aware of that and was relieved she'd asked Saj to wait for her outside. She suspected she might get more information from Sabeekah without his presence and she didn't want her to feel the need to cover her face in her own home. Now that she was inside, Nikki's breathing eased. The house was nothing like how she'd remembered it. This house was a home, filled with love. It was clean and well looked after. It smelled of vanilla and spices, not damp and fear.

Sabeekah led the way through to the kitchen and indicated that Nikki should sit at the table. Like Nikki's mum did, Sabeekah boiled up milky chai in a saucepan on the hob. The main difference being that Sabeekah made tea the Pakistani way. She only added cardamoms and used a small ladle to scoop up chai and pour back into the pan. It was relaxing to watch her at work and the fragrance, although more delicate than the Gujarati chai Nikki was used to, calmed her.

With the steaming sweet tea in front of her and Sabeekah perched on the chair opposite, Nikki began. 'Can you remember exactly when you saw this man? Which day? What time?'

'You know, I can't be sure but I think it was that really hot day, last week. The one that ended with that massive thunderstorm later that evening. I could be wrong though.' She took a sip of her tea. 'I'm sorry I can't be more accurate. It was morning, probably around eleven or eleven-thirty because Zain hadn't long woken up from his nap.'

The tea was delicious – sweet and just what Nikki needed to

settle her stomach. 'What did he look like? Tall, short, ethnicity, age, build, clothes?'

'I told you about his cap. He had long-sleeved clothes on and a jacket, which I noticed because it was so warm and most people wore T-shirts and suchlike. I think he was white, or a very pale Asian – but again I can't be sure. When he glanced over, his eyes were hidden by the cap and I could only really see his lower face.'

'Clean-shaven or not?'

'Stubbly. I don't think he was that young though. He didn't walk like a kid – you know with that strut they all have. Middle-aged maybe – maybe even older?'

'This man could be quite important to our investigation, so I'll get a female officer to come round with some photos to show you. See if you can identify him. Would that be okay?' When Sabeekah nodded, Nikki stood up. 'Thanks for the tea; I needed that.'

Struggling to get to her feet, Sabeekah moved round the table and then placed a hand on Nikki's arm. 'I hope you don't mind me asking, but I watched you arrive and, although the crime scene was Mr Hudson's house, you seemed mesmerised by my house. Did you know someone who lived here? Was there a crime committed here in the past?' Sabeekah's voice was shaky and a furrow pulled her delicately shaped eyebrows together. 'You seemed reluctant to come inside – you looked pale, anxious. You kept glancing round as if you expected my home to look different.'

Nikki forced a smile to her lips. She was about to downplay one of the most traumatic times of her life because she was compelled to wipe the worry from this woman's face, yet prepare her for the barrage of media analysis that would descend on her when the full story came out. 'Truth is Sabeekah, I lived here as a child and today is the first time I'd set foot in Gaynor Street since. It just brought back memories.'

Sabeekah nodded, her face clearing into a smile as she made the judgement that Nikki's childhood had been happy. Most people assumed that about people who were professionals. They assumed a lot, but Nikki had learned long ago that you couldn't see people's inner scars – they were invisible. She grabbed Sabeekah's arm to stop her opening the door just yet. 'The truth is, Sabeekah, my childhood was not happy, but you've made this into a happy place for your family. Filled it with joy and comfort and love.'

'But …?' Sabeekah was clearly an intelligent woman who had read between the lines. 'That man kept glancing over here.'

'Yes, he did. Look, Sabeekah you need to prepare yourself for some media attention – not you – but this house as well as Mr Hudson's.' Nikki knew she was breaking protocol, but humanity won out. 'I'd appreciate it if you kept this to yourself for now. Give us time to do our jobs.'

Nikki stared into Sabeekah's eyes, willing her to appreciate Nikki's confidence. With a single nod, the pregnant woman opened the door. 'I'll expect your officer, Nikki, and good luck with your investigation, wherever it may take you.'

Saj was waiting outside, his tie loosened and his shoulders hunched, clearly deep in thought. When he spotted Nikki descending the steps from Sabeekah's house he took a step towards her, eyes scouring her face. *Trust Saj to be concerned about me.*

'You okay, Nik? That couldn't have been easy. Going back in there after all this time.'

Nikki glanced back at the house. For a moment she imagined two little faces peering out the upstairs window. 'No, it wasn't, but it was useful – made me realise that when Ani, Mum and I lived there it was just a place we slept in – bricks and mortar. The only place with any love was up in that bedroom when the three of us locked ourselves away from his poison.' She smiled. 'Now, it's a home. The only monsters there are in my mind – and probably in Ani and Mum's too. Number 86 Gaynor Street has only love and happiness and hope left. Whatever toxicity Downey wallpapered that house with has been stripped away and chucked out. There's no trace of it left – none at all.'

# Chapter 33

Nikki had expected her boss, DCI Archie Hegley, to be annoyed – possibly even angry. What she hadn't expected was for him to be incandescent with rage. As she explained about the letters containing the article and the diary pages, his face had reddened to the hue of a strawberry, but when she came to the part about finding similar diary pages under their current murder victim's pillow, the colour deepened to a beetroot shade and his breath came out in audible pants. Casting a quick glance at Saj, who'd accompanied her for moral support, she worried that she'd exacerbated the heart condition he'd been diagnosed with earlier in the year.

Archie stood up and, despite his recent weight loss, he seemed to fill the room as he huffed and muttered and stalked around behind his desk. His reaction was confusing. In the past, Nikki had done much worse than delay telling him about a couple of non-threatening missives sent to her place of work. She didn't understand why he was so angry about this.

She cleared her throat and swallowed hard and, avoiding the laser glare he focused on her, as he fisted his hands and used them to brace himself against his desk, she explained about her history with Gaynor Street.

By the time she'd done, the silence in the room was palpable. A shiver trickled down her spine as she exhaled, tensing herself against the tongue-lashing she was sure was about to descend on her. Instead, Archie collapsed onto his chair, fingers rapping on his cluttered desk, and in slow damning movements he shook his head from side to side. His eyes were dull with disappointment and a combination of remorse and indignation flooded Nikki. On the one hand, she should have mentioned the letters to Archie, but on the other – there had been no overt threat and, at that point, nothing tangible to link them to her in a more insidious way. Besides, she'd only just received the second communication recently, which was the one that had potentially linked the killing of the Cambridge student with the diary excerpts, and she'd promptly sent them off to the forensic lab.

Besides, Archie had been interviewing prospective DIs for most of the day, then, by the end of the day, they'd all been blindsided by Felicity Springer's transfer to their team. As soon as she'd seen the diary extracts at the Hudson crime scene and realised that it was more than likely personally linked to her in some way, she'd come clean – well, after interviewing the care giver and the neighbour. She opened her mouth to speak, but Archie glared at her and waved his hand. Aggrieved, Nikki clamped her lips together and straightened up in her chair.

'You ken, Parekh, I gie you a degree of latitude because you're a damn fine detective. However, has it escaped you that only a few months ago we very nearly lost one of oor own? …'

Again she opened her mouth to reply, but again was shut down by another angry hand wave. 'You're no a team player, Parekh, and that really gets on mah proverbials. Not only did we almost lose Springer, but the city went into meltdown and we've had tae pick up the debris. We've had a corrupt officer in our midst as well as trusted officials arrested, awaiting conviction for heinous crimes. The time for you tae play the vigilante sole hero has long gone. From noo on you act like part of a team. Ye keep me updated on anything ... and ah mean anything that could even remotely impact oan officer safety. Got it?'

Nikki wanted to rail against the unfairness of Archie's words. She'd been instrumental in finding Springer and in bringing down the huge trafficking operation, but deep down inside she knew those words came from a place of caring. They'd been through a lot – her, Archie and Saj – and she identified hurt in his eyes, now that some of his anger had abated, so she bit her lip and bowed her head. 'I'm sorry, Archie. I just didn't expect it to blow up like this. The last thing I ever expected was for this to take on a personal slant ... if it has – I mean we're not sure about that yet, are we?' Even she knew her words were a lie.

Beside her Saj snorted. 'Coincidences ...'

With a quick nod, Nikki had the grace to acknowledge that Saj was probably right. *Marcus would be so proud of me behaving like a grown-up for a change.*

'Exactly. Malik's right, Parekh. Nae such thing as coincidences, you mark mah words. Noo, what are your thoughts about what all of this is aboot? So, you've told us aboot your mum's link to Peggy Dyson, but what aboot this student, what's his name – ach, aye, Liam Flynn?'

'Ever since it arrived, I've been keeping up with the story. It's not made a massive impact nationally, but I've followed the local papers. I don't recognise him, his name or for that matter, his boyfriend.'

'His family?'

'By all accounts it's the older lad who's been doing the public appeals. The parents are estranged from Liam. I put the entire family's names through HOLMES but got nothing and I've never locked up anyone from that family.'

Nikki took a deep breath. Now was the time to come clean about their trips to Cambridge and Manchester and she doubted those would be received any better than her earlier revelations. She wished that she could retrieve from the bottom of her drawer the bottle of whisky Davy Jones had sent for Archie. Maybe that would butter him up a little. He was partial to a good malt. A quick glance at his tight lips dashed that hope and Nikki decided to plunge right in. 'We, that is, I decided to reach out to the Cambridge team investigating Flynn's murder.'

Archie nodded. 'Well, that goes withoot saying, Parekh. A wee phone call tae touch base is only good policing. What did that throw up?'

'Well, that's what I'm trying to tell you, boss. We ...'

Saj cleared his throat loudly and Nikki rolled her eyes at him. *Okay, Judas, I won't throw you under the bus with me.* 'I mean, I ... Saj was only acting under my direct orders. Well, we took a trip down to Cambridge on Friday.' She smiled, and rushed on. 'Turns out the lead detective was an old mate of yours, Davy Jones. Sent you a bottle of Scotch. I'll go and get it ...' Desperate for a little breathing space, she half stood, but fell back into her chair when Archie yelled.

'WHAT?' The single word reverberated around the room and immediate silence fell in the office space outside. She didn't need to look to know that the entire office had stopped working and that all eyes were now directed through the blinds of Archie's office at the three of them. Oh, how she wished those blinds were closed.

Shifting in her chair, Nikki wanted to twang her elastic band, but managed to refrain. Saj, eyes cast down towards the floor, slumped as if waiting for the sword to fall. 'Look, boss. We ... I ... didn't realise that the personal link would be so strong. How could I? All I'd got was a couple of diary extracts and photocopies of news reports concerning two seemingly unrelated murders.'

'Well, they're no so bloody "seemingly" unrelated noo, ur they?' Archie's roar had increased in decibel, his Scottish burr more pronounced, and Nikki half expected the DCS to come bounding down from upstairs in response.

All she could do was shake her head. When Archie was as mad

as he was now, the only way forward was to give him the space to sort things out in his head. He pushed himself back to his feet and resumed pacing. Glancing through the window into the outer office he muttered under his breath, 'Bloody nosy bastards,' and strode over, flicking the blinds shut.

*If only he'd done that earlier before he decided to tear a strip off me.* Archie's pacing seemed to go on forever, but was in fact only a minute or so. It was a minute during which Nikki had to bite her tongue, for all she wanted to do was argue her case … and she was woefully aware that she hadn't touched on her and Saj's little foray to the Flynns' homes yet. Who knew what anger that would unleash?

Opening a bottle of water, Archie sagged onto his chair and took a long drink before speaking. 'How is Davy?'

'He's fine. Asked after you, but they're stumped with the Flynn murder.' Nikki took a deep breath and spoke her next words in a rush. 'That's why we headed over to Ashton-under-Lyne, to interview the Flynns on Saturday.'

The silence following her rushed words lay heavy as Archie, eyes closed, muttered to himself, the only discernible words being "proverbials, idiots and insubordination". Eyes still shut and in a quiet tone that affected Nikki much more than his earlier loud anger, he wafted his hand towards the door. 'Get both the Cambridge and Ashton interviews written up. I want a full report on mah desk within the hoor … And, Malik, get the Hudson crime scene report written up, ready tae share at briefing … and you, Parekh …' He didn't even make eye contact with Nikki. 'Consider yourself aff the Hudson case.'

Sajid jumped to his feet and reached the door in record speed, Nikki trailing behind. Relieved to be leaving the charged atmosphere of Archie's office, Nikki was gutted by her boss's next words. 'Send Springer in. Ah need a DS ah can trust leading this case.'

# Chapter 34

'Well, that went well.'

Nikki scowled. Saj's blasé words were belied by the way he loosened his tie and all but fell onto his seat. Standing next to him, shoulders hunched, Nikki didn't know what to do with herself. When they'd exited Archie's office, silence had once more fallen on the rest of the team and everyone seemed to be engrossed in their work. That they'd overheard her rollicking from the boss would ordinarily have pissed Nikki off, but today what upset her most were Archie's parting words: "I need a DS I can trust." *Springer, really? He thought he could trust Springer more than me?* That hurt, really hurt. After all they'd been through, her and Archie, and now he was throwing her on the compost heap, like a sack of potato peelings.

Sliding into her chair opposite Saj, she stared into space. Springer's expression when her partner had told her Archie wanted to see her was one of puzzlement and Nikki didn't want to witness the change from confusion to smug satisfaction when the other woman came out. Chest tight, Nikki tried to breathe through the tension that held her body like a vice. She was a far better detective than Springer could ever hope to be and yet here she was being side-lined. If it was any other case, it wouldn't matter quite as much, but this one … this one was personal. This one was about her past – her family's past and she couldn't trust it to Springer – not when so much was at stake. Not when she had her kids to consider.

She leaned closer to Saj round the side of the monitors, and keeping her voice low said, 'Can you believe this? Springer? I'm supposed to just let Springer take over? What the hell is Archie thinking?'

Hesitating, Saj rolled his neck and then with a sigh responded. 'Look, Nik. I know this isn't what you wanted. I know you find it hard to let go, but on this one Archie's right.'

Nikki's mouth fell open, but Saj continued speaking before she had a chance to vent. 'No, he's not right about Springer being better than you – that goes without saying. *However*, he is right about keeping you in the background on this one. You know he is. People have been murdered, Nikki, and for all we know, this bastard may have more planned. All clues lead back to you and so we need to make sure you're out of the equation as far as documentation, witnesses and the press and public are concerned. I think Archie's done you a favour. He hasn't sent you home. He hasn't banned you from the office. He hasn't sent you to the dungeon to computerise documents from fifty years ago. No, what he's done is protect you and the victims and their families by keeping you publicly out of the investigation. He's done his job, yet in typical Archie style, he's allowed you access to the ongoing investigation … okay, it's from behind a desk – but it's the best of a bad situation and if you just take a deep breath and stop letting your self-righteous indignation get the better of you, you'd accept that. Besides, how the hell do you think I feel? It's not all about you, you know. How the hell am I supposed to cope with working with Springer? It's my worst nightmare. Now crack on and help me with these reports. Last thing I want is another Archie tirade.'

For a moment Nikki glared at Saj, who, tapping away on his

keyboard, ignored her. She hated it when he was right. Poor Saj wasn't going to find it easy adjusting to working with another DS and Springer wasn't going to be easy for him. Folding her arms over her chest, she slumped in her chair. How the hell was she going to manage to stay in the office? A quick glance around at the four beige walls and the rows of desks filled with officers who were better on computers than she was, filled her with dread. Biting her lip, she considered her options. She would be able to offer her unique insight into the case – after all the missives had been sent to her, hadn't they? She might, with Sajid's assistance, be able to direct the investigation in the way she wanted and, when she was out of the office, in her own time of course, she could use her own resources. Maybe things wouldn't be so bad after all.

Archie's door opened and DS Springer, Archie trailing behind her, walked into the middle of the room, clearing her throat. 'Just to let you know that I am Senior Investigating Officer on the case of the man, Gerry Hudson, discovered this morning. Information has come to light that may link this investigation with the murder of Peggy Dyson. I would like you …' she pointed at DC Anwar '… to collate everything we have on the Dyson case ready for a briefing at 4 p.m. Today. In the meantime, I am heading over to the crime scene to view it for myself. All reports from door to doors et cetera should be ready for the briefing. Clear?'

All the time Springer spoke, she had avoided looking in Nikki's direction. Now, she straightened her spine, looked straight at Nikki and with an abrupt nod, walked out of the room, leaving, for the third time that day, a stunned silence behind.

# Chapter 35

After dropping Isaac off near the café, Lalita had driven to her own work. As she approached Tyersal Library, she found herself slowing the car. Glancing round, she looked for any suspicious characters, before indicating and turning into the car park. Instead of driving to her usual parking spot at the back, Lalita had eased the car into one of the bays nearest the entrance to the library. She was being overly cautious, yet she couldn't shake the sense that she was under threat. No matter how much she berated herself for her stupidity, Lalita was nervous.

During her shift, Lalita had been distracted, so much so that her manager had pulled her to the side. 'You okay, Lalita? You look a little tense.'

Lalita had smiled and waved off the other woman's concerns, determined to ignore the knot of anxiety that had lodged in her tummy. 'I'm fine. Just tired.'

Still, she couldn't help herself studying any visitors she hadn't seen before. Did they look likely to have put a mildly threatening note under her windscreen wiper? When she found herself scrutinising an 80-year-old who was returning his wife's books, she gave herself a mental shake. *Come on, Lalita, get a grip.*

When the end of her half-day shift arrived, Lalita was reluctant to leave the safety of the library and stayed on returning books to shelves until her manager pointed out the time. Lalita had no choice now but to return to her car. With her heart thurrumping, car keys in her hand, one protruding between her middle and index fingers like Nikita had shown her, she forced herself to straighten her shoulders and walk smartly to her car. Seeing the windscreen was bare, Lalita collapsed into the driver's seat, relief flooding through her. With a laugh, she inserted the key in the ignition and edged out of the bay. *What an idiot. Of course it was just kids pratting about. Who else could it have been?*

Relaxed, and feeling ever so slightly foolish, she switched the radio on to Bradford Asian Network and sang along to some of her favourite Hindi songs as she drove home. The sun was out, the sky was blue and she looked forward to preparing a meal for her and Isaac to share. It was so good to have someone to cook for. Although she frequently cooked for both Nikita and Anika's families, having someone to share a meal with at her own table in her own house was special.

As usual, she pulled into the small parking space Marcus had created for her in her backyard and was soon indoors, throwing open windows to let the late summer's warmth heat up the house. Stopping only to flick the kettle on, she walked through the hallway, meaning to go upstairs and change into something more comfortable. A pile of mail lay on the doormat and, humming to herself, Lalita picked it up and began to sift through it. Bill, bill, flyer ... and *Oh my God!* The unopened letters fell to the rug as Lalita clutched the scrap of paper, her eyes glued to the words as if to memorise them, when in truth they were already tattooed into her brain. *I Am Watching You.*

Sliding onto the bottom step, one hand clutched to her throat, Lalita dropped the letter on the floor, watching it flutter down to land on top of the others, the threatening words face upwards, taunting her. Tears sprung to her eyes. The other note hadn't been left by kids. The presence of this one proved that. Her fears hadn't been unfounded and now, whoever was behind the note, had visited her home. Her faceless tormentor knew where she lived. Lalita jumped to her feet and flew back down the hallway to the kitchen where she slammed the windows shut and double-checked that she had locked the back door before doing a round of her home, closing curtains, checking windows and doors.

Sitting in the dark living room, she tried to control her breathing. She was safe. No one could get in. She had nothing to worry about. The one thing that was clear to her though was that there was nothing else for it: she'd have to tell Nikita now – but later. When she got back from work.

# Chapter 36

The briefing started promptly at 4 p.m. Springer, standing in Nikki's usual spot at the front, the boards ready behind her courtesy of Williams and Anwar, looked efficient and ready to lead.

Saj wheeled his chair closer to Nikki and spoke in a whisper from the corner of his mouth. 'It'll stay like that.'

'Eh?'

'Your expression. It'll stay like that if the wind changes. And let me tell you, you do *not* want that as your resting bitch face.'

Nudging him sharply in the ribs, Nikki attempted to rearrange her features into a less scowly combination and tried to focus on the blah blah blah stuff that Springer was regurgitating about the crime scene and the carer and the boxes found at the scene. Her stomach gurgled and Nikki realised she'd missed lunch. Thoughts of a bacon sandwich from Lazy Bites made her wish this damn meeting was over, then she realised everyone was looking at her. 'Sorry, what was that? I must have zoned out for a second.'

Springer's smile was forced as she repeated her words. 'If it's not *too* much to ask, I was asking you to update the team on the possible links to the death of Peggy Dyson, one of

175

Bradford's rough sleepers, Liam Flynn's abduction and subsequent murder in Cambridge and Gerry Hudson's murder this morning.'

*Ouch! The Spaniel is back in town!* Despite the other woman's hostility, Nikki detected an underlying nervousness. A frown was embedded across Springer's forehead and her knuckles clutching her notes were white, as if her grip was excessive. Standing up, Nikki strutted to the front of the room and stood between the two boards positioned beside the one topped with the morgue photo of Gerry Hudson. One board was headed with a police photo of a scowling, mucky-faced, Peggy Dyson, presumably taken during one of her arrests for low-level disturbances or soliciting. On the other, by sharp contrast, was an image of a smiling fresh-faced Liam Flynn. Below each image were copies of the diary extracts and news clippings sent anonymously to Nikki. Pointing to the boards, Nikki, choosing her words carefully, began with a warning. 'What I am about to reveal does not leave this room. This is all highly confidential and as such we don't want the press to get wind of it.'

Taking a deep breath, she continued. 'This first photo is of Peggy Dyson, a rough sleeper, drug addict and prostitute known to Bradford police. She was found with multiple stab wounds under the Forster Square arches, where she tended to spend her time, at the end of August. These ...' Nikki pointed to the clippings and extracts below '... were delivered to me shortly after her death, sent by an anonymous sender.'

Buoyed by the charged atmosphere in the room, Nikki momentarily forgot she wasn't the lead investigator as she moved on to the second board. 'This is the research student, Liam Flynn, who was abducted and then later found dead in a field outside Cambridge, earlier in the month. His cause of death was also multiple stab wounds and ...' she pointed at the extracts and news clippings beneath Liam's image '... a couple of weeks ago, I was sent this. Again, they came through the post, addressed in a handwritten envelope to me at Trafalgar House. Naturally I had everything processed.'

She ignored Saj's raised eyebrows and smirk. She wasn't lying, she *did* have it processed, just not when it first arrived. 'There were no forensic traces on either the envelope or the photocopied articles. No doubt you have all made the link between these diary extracts and the ones discovered at the Gerry Hudson scene.'

'Where were the articles from?' Williams had raised his arm, the words tumbling from his lips at the same time.

Nikki smiled at him. 'The Peggy Dyson article, which was basically an obituary, was from the Bradford Chronicle and the Flynn article was from an online Manchester newspaper. Flynn as you know was born and raised in the Manchester area. And before anyone asks, there was no note. So, the only thing we have is the handwritten envelope, the diary extracts and the questions posed by the missives themselves.'

Anwar frowned. Her Bradford accent was pronounced as she spoke. 'If there's no forensics or owt, why is it of interest to us right now? Shouldn't we be focusing on the Hudson murder?'

'Yeah, you're right. However, it turns out that the three murders may well be linked. Cause of death is consistent with all three, although we must await confirmation of that from Dr Campbell. If the three deaths are the result of the same killer, then we have a serial killer on our hands, and as we well know from past experience, these sort of killers generally don't stop till they're caught. But let's not get ahead of ourselves. At this point we need to find links between the three victims. DC Malik has uploaded interviews conducted with Flynn's contacts both in Manchester and Cambridge to the police file. Please study it carefully. We need to find out what the link between these three deaths is. Anwar has uploaded the police file on Peggy Dyson. Again you need to scrutinise it and we need to find the crossover, if it exists, between the three.'

Eager beaver Williams' hand shot up again. 'Could it just be someone yanking your chain, boss?'

Before Nikki could respond, Springer had jumped to her feet, clearly irked by Williams addressing Nikki as boss. Her face was flushed and her words came out as more of a plea than a bald statement. Springer was well and truly rattled. 'I'm the boss here, Williams, and to answer your question, yes, it could be someone yanking DS Parekh's chain, as you so eloquently put it, However, there's an old adage about coincidences: never trust them.'

Moving closer to Nikki, in a move designed to make a statement and show who the real boss was, Springer smiled and leaned her elbow on Nikki's shoulder. Next to Springer, Nikki looked tiny. However, her stature didn't bother Nikki. What really irked was that Springer had had the audacity to *lean* on her. *How dare she!* It was a cheap move to show her authority, but in reality, all it did was show how insecure Springer was. When she spoke, her words were stilted. 'Thankfully, DS Parekh has agreed to share some more information with the team, which may move the link from tenuous to suspicious.'

Easing from under Springer's shoulder, Nikki swallowed the urge to jerk her shoulder upwards. She sighed. This was the part she was dreading, and Springer's overt challenge had set her off kilter. Privacy was something Nikki valued above most things – privacy and loyalty. Now, circumstances beyond her control forced her to break her privacy mantra. She only hoped that the officers before her were loyal enough to keep her revelations between them. She glanced first at Archie, who, head down, didn't meet her eye. Her heart sped up. She was on her own – no support from her boss on this one. He was clearly still smarting from her "rogue" actions. Her gaze moved to Saj and seeing his encouraging smile and cheeky wink, made her want to hug him. She had friends in this room.

Stepping away from Springer, Nikki faced the expectant audience, hoping that her face didn't betray the blind panic that flooded her body. Officers had been pulled in from all over to create an extended team and their presence, filling all of the space, was claustrophobic. For a second, Nikki wondered if she might just rush out past them and wash her hands of the whole damn thing – then sanity returned. She was in an ideal situation to do damage limitation and so she would just have to bite the bullet and crack on with it. 'The fact that they were sent to me creates another link. One I'm afraid we can't ignore. Initially, I thought it was an arbitrary thing. Some idiot who'd seen me on the news during the trafficking investigation and ...' She bit her lip. Springer might be a bitch, but Nikki had no desire to rake up the other woman's abduction and her part in the rescue.

Setting her gaze to a spot on the wall behind the watching officers, she began, 'Well ... I'm just gonna jump in with this. I lived on Gaynor Street myself till I was about twelve. In fact, my house was the one directly opposite Gerry Hudson's. Like many kids in the city, they weren't particularly happy years because my mother was in an abusive relationship and suffered a great deal of trauma. Obviously we've moved on as a family and I would like to keep our past as low-key as possible. I hope you can respect our privacy. It is because of my link to Gaynor Street and the fact that I received the anonymous communications outlined earlier that DS Springer will be SIO on this case. Of course any information pertaining to the investigation will be shared with the necessary officers.' Nikki paused to let her words settle. 'So – it seems clear that we need to explore the efficacy of the diary ...'

Stepping forward, Springer indicated the seat Nikki had vacated earlier and grabbing her arm all but directed her to it. Nikki jerked her arm away and turned to Springer. She leaned over and spoke in her ear. 'Don't you ever touch me again or I *will* react.'

Colour suffused Springer's face, but she held Nikki's gaze for a moment and then gave an abrupt nod. 'Naturally we have sent the diary excerpts for analysis and we're awaiting results from those. We've also employed a forensic consultant to try to make some sense of the chronology of the excerpts – again we're awaiting feedback from that. In the meantime, you all know what you have to do, so go and do it. Next briefing tomorrow at 8 a.m.'

Springer waited till the uniformed officers had begun to leave the room before addressing her detectives. 'Williams, Anwar and Malik, I would like you to join DCI Hegley and I for a private meeting.' She began to move towards Archie's office, then turned back. 'Oh and you too, Parekh.'

Walking into Archie's office, Saj had whispered into Nikki's ear. 'What a bitch – guns drawn at dawn, do you reckon?'

His levity, despite the anger bubbling beneath the surface, made Nikki smile. Springer was exerting her authority and being a bitch about it, but Nikki understood it was because the other woman expected Nikki to try to undermine her. And that, if she was honest, was what annoyed her most. The thought that Springer would think, even for a nanosecond, that Nikki might jeopardise an active investigation to fulfil some sort of power play was disheartening.

Arms crossed, Nikki slouched in the same chair she had occupied earlier in the day and not for the first time since her rollicking, wondered how she could mend her bridges with Archie. She valued him both as a friend and as a boss and his obvious hurt and anger were killing her. However, right at this moment she had other things to think about – she was about to expose her soul and the very thought of it freaked her out. Nikki had rehearsed what she'd tell the team with Marcus the previous evening, yet now all her carefully planned phrases seemed hollow and inappropriate.

When Williams, Anwar, Springer and Malik were all seated in Archie's room, Archie spoke. 'Close the blinds, Williams.'

Williams and Anwar exchanged puzzled glances, but he jumped up without a word and closed them.

Instead of Springer leading the meeting, Archie stepped up. 'Some of you will be wondering about all this cloak and dagger stuff.' He made eye contact with each of them. 'Everything that is discussed within these four walls is to be treated with the utmost sensitivity and discretion. Information from here will be fed to the wider investigative team, only ... and I repeat, only when either myself or DS Springer deem it as necessary to furthering the investigation.'

Settling himself into his chair he opened a bottle of water. 'DS Parekh has information to divulge ...'

For the first time since she'd been demoted, Archie looked straight at Nikki and nodded. Although his face was taut, his eyes signalled their support to her. Taking a deep breath as the words built up in her throat, battling to get out now that it was time, Nikki thought of her own mother and the abuse she'd suffered over the years. 'Like Archie, I trust that none of this will leave this room.'

When everyone nodded, she took a sip of water and began pacing the room. When she spoke, her tone was low, almost robotic, but there was no other way she could deliver it.

'When my mother and her parents came to the UK, my mother was only thirteen or so and confronted with other children who had much more freedom than my grandparents allowed her, she rebelled. At fourteen, she was groomed by a man called Freddie Downey – my father.'

Grinding to a halt, Nikki tried to control the hatred she felt for the man who had abused her mother. Archie poured her more water and patted her on the shoulder and returned to sitting behind his desk. Nikki took a sip, glad of the coolness as it soothed her throat. She'd give the salient details. Who her father was, how he'd groomed her mother, how he lived in Scotland now having served a pitiful sentence for abusing children. Each word ripped at her and she twanged her elastic band again and again as she walked. She'd share the bare details, but she couldn't allow them

181

to see her scars – not the invisible ones anyway. 'Downey thought because she was Indian, she was exotic and …' she snorted '… it seems that there was a taste for "the exotic" among the men my father worked for. Soon she was dependent on him, manipulated and vulnerable – a victim of Stockholm syndrome. When I came along, followed by Anika a couple of years later, he used *us* to control her.

'We were all subjected to his manipulation for a long time. Until, one day when I was about twelve, Anika would have been ten, my mum made a friend in the school playground. When Downey started to show an interest in me … and my *saleability* …' she spat out this word '… my mum worked up the courage to confide in her friend.' Nikki took a swig of water, wishing her throat wasn't so dry. 'Her friend helped us escape and report Downey.

'So, you see. I'm almost sure that my father was working with this Gerry Hudson. I was too young to remember everything that went on, but he was a bastard. I'm also wondering if Freddie Downey is behind these deaths and the diary excerpts. Terrorising people is sort of his thing, after all. For years I've been keeping tabs on his whereabouts. Making sure he was nowhere near us. I'll get my private investigator to check out that he's still in Scotland. And, of course I'll give you access to all the PI files I've accumulated over the years.'

Slowing her breathing down, Nikki snapped at the elastic band on her wrist, trying to synchronise each snap with the start of a new breath as she waited for a response to her revelation. She'd confided to Khalid, Charlie's father, before he left and to Marcus, the father of her other two children. Every so often she'd add bits and pieces to the tapestry of her life story and Marcus didn't probe – didn't force her hand. He was just there. Her rock – her indestructible mountain. Now, a massive earthquake was going to hit her tight little family and she only hoped they'd have the strength to survive.

Sajid's one-word response, 'Fuck,' was followed by a huge hug that helped ground her. She stopped twanging the elastic band and looked at Archie. His face had paled and his fists were clenched on the desk top. The rest of the room's occupants were shocked into silence.

'I hope that fucker an' all of his damn mates are rotting in jail now.' Archie's voice burst into the stunned stillness.

Nikki snorted. *Yeah that'd be right.* 'Unfortunately not. He only got a few years …'

The British Justice System had allowed her father to serve less time in prison than her small family had suffered at his hands. It angered her and it was this anger that drove her. She detested injustice. 'He's living in Scotland … I have a PI who keeps a regular eye on him to make sure he's nowhere near my mum.'

'Maybe a couple of uniforms can chat to your mum and sister. They might have a better recollection than you.'

Nikki raised her hand to the scar on her throat and was unable to keep the panic from her voice. 'No, no. Don't send a uniform. I'll speak to my mum and Ani. It's got to be me.'

When she paused, she realised that both Archie and Sajid were focused on her fingers, which were moving back and forth over the ridged scar on her neck. She lowered her hand and shoved it in her pocket, ashamed to have been caught out like that and wondering what the rest of the officers present made of it.

'Look, Parekh …' Archie spoke in his "gruff kindly" voice. 'This is clearly upsetting you. Are you sure you're up for this? Maybe I should send you to work on another team. Perhaps you're too close to things.'

Her stomach lurched as if filled with wriggling worms as panic took over. She badly wanted to twang the elastic band on her wrist to ground herself, but couldn't show weakness. Not when so much depended on it. The last thing she wanted was to be on the outside, not even able to watch as her team dissected her childhood. She couldn't just be side-lined to another investigation entirely. Not without a fight anyway. However, she'd no idea how to convince Archie – no idea how she would be able to get the words out without tearing up, without breaking down – and that would have the exact opposite outcome from the one she wanted.

Sajid stood up and moved in front of her, effectively obscuring her from Archie's vision. 'Thing is, boss, I reckon Parekh's proximity to the case gives us a better perspective. She's been getting these letters for a reason and to remove her completely at this stage would be detrimental to the investigation. Of course, if at any point we think her presence compromises anything, then we'll have to think again.'

Nikki could have hugged him. Saj didn't know the full story of her childhood – not yet anyway – but still he had her back and right now she needed that more than ever.

'Och sit doon, laddie. I ken what you're doing. You're backing up your partner and that's good. You two make a good team. But I want to see Parekh's face. I want something from her to convince me.'

Saj turned, hands out in a "well, I tried" gesture and sat down. The short interlude with Saj had been enough for Nikki to collect her thoughts and compose herself. 'Look, you all know now, mine and Anika's childhood was crappy. As a family, me, Anika and my mum have moved on – put it behind us ...' She hesitated before continuing, choosing her words carefully. 'However, I suspect that some things are going to come out about Freddie Downey and my family, during the course of this investigation. Things we've locked away for years are going to come out into the open. It might be fodder for the media and I've got to think about the fallout from all of this on my immediate family and on my mum and Anika and Haqib. Particularly Anika and her son Haqib. They're still very fragile after all that's come to light about Haqib's dad.

'I'd like to work with my own team on this. I think I have

184

their respect and they'll deal with what they find out with sensitivity – of course, I can't control the extended team's thoughts and actions, but I am strong enough to deal with it. I've been through worse.'

She swallowed on the next words, but knew she had no choice but to say it. 'I can offer a lot to this investigation and I promise I'll work just as hard for DS Springer as I would if I was leading it. She's the SIO and I know I'll have to take a back seat, but I need to be the one who breaks this to my family. They've been through so much already. They can be interviewed officially afterwards – that's not an issue – but please let me be the one to break the news first. I have to give them a heads-up on what's going to happen and I think I'll get more out of them. Anika's fragile. I'll need to go gently with her.' Another thought occurred. 'I also need to help the kids make some sense of it all too.' She looked at Springer. 'Is that okay?'

Springer gave a brief nod. 'But, Parekh, I will be keeping an eye on you. I'm all too familiar with your propensity to head off on your own. I won't stand for it. Got it?'

Nikki lowered her head and did the only thing she could. She nodded.

# Chapter 37

The last thing Nikki wanted to do was to have these conversations with Anika and their mum, but she had no choice. She couldn't leave it till it hit the news and, although they'd not released the name of this morning's murder victim, it wouldn't be long till one of the local journos found it out. The more she'd thought about it, the more it seemed likely that her mother would have some sort of information on Gerry Hudson and she was reasonably sure that that information would link back to Freddie Downey.

She whizzed off a quick text to the private investigator she employed to keep an eye on Downey. Since Downey's release from prison, Nikki had made sure she knew exactly where Downey was. At the moment he was in Scotland. She could just about stretch to a bit of additional surveillance – she couldn't really afford not to, not till she had more of a handle on what was going on.

Springer was organising things back at Trafalgar House. She'd set a team on the massive task of going through all the boxes they'd taken from the crime scene. Anwar and Williams were attending Gerry Hudson's post-mortem and a team of uniforms were still taking statements at Gaynor Street. So far, Nikki could find no fault with Springer's handling of the investigation. The fact that Springer being on top of things irked made Nikki feel like a real cow. She should be pleased that Springer was stepping up to the mark.

Pulling into Listerhills, Nikki resisted the impulse to drive straight down the road and back to Trafalgar House. Instead she parked up. She could leave it to a uniform, Archie had suggested that, hadn't he? But a memory of her mother, tears streaming down her cheeks, her eye swollen and bruised as she grappled with Downey, to stop him entering their bedroom, put paid to that idea. She couldn't allow anyone else to deliver this news to her mum. Back then, Nikki hadn't been strong enough to protect her mum and sister.

*That particular day, Downey had grabbed Nikki's mum and flung her to the floor. The sound of her mum's head cracking onto the dresser had made Nikki feel sick. Nikki had pushed 8-year-old Anika behind her, raised her chin and said words she'd never before or since uttered in front of her mum. 'Fuck off and leave us alone.'*

*Downey's face had darkened, his eyes flashing, lips thin as he lunged for Nikki. Nikki darted to one side and yelled for Anika to run, but Anika was too scared and she'd stood there, wee dripping down her leg.*

*'You dirty fucking little slut.' Downey's fist hit the side of Anika's head just as Nikki grabbed his arm. Still, the power behind his fists sent Anika toppling onto her bum. Their mum, groaning, a smear of blood dripping from her temple, had yanked him back, but he'd swivelled and wrapped both arms round Nikki's chest and dragged her screaming and kicking from the room.*

*'Leave her alone. She's too young. Leave her.'*

*Nikki hadn't been entirely sure what she was too young for, but she had a pretty good idea. She'd struggled more furiously, determined to get away as he pulled her downstairs, her mum following, pleading and beseeching him.*

'Shut up, the two of you, or I'll bloody go back and take the other one too.'

Nikki stopped struggling. The last thing she wanted was for Ani to be grabbed too.

Entering the kitchen, he flung her onto one of the chairs and grabbed a rope that he always left there in case any of the women needed "teaching a lesson". He'd bound it so tightly round Nikki that she could still feel it now, all those years later.

Her chest clogged up and she began gasping – quick short gasps – dizzy and sweating. She forced her hands onto the steering wheel, closed her eyes and began to count her breaths. After a while, although still shaky, Nikki was calmer. She hated that Downey still had the power to make her feel like this. Hated that she couldn't just let it all go, no matter how much she tried. She raised her fingers to the rough scar that ran across her neck. He'd done that to her that same day; the day that they started to plan; the day they began to snatch back control little by little. The day they became stronger.

The unwelcome memories kept breaking in on her.

Two others had been there that day. She couldn't remember their names; in fact, she seemed to remember that they lived there too ... Downey in a rage was something to be scared of and Nikki didn't blame the other women for leaving.

'Sit down and listen.' He kicked a chair over to Nikki's mum who wrung her hands, shaking her head from side to side, making all sorts of promises if he'd just take her instead of Nikki. Talking right over her mother, he grabbed a bottle of bleach from under the sink, opened it and yanked Nikki's head back. 'You shut right up, right now, or I swear I'll pour it down her throat.'

As he spoke, he wafted the bottle in front of her; droplets landed on her lips and face, the smell was so strong she retched, but it did the trick. Her mum shut up bar the odd gulping sob.

'I've got an order in for a young girl and she's gonna have to do it.' He turned to Nikki. 'You know what'll happen to your *mum and sister if you don't do whatever my friend tells you, don't you?'*

*She looked at her mum, rocking back and forth on the chair and thought of Ani who was probably hiding under the bed upstairs, right now. As she nodded, a little part of her heart curled into a ball and died. He dragged her up and through to the living room. The room they were never allowed in. The room with the dark curtains and the great big padlock on the door. But it wasn't locked then. As he thrust Nikki in, her nostrils were filled by the stench of sweat and some other underlying scent she couldn't identify. A man – an old one, sat on a double bed that was covered only by a sheet. He patted the bed beside him and as he smiled at her, the door slammed shut behind her and her bowels loosened, adding to the room's putrid stench.*

It was her fear that had saved her being raped that day, but her punishment was a lasting one ... Again she touched her scar before stepping out of her car and with leaden feet made her way over to her mum's house.

The street was nearly empty; all the kids were back at school now and apart from Mr Ayub making his way home from mosque and a couple of women doing a bit of gardening, Nikki was alone. She looked up at her mum's house, just three doors along from the two that she and her sister lived in. Plant pots filled with late summer blooms, which Nikki didn't know the name of, were scattered around the small square of front yard. A wooden bench with a small matching table sat at an angle throughout the summer. Nikki had got used to seeing her mum sitting there with a cup of something in her hand, watching the kids playing on the street, as Nikki pulled up after work. She'd enjoyed grabbing an occasional half-hour with her mother, with the fading sun warm on her back, before she made her way along to the chaos that was her own house.

Today, she'd give anything to walk right on by, storm upstairs into her bedroom, drag the boxes containing the PI photos and reports on Freddie Downey downstairs and burn the lot of them. She could just pretend none of it had ever happened. That her childhood had been the feel-good Disney, ice cream and trips to the zoo one that other kids had.

She sighed and braced herself. Life was not always a box of fucking chocolates – today it was more like a rat poison sandwich. She got her key out, but suspected that her mother would have forgotten to lock the door behind her, regardless of Nikki's repeated warnings. She was wrong. The door was locked so she took her key and unlocked it. As the door opened, a waft of spicy masala tea and the muted sounds of Anika and her mum talking drifted through from the kitchen. Nikki wandered down the short hall and pushed open the door and looked at them. Her mum, despite everything, was good-looking. People said that Anika and Nikki looked like her and Nikki was glad of that, for the alternative would have been too hard to bear for any of them. Her mum was nearly fifty, with her hair styled into a shoulder-length bob whilst Anika's was long and straight. The likeness between the three ended at looks, for, whilst Lalita was good-natured, organised and full of vitality, Anika could be unreliable and easily led. She was prone to bouts of depression and unlike Nikki, trusted far too easily, which was one of the reasons for the current disagreement between the sisters. For a second, neither of the two women noticed her. Then the smile faded from Anika's lips and a frown appeared. 'Thought we were just meeting for a catch-up, Mum. Didn't realise you were staging an intervention.'

Lalita Parekh wafted nail varnished fingers. 'Oh for goodness' sake, Ani. It's not an intervention. Nikki wanted to talk to both of us and so I invited you over for tea. Surely a mother can have her two daughters in the same room without them scratching each other's faces off?'

Nikki studied her mum. She looked pale – strained even. A

pang of guilt jabbed Nikki, for here she was about to bring her mum's worst nightmare back to life.

Anika turned her glare to Nikki, sarcasm dripping venomously from her tongue. 'Oh, of course if Princess Nikita calls, we all have to jump. Can't have the princess waiting, got to put everything on hold to accommodate her.'

Biting the sharp retort that sprung to her lips, Nikki instead pulled out a chair and accepted the cup of spicy chai her mother poured from the saucepan on the stove. Not sure her stomach could handle the milkiness at that moment, Nikki placed it by her side, leaned her elbows on the table and got straight to the point. 'I got called to a murder in Gaynor Street this morning.'

Her words hung in the air; the only sound was a quick gasp from her mum. Nikki gave them a moment to absorb the implications of this. They'd realise that if it didn't concern them in some way, Nikki would never have mentioned it. Her mum's face paled even more. A pulse began to beat at her temple and Nikki jumped up and got her a glass of water. Anika bowed her head, probably to avoid Nikki seeing her expression, but she systematically pulled each of her fingers in order until they cracked. This was her "tell" – Anika had done this ever since she was a little kid and although Nikki usually chided her for it, today wasn't a day for chiding.

Her mum spoke first. 'Does this concern us in some way?'

Slamming her palm down on the table, spilling Nikki's tea in the process, Anika snorted. 'Of course it does. 'Course it bloody does. Why else would she be here talking about Gaynor Street, Mum?' Anika's voice got louder so that by the end of her speech she was almost spitting the words out. She jumped to her feet and headed to the back door, ready to run, like she did from every problem life gave her.

Using every ounce of patience she had left, Nikki kept her own tone low. 'I didn't want you to hear about this on the news – *and* I didn't want you to be interviewed by a uniformed officer before

191

I'd spoken to you. I had to mention that I'd lived there – that we had.'

Ani spun round, her face twisted in rage, her eyes flashing. 'That's just it, Nikki. You didn't. You didn't need to do a bloody thing. You could have just shut up and said nowt and we wouldn't even have to think about it all.'

'Further down the line they'd have looked at previous residents of the street and it would have looked suspicious if I hadn't come clean at the time. You know that. This is a murder, Anika. Look, sit down and let me explain everything.'

Anika looked from her mum to her sister, her chest rising, her breathing loud and fast.

'Come on, Ani. If Nikki thinks we need to hear this, then that's what we should do. Sit down and listen, *beti*.'

Scraping the chair she'd vacated moments earlier away from the table, Ani sat down, arms crossed over her chest, face set in stone as Nikki told them everything: about the anonymous letters she'd received, about the diary extracts, the newspaper articles about Peggy Dyson and the young lad murdered in Cambridge, Gerry Hudson's murder and the diary extracts they found under his pillow.

'We're still trying to piece everything together, but it seems fair to assume that the two cases are linked and by involving me, someone seems to be indicating it's to do with when we lived there.' Nikki took a sip from her tea and when it settled in her tummy with no ill effects, she took a longer sip, savouring the sweet spicy warmth as it trailed down her throat. 'Do either of you remember him – Gerry Hudson?'

Lalita looked at her eldest daughter, her eyes moist with unshed tears, her fingers clasped tightly in her lap. 'He was a vile man. Lived opposite us. He and your father were as thick as thieves – I sometimes wondered if Hudson was propping Freddie up – you know like a silent partner or something. Rumours were always flying about him, but in those days, what happened on the street stayed on the street.'

Anika was calmer now and she too sipped some of her tea before speaking. 'I was too young to remember much of anyone outside the house. I remember all the women coming and going, the kids – but that's about it.'

Nikki took out the photocopies of the diary extracts and handed them over. 'Ever seen these before?'

When both shook their heads, she took out the copies of the real photos she'd taken from Gerry Hudson's house. 'What about these. Any of these kids seem familiar?'

Huddled together, Ani and her mum took their time studying the photos without saying a word. Finally, Lalita raised her head. 'I do recognise some of these as kids from the street. You two aren't in any, but I do recognise some of the kids – can't remember any names though. Let me think about it. Can I keep them? Maybe something will click later on?'

Nikki nodded. 'Sure, I've got copies. Don't show them to anyone else though. This is all between us for now.'

With a frown, her mother picked up one of the photos again. Nikki made a mental note of which photo it was, for she was as sure as she could be, that her mother was keeping something from her – and that didn't bode well.

# Chapter 38

After her daughters left, Lalita Parekh sat for a long time at the kitchen table, her chai going cold in the cup before her. Everything she'd been feeling for the past few days was explained. She still hadn't told Nikki about either the note on her car or the one that had been pushed through her letterbox, but she was now convinced that it was from Downey. Who else could it be from? With leaden limbs, she pushed herself up from the chair, stumbled, then righting herself, she double-checked the back door was locked before closing the kitchen blinds. In a trance she walked through the hallway to check the lock on the front door, her fingers trailing against the walls on either side as if to help her balance. For double safety she slotted the security chain over too, then made her way to the living room to close the curtains she'd opened after receiving Nikki's call earlier.

She hardly noticed the tears streaming down her cheeks as, holding on to the banister, she hefted her weary bones upstairs. Once in her bedroom, she locked the door and leaned against it, eyes closed. She'd always suspected this day or one very similar would come, but as time passed she became complacent and less vigilant. Years ago, had she found a note like that on her windscreen, her mind would automatically connect to Freddie Downey.

Now, after Nikita's revelations about Hudson's death, Lalita was convinced Downey was behind it all – the letters to her daughter, Peggy's death, the notes, and even Hudson's death – just like he'd been behind everything all those years ago. As he'd promised, he'd come back for her – for revenge – and Lalita doubted she'd be able to escape this time.

Scrubbing the tears away, she walked over to the window that looked out onto the street below. Standing first to one side, then the other, just out of sight of anyone looking up from the street below, she perused the area. Would she recognise Downey now? After all these years he'd have changed and Lalita wasn't convinced she'd spot him quickly enough to escape from him. He was a violent man – ruthless, sadistic. Both she and Nikita bore the physical scars to testify to that. All three of them bore the emotional ones too – sometimes she thought that that kind were even more destructive.

She blamed Downey for Anika's propensity to choose the wrong man – her inability to put herself, or even her son before the love of her life. She'd been a doormat to Yousaf, Haqib's dad, for years – always seeking his approval, changing herself to suit him. Both Nikita and Lalita had tried so hard to make her see how worthless he was, how she deserved better than that, but the lessons learned from her father had left their mark. Nikita was the opposite. The elder daughter, she'd taken on the role of protector to both Lalita and Anika from such a young age. Nikita kept her emotions under wraps. Like a hedgehog, her prickly nature was her defence against being hurt. Lalita was just pleased that finally her eldest was beginning to let people under her prickliness. Marcus was good for Nikki, as were Sajid and Langley and, if she'd only allow them to be, Stevie and Felicity Springer would also be good for her.

Flicking the bedside light on, Lalita settled herself on the floor beside her bed and pulled a suitcase out from underneath. It had been a long time since she'd looked in it and she hesitated before unzipping it. Still, she was reluctant to flip the lid open, for when she did, she'd be transported back to there. Back to that horrible time in her life, back to the life she had thought she might never escape.

Lifting the lid, her hands shaking, she flipped it open and just sat for a while studying the contents. Right at the top was a clear plastic bag with a tiny Baby-gro inside and a hospital baby wrist tag. Tears filling her eyes, she reached out and lifted it. She opened the seal at the top of the bag and after slipping the tiny garment out, held it to her face, inhaling deeply, imagining the baby smells that had long since evaporated. Nikita – a tiny red-faced squalling baby – even then she'd been strong. She'd had to be and sitting there on the floor of her bedroom, the smell of her baby filling her nostrils, Lalita drifted back in time ...

*'I told you to get rid of it, didn't I? No one wants to screw a fat bitch, do they? How are you supposed to pay your way with a sprog in your belly, you stupid slag? As if I don't have enough mouths to feed. I've already got them two feckless sprogs with Peggy – don't want any more with you.'*

*'Freddie, no please, Freddie, don't.' But he had a hold of her hair and was dragging her through to the kitchen. He pulled her round and with a final thrust propelled her against the kitchen table. It caught her right in the stomach, and she yelped, falling to the sticky lino floor. 'No, Freddie, no, you're hurting the baby.'*

*'Damn right I am. If you won't get rid of it the way I told you to, you'll get rid of it my way.' He raised his booted foot and before she had a chance to roll into a ball, he landed it right in her belly. The baby kicked a few protesting flutters in her abdomen and then ... stillness. Lalita groaned, the pain was excruciating, but somehow she managed to curl up, her arms cradling her slightly swollen belly as Freddie took aim again. This kick caught her hand, scraping it, breaking two of her fingers, but she didn't care. She had to protect her baby, for he wasn't done. She recognised the look on his face – that dark, gloating anger. Freddie Downey wasn't done,*

*not by a long chalk. Bracing herself, Lalita shut her eyes, and waited,*
*sobbing and squirming on the floor.*

*Then, there was hammering on the door and she recognised the*
*voice. It was Mr Moretti from next door. 'What's going on in there?*
*Do I have to phone the police again, Downey?'*

*With a final ill-aimed kick that caught the top of her legs, Downey*
*marched to the front door, yanked it open and stormed past Moretti,*
*slamming it shut behind him. 'Mind your own fucking business,*
*Moretti. Nowt going on here for you to worry about. Now piss off*
*back home and mind your own business!'*

*'Or what, Downey? Or what?'*

*'Or I'll fucking kill you. I promise you, I'll kill you.' Downey's*
*voice faded as he headed down the road and then Mr Moretti was*
*pushing the door open and peering inside.*

*Lalita tried to get to her feet, but doubled over at the pain in*
*her abdomen, until gentle hands helped lift her – Peggy and Mr*
*Moretti, one at either side. Lalita could have cried with relief. Peggy*
*was always kind to her, always tried to keep an eye out for her –*
*when she wasn't high on drugs, that is. And Mr Moretti was a saint.*
*He stepped in whenever he could on her behalf and gave the kids*
*ice cream from his van. 'I phoned an ambulance, Layla. You're*
*bleeding.' Peggy's voice was frantic.*

*Layla looked down at the lino and saw a small pool of blood.*
*She looked up at her friend. 'He's killed her – he's killed my baby.'*

*'Ssh, ssh, sweetie. We don't know that. Let's just get you to hospital*
*and we'll see. If she's as strong as her mummy, then she'll make it.'*

Lalita pressed her fingers over the soft fabric and smiled. Peggy
had been right. Nikita was tough – not that she should have had
to be and that was something Lalita couldn't forgive herself for.
She shouldn't have gone back to him after she had Nikita, but
then she wouldn't have had Anika, would she?

The life they had with Freddie Downey had been like a constant
thundercloud with only her two children giving it its silver lining.
They'd deserved better than that. For twelve years Nikita had seen

the things that man was capable of. For twelve years she'd allowed her children to be subjected to all sorts of things. That was something she could never forgive herself for and now, when they'd moved on with their lives, Downey had come back into them – and this time, Lalita wasn't sure they'd come out the other side in one piece.

# Chapter 39

Now that she was out of the house and back in the sunlight, Nikki drew in deep breaths. Someone was making pakoras and the hot spicy frying smell grounded Nikki. Things all around were normal – it was just her mad life that was in chaos. Stomach gurgling, she breathed in the aroma, and realised she was starving. Food had been the last thing on her mind all day. Although eating something now was tempting, Nikki still had that unsettled sensation in the pit of her stomach that told her if she ate anything, she'd hurl. The meeting with her mum and Ani had been awful. Her mother's hopeless expression – the way her face paled and the worry lines across her forehead had deepened, made Nikki want to kill Downey for all he'd put them through. Anika's animosity was hurtful, but she could cope with that. It was Ani's way of coping – deflecting the blame onto Nikki was par for the course with Ani. What she couldn't cope with was the vulnerability of the two women she loved most in the world. If Downey was behind all of this, then Nikki would make sure he paid.

Before heading over to her car to retrieve the documentation she wanted to study that evening, she glanced towards her mother's house. Her mum had pulled all the curtains closed and Nikki's heart contracted. Her mum was cocooning herself in darkness like she'd done when they first escaped Downey. Nikki started to walk across the road, determined to take her mum back to her house, but then stopped. She'd piled a lot on her and Nikki needed to give her space to process everything – space and privacy. Marcus's words – "You can't always take away the hurt" – came to mind. She'd just turned back to her car when a large, flashy BMW drove up the street and glided into a parking space outside her mum's house.

Opening her own car, which was parked on the opposite side of the road, Nikki cast a glance towards the vehicle. The driver had remained inside and the engine was still humming. Perhaps it was all her thoughts of Downey, all her memories that had resurfaced or perhaps it was just her copper's instinct. Whatever it was, instead of grabbing her stuff and heading home, Nikki slid into the driver's seat and using her side mirror, observed the car. Her vision of the driver was obscured, but he still had made no attempt to leave the car. Nikki glanced up and down the street trying to work out who the man had come to visit.

That was when she saw Isaac, head down, shoulders hunched, walking up the road from the bus stop. She smiled. Isaac always made her smile. She'd intended to pop in and see him at Lazy Bites today but events had overtaken her. She made a promise to herself to do just that the next day. As she watched Isaac draw level with the BMW, a short Danny DeVito lookalike, in a smart suit with gold dripping off his wrist, got out of the car and extended an arm to Isaac. *What the hell did this bloke want with Isaac?*

As Isaac pulled his headphones from his ear and gripped the older man's hand, Nikki got out of the Zafira and ambled across the road. 'Hi, Isaac.'

In different circumstances Nikki would have been tempted to take a photo of Isaac's dismayed expression. The smile faded from his face and his eyes darted around as if he was looking for an escape. But right now, with this smarmy gold-adorned man in the smart BMW talking to her friend, she wasn't amused.

Eyes narrowed, she allowed her gaze to rake over the man, not bothering to hide her distrust. 'What's going on here, Isaac? Who's your friend?'

Before Isaac could reply, Gold Man held out a card to her, which she took and studied for a moment – Gold Man appeared to be a lawyer.

'Cliff McIvor. I've got business with young Isaac here. Now if you don't mind …' He began to guide Isaac round the side of the swanky car, the false smile still on his chubby face.

Nikki moved to block their way. 'Ah, but you see, Mr McIvor, I do mind.'

McIvor's smile was still in place. *How did he do that?* He attempted to wave her away with his hand. 'This is nothing to do with you, miss … Isaac and I have business to conduct in private.'

The rage that Nikki had suppressed all day threatened to engulf her as she looked at Isaac, red-faced and uncertain, and McIvor sleazy and pushy. With great deliberation she stepped closer, eye to eye with the small man, her eyes flashing. 'Well, that's where I disagree. Taking advantage of a vulnerable adult is very much my business.'

She took out her warrant card and thrust it under McIvor's nose. His many chins began to wobble, his pupils dilated and his breath hitched a little as he splayed his hands out. 'I'm not taking advantage of Isaac. He needed a conveyancing lawyer to facilitate his house sale and I was recommended to him. That right, lad?'

Isaac glanced at Nikki, tears in his eyes. 'I got to sell the house, Nik, Nik. I pinkie promised. I don't want my mum going to hell. She can't go to hell, Nik. Let me sign.'

Trying to make sense of everything, Nikki directed her next question to McIvor who was now edging back towards the driver's door. 'What was Isaac going to sign?'

'Nothing, nothing. The lad's confused.'

But Isaac, who hated being told he didn't understand, stepped forward. 'You told me I had to go into your car to sign the documents in your briefcase. You did, Mr McIvor, I'm not confused.'

Nikki quirked an eyebrow at McIvor. 'I suggest you show me these documents.'

When McIvor hesitated, Nikki again stepped forward. 'NOW!'

McIvor opened the door and leaned in. 'My other clients had me make up the documents – it's all perfectly legal.'

Nikki flicked through the pages. She was by no means into all the legalese, but even she could tell that the document, when signed by Isaac, would pass the deeds of his old house over to McIvor.

Before she could reconsider, Nikki grabbed McIvor by his lapels. And drew him right up to her face. 'This might not be illegal, but it sure as hell is immoral, you sleazy little scumbag. Where the hell do you get off trying to exploit a young lad? You're despicable.'

Isaac pulled at her arm, and Nikki, loosening her grip on the lawyer, glanced at him. Tears poured down his cheeks, his chest heaved. 'Nikki, Nikki, leave him alone. I gotta sign. I gotta sign or my mum will go to hell.'

Coming to her senses, Nikki thrust the lawyer so he landed against the door of his posh car. 'You get the hell out of here, now. And be sure I'll have some of my colleagues from fraud check out your outfit in minute detail.'

Then she turned to Isaac and pulled him close to her, smoothing down his hair, whispering in his ear. 'Oh, Isaac. There's no way your mum could ever go to hell. She was far too good a mum and friend to end up down there. I promise you.'

She held Isaac at arm's length and looked right into his eyes and repeated her words. 'I promise you, Isaac, and you know I keep my promises, nothing you could do would ever send your mum to hell.'

Isaac sniffed and Nikki wished for a moment she had one of Saj's posh hankies to offer him. Instead all she could find was a dubiously crumpled tissue from her back pocket. When Isaac had sniffed and scrubbed his face, Nikki linked her arm through his. 'Come on, let's sit in my car for a bit and you can tell me everything. Last thing you want is for Lally Mum to see you in this state.'

They sat in the front seat of Nikki's car, Isaac insisting on putting on his seatbelt although Nikki reassured him that if they were stationary there was no need. 'You going to tell me what's gone on?'

Isaac looked down. 'I missed being here. Missed seeing Lally Mum and Sunni and everybody.' He hesitated a moment and added, 'Even Ani – I even missed her.'

Nikki's lips twitched. Ani didn't bother spending time with Isaac. Too impatient and too wrapped up in her own world to bother giving him the time of day. 'We missed you too, Isaac. We're all glad you're back and you know you can stay at Lally Mum's as long as you want to. I want to help, so why don't you tell me what's gone on.'

'I had to pinkie promise. Calum made me. He said if I didn't pinkie promise to give him all the money from the house, he'd make sure my mum went to hell. He said if I broke the promise, she'd go to hell.'

It all made sense to Nikki now – all Isaac's questions about hell and pinkie promises were because of this. Choosing her words carefully, Nikki said, 'I meant it when I said your mum would *never* go to hell. This Calum was lying to you. God would never send someone to hell for breaking that sort of promise. This Calum was being unkind. He was bullying you. You understand?'

And after Isaac nodded she continued. 'Where does he live, this Calum?'

Tears rolling down his cheek once more, Isaac shrugged. 'Dunno. Him and his mates find me.'

Nikki nodded. 'They sent you to meet this McIvor man?'

'Yes.'

'From now on, till I find them, me or Lally Mum will drop you right outside your work and ... no more arranging to meet folk you don't know, okay?'

'Yes.'

Nikki smiled and held out her hand. 'Pinkie promise.'

This raised the first slight smile she'd got from Isaac since she confronted him. But she wasn't off the hook yet. She still had some bad news and who knew how Isaac would take it? How she wished this day was over. 'Just one more thing, Isaac. You and your mum lived next door to Lally Mum for a long time, but ...' She paused, unsure just how much to reveal to Isaac, then decided to take the coward's way out for now. 'Well, your mum didn't own the house. Someone lent it to her to live in.'

'Okay.' He smiled. 'So I can't sell it anyway?'

Pleased that he'd understood so easily, Nikki grinned. 'That's right. It's not yours to sell.' She dreaded him asking who owned it. The last thing she wanted to tell this lovely boy was that his own dad wanted nothing to do with him, but Isaac just nodded and undid the seatbelt. 'Better get home now. Lally Mum's waiting for me.'

Nikki watched him cross the road to Lalita's house, pleased to note that the curtains were open again. It was good that her mum had Isaac to focus on.

# Chapter 40

Well, well, well something was definitely afoot around the Parekh residences in Listerhills. All that coming and going was enough to make a man dizzy. After his curry at the Kashmir, Freddie Downey had borrowed a car from his mate Jimmy, and although nobody had noticed him so far he'd have to be a bit more careful because things were hotting up. Last thing he wanted was to get spotted before he was good and ready to make his presence known. Freddie, seat inclined and cap on, was parked a good six houses away from the Parekhs'; still, he had a good view. Layla's curtains were being closed and opened at intervals all afternoon. Did the stupid bitch really think shutting her curtains would protect her from him? If he wanted in, he'd manage it no problem.

First, the skinny bint with the long hair had gone into the house. Layla had opened the door, barely enough to let her younger daughter squeeze through, then she'd poked her head out peering up and down the street before shutting it again. Slapping his palm on the steering wheel, he laughed aloud. The bitch was running scared. Well, he'd warned her, hadn't he? Told her, he'd be back. Told her, he'd get his revenge and boy, was he looking forward to it. If she was scared now, then when she finally realised what he had planned for her, she'd be bloody petrified.

When he'd been in the nick, he'd spent months brooding on all the things he'd do to her … and to that Nikita. He'd made big plans, but he was smart enough to know that if he took his revenge too early, they'd trace it back to him and he'd end up right back there, dodging the faggots and the gangs. He was too smart for that though. Once he'd got into the routine of prison life, he'd fine-tuned his plans. He was prepared to wait. Build up his network, get a bit of money behind him and then, when the time was right, he'd exact his revenge. The diaries were just a bit of fun to him. So were the letters to Layla. Fun Fun Fun – he was such a fun-loving guy. It was the rest of it that was serious. There were so many of them he needed to get his revenge on but slowly but surely he was making progress.

Soon after the younger whore arrived, the other one pulled up in her battered old Zafira. What a mess she was. He hated her with a vengeance. She'd always had an insolent look in her eye, that one. Even when he gave her a hiding and tears poured down her face, she never made a sound – just stared right at him, a sneer on her face. He'd enjoyed marking her. Enjoyed the feeling of power when he'd put that rope around her little neck and pulled. She'd coughed and spluttered, her entire body jerking around, her skinny little fingers trying to pull the metal away. For a second – just one second, he'd been tempted to finish her. Then he saw the blood seeping through the rope. Her eyes bulged, her lips were turning blue, and all around him they were yelling at him, hammering their stupid women's fists on his back – Peggy and Layla. Stupid whores, as if they'd be able to stop him.

Then that hammering on the door. Fucking Moretti. It was always fucking Moretti. He'd let the girl go. Went down the pub whilst they took her to Bradford Royal Infirmary. He wasn't worried that they'd snitch him out – why would they? For years they'd made excuses for all their injuries, why would this time be different?

But it had been.

His hands tightened on the steering wheel as he watched her cross the road and enter her mum's house. That fucking ponytail bobbing up and down like she hadn't a care in the world – taunting him. Oh, she'd pay – he'd make sure of that. Nikki Parekh would pay big time – they all would.

He waited till she left Layla's house and was just about to drive off, when he saw the BMW drive past, followed moments later by the retard walking up from the bus stop. Why the fuck did they bother with the likes of him? Freddie enjoyed the contretemps that followed. Nikita hadn't lost any of her feistiness – not yet. But soon, very soon, that bitch would get what had been coming to her for a long, long time.

# Chapter 41

Once Sunni was in bed and Ruby and Charlie were doing their own thing in their rooms, Nikki opened a bottle of wine and sat on the sofa with her legs sprawled over Marcus. It had been hard telling them that they had to be careful for the moment. She hadn't wanted to be too explicit, about the possible threat from Downey, but she did want them aware that they had to be careful for now. They accepted it as par for the course and Nikki, with a momentary pang for misleading them, consoled herself that it wouldn't be for long. That as soon as she had a handle on things, she'd talk them through everything.

As she gave Marcus the run-down of everything that had gone on that day, he gave her a foot rub. One of the things she loved most about him was that he was unflappable – solid. He had her back no matter what and he could listen and really hear what she was saying. He already knew most of Nikki's history and so none of it came as a shock to him. When she'd finished, he refilled their glasses before speaking.

'So, do you think this has something to do with Freddie Downey?'

Nikki could have kissed him. Earlier her mum had referred to him as her father and it made Nikki want to lash out. She let it go – that time – because of the circumstances, but she was relieved that Marcus just got it. She'd never had to tell him that she didn't consider Freddie Downey as anything other than a sperm donor. He'd just got it and he never referred to him by anything other than his name. 'Dunno.'

'He still up in Scotland?'

Nikki sighed. 'Again, dunno. My PI is checking it out. He only goes by Downey's flat once a month nowadays and it's been three weeks since he last checked him out. I'll know tomorrow where he is.'

'But you think there's a link, don't you?'

'S'pose so. Too many coincidences for there not to be. Though I just don't see what's happened to spark things off *now*. So far we've found no link between Peggy Dyson, Liam Flynn, the Cambridge student, and Gerry Hudson. Or me, for that matter – other than Gaynor Street. The team are still looking though. Hudson himself doesn't seem to have travelled in the last twenty-five years, so it's all a mystery. Those diary extracts are a bit chilling though. Difficult to work out exactly what's gone on – but I have a horrid feeling about them.'

'You told Saj everything yet?'

At that point the doorbell rang and Nikki swung her feet from Marcus's lap. 'Hope you don't mind, but I invited Saj and Langley over so that we four could maybe go over things – you know, fresh eyes and all that.'

Marcus leaned over and kissed her on the lips. 'Of course, this is nothing to do with you not trusting Springer to get things done?'

'You know me too damn well, babes.'

Looking into Marcus's eyes gave her strength, but she would be glad when this day was over. When she had to delve into her past, who else would she want by her side than these three? 'I think we may need more wine.'

Marcus grinned. 'You get the glasses; I'll get the door.' As she jumped to her feet he grabbed her arm and pulled her to him in a bear hug. 'I'm here for you, Nik. Always.'

A half-hour later, when everyone's glasses had been filled and the kitchen table was covered in documents, Nikki looked at Langley. 'I know we'll get the PM report on Gerry Hudson tomorrow, but is there anything you can tell us at all?'

Langley had been studying the post-mortem report on Liam Flynn that Davy Jones had copied for Nikki. He pushed his reading glasses up his nose and nodded. 'Hmm, well yes, there are bits I can share. Firstly, I confirmed earlier today that the weapon used to kill Peggy Dyson and the one used on Gerry Hudson could conceivably be the same one – a large heavy-duty flat-head screwdriver with a two-centimetre blade and a long – perhaps a six-inch – shaft, would be my best guess.' He sipped his wine and leaned back. 'Of course, this is all speculation, you understand. It could equally be an ice pick, but in my experience a screwdriver seems more reasonable. Anyway, the weapon, unless you find the specific one, won't in itself drive the case forward much. However, something interesting has just come to my attention from the Flynn murder – it looks very much as if the same or a similar weapon was used on that victim too.'

'So, a possible direct link between all three murders?' This was the sort of confirmation Nikki needed. Although in her own mind, she was sure all three cases were linked, until now, she had only an anonymously sent news clipping pointing that way. The strong possibility that the same or at the very least a similar weapon had been used was a step in the right direction. But Langley wasn't finished.

'Ah, but that's not all. As we pathologists do, we measured the depth of each wound and counted them. So, considering the number of penetrating wounds first – ten for Peggy Dyson, fifteen for Liam Flynn and a whopping twenty-five for Hudson – it's fair to say that the perpetrator is either accelerating, getting more angry or that Hudson was more personal than the others – or, maybe even a combination of all three. Believe it or not it takes a lot of strength to deliver multiple stab wounds – especially to a living victim. Of course, we already know that Peggy was off her skull on benzo, so maybe she didn't put up much of a fight. Liam Flynn, from the angle of some of the wounds penetrating his body, did try to protect himself, whereas Hudson, perhaps because he was so frail, barely moved.'

Well into his swing now, Langley leaned forward. 'The depths of impact varied, although the one identified as being the "kill" wound on each victim was straight to the heart and around the same depth of four to five inches. It's this that tells me the shaft of the weapon must measure around six inches. Our killer had clearly done their homework. It seems that was followed up by stabs to the carotid, groin area and repeated hits to the bodies. So, impassioned – perhaps – but also clear-headed enough to know where to strike for maximum effect.'

'What about spatter? Surely there'd be a whole load of blood flying about?' Saj enjoyed the science of blood spatter and was always keen to hear more about it. 'There was definitely spatter in Hudson's case.'

Langley laid out a series of images on the kitchen table. 'This first one is from Peggy Dyson's murder – of course we can't do any further forensic examination of her body as she's been cremated, but the CSIs did their job. Unfortunately, because of all the debris and the disturbance of the crime scene by the other rough sleepers, it's difficult to detect a pattern, but, in my opinion, the spatter would have been quite extensive and certainly our perp would have had a sizable amount of spatter on him.'

Langley tapped an image of Liam Flynn's body at the dump site. 'Now we can't see any spatter here because this was not the kill site, but from the wounds, I'm certain the perpetrator would again have spatter on his person.'

Pointing to the images taken at the crime scene that morning, Langley reiterated that here too, the killer would have been unable to avoid spatter when inflicting the injuries to Hudson. He gave them a moment to digest the information before continuing. 'Your genius pathologist – that's me – also discovered something else today. In a couple of the wounds – notably the ones that I suspect were cause of death, I found some debris.'

'You got it analysed?'

Langley's look was enough to quell any further questions from Nikki. 'Of course I sent it for analysis. You just stick to the day job, Parekh, and leave the tricky business of extracting evidence from dead bodies to me, eh?' His wink softened his words and Nikki shrugged apologetically and then sent a withering glance to her partner when Saj snorted.

'Moving things on, children,' Langley continued. 'The report from Cambridge also shows that some debris was extricated from wounds on Liam Flynn's body. Although we've not yet had the analysis of ours back yet, so far I see no reason to assume that the traces will not be similar. Of course, till our results come back, we have to keep an open mind.'

Whilst Marcus poured more wine, Saj nudged Langley. 'Go on then, smartarse. Tell us.'

But before Langley could respond, Marcus jumped in: 'Paint specks or metal shavings.'

He stopped pouring and looked round at the three of them who were staring at him. 'What? It makes sense, doesn't it? The only thing any self-respecting person uses a flat-head screwdriver for, apart from offing people that is – is, well, screwing screws – hence the metal shavings. Or …' Marcus grinned '… opening paint tins, which again gives you metal shavings and/or paint.'

Three pairs of eyes looked expectantly at Langley who frowned at Marcus. 'Stealing my thunder, Marcus. But yes, you're right. Traces of paint and metal shavings were discovered in some of Liam Flynn's wounds and I suspect we'll find that the debris I sent off from Gerry Hudson's wounds will be the same. Now don't get all overexcited about this. The analysis will probably show up a generic paint supplier, so you can't use that to track down this bastard. But, if you find that sort of paint et cetera and a screwdriver ...' He splayed his hands. 'Well, that'll all be contributory evidence – it could help you tie a bow on your case when you submit to CPS.'

This was huge. Okay, it might not push the case forward in terms of suspects, but it did give a concrete link, depending on the test results. It wouldn't lead them to a screwdriver-wielding person's door, but this was strong circumstantial evidence that would help in court. For the first time since that awful phone call directing her to Gaynor Street this morning, Nikki felt a shadow lifting. Things were moving forward. Now, all she had to do was make sure Springer did her job.

# Chapter 42

For once, Lalita had been relieved when Isaac said he wanted to watch *Dr Who* in his bedroom. He had a bit of a crush on Jodie Whittaker and had watched the first series featuring her numerous times already. The lad had been subdued over dinner, but a phone call from Nikita had explained that and, taking her daughter's advice, Lalita pretended not to notice his mood. Her qualms that, yet again, she was leaving it for her daughter to sort something that she should take responsibility for, nagged her. It had only been Nikita's insistence that she'd be able to find out more from the other officers at work than Lalita herself could, that had finally convinced her to give in.

About an hour after her daughters had left, DC Williams had turned up at the door. He'd been pleasant, courteous, but Lalita's shame had made her responses abrupt and a little aggressive. Poor Nikita. She'd fought so hard to leave all this behind, got a job where she was well respected and now, her own mother's shameful past was known to all her colleagues. This wasn't fair – it just wasn't fair at all.

Although Williams had been thorough, noting down all the names Lalita could remember from Gaynor Street and showing her a few more images that Nikita hadn't shown her earlier, Lalita sensed that he was as embarrassed as she was. He hadn't shown her the diary extracts that her daughter had and Lalita wished she'd been able to have another look at them. There was something about them that tugged at her memory, and if she could just focus, instead of being all over the place, she was sure she could work it out.

Before he left, DC Williams had asked if there was anything else she wanted to share – anything else, no matter how small, she could add to their investigation – and Lalita, clasping her hands so tightly together that her fingernails marked her palms, had shaken her head.

Now, cup of cold coffee on the table beside her, she berated herself. The notes were relevant to this investigation. Deep down she acknowledged that. She had no doubt they were from Downey and, equally, she had no doubt that he was behind these murders. So, the next logical assumption was that he would come for her. Then, as another more appalling thought struck her, she jumped to her feet and began pacing the living room. Perhaps he'd come for her daughters first – or perhaps her grandchildren.

Flinging herself back down on the sofa, Lalita Parekh cried and cried and, when no more tears would come, she made a decision. A decision that would sort things out for everyone.

# Tuesday 22nd September

# Chapter 43

'It's Anika's birthday today.'

Nikki blinked, rubbing sleep from her eyes, and gratefully accepted the coffee Marcus had brought her. After Sajid and Langley had gone home the previous evening, she and Marcus had spent time going over the files on Freddie Downey that she'd accumulated over the years and now it seemed like she'd only been asleep for two minutes. Groggy, she glanced at the clock. *Six o'clock!* She rolled over, wanting just another half-hour, but Marcus shook her shoulder again. 'Did you hear me? It's Anika's birthday and your mum's making a birthday tea with Isaac. She wants us all there this evening before Haqib takes her to the cinema.'

Nikki opened her eyes and reached for the coffee. It was delicious. Now, if only Marcus had thought to bring some toast too.

'You hear me, Nik? You can't ignore it. I know she's being a bitch but, with everything that's going on, maybe now's the time to reach out again.'

Realising that Marcus wouldn't let this one go, Nikki took another sip before grudgingly nodding. 'Look, I'll try, okay? That's all I can promise. I've got a busy day ahead. Briefing at eight ...'

'You've been grounded, Nik. Your day will be a rare one, spent in the confines of Trafalgar House, so you'll be able to nip into Broadway and grab something nice for your sis.'

Nikki put her empty cup on the bedside table and got out of bed. 'Need to pee.'

But Marcus grabbed her arm. 'You've no intention of trying have you?' He stared at her with those eyes that seemed to penetrate her soul.

She shrugged. 'It's too much right now. I can't face seeing Mum all agitated and it's only made worse with Anika's bitching. Best if I steer clear. It's Ani's day after all.'

'Okay, I'll go and I'll take the kids, but *you* can get the present *and* a card, and none of that petrol station crap – get something nice for her – something that shows you care. Oh, and get a cake too.'

*Pressure, pressure, pressure! When will it all stop?* She raked her fingers through her hair. She'd forgotten to take the bobble from her hair when she'd fallen into bed and now it was a tangle caught up in a clump of hair. She yanked it hard, grimacing when a clump of long black hair came loose. Bloody great start to the day.

The images and reports about her father's activities, which she'd received from her PI over the years, were still all over the floor. The previous night, she and Marcus had dragged them from the bottom of her wardrobe and began the long, drawn-out task of scrutinising them. She wanted to go through them herself before she came clean to Archie and Springer. He'd no doubt confiscate them. Over the years, since his release from prison, Downey had stayed in a variety of cities – always monitored by a parole officer, still on the sex offender's register – but only for what he'd done to her mum and a few other women whom he'd groomed and prostituted. The police had been unable to nail him for anything else and, at that time, Lalita Parekh and the other women had been too traumatised to give up anything more. He'd had a stint in Birmingham, then moved to Manchester for a while before heading up to Scotland where he stayed in Glasgow before settling in Livingston near Edinburgh. Nikki had wondered at the time if this was to physically distance himself from some unsavoury criminal activity that he'd managed to keep from his parole officer.

Each of the places he lived in would have to be investigated – associates, work colleagues, employers, neighbours, all questioned and that was the first investigative action she'd start this morning.

With Marcus's help, she began to put the files back into their boxes; whilst she had her shower, he lugged them out to the Zafira. Fifteen minutes later, hair still wet but dragged back into a dripping ponytail, Nikki grabbed her leather jacket from the banister, pulled on and tied her Docs and ran into the kitchen to drop a kiss on each of her children's heads before she left. 'Remember, nobody wanders off alone – you all report to your dad.' She looked at Charlie. 'Don't try to slip away. This is for *your* safety – whoever you're seeing in secret will just have to wait.'

As Charlie rolled her eyes, Sunni began to chant: 'Charlie and someone up a tree – K.I.S.S.I.N.G ...'

'Give it a rest, Sunni. Leave your sister alone. She's allowed her privacy.'

Ruby snorted. 'What privacy? If we've got to report our every move to Dad, none of us have privacy.' She pouted. 'It's state control – that's what it is. Big Daddy watching us.'

Nikki shook her head, laughing. 'You know it's not that, Rubster. You know that occasionally I'm working a case that I want to protect you lot from. That's all it is, so stop being a pain. Just look after yourselves – yeah?'

Nikki turned to leave, her damp T-shirt sticking uncomfortably to her back, but Charlie followed. 'Mum!'

Nikki turned. 'Yeah I know, Charlie. Marcus and I will explain it all tonight – I'm not shutting you out – just been really busy.' She moved closer to her eldest daughter and held out her little finger. 'Pinkie promise?'

Charlie laughed, but linked her own pinkie finger with her mother's. 'Okay.'

# Chapter 44

I'm famous! Well, okay nobody knows it's actually me who offed the old pervert, but at least it's all over the news now. Was beginning to think they'd never find him. Wonder what they made of it all. It seems like they're beginning to put two and two together now – linking the old bitch with this one and the Cambridge one.

It feels so good, but I've got a bit of a problem and I'm not sure what to do about it. I've had to hide the clothes I was wearing – that's why I started to wear them disposable all-in-ones. I don't have money to squander on buying new clothes. I could boil-wash my clothes, but last thing I want is to leave even a little bit of blood on them.

I get up and head out, yelling that I won't be long – not that she cares. Not sure anybody does – not today. Still I'll make sure I'm back in time.

The library's only a half-hour walk from here and I take my time. No need to rush; besides, walking lets me think. I've decided on my next target. It wasn't hard really. I wanted another easy one first, but that's not the only reason. No – this one's dangerous. Got a lot of information that could fuck everything up and I'm not going to let any of that get out. I've decided that all this moving around could be risky, so I'm moving into a hotel. I've used a false name and will pay with cash – it's one of those sorts of establishments, so if I get lonely, I can sort that out quick like. It'll make everything easier. Still leaving my phone at home – no way I can be traced – no way at all. My bags packed under the bed, all ready to leave. Just need to get through the rest of the day and then I'm off. By the time I return it will all be sorted and we can move on.

Thing is, I can't drag the bloody clothes with me. That would be a dead giveaway if I got stopped, so I need to dispose of them somehow and I need to do it today. Thought about shoving them in the river – but wasn't sure how much forensic stuff they could retrieve. Could use bleach I suppose and then dump them in the river. Or burying them. That could be an option. I like the idea of bleach first though. Whatever I do, I'll bleach them first to be doubly sure. But I won't make a final decision till I've been online. I smile at a mother whose kid's having a tantrum. If it were mine, I'd smack its arse for it, but now the stupid bint tries to reason with it. 'Give it a smack, love.'

She looks at me like I've just asked her to hang, draw and quarter the squealing brat – her eyes all round and spacy. Grabbing it by the arm she scurries along casting venomous glances my way. I growl and take a step in her direction, laughing aloud when she whips the kid into her arms and skedaddles at full throttle down the road. *Stupid bitch!* Like I'd do anything to her in broad daylight.

I smile at the old lady who witnessed my little interaction, and she flinches and looks away. I try to make my smile look less threatening. What am I playing at? I should be keeping my head down, not strutting around drawing attention to myself. But I feel good for once – not the reason for her disappointment, not the meek little "say nothing and shut up" creature they all think I am. I'm strong and facing things head on. I'm taking control for once. What a great day to be famous!

# Chapter 45

The pelting rain suited Nikki's mood as she headed to Trafalgar House and, for once, she didn't care that the rain dripped onto her leather jacket from the leaky window, splashing up onto her face as she drove. Still, she was achy tired, like she could still sleep for another few hours. It was a reaction to all the adrenaline that had flooded her body the previous day and she knew the best remedy for her lethargy.

Once she'd parked up in the car park, Nikki ran along, dodging puddles, uncaring that her ponytail was getting wetter, and she almost crashed through the Lazy Bites door.

Elaine, glorious in pink as usual, welcomed her with the biggest smile, whilst Isaac practically dived from the kitchen area to greet her.

'Lally Mum dropped me off, Nik Nik.' He squeezed her tight. 'I wondered if you'd come in to see how I'm doing. I'm doing grand aren't I, Grayson?'

Grayson winked at Nikki. 'He sure is – a natural. He's just been frying up some bacon and eggs and they're spot on. You sitting down?'

'Can't stop, I'm afraid; got a briefing in ten minutes. But what about twelve butties, half bacon and half just egg, to take away?'

Shoulders back, face flushed with pride, all business and efficiency, Isaac went back into the kitchen. 'I'll get them, Nikki. Got enough on the hotplates already.'

As Nikki paid Elaine for the butties, the doorbell jangled and two lads walked in, nudging each other and talking loudly. 'This must be that retard café. Look there's the moron looking like a right ponce with that stupid hat and apron on.'

Nikki glanced at Isaac. The colour had drained from his face and his eyes were flitting all round the room. A sure sign that he was nervous. He dropped two eggs on the floor and Grayson put a hand on his shoulder. 'Never mind those idiots, I'll deal with them.'

But Nikki spun round, her anger palpable. These must be the lads who were bullying Isaac. Well, that saved her some time. Now she didn't have to seek them out. They'd landed right on her doorstep. 'Watch your mouths.'

The taller of the two, nose covered with a slick of blackheads, cap on backwards, sidled up to her. 'Oh and what are you gonna do if we don't?'

Rather than backing away as the lad seemed to expect, Nikki took a step forward and flashed her badge. 'You know I can arrest you for hate speech?'

Looking at her badge, the shorter of the two raised his arms, palms out in a placating gesture. 'Now, no need to get your tits in a spin. We're only joking. We know old Isaac here, don't we?'

Isaac, busy with the mop, cleaning up the dropped eggs, nodded once, refusing to meet Nikki's eyes.

'There, told you. He's not offended.'

Elaine had scurried to the back of the café and was sobbing into her hands. Grayson stood beside Nikki. 'You're both barred. We don't want your sort in here. Please leave.'

'Yeah, yeah, yeah we're going.' The tall one raised a hand and waved towards Isaac. 'See ya soon, retard. We got unfinished business.'

Nikki followed them outside and grabbed the tallest one by the arm.

'Oi, that's police brutality that is. Get your phone out, Lenny, and record this.'

Nikki pulled him closer. 'I know exactly what you've been cooking up with McIvor and I'm not happy about that.'

The lad's sneering grin made Nikki want to slam his head against the wall.

'What, you after a cut like? Heard about bent coppers.'

Nikki squeezed his arm tighter. 'You go near him again and I'll arrest you, got it? This café's right opposite the station and we have some really cold and crappy cells that we reserve for the likes of you. So, unless you want to end up in one, I suggest you toddle away and steer clear of this café and all the people in it.'

She watched the boys walk off until they were a few metres away and then added. 'Oh, by the way. I'm going to make sure every beat copper has your faces tattooed on their retinas. Any of you make one step out of line and I'll make sure they bang you up. Got it?'

With mock bravado, they jostled each other, jeering and laughing as they walked out of sight. Nikki waited till they'd gone, before walking back into Lazy Bites.

'Thanks, Nik, good job you were here; maybe those tossers will stay clear of us now.' Grayson looked well pissed off. 'We always seem to attract idiots like that. I'd hoped we'd be a bit safer here opposite the cop shop.'

'Always a pleasure to put idiots in their places and I'll put the word out at the station for everyone to keep an eye out. Now, how are you, Elaine?'

When Elaine blew her nose and smiled, her tears nearly dry, Nikki turned to Isaac. 'And you? I take it they're the scum who put that McIvor up to his trick yesterday.'

'They're not nice, Nik. You should be careful how you speak to them. They might beat you up.'

'Is that what they threatened to do to you?' Nikki waited but Isaac avoided her gaze and cracked on with making the butties she'd ordered.

'Come on, one of them must be Calum, but you must know the other lads' names too.'

Silence.

'You know I'll look out for you. Me and Marcus and Mum and Anika – we've all got your back. Just tell me their names.'

A slight shrug this time, yet still he dug his heels in and wouldn't say any more.

Nikki picked up her carrier bag of delicious-smelling butties and indicated that she wanted a quick word with Grayson outside. 'Keep an eye on him, will you. She handed him a fiver. Get him a taxi home tonight, yeah? I need to try to track down these louts and make sure they don't come back.'

'I'll see if he'll say owt else later on, Nikki. Poor lad looked petrified.'

Nikki nodded. 'He did. You got CCTV?'

When Grayson nodded, she said, 'Look, make a copy for me of the last couple of hours' footage and I'll send someone over for it later.'

228

# Chapter 46

The smell of the warm butties had the team descending on her like a flock of vultures on a dead deer. Nikki was glad she'd made the effort. It was not often that she thought of these things; must be Marcus and Saj rubbing off on her. She dismissed the thought with a smile and walked over to examine the incident boards at the front of the room, painfully aware that this should be *her* investigation – not Springer's. Still, she had to show willing. Had to rein in her frustrations and play the game. As Marcus had pointed out, she was lucky to be here at all.

Anwar had done a grand job, adding to the boards as information was forthcoming – not that much had come forth overnight. In the middle of the larger board was a mortuary photo of Gerry Hudson with his name and date of birth above it. He'd have been in his mid-seventies, if Nikki's quick calculation was accurate, which made him in his late forties/early fifties when she'd been living in Gaynor Street. *What did you do to deserve this now? Why not years ago?* It wasn't often that Nikki found it difficult to summon some empathy for a victim, but something about Gerry Hudson made it impossible. A niggling thought that she remembered him as a bogeyman from her childhood, combined with her mother's as yet unsubstantiated suggestion that he was in cahoots with Freddie Downey, had leached all sympathy for him from her thoughts.

True, no one should have to die the way he did, but it was equally true that no child should have to go through what they had at a grown man's hands. She'd still do her job – of course she would – but she had to find a way to depersonalise the investigation. *What am I talking about? This isn't my investigation. It's Springer's. I'm only a flunkey this time.* Still, she'd need to distance herself personally from it. All eyes were on her on this one. Everyone would be watching her, trying to work out how this was affecting her.

As it was, she was well aware of Springer's watchful eyes appraising her from the other side of the room. It was a wake-up call that not everyone in the room was on her side and a coil of anger fizzed like a Catherine wheel in her stomach. Swallowing, she forced it away and turned and smiled at Springer. Archie had informed her that he would be keeping up to speed on how cooperative Nikki was being. The unspoken implication being that if he got a single whiff of dissent from her, he'd whip her off the case completely and send her home to twiddle her thumbs. She was lucky she was allowed to contribute even the small amount she was.

Springer walked over to join Nikki, and, standing shoulder to shoulder with her, it was impossible for Nikki to assess the other woman's expression when she spoke – even so, Springer's words surprised her. 'I've got your back on this one, Parekh. I know this isn't easy for you – playing second fiddle to me. But I want you to know that I respect your input and if you stick to the deal we made yesterday, then things will work out. We got off to a bad start.' She lifted her shoulders. 'Probably my fault as much as yours, but I want us to put that behind us. After all, we both want the same things, don't we?'

Springer gave a weird little laugh that turned into a cough. 'That bastard Hudson may well have deserved all he got, but we'll find who did it anyway. We'll also do our damnedest to identify some of those other sick fuckers and get them locked up too.'

Springer gripped her shoulder and squeezed – just once – and then moved away. A flood of emotions swept through Nikki. Apart from the "second fiddle" bit and the weird laugh/cough, Springer's tone had seemed sincere. However, was it possible that her attitude could do such a turnaround from yesterday? She'd been raped not so long since and gone through a really rough time. Despite Nikki's part in Springer's rescue, this was the first time she felt that she and Springer had connected on a personal level and although instinct warned her to be careful, a wave of optimism lightened Nikki's mood.

She shrugged and moved her gaze over the information that had been added to the board since the previous day. By the time she'd absorbed it all, Springer had called the room to attention and Nikki moved away. Saj was sitting on a desk near the front, with Anwar and Williams standing behind him, like a pair of henchmen. Nikki made her way to the back of the room among a crowd of uniformed officers, and just as the briefing was about to start, DCI Hegley walked in. It seemed that his eyes went straight to Nikki and as a result everyone else's head swivelled in her direction too. *So, all eyes on me!* As far as Nikki was concerned, his scrutiny had told the room that he was surprised she hadn't defied his orders and taken off, chasing down a lead vigilante style. Of course, with everyone watching her, during the briefing, there was even more pressure on her to remain composed. Sweat gathered at the back of her neck, and she was glad her hair was pulled up into the ponytail she favoured, giving her some air. Ignoring all the attention as best she could, Nikki focused on Springer.

Although Langley had updated Nikki on Hudson's post-mortem the previous evening, she was happy to reabsorb the pertinent information. What she wasn't happy with, was the way her skin crawled with Springer's stuttering, stammering briefing.

The other woman seemed less in control than she had at the previous briefing, more nervous, less sure of her facts. Springer's frequent glances towards Archie made Nikki suspect Archie had spoken to her – told her he was watching her. Having been on the receiving end of Archie's displeasure on many occasions, Nikki knew how unsettling that could be. She found herself crossing her fingers and hoping Springer would hold it together.

'Right, em … well. For those of you who haven't had a chance to check out the crime board, here's the update from Dr, em Campbell. Time of death established at … hold on a minute … oh yes here it is … between 1 and 3 a.m. Multiple stab wounds, death caused by, em … where is it? Oh yes, stab wound to the heart.' Springer's face was red as she flipped back and forth over the typed report, when all she needed to do was look at Anwar's concise notes on the crime board.

'Dr, em Campbell intimates there were no defensive wounds.' Springer looked up at the officers crowded in the room and without making eye contact with anyone, lowered her head. If the way this investigation was progressed wasn't so important, Nikki would have laughed out loud. But this was ridiculous. Archie should have got an experienced DS in from another team if he was going to replace her, not this incompetent woman, who would never be able to inspire the team to push forward. This was a fuck fest and Nikki was pissed off. Adrenaline coursed through her and it was all she could do to remain standing at the back of the room.

Springer continued. 'So either Hudson had been asleep or unconscious when he was killed. We're waiting for forensics on the blood, on the off-chance our killer managed to nick himself, but em, well, the early reports from the CSIs indicate that our killer wore gloves. Any questions?'

A communal headshake seemed to relax Springer a little as she proceeded with more assurance. 'Statements from neighbours were sparse. Nobody had seen him for months – some of the newer residents hadn't ever seen him except sitting in his window. No unusual vehicles in the street, no unidentified people either. Few houses had CCTV and none near Hudson's house.'

Springer, more definite now, although still consulting her notes, nodded to Anwar who was now standing near the crime board, marker in hand ready to write down any actions resulting from the briefing.

'Get a couple of officers to obtain and trawl the CCTV footage from any houses further down the street whose camera covered the road or pavements. A thankless job, but it could pay dividends. If the killer drove or walked up the street to Hudson's house, they might get lucky – especially as the road could only be accessed by car from the Leeds Road side. If he accessed the street from Leeds Old Road, there are no cameras to catch him entering or leaving the crime scene.'

An officer standing near Nikki raised a hand. 'Ma'am, I hope it's all right, but when I was taking statements yesterday I took the liberty of asking those houses with CCTV to forward their recordings to us. I've made a list of the ones that have come through so far.'

For a moment, a frown passed over Springer's face as if taking the young officer's initiative as a personal slur, then it cleared. 'Yes, well done – em, good thinking. That's what I like to see – someone thinking for themselves, making logical decisions and thinking ahead. Well done PC ...?'

Her face flushed as she stammered, 'Richards, ma'am.'

'Brill. Pass your list to DC Anwar.'

Nikki raised a hand and, aware that her action had once more prompted scrutiny from the entire room, kept her tone neutral. 'Might be an idea to grab CCTV footage from the shops on Leeds Old Road that were near to Gaynor Street. Might as well cover all eventualities.'

Springer's face fell, then she smiled. 'Thank you, DS Parekh.' She turned to Anwar. 'Action that too, please.'

Studying her notes again for a moment before squinting round the room, Springer looked at Williams. 'DC Williams, what have you found so far in those boxes?'

Exhaling loudly, Williams, face serious, walked to the front of the room, whilst Springer sank into a chair next to Sajid. *My chair, my partner.* Nikki was being petty, but it stabbed her to think of Saj working with Springer whilst she was holed up behind a bloody computer.

Williams cleared his throat. 'We've not had the chance to go through all of them. I think we'll need a few more pairs of hands and eyes if we're going to make a dent in it anytime soon.'

Anwar added that to the list of actions as her colleague continued. 'Each box has a date on it, going back years, but we've yet to find any boxes dated after May 1994. Whether that means our killer took them or whether Hudson just stopped his activities, I'm not sure.' He screwed up his face. 'Actually, I don't reckon the killer took any later boxes because they were all higgledy-piggledy, although the month of each box was written on the outside in the top right-hand corner. We sorted them by date when we got back here.'

'What was in the boxes, Williams?' Nikki couldn't help herself – she just needed to know. After all, those boxes could reference her and her family.

Williams closed his eyes for a moment and then shook his head. What he'd seen in those box files would stay with him for a long time. Then, he opened his eyes, straightened his shoulders and began. 'Each box contained photos of children being abused. The abuser's faces were hidden from view but we did see a few identifiers like scars, tattoos and on one a birthmark. One tattoo, we matched to our deceased and it appeared in numerous photos with both male and female children.'

The young officer hesitated, letting his words sink in and as Nikki looked round the room, she saw varying degrees of disgust on the team member's faces.

'There were also what looked to be handwritten receipts, written in code.' Williams pressed the clicker he held and an enlarged example of the receipt flashed on the large screen.

Written on lined A4 paper each "receipt" had a date, which corresponded to the month on the box in which it was found. Written on the left was "Invoice for TL for the use of DD" and underneath was a list of codes with amounts aligned with them.

---

1st December 1993

**Invoice for TL for the use of DD:**
**AP £25**
**OS £10**
**HC x 2 £20**
**Total £55**
**DW – £10**
**TP £45**

---

'I'll print them out and put them on the board so if any of you are good at cryptic stuff please have a go at breaking them. Some of them are obvious – like TP more than likely means total paid. Having spoken to VICE, who have now taken copies of all the contents and are working to match the photos of the victims and abusers to their database, they believe that the initials at the top refer to the abuser and the victim. In this case, this TL is the abuser and DD is the victim. They hope to have some names for us before the day's end.'

'Bastard got off lightly, if you ask me,' a voice from the crowd spat out.

A series of muffled whispers followed this observation and a sourness settled over the room. The scent of disgust was so strong it was palpable. Nikki had experienced it before. Coppers hated paedophiles and now they were conflicted. On the one hand they thought the bastard deserved all he got; on the other, they were there to uphold the law as this sort of vigilantism, when left unresolved, could lead to total chaos. It was Springer's job to keep them focused on the task in hand.

It took just a moment too long before Springer reacted and hopefully only a few saw the exaggerated sign Archie made, telling her to stand up. Jumping to her feet, Springer faced the officers. 'Look, I understand how you all feel.' *Understatement of the decade.* 'But, I need you focused on this case. Our job is to find the person who killed Gerry Hudson. It's that simple. We are looking into his lifestyle and, as we often do, we're discovering some very unsavoury things about him. These things will ultimately help us catch his killer ...'

Nikki looked round the room and saw that many faces were unconvinced. *Motivational speaker she's not!*

But Springer went on gamely. 'They'll also help us identify the other men who are out there, possibly still abusing and ...' she glared at the officer whose earlier outburst had caused the tension in the room '... we'll be able to get justice for the real victims in the process. So ... anyone who wants to ditch this investigation – have at it. You won't be disciplined or written up for it. I only want officers here who will do the job they're paid to do and dig deep to bury any thoughts like those just expressed.'

The room was silent. A chair shuffled and Nikki saw the officer in question, an older guy with a beer belly and a frown, stand up. He was going to walk and Nikki's heart sank. What if they all walked? What if Springer ended up losing her team on day one?

The officer, she remembered his name – a DC Marley – stepped forward and then his big hairy hand was extended towards Springer, a self-conscious grin on his stubbly face. 'You're right, boss. You're right. I just got a bit worked up then. My apologies and I promise it won't happen again.'

Springer looked at his hand and then into his eyes before she extended her own hand to him. The tension in the room broke and just like that Springer's extended team were all on the same page again. As Marley returned to his seat, Springer resumed the briefing. 'Okay, in light of these names, it would be prudent to track down past residents of Gaynor Street – particularly those with children. We already have some names, but, Williams, you can do that, please. If any of the initials match any found in Hudson's box files, I want you to alert me immediately. Questions?'

'What about the carer who discovered the body? She well enough to be interviewed?'

'Yes, we interviewed her yesterday. The interview report is in the file on the PCs. I'll be out of the office with DC Anwar for the rest of the day, as it's Liam Flynn's memorial service in Manchester, but DS Parekh and DC Malik will be in the office going over all the CCTV footage and they should be your first ports of call should you need to report anything important. Right, off you go.'

# Chapter 47

He was out there. She knew he was. All this with that scumbag Hudson and poor Peggy's death was no coincidence – he was behind it all. After all these years he'd come back and cast a cloud over everything her little family had achieved. They'd managed to cover up their inner scars, make lives for themselves and now on some whim or other he'd turned up again. Well, this time, he wasn't going to get the better of her. This time, she wasn't a silly little teenager with no self-respect and a desire to try to fit in with all the white girls. This time she was an adult – a grown woman with self-respect and she wouldn't let him cheat that away from her.

So, Lalita had to make plans. She had time. Today was Anika's birthday and although she suspected he'd love to throw a cog into a family celebration, Lalita knew he'd have no idea that it was his youngest daughter's birthday. But she did and, if this was perhaps going to be the last celebration she ever shared with her family, then she was going to make it a good one.

Marcus told her Nikita wasn't going to come. Lalita snorted, hands on hips. She'd see about that. No way was her eldest daughter going to miss this. Despite everything, they were a family and if the worst came to the worst, she wanted to make sure that they didn't forget that. Today was for cooking, which would also give her time to plot. There was nothing that soothed her more than delicately mixing her spices and creating food for her family to enjoy.

As she kneaded the paratha dough, with half an eye on her samosa mix and a Hindi CD playing in the background, Lalita considered the best way to lay her trap. She'd been awake most of the night thinking about that. Where would be the best place to lure him?

Initially, she'd considered trying to lure him down to the arches where he'd murdered Peggy Dyson. But the very thought of going down there scared her almost as much as Downey himself did. Besides, there was no guarantee the rough sleepers or drug addicts who hung out there would come to her aid, if she needed them to. Ultimately, she'd realised that much as she was loath to have him anywhere near her beautiful safe home, that was the only sane solution. There were many benefits to it. Firstly, it was her own turf. She knew the lay of the land. She could secure hidden weapons all over the house. Yes, he was a big man and she was small, but, she had taken a self-defence class with Nikita and Anika and, courtesy of her eldest daughter, she wasn't weaponless. On the contrary, she had enough MACE and pepper sprays to have two in each room. Plus, she had knives – sharp ones. But her coup de resistance was the Taser Nikita had given her. Lalita had protested, knowing it was illegal, but Nikita had insisted that she take it. 'We need to be safe and you never know when you might need it, Mum.'

At the time Lalita had known Nikki was referring to the threat that Downey might turn up one day, and although time had passed, the thought of the Taser was reassuring. She'd got up in the middle of the night, retrieved it from its hiding place, checked the batteries and familiarised herself with it. It was easy to use – aim and fire. She could do that.

To minimise the risk of her plan going awry and Downey

snatching her on her way to or from work, Lalita had phoned in sick. Nobody would suspect anything. Her manager had been concerned about her during her last shift, so a few days' sick leave wouldn't raise any eyebrows. The only concern she had was Isaac. She had to make sure that Isaac was safe no matter what. The best plan she could come up with was to lay the seeds for a *Dr Who* sleepover with Sunni. Nikki wouldn't be keen on a school night sleepover, but if she primed the boys well enough, she reckoned Nikki would give in to their combined pressure.

She settled down to make the pastry for the samosas, content that she had a plan in mind, and put all thoughts of Freddie Downey to the back of her mind.

# Chapter 48

*Scut work!* There was no other term for it. Nikki's eyes were blurring and on occasion she'd had to nudge Sajid when he'd started snoring. CCTV viewing was a thankless task and she wished that Springer had had the sense to split it into two-hour blocks, but so keen had the woman been on exerting her authority over Nikki and her closest ally, she'd ordered them to have it done by the end of the day. Well, she could swivel on that one. No way could they get through this lot in one day. Although fed up and angry – adamant that this was not a good use of her time or experience – Nikki was more indignant on Saj's behalf. He'd been directed to this task purely on merit of being her partner, and that was crap. He should have been at the Flynn memorial with Springer.

Hell, Nikki wished she could have gone. There was something not sitting right with that family and, unbeknownst to Springer, Nikki had tasked Anwar to dig deep for as much information on them as possible – from birth certificates to work records to social media interactions. The memorial would have been a fantastic opportunity to scrutinise the family and check out any suspicious characters who attended.

Moving her head closer to the screen, she nudged Saj again and took a note of the time on the recording. 'You see this bloke,

Saj? Does he look like he's trying not to be noticed?' The CCTV footage they were currently watching was from one of the houses near the bottom of the street. They'd started from Friday lunchtime and were now at nearly midnight on the Saturday.

Stretching, Saj rolled his shoulders, blinked rapidly a few times, and then peered in at the shadowy black and white figure Nikki had paused on. 'Well, yes. He looks dodgy to me. Hood up covering his face, bag on his back, shoulders hunched … but how many similar figures have you noted on Gaynor Street so far?'

Nikki got his point. From this one camera, they'd already paused and noted the times of around twelve figures who could be their perpetrator. 'Trouble is, they all wear hoodies these days and they all look suspicious and they all walk like that.' Throwing her pen down, Nikki jumped to her feet. 'I need a bloody break. I'm going for lunch.'

Saj jumped up too. 'Lazy Bites?'

'No, I got a job to do, so I'll just grab a sandwich on my way back.'

Saj hesitated, then said, 'I'll come with you if you like.'

Nikki frowned. What was he playing at? Couldn't he have lunch on his own for once? Then it hit her. 'Archie!'

Trying to look his most innocent, Saj began putting pens back in his pen pot. 'Eh?'

'You're busted, Saj. Archie put you up to this, didn't he? You're my minder.' She laughed. 'Not that he could have chosen a scrawnier minder if he tried. What you going to do, rugby-tackle me to the ground if I go rogue?'

Saj tutted, but she shook her head. 'I'm not going off Gangnam style. I'm getting Ani's birthday present and dropping it off at her house whilst she's at her counsellor, so I don't have to hear her carping at me again. That means *you* can go and enjoy a break from *me*.'

She grabbed her bag and had almost made it out the door when it burst open. A young officer in uniform barged straight into her. 'Oh good. I caught you, DS Parekh.' He thrust an envelope towards her. 'Thought it looked like the same envelope the other stuff arrived in.'

Nikki, pleased to see the young officer was wearing gloves, dipped her hands into her jean pocket and pulled out a pair of her own. *Not another one!* Saj watched as Nikki placed it on her desk and then they just stared at the envelope. It had the same scrawled name and address on the front. No postmark this time though. The lad was still by the door, so Nikki asked, 'How was it delivered?'

'A young lad came in and dropped it on the front desk and then took off.' Face flushing with pride, the officer continued. 'I ran after him and when I caught him, he said he'd been paid a fiver by an old git to drop it off.'

'He still downstairs?'

The officer nodded.

Nikki grabbed one of the photo packs they'd prepared earlier, which included the most recent one they had of Freddie Downey. 'Okay, get his name and address, show him these photos and ask if any were the man who paid him. Then find out where the exchange took place. Check for CCTV around that area and claim any you find, okay?'

This felt too damn close for comfort. If Downey was behind this, then it meant he was in Bradford. Of course, he had an entire network of friends and contacts in the area and he could have put any of them up to dropping the parcel off … Still … it left a bad taste in Nikki's mouth.

'Open the damn thing, Nik!'

Nikki started, and glanced round. The few officers still working on computers had gathered round and were looking at her expectantly. Had she zoned out for long? She switched her gaze to Saj, who inclined his head slightly and grinned.

Taking a reluctant step forward, the last thing she wanted was to lift the letter – to open it. Touching it made it all too real.

Inside the gloves her hands sweated uncomfortably as she took it and opened it. Aiming for the least contact possible she let the contents slip onto the desk and then inserted the envelope into the evidence bag Saj had ready for her. There would be no forensic evidence of use, she was sure. There had been none on the previous envelopes and it didn't look like her anonymous sender was about to slip up anytime soon – but on the outside chance that he might have, Nikki would be meticulous.

There were two items inside the envelope. The top one was a printed newspaper report from the online *Bradford Chronicle*, dated that morning. The headline followed by the picture beneath was like a neon light taunting Nikki.

*Disabled man murdered in his own home! Can we trust Bradford police if they can't stomach it?*

Underneath was a picture of Nikki, hands resting on her knees, hurling up into the gutter outside Gerry Hudson's house. As expected, the article was credited to the journalist Lisa Kane. Using a finger and thumb, Nikki transferred the photocopy to another evidence bag before turning her attention to the diary extracts. She'd been expecting another extract and by the look on the faces avidly reading the extract, so had everyone else.

*Saturday 27th February*

*I hate Saturdays. Tried to tell them I was poorly. Nobody would listen. I threw up all over Mr H and he beat me. Now I can't move. Everyone's angry everybody's shouting. I hate them all hate hate hate them.*

*Friday 8th October*

*Teacher, that old cow, told me off for not having my PE kit. Told her I couldn't do PE. She was a bitch. A right bitch. How am I supposed to put shorts on with all them bruises? Told them about that, but nobody listens. Nobody but D. He listens.*

Like the others, the extracts had been ripped from whichever diary they'd been taken from and only had the month and date on them, which gave no indication of the order of the entries. This was a real puzzle and Nikki still couldn't work out how they fitted with everything else. Her best guess was that they belonged to one of the children, probably a girl, whose details were in the boxes Williams was steadfastly working through.

'Right, get these up to forensics and ask them to send copies down ASAP.' Nikki's voice was brusque, yet nobody seemed to care. In silence, one of the officers collected the evidence bags, labelled them and took them upstairs. Nikki needed to escape from Trafalgar House. She needed space to think, space away from here. 'Phone Springer and update her, Saj. I'll be back in an hour.'

# Chapter 49

Driving home calmed Nikki. The sun was out and the day was bright. Who would believe that so much evil was in a world as beautiful as this one? Her plan was to drop off Anika's birthday presents and card whilst her sister was at her counselling session. And that left only a narrow window of opportunity and she was already running late. Swinging into the Morrisons' petrol station on Ingleby Road, she grabbed a bunch of flowers before heading to Listerhills.

After parking up beside her mum's little Mini in the back alley, Nikki took a moment to scan the street. She admonished herself. Being jittery was not something she was comfortable with. Seeing nothing unusual, Nikki got out and with Anika's back door key in her hand, headed to her sister's house a couple of doors down. She inserted it in the lock and then cursed. The damn door was unlocked. *Bloody Anika.* She was always forgetting to lock her back door – but you'd think that with her little pep talk the previous night, she'd be a bit more careful. Nikki dumped her stuff on the table, then, hearing a murmur of voices from the front of the house she eased open the kitchen door. *Surely Anika hadn't cancelled her appointment.*

But it was Haqib's voice, followed by a female voice, raised and angry-sounding. 'You can't finish with me, Haq. I'm dumping you – got it? I dumped you first.'

Nikki tried to ease the door shut and backed off. Much as she was pleased that Haq was coming to his senses and dumping Michelle Glass, the sister of a racist thug who had been killed earlier in the year, she didn't want to be caught eavesdropping. Before she had a chance to dodge into the backyard, the kitchen door swung open, and as Michelle barged past, it clattered against the wall. Haqib followed at a slower pace, his face flushed but determined. Catching sight of his aunt standing by the back door as his now ex-girlfriend elbowed her way past, he raised a hand in greeting and exhaled as the back door slammed shut, leaving the room silent.

Needing to make sure Haqib knew she hadn't been spying on him, Nikki walked over to the table and began fiddling with Anika's gift. 'I was just dropping these off for your mum.'

Haqib pulled up a chair and slumped into it. 'I can see that. What you got her?'

Nikki was quite proud of the gifts she'd got her sister. Marcus had told her to get something meaningful, something that showed she cared, and she thought she'd done exactly that. 'Wait and see.'

She risked a glance at her nephew. When had he got so tall – and broad? He was turning into quite a handsome young man, yet, despite having ditched the deadweight girlfriend, he looked like he carried the weight of the world on his shoulders. Nikki paused what she was doing and filled the kettle. 'Cuppa?'

Haqib's face lit up as if she'd offered him free ice cream for a year and Nikki felt a pang. She should have been there for her nephew over the past few months. Just because Anika had shut her out didn't mean that she should have neglected her nephew. He'd been affected by Yousaf's behaviour too – and he'd had to live with Anika whilst she came to terms with realising that Yousaf was a child trafficker. He wasn't even seventeen yet. Too young to have to be his mother's support mechanism.

He got to his feet, opened one of the cupboards and brought out a packet of chocolate Hobnobs. 'Might as well treat ourselves, eh? Not every day my auntie makes the tea.'

'Cheeky sod. I make tea.'

'Yeah, when? It's always Marcus who makes the hot drinks.'

Pleased that they could indulge in this gentle teasing, Nikki shoved teabags in two cups and filled them with boiling water. She shoved Haqib's towards him and grabbed the milk from the fridge before sitting down. 'So, what's been going on – apart, of course, from you dumping the delightful, if not very intelligent and really quite racist Michelle Glass.'

Haqib snorted, sending a load of Hobnob crumbs flying across the table. 'Good one.'

He hesitated for a moment, took a swig of tea with the teabag still in and glanced at Nikki.

Nikki recognised that look. It was his "should I? shouldn't I?" look. 'Spit it out, Haqib. I'm your auntie and I want to help you. I know me and your mum haven't been close recently, but that doesn't mean I'm not here for you.'

'She's going to visit him.'

Nikki frowned, momentarily confused, then it dawned on her and she placed her mug back on the table before she dropped it. 'Yousaf? You mean Yousaf? She's going to visit that bastard?'

'Please don't get all aerated, Auntie Nik. And please don't tell her I told you. She wants to visit him for "closure".' He made air quotes with his fingers and shrugged. 'Or that's what she says, anyway.'

'*Closure?*'

'Look, if all you can do is repeat what I say, then I'm not going to talk.'

'Fair point. Look I understand that she wants closure, but …' Nikki went to twang the elastic band on her left wrist, but realised she'd broken it earlier. 'He'll make mincemeat of her, Haq

– he really will. He's a monster and she's always been blind to his faults – too easily led by him.'

'Tell me about it. Look, don't worry. I'm going with her.'

Nikki looked at her nephew. His eyes were worried, his expression resigned as if there was no other option. She reached over and grabbed his arm. 'You're a good lad, Haqib. But you don't need to do this. I'll go with her.'

But Haqib was already shaking his head. 'She won't go with you. You know she won't.'

Nikki smiled. 'Well, we just won't tell her that I'm the one going in with her till she gets to the prison.'

For a second Haqib just looked at her, then he jumped up and hugged her. 'You're the best auntie ever.'

Nikki batted him away. 'Leave me alone and tell me why you dumped Chell-to-my-friends. Got your eye on someone else?'

The flush that coloured his cheeks told Nikki she'd hit the nail on the head. 'Okay, who is she? Please say it's not some racist shit's sister. Anybody else and I'll be happy.'

'Look, you got to keep it secret, right.'

Nikki nodded, envying him the joys of dating and falling in and out of love.

'It's Fareena.'

All indulgent thoughts flew from Nikki's mind. 'Fareena? Fareena who – Please tell me it's not …?'

But Haqib was already nodding and it was as if a thundercloud had appeared and pissed on her parade.

'Yes, Fareena Shah who lives down the road.'

'Oh no, Haqib – no. Do you know what you'd be getting yourself into?'

Straightening in his chair, Haqib pouted like the sulky adolescent he was. 'We love each other.'

*For now. You love each other for now, but if her brothers find out or her dad, you'll be dead meat.* Nikki didn't utter the words – she couldn't. Images of Haqib chopped up in a suitcase refused to fade. 'Her parents are very strict Muslim. Fareena wears a niqab.'

'Only because they make her ... She takes it off when she gets to school. Loads of the girls do.'

Charlie had told Nikki that, so it came as no surprise. Fareena was Charlie's friend and Nikki was aware that the friendship lasted despite Fareena's parents' objections. This relationship with Haqib, who was only Muslim in name, would not be tolerated. Fareena's brothers were massive and extremely overprotective. Fareena was chauffeured to school and back again. This was a relationship doomed to hell, but Nikki had the sense to realise that there was little she could do about it other than look out for Haqib. She resolved to have a word with Charlie when she got home.

Smiling to take the sting out of her words, Nikki laid her hand on her nephew's arm. 'I think you need to consider this relation-ship very carefully. I know you will. You have to really think things through. A relationship with Fareena Shah could be very dangerous for you.'

She held his gaze for a moment and then jumped to her feet. 'Right, get a vase for those flowers. I need to get this stuff out on the table before she comes back and catches me here.'

Haqib filled a vase with water and took his time to place the flowers in one at a time, which Nikki had to admit was more than she would have done. Presentation wasn't her strong point. When he placed the vase on the table, behind the rest of Nikki's gifts, he started to laugh. 'Really?'

But Nikki was determined. 'Yes really. Your mum will get it.'

She opened the pack of Rolos, pocketed all of them bar one and placed the remaining sweet on its wrapper before the cake she'd had made at Lazy Bites. It had been decorated as per her instructions with 3D Teenage Mutant Ninja Turtle characters.

Haqib shook his head, still grinning. 'Okay then – if you're certain.'

'I'm sure. Trust me, she'll love this.' Nikki opened the card and wrote inside, with Haqib hanging over her shoulder.

'What's that mean – "I still love you enough to give you my last Rolo." You haven't even signed it.'

'I don't need to sign it. Nobody else would ever leave her these gifts.' And Nikki reached up, kissed Haqib on the cheek and left. Contrary to Marcus's belief, these birthday gifts had been planned well in advance.

# Chapter 50

Still thinking about all of Haqib's revelations, Nikki made her way back to her car, her steps heavy. Why did life always have to be so complicated? When her phone rang, a glance at the screen told her it was her PI, Douglas Shearer. After her earlier text to him, Nikki was on edge. Stomach clenching, she answered the call. 'Hey, Dougie. What have you got for me?'

'Bad news, I'm afraid, Nikki. The bastard's flown the nest. Well, if you can call the shit heap he's been living in a nest, that is.'

She turned away and opened the car door, allowing some of the heat to escape whilst she was on the phone. Freddie Downey, the man who was her biological father had gone AWOL from the house in Livingston, where he'd resided for the past few years. Till now Nikki had always been reassured by regular photographic evidence and reports from the PI that Downey was hundreds of miles away from her family. However, she wasn't surprised by Shearer's news. She'd expected it – that's why she'd got him to double-check. Now, Downey could be anywhere and although there was a restraining order against him making contact with Nikki, her sister or her mum, this didn't reassure Nikki in the slightest. Freddie Downey had never been a man to conform to the rules and now, all these years later, his disappearance from the place he called home, where he had a job, set down roots, was ominous. The fact that his disappearance coincided with Gerry Hudson's death and the anonymous letters sent cold shivers down Nikki's spine.

The link she'd been looking for between Liam Flynn's death and Peggy Dyson's might be closer to home than Nikki had first suspected. Struggling to maintain a non-committal tone, Nikki finally responded. 'Any ideas when?'

'Yeah, about three weeks ago, according to the neighbours – just after my last surveillance. Word is he left with a suitcase in a taxi. I'm going to track that down in a minute, but just wanted to let you know, he was onto me.'

'What?' Nikki's tone was sharper than she'd intended, the single word spat from her lips like lightning. If Downey was aware that she was keeping tabs on him, this could prompt him to act; to maybe seek to insert himself into their lives and in the worst-case scenario to take the revenge he threatened against them before he ended up in prison. Nikki was in no doubt that Downey's desire to get even would not have diminished after seven years in prison and a further fifteen in different cities. Downey was nothing if not tenacious – Nikki knew that to her own detriment.

'There's printed photos of me all over the manky old coffee table in his living room – taken from the upstairs bedroom window mostly, by the look of them. Some from the last surveillance, but some much, much earlier ones dating back to when I first started watching him.'

'Bastard knew I was keeping an eye on him?' Nikki's fists clenched. She wanted to rage at her PI for being so stupid as to get caught, but she knew how devious Freddie Downey was.

'There's more, Nik.'

*More? What more could there be?* 'Go on.'

'Thing is, Nik, I also found images of you and your sister and your mum – some of them going back years and some of them more recent – at your house, at your places of work, just doing day-to-day stuff. Your kids are in quite a few and in the more recent ones another Asian lady whom I don't recognise – well dressed, fifties, and a kid with Downs.'

*Enaya*. He'd even got images of her dead husband's mum and Isaac.

'Looks like when he got wind of me checking him out, he decided to reciprocate and have you checked out. I'm sorry, Nik, truly sorry.'

Her mind was all over the place. Freddie Downey knew more about her and her family than she knew about him. The bastard had the gall to taunt her. He was doing what he'd always done in the past. He was playing games with her; like a fisherman dangling a fish on the end of his line, Downey was toying with her. Her family were vulnerable and even more so because she suspected that with Downey AWOL he would make his way back to Bradford. Shit, everything that had happened pointed to the fact that he was probably already here.

'Get in touch with his parole officer – he's in breach of his licence. I want them on his tail. Also, find that taxi driver – I want you to trace his movements from when he left his home. I need to know for sure if he's in Bradford.'

'Will do. Also, Nik, I'll send you the images he's taken in a file when I get back to the office, but I'm sending you this now. It's really strange and I'm not sure how it fits in.'

Sounds of Dougie fiddling with his phone drifted down the line for a couple of seconds. 'Sent.'

Nikki's phone buzzed and she opened the image from Dougie. In silence, she studied the images. The photocopied ripped pages of diary excerpts written in the same familiar hand as the previous ones made her heart sink. Now there was no denying Downey's involvement in all of this. They had to find him … and fast.

Unsure how she managed to keep her voice from trembling, Nikki inhaled before responding. 'Were there only these two sheets?'

'Yep, just those two sheets. Looks to be ripped out of a note-book or diary.'

'Okay, Dougie. Get them bagged as evidence and couriered down to me ASAP. But email me the images you've just texted me. Keep me informed.'

After hanging up, Nikki slipped into her seat and rested her hands on the steering wheel as she thought through everything she'd just learned. She couldn't be sure that Downey sent the anonymous notes. He could just as easily have been sent the diary entries, just like Nikki was. But Downey was a known risk to her and her family and she needed to get eyes on the street looking for him, chasing up some of his old known acquaintances, checking out his old haunts. Instead of hotfooting it back to Trafalgar House, Nikki got busy on her phone.

Nikki: *Ali, need some backup to keep my family safe. You able to sort that ASAP?*

Ali: *Sure thing. What you thinking? Who we looking out for?*

Nikki: *Need to guard Marcus and the kids as well as my mum and sister. A bloke called Freddie Downey might have it in for them. I'll send you the most recent image I have.*

Ali: *Sure thing. I'll get two teams over to yours ASAP.*

Nikki sent her friend Ali, who owned a taxi service in Heaton, the latest images of Freddie Downey, updated Marcus on the threat and relaxed a little. She'd done all she could at present. With Ali's mates and Marcus aware of a possible threat, her family were safe for now. Despite her reluctance to leave Listerhills before Ali's men were in situ, Nikki had no option. She needed to get back to work and make sure that Springer implemented a "Be On The Look Out" for Downey. There was now no doubt in her mind that he was in Bradford.

# Chapter 51

Duty is a complete ball-ache. It's not like I've not got better things to do with my time. But needs must. After my little slip-up earlier with the mother and kid, I've been on my best behaviour all afternoon. Dutiful, attentive and bored out my mind. Still, it has to be done and it's worth it. No point in drawing attention to myself. The thing is, when you're a killer, even if you never really had aspirations to be one before, you've got to play the part.

Now I'm getting into it, I realise I'm proud of my achievements. Taken me a long time, but I've found my forte. Three down – and a whole list more to go. When I hit that giddy number three, it really hit home. I'm no bog-standard killer anymore. I'm a serial killer. But, not a pervert like the likes of Sutcliffe or Bundy. My killing, although becoming more enjoyable every time, is the result of necessity. Wonder if that makes a difference? Wonder if somewhere some clever arse has another label for me.

It took a bit of smooth talking to get away. But, now I'm here in the hotel – if you can call it that, more like a hovel than a hotel – I can relax. I've got a busy few days ahead of me. I aim to complete my work, finish the job and then just get back into life. It'll be hard. I know it will. But I've no choice. It was always all about preservation and, just because I've got a taste for it, that hasn't changed. Once I've obliterated my list, we can all get on with it. I'll still have my little interests, my hobbies to keep me amused and, if that's not enough, I've heard there's places you can go where human life isn't as valued as it is here. I can always go and explore that, if I need to get my kill thrill.

I lie on the bed and try to not dwell on the forensic knowledge I've gained through all my research. Apparently, forensically speaking, hotel bedrooms are a cesspool of DNA from bodily fluids – yuck, doesn't bear thinking about. Instead, I close my eyes and go over my plan for later on. Today's another surveillance day. I'll spend a few hours checking out my next target. I've got an address and, for now, that's all I need. This one should be another easy one. The hard ones I've left for last.

With the thump thump thump of the headboard from the next room banging against the wall, accompanied by exaggerated moans of faked orgasms, I pull my jeans zip down. It's been a busy few days and I deserve a bit of me time – no reason I shouldn't add to the forensic mix now, is there?

# Chapter 52

Nikki had taken a moment to phone Marcus to update him on Shearer's findings and to make sure he would be able to collect the kids and also move Enaya into her mum's house. If everyone was together, keeping them safe would be more manageable. Then she hotfooted it back to Trafalgar House and brought Sajid up to speed about her PI's findings.

Although they'd been expecting this, a frown furrowed Saj's forehead. 'Even if he's not part of the equation, that bastard needs to be brought in. I'm sure we'll find something to detain him with. How's your mum?'

Nikki had briefly considered telling her mum. After all, she was parked just outside her house, but she just hadn't been able to face it – not when she was still processing everything. Instead she'd copped out and asked Marcus if he'd do it. She wasn't proud of herself, but she brushed that aside with a light, 'Marcus is telling her.'

'We need to let Archie and Springer know about this.'

That was a no-brainer. Of course she'd have to let the team know so they could direct resources to finding out Downey's whereabouts. However, although she hadn't confided in Saj yet, she was sure police resources wouldn't be able to run to round-the-clock protection for her family – and that's where Ali came in. She trusted him implicitly. They'd been through a lot together over the years and if anyone could keep her family safe then it was Ali and his men.

Her phone rang and before the first ring had ended, Nikki had answered. 'You got them protection, Ali?'

'Located everyone, Nikki. Marcus took the kids out of school and they're altogether at home. Your mum, Anika and Haqib are at home too and Enaya is going to stay with your mum and Isaac for the time being. So, all your family, extended and immediate, are safe. I've put two men outside the front and another two positioned at the back for now and we're looking for a safe house for you all. Have to say, Nik, with you all living in the same street it makes it easier to look out for you.'

As she hung up, Nikki risked a glance in Saj's direction, knowing he'd have been listening in to her side of the conversation. His face was set in a frown. 'Ali? Really? You've got Ali to bring in some heavies to protect your family?'

Nikki glowered and turned away. 'Gotta do what I gotta do, Saj. You'd do the same if it was Langley at risk.'

Exhaling, Saj nodded. 'S'pose you're right. But soon as they get back you tell Springer to arrange protection and call off Ali's heavies.'

Plucking at her new wristband, Nikki disagreed. 'Us all living on the same street made us an easy target for Downey.' She punched her leg. 'I fucking made it easy for the bastard, Saj. If I'd wrapped them all up in a box and sent them to his house, I couldn't have made it easier for him. I should have thought ahead. Should have realised that if I was keeping tabs on him, then the chances were that he was keeping tabs on us too. But, we both know that Springer's budget won't cover it. So, Ali's my only option.'

She stared blankly at her computer screen, trying to piece all the information they had together in her mind. She had to consider whether Downey would have killed Peggy Dyson and, if so, what was the link to Liam Flynn? Right now she couldn't see one and didn't want to start creating imaginary links that might skew her analysis of the facts. The other question was, who the hell was sending the anonymous letters?

This was truly confusing. Perhaps the Liam Flynn letter was a red herring – but what could possibly be the purpose of that?

She sighed. Liam Flynn's murder was an anomaly. Bradford seemed to be the centre of it all and, although she really didn't want to go down that route, Nikki feared that her family's past was integral to this. All the more reason to get to the bottom of things before someone else ended up dead.

# Chapter 53

It was nice having Enaya and Isaac in her home, but the presence of the young lads outside her back door made Lalita both nervous and annoyed. Marcus had tried to keep her calm, tried to tell her it was nothing to worry about. But that was all platitudes. Of course there was something to worry about – she knew that only too well. Why the hell else would Nikita have holed them all up in one place with bodyguards outside both front and back? But what was worse was that, by putting her under guard, Nikita had scuppered Lalita's plans and now, she not only had Isaac under her roof, she also had Enaya. How was she going to put an end to this once and for all with so many people around?

Soon after Marcus had told Anika what was going on, her youngest daughter had also descended on her and now she paced round the kitchen moaning about Nikita's high-handedness. Lalita's head throbbed and her nerves were frazzled. She'd already cut herself once when chopping onions and now sported a bright blue Band-Aid on her finger. Usually able to tune out Anika's whinging, she found that today it irritated her beyond measure. And for once, Lalita could see her younger daughter's point. It was irresponsible for Nikita to disappear, leaving them grounded without a proper explanation.

'She makes me mad, Mum. Really damn mad. I've got Haqib moaning on at home about Marcus telling him he's to stay in, but not telling us why. She's such a control freak. It'll be her bloody job that's got us in this mess – making us targets and meanwhile *she's* not even here.'

Torn between contributing her own tuppence worth to the bitching, or pacifying the already strained relationship between her daughters, Lalita did what she always did in times of stress and started to pile more ingredients on the table and work surfaces. Anika's birthday tea was not going to be the nice time she'd hoped for, but at least nobody would go hungry.

'She left me a stupid cake too. If she thinks a cake with a couple of Ninja Turtles on it and a single Rolo are going to win me round, then she's got another thing coming. It's not like we're kids anymore.'

'Aw, Anika. You're too harsh on her. It's sweet. You two were always role-playing those turtles when you were little.'

Anika tutted, clearly not impressed, but at least for now she was quiet, lost in her own thoughts, which left Lalita free to indulge in her own. The note left on her car windscreen preyed on her mind and she now wished she'd spoken to Nikita about it. 'Look, Nikita just wants to keep us safe. We should be grateful.'

Anika spat out a loud hmph. 'Oh yeah. Saint bloody Nikki looking after us all. When's she going to realise that we're adults? That we don't need her protecting us all the time?'

She peered out the kitchen window at the car parked beneath it in which two burly men were sitting, the strains of Bradford Asian Radio tunes drifting through the slightly open window. 'What's she up to, Mum? This is all very dodgy. Not like she's got police officers keeping an eye out. Those are Ali's taxi drivers. That's not official, you know?'

Lalita had hoped that Anika would be too self-absorbed to comment on the fact that Nikki hadn't arranged police protection. Relationships between the siblings were already strained without Anika having more ammunition to use. It wasn't that Lalita didn't sympathise with her younger daughter. On the contrary, she was well aware of how difficult Anika was finding things since her lover had been imprisoned earlier in the year. Lalita hadn't liked Yousaf. He had been bad for Anika and, as it turned out, an evil bastard into the bargain. Still, Anika was grieving and angry and all her anxieties were finding an outlet – someone to blame: Nikita. Every emotion was poured out in a torrent of hatred and anger on Nikita's shoulders. Lalita had tried to smooth things over, but it had been too early. Anika needed to vent and process everything before she could make her peace with her sister. 'Look, Anika. Your sister always does the best she can for us. If she's decided that we need Ali's friends to protect us, then that's what we need. When she comes home, she'll explain everything to us, okay?'

Flouncing over to the table, Anika pulled out a chair and flopped onto it, exhaling loudly as she did so. Enaya, whom Lalita had settled in her second spare room, came in and looked at the packets of gram flour, spices and vegetables on the table. Seemingly unaware of the tension in the room, she said with a bright voice. 'Great, I'm in the mood for a cooking lesson, Lalita. Can't wait to learn some of your Gujarati recipes.' She poked her head back out the door and yelled upstairs. 'Isaac, come on. Lally Mum's going to teach us some recipes.'

Anika rose, frowned at Enaya and her mum, and headed to the back door. 'I'd better get back to Haqib. I'll speak to you later.'

# Chapter 54

'I need your car for the day.'

'Eh, well, the thing is, like, I need it. Got deliveries to make, you know.'

'You're not hearing me. I said I need your car.' Downey clenched his hand into a fist and pressed it against the palm of his other hand. The sound of his knuckles cracking darkened the atmosphere in the small garage.

Downey's friend, a small man in overalls and a greasy oil smear on one cheek stared at Downey's huge fist and swallowed hard, but still he resisted. 'I need it. Can't you borrow one from someone else?'

Leering at the other man, Downey picked up a car wrench and took a step forward. The mechanic took a step back, glancing round looking for a weapon he could use, but he was too late.

Downey slammed the wrench onto the man's shoulders and then when he was on his knees, he slammed his fist into his face, waited till he fell to the ground and rounded off his attack with a kick to the guts. Whilst the injured man rolled about the floor, moaning, Downey searched through his pockets till he found the keys. He grinned and threw them in the air before catching them again in his open palm. 'Amazing what a little bit of gentle persuasion can do, eh?'

The car was a wreck. The clutch grated with every gear change and the brakes were slow to respond, but it served Downey's purpose just fine. He needed wheels for the day and although he could well afford to rent, or even buy a car, he wanted to stay under the radar. So, a few minor inconveniences like the pervasive stink of weed – no doubt the delivery the lad had referred to, the overabundance of empty pop cans and empty takeaway wrappers in the foot-well, were a small price to pay.

Downey turned into Nikki's road without indicating. During his time in Bradford, he hadn't spent much time in this neck of the woods. BD3 had been his stomping ground, but it seemed that his girls, as he liked to call them, had moved to the other side of the city centre. Driving down the road, Downey's face split into a wide grin when he saw the two bruisers parked up outside Nikki's house. One leaned on a souped-up Ford Escort all bulging biceps, tattoos and a stupid durag on his head – tosser wasn't even black – while the other sat on the doorstep, shades on, head back, lapping up the sun.

Well, well, well. Seemed that the weaselly whippet PI, Dougie Shearer, had finally realised that Downey was AWOL from his home in Livingston. About time too. Driving past, taking care not to look at the two men, Downey drove to the very bottom of the street and tucked his car between a van and a Mini. This development was very interesting. Very interesting indeed. Angling his side mirror so that he could see the two men, Downey considered what the presence of the two thugs meant. Clearly, Nikita had decided not to go all official on him – yet. She'd called in the heavies to protect her family and that pleased Downey. Seemed his oldest lass was a chip off the old block after all – prepared to do whatever was necessary even if it wasn't within the scope of the law. When he'd first realised she was a copper, he'd swayed between anger and amusement – cursing the fact that any daughter of his could be part of the Old Bill. Now, it seemed that she might in fact be a dirty cop. Downey wondered who she'd called in the favour from and made a mental note to check it out.

Settling down, windows open, Downey pushed his car seat back and, allowing his mind to wander, kept an eye on the two bodyguards. He wished he'd been a fly on the wall when Shearer finally got wind of his departure. He'd have paid a lot to have seen the idiot's smarmy face when he found the images Downey had left behind for him to find. Stupid little tosser wasn't as smart as he thought he was. Granted, it had taken Downey a year to realise he was being watched. But hey, it was only every so often and at first, Shearer had been very professional. However, towards the end, he'd become complacent – just getting his few photos and cashing his paycheque. It amused Downey to think that he'd not only got the better of the PI, but also of that little bitch Nikita. From the day she was born, she'd done nowt but cause trouble for him, and before long he'd make sure that she got her come-uppance.

In a way though, him working out that he was being surveilled had led him to keep an eye on what he called his assets. He had a lot of grudges that needed to be settled and he'd used the last few years compiling his own evidence, getting his own intel and, of course, that's what had led him back here to Bradford. He was content, for now, to watch with interest to see what his bitch of a daughter would make of all his clues. Would she be smart enough to put it all together? He doubted it – but that was okay. For now, he was happy to have his loose ends tied up for him. Happy as long as none of this came back on him. But he'd be well out of it by the time he was under threat.

The dark days of those seven years in prison still weighed on him. He'd avoided repeating the experience. Had used the time to educate himself. To find out sure-fire ways to earn money on his release – all under the wire of course. The sun warming his

266

face through the windscreen reminded him of his release from HMP Oakwood in Birmingham fifteen years ago. His contacts inside the nick had made it easy for him to forge a new trade – one which kept him away from vipers like Layla Parekh and Peggy Dyson. It wasn't long before the trade he built in transporting drugs throughout the country paid off. He was smart though. Kept himself high up the chain but with no direct links. Expanding into Manchester and then later Glasgow had made him more than comfortable and now, approaching his sixtieth birthday, he was all set to cash in and retire. But, of course he had a few things to sort out first.

# Chapter 55

The rest of the day had been a blur for Nikki. She'd had to suffer explaining her PI's findings to Springer and then again to Archie when he came in. Plus, she'd had the added mortification of being teased at throwing up at the Hudson crime scene and no amount of denying that it had been the sight of the body that had made her vomit would get them to ease up. In the end, she'd grinned and held her hands up, laughing alongside her colleagues, whilst mentally cursing the journalist. Lisa Kane: the bitch had done her job well.

She'd deliberately stayed late at work, wanting to avoid Anika's birthday tea and had spent hours poring over the CCTV footage in the near-empty room, determined not to give Springer any excuse to haul her over the coals. They didn't seem to be any further forward and no sightings of Downey had come in. Officers had been dispatched to interview any of Downey's contacts on record, but so far zilch.

Eventually, she'd given in and headed home. Weariness penetrated right down to her bones. Her neck was stiff, her back achy. It had been a long day – and emotional. When she pulled into her street, Nikki debated knocking on her mum's door before going home – just to check she was okay, but she just couldn't face it.

Instead, she drove down the cobbled back alley that separated her street from the adjacent one, cursing under her breath at the potholes that made the car lurch. She wanted to be sure that Ali's guys were in situ at both the front and back of her street. There wasn't space for a car to park in the alley so Nikki had instructed Ali to ask his men to park in the parking space Nikki's mum had paved out in her backyard. She'd also stressed that they needed to do frequent foot patrols up and down the alley.

With no streetlights at the back of the houses, the area was only illuminated by lights from inside the houses. Evidence of urban fox activity was all over the street with ripped bin bags spewing rotting garbage across the cobbles. She swore that these animals, to her no more than large rodents, were getting more and more wily as they managed to topple the bins that were only half full and scavenge in them. Marcus had secured their wheelie bins with padlocked chains for just this reason.

Before she got close to her mum's home, a bulky figure with a torch stepped forward, shining the beam inside her car. His partner stood behind, hand hovering over his radio, ready to phone for backup if necessary. It was Haris, one of Ali's right-hand men.

When Haris recognised her, he averted his flashlight from Nikki's eyes and she opened her car window, smiling. 'All okay out here?'

'Apart from the foxes, it's been dead.' Haris's voice rumbled through the darkness, strong and reassuring.

Nikki's shoulders untensed and her face relaxed into a smile. 'Good, let's hope it stays that way. You need anything? A loo break or owt? Might as well have one now if you need it whilst I'm here.'

The other heavy approached. 'No need, your mum's been in and out giving us cups of spicy tea and samosas and something she called dhokla – loved that. We've been taking it in turns to nip in for loo breaks.'

Nikki grinned. Her mum was doing what she always did when stressed or anxious – cooking – and Isaac would be in his element helping her. He loved nothing more than being in the kitchen making things. 'Pity you'll have changed shifts before morning. You'll miss the full Indian breakfast.'

When the impromptu bodyguard looked suitably crestfallen, Nikki grinned. 'Don't worry I'll tell her to keep some for you for tomorrow night if you're still needed. When do you change shifts?'

'Three a.m.'

'Well, keep sharp till then – need anything, just ring me okay?'

Reassured that the two men were on their toes, Nikki decided to set her phone to waken her at half three – assuming she was actually asleep by then – so she could just see how efficient the next two guys were. By the end of this she would owe Ali big time, but it was worth it to keep her family safe.

She drove on to the bottom of the alley and turned right into the front of her street. With its streetlamps on and lights from living-room windows, this side of the street had a distinctly less threatening feel to it. She spotted the rest of Ali's guys straight away. Their car was parked opposite her house giving the men inside a clear view of Anika's house through the windscreen and her mother's through the side and back mirrors.

Ali was a close friend. Straight as a die, quick to help if there was any crap going down on the streets and completely loyal to Nikki. She'd helped him out on more than one occasion, and they didn't normally keep tabs on who owed what. However, this extended surveillance was a big ask. Whilst four of Ali's men were keeping watch here, they weren't out earning money in their taxis. Ali wouldn't allow them to be out of pocket, so Nikki was aware she'd have to find some cash to pay her friend back. Looks like the leaky car window would have to wait another few months, to say nothing of the double glazing she'd been pricing up for the kitchen.

As expected on a week night, it was quiet. Mr Hampson from

the end of the street was walking his dog. Mr Bhullah was just setting off for his night shift at the Farmer's Boy factory and a tabby cat, which she frequently saw exploring the area, crossed the street carrying something in its jaws. Satisfied that there was nothing to see, she exhaled, rolled her shoulders in an attempt to loosen up and got out of the car.

Nikki slammed her car door shut, she crossed the street and slid into the back seat of the undercover car. 'Anything?'

Both men turned sideways so they could speak to Nikki. 'Just the usual comings and goings – nothing of note really.'

The car smelled of samosa and dhokla, a spongy savoury Gujarati snack, and Nikki grinned, raising her eyebrows in mock innocence. 'Any visitors bearing gifts?'

The guy in the driving seat, slapped his hand on the steering wheel. 'Told you we should have opened the window for longer – she's sussed us out.'

The other one returned Nikki's grin. 'Your mum's a bloody star. I could do stakeouts like this every night, if I was getting fed like this.'

Nikki shook her head. 'If my mum fed you every night you wouldn't fit behind the steering wheel. Keep alert, yeah, and call me if you need owt.'

The living-room light was still on and the TV flickered through a crack in the curtains. Marcus was still up, waiting for her as usual. She hesitated by the gate. She wanted to go in – to allow Marcus to pamper her, to vent and let his broad shoulders take some of the weight, but another part of her wanted to get into her car, pretend it was Saj's Jag and just drive and drive and drive.

Despite Saj's reassurances earlier and her own logic telling her she wasn't to blame for bringing yet another threat to her family's doors, she couldn't dispel the gut-wrenching guilt that made her want to scream and yell and destroy something – herself? She was on the point of heading back to her car, to drive to the nearest 24-hour supermarket to buy a kit – razor blades, gauze, cotton wool. Her breath came fast and deep and no matter how hard she twanged her wrist, she couldn't squash the urge. Harder, she twanged – harder and harder, her heart pounding, her body near collapse and then she reached out and gripped the wooden gate – the one that she and Marcus, on Sunni's instructions, painted a jaunty red earlier in the summer. Some of the weight lifted. She slowed her breathing, until the twangs on her wrist stopped.

A sound startled her and her head swung up to the door. Marcus stood, the light from the hallway illuminating him. 'Bad?' he asked, walking down the stairs.

Nikki nodded and allowed him to help her into the house. She was home and she was safe.

# Chapter 56

Marcus helped her into the house and guided her through to the kitchen, sitting her down at the table. Without saying a word, he removed the elastic band from her wrist, bathed her wounds, put cream on them and then sat opposite her. 'The kids are still up, but you don't have to do this tonight, Nik. You look done in.'

Nikki exhaled, grabbed his hand and held on tight. She'd asked Marcus to keep the kids up despite it being a school night so she could update them. Memories of Charlie finding out about her dad on a radio news report had taught her that being up front with her kids was the best policy. She'd already waited too long – maybe even years too long – to tell them about her past. 'Haqib here too?'

Marcus nodded and she smiled. 'I need to do this tonight. Can't risk them finding out from some sleazy article or a social media smear campaign.'

He lifted her hand and kissed her palm. 'I'll call them down then.'

Ten minutes later they were all in the living room waiting for their mum to come through from the kitchen. Nikki had rehearsed it all in her mind on the drive home. *She'd sit the kids down in the living room, Haqib included, telly off, Marcus and her on the chairs either side of the stove, Sunni on the floor, older kids on the couch – the smell of home-baked brownies wafting through from the kitchen – well, perhaps not that last bit – Nikki wasn't the best cook in the world. She'd pave the way slowly, describing all of Marcus's contributions to their family life, how much of a loving family they were, how safe she and Marcus had made their home, then she'd move on to how her and Anika's childhood had not been safe, not been secure, not been happy and full of joy.*

The reality was vastly different. She walked in to the living room to Ruby yelling, Charlie moaning, Sunni crying and Marcus shaking his head in dismay.

Ruby glared at her brother. 'I told you not to touch my pens, Sunni. They're my special ones and well you know it. You're such a little prick – you know that?'

'Ruby – language.' Marcus's tone was mild, clearly trying to smooth things over before Nikki came in – but too late.

All Nikki's deep breaths and calm thoughts flew out the window as the imaginary scene she'd created disapparated before her eyes. Her tone was cutting and cold – too cold for the situation, but she couldn't help herself. 'They're only bloody pens.'

'No, they're not, Mum. They're not *only* pens – they're my special gel ones. The ones I use for my artwork. That little brat shouldn't even be in my room. He needs to learn boundaries.'

'Do not, Rubster. I just wanted to borrow them.' Sunni picked them up and threw them across the room, scattering them all over. Charlie tutted loudly and curled her feet up onto the sofa. 'This place is like a damn zoo. Why can't we have a normal family? Why does everything have to be such a drama?'

Haqib, headphones on, frowned. 'You should live in my house, Charlie. Drama from dawn till dusk – that's how I live.'

Nikki closed her eyes, trying to grasp a fleeting memory of the scene she'd hoped for, but when she reopened them, all she saw was chaos and, just like that, she lost it. 'SHUT UP! The lot of you, just damn well shut up. If you'd had the sort of childhood your Auntie Anika and I had, you'd know all about it. Every night your Ajima had to lock us into the dingiest, crappiest room in the world just to keep us safe from our own father. We never had bloody gel pens. Our clothes were second and third hand and *never* fitted us properly. Our dad hit us – not with his hand, but with his belt, or his fists or his feet so ...' Nikki took a deep breath and looked at the stunned faces of the four kids. Twanging the elastic band, she'd placed on her other hand, the blood drained from her face. She sank onto the couch next to her eldest daughter Charlie and cradled her head in her hands. 'I'm sorry – so sorry. I shouldn't have told you like this.'

Before Marcus had the chance to comfort her, Charlie and Haqib each put their arms round Nikki's shoulders and Sunni climbed onto her lap, arms round her neck hugging her tightly, whilst Ruby stood in front of her saying. 'Don't cry, Mum. Don't cry.'

Nikki tried to staunch the tears that flooded her cheeks. She never ever cried in front of the kids. Hell, she rarely cried, full stop, but now the floodgates were open, she just couldn't stop. Ruby handed her a fistful of tissues and Charlie looked up at Marcus. 'We got this, Marcy, you get the kettle on.'

Haqib looked up. 'Nah – get a bottle of wine. I think Auntie Nik needs something a bit stronger than tea.'

Nikki laughed. Trust Haqib to lighten things. Scrubbing her face with the tissues, wishing she'd had the foresight to swipe one of Sajid's lovely soft hankies, she sat up, exhaled and looked at her kids' worried faces. 'I needed to talk to you about something tonight and it all came out wrong.'

Marcus returned from the kitchen, carrying an opened bottle of white wine and a full glass, which he pushed into Nikki's trembling hands. With a grim smile, Nikki scrutinised his face before accepting it. As usual, there was no judgement in his eyes – only love and support. His mouth quirked up in a half-smile as he settled himself into the space left by Haqib. 'You all need to listen to your mum. She's got to tell you something really important and it requires you all to be really sensible, and do what we tell you, okay?'

All four nodded and Nikki took a gulp of the wine, savouring its coolness on her throat as she swallowed. 'Okay, I had it all planned how I was going to broach this with you tonight and it was nothing like the way I did. I'm sorry if I frightened you all.'

Four pairs of dark eyes, each a slightly different shade of brown, stared at her, each pair filled with love and compassion. Smiling slightly, Nikki reached out and ruffled Sunni's hair. 'What I actually wanted to talk to you all about was Aunty Anika's and my biological father. He's called Freddie Downey and he's a really, really bad man. The things I blurted out earlier are all true. He went to prison for some of the things he did to us and Ajima, but was released after a short time and has been living in Scotland since then.'

She took another swig of wine. 'Thing is, we've discovered he did much worse things too and we now believe he's made his way back to Bradford.'

She took a photo from her bag and handed it to Charlie. 'This is the latest image we have of him. I want you all to be really vigilant. If you see anyone suspicious hanging around, you need to let the police and me know immediately. If you see him, you need to report it to me. He's dangerous and he might see you four as a way to punish Ajima, Anika and me. The cars will remain at the front and back of the street, but until further notice, none of you will go anywhere unless accompanied by me, Marcus, Ali's men or the police. Don't trust anybody – promise?'

With serious expressions, they all nodded and then Sunni, face scrunched up in anger spoke. 'Did he hurt you, Mummy?'

Nikki smiled and hugged him. 'Yes, a little – but it's all in the past now, Sunni. We're all safe now. If you do what I ask, we'll all remain safe too.'

'I hate him, I hate him, I hate him.' Sunni's small face was scrunched up and red, his hands fisted. His phraseology reminded Nikki of the diary excerpts and she wondered if the person who wrote them was also directing their anger at Freddie Downey.

Marcus threw Sunni a cushion. 'Punch it out, Sunni. Punch it out.'

It didn't look like any of them were heading to bed anytime soon and Nikki understood that. She'd given them a lot to think about and she was aware that there would be a lot of questions to answer after they'd processed the information she'd given them. Her head throbbed, so, glass in hand, she stood up. 'Now, much as the wine hit the spot, I think I really need a cup of coffee.'

She walked through to the kitchen and tried to ignore the excited chatter that had broken out in the living room as soon as she'd left. Marcus would handle it – he always did. Leaning against the sink, she looked out the window as night settled over Bradford. She had never wanted to bring her childhood experiences into this house. Never wanted her children to know the sorts of things she'd experienced and then, when it came down to it, what had she done? *Stupid!* She'd just blurted it out like lead bullets peppering the living room with her baggage. Baggage she should have kept locked up.

Hearing footsteps entering the kitchen and expecting it to be Marcus, she said, 'I'm so crap at this mothering business. The more I try to protect them, the more I seem to fuck them up.'

'You're not a crap mum and you haven't fucked us up.'

Nikki's heart plummeted as she glanced at Charlie. 'Case in point, Charlie. I've yet again not been the perfect mum because my eldest daughter doesn't think twice about swearing in front of her mum – twice in the one sentence, I might add.'

Charlie laughed. 'Aw, don't get all maudlin on me, Mum. Who says what's perfect? Who makes that decision, eh?'

Nikki grinned, pushed herself away from the sink and hugged her daughter. 'You know, Charlie, you're turning into a quite exceptional young woman.'

'Yeah, I got a kick-ass mum to thank for that.'

Nikki put the kettle on and spooned coffee and instant hot chocolate into various mugs. 'Hm, I suppose I'm to blame for your sassy backchat too.'

'Yeah, I reckon so. Ajima say you've always been a bit gobby.'

Pouring water into the mugs, Nikki pushed one across the work top to Charlie and picked up the tray with the others on.

'Mum ...'

Nikki hesitated by the door. Charlie was looking out the kitchen window, coffee mug in her hand, and casting surreptitious glances at her mother.

'Your scar? Did he ...?' Charlie, eyes averted, bit her lip.

If this was some sort of motherhood test, Nikki felt woefully inadequate. Did she spare her 15-year-old daughter from the horror of her own childhood? Should she give her some diluted version of events or perhaps just tell her how it happened in a matter-of-fact, no-nonsense way? Nikki placed the tray on the kitchen table and moved closer to her daughter. 'Yes, Freddie Downey did this to me. I was 12. He wanted me to do something.'

Nikki swallowed the lump in her throat. 'Something sexual with one of his friends. And when I refused, he tied a thick hairy rope round my neck and pulled it tight. He kept pulling it tight and then releasing it ... again and again. He was an animal. By the time Ajima managed to get Ani and me out of there and into hospital, I was hurt quite badly. They didn't know if there would be damage to my vocal cords, but I recovered. We went into a refuge after that and he was imprisoned.'

'Why don't you have it removed?'

Nikki put her arm round Charlie. 'It's a reminder that I'm a survivor. A reminder to make sure that I bring you three up to be strong and not to get into the position Ajima got into.'

'She should have protected you and Auntie Anika.'

'She was barely 15 when she had me and 17 when she had Anika. Her parents were new to the country. She was just a kid who made some mistakes and slid through the net. She's not to blame.'

She picked up the tray and then frowned. 'Women are never to blame for male violence against them, Charlie. Never.'

With a smile, she used her bum to open the kitchen door and was nearly through when Charlie spoke again. 'I love you, Mum.'

Nikki hesitated, then nodded, her eyes filling up again. What the hell was happening to her? 'Love you too, Charlie.'

Then a thought occurred. 'Charlie, what's with Haqib's new girlfriend?'

Charlie tutted. 'I told him it was risky, Mum, but you know what he's like. I've got his back. I'll make sure he's careful.'

Not one hundred per cent reassured, Nikki realised that was probably the best she was going to get.

# Wednesday 23rd September

# Chapter 57

The house was silent for the first time in a couple of days and Lalita welcomed it. Much as she loved Isaac, it was hard to maintain a laughing demeanour, so she was glad Marcus had dropped him off at work for her. He needed the distraction and she needed the peace. Late the previous evening, Enaya had surprised her by announcing she had not only booked a flight back to Palestine but had also booked a taxi to take her to Manchester airport that evening.

'I can see you've got enough on your plate right now, Lalita, and you need space. I'll come back before Christmas when this is all over with.'

Despite her relief at having one less person to worry about, Lalita had clung to the woman who had become her friend and cried when she waved her off into the night. Now, in the bright daylight, Lalita had time to reassess her options. Much as Nikita's decision to have Ali's men staking out the street came from a good place, Lalita wanted to curse her eldest daughter's sense of responsibility. Nikita had scuppered all her carefully laid plans, and now Lalita was going to be forced to work out an alternative. Touching the pepper spray she kept in her pocket at all times now reassured her that she wasn't only a weak older woman – she had weapons and she would use them.

She'd spent the night pacing the living room, contemplating her options. Once before she'd trusted in the legal system to provide justice for her and her family, only to have her hopes dashed by the measly sentence doled out to Downey. She would not make that mistake again. This time, she would end it, once and for all. This time she would do what she should have done all those years ago.

A photo lay on the kitchen table. She'd looked it out from the albums the previous night when Haqib had appeared holding the Ninja Turtle cake Nikita had bought. Anika had pretended to hate it, pretended it meant nothing to her, that she thought her sister was an idiot. Yet, Lalita knew that deep down Anika was touched by the gesture. The photo was a rare one – two little girls with wonky haircuts, dressed in Ninja costumes, arms round each other. Their huge smiles belied the squalid life they led. Lalita pulled it towards her and with her index finger traced each of her daughter's faces. Amid all the fear, these two little girls had somehow survived and grown up into beautiful women. All right, they both had issues, but they were still here, still fighting and now at last Lalita Parekh would protect them in the way she should have when they were little.

With care, as if it was a precious and very fragile work of art, Lalita kissed the faces on the photo before placing it on the table. Heart pounding, she picked up her phone and with a single phone call to a number she hadn't phoned in years, she put in place a plan that would hopefully rid them, for good, of the evil that was Freddie Downey.

# Chapter 58

The team Saj had taken to calling the inner sanctum gathered in DCI Hegley's office. Williams, Anwar, Archie, Springer and Nikki all gathered together to discuss progress on locating Freddie Downey, the diary extracts and the link to the Cambridge murder.

Sajid was concerned about Nikki. She wasn't as tough as everybody thought and this investigation was very personal for her. He wasn't sure it was good for her to be here, even if she wasn't SIO. On the other hand, he knew they'd need a chainsaw to dissect her from the case if she dug her heels in. Marcus had asked him to keep him updated for he too was worried about her. She wasn't sleeping, was on the go all the time and was anxious about her family.

He studied her as Springer updated them on their enquiries into Freddie Downey's whereabouts. Her right eye twitched and that, along with the way she kept cricking her shoulder told him she had one of her headaches. She hadn't noticed, but her T-shirt was on inside out. But what concerned him more was the bandage around her left wrist and the elastic band on her right. Marcus had told him about it, swearing him to keep it to himself. He'd never seen her wrist bandaged like that. Usually the occasional twang of the elastic band was enough to ground her, but last night, Marcus had had to tend to it.

They were still debating whether it was time to confide in the rest of the team about Nikki's dad, Freddie Downey. Nikki had kept remarkably silent on the matter, whilst Springer was all for sharing it with the team. When Springer finally ground to a halt after outlining a host of very valid reasons for sharing the info, Nikki nodded. 'She's right. Transparency will be good for the team. If they don't have the full picture, they might miss something useful. I'll forward all my PI's info to the team.' She looked directly at Springer. 'Could you ask them to refer to him only as Freddie Downey?'

# Chapter 59

As soon as the private briefing was complete, Williams was by Nikki's side. His eyes were red-rimmed and he wore the same clothes as the previous day. 'Got lots of initials of possible victims and abusers from the box files. I've made a chart of them all, which I've attached to the main file.'

He shuffled a little, his eyes flitting around the room. 'There were hundreds of victims – but only about fifteen abusers that I could account for, going by distinctive marks – a few tattoos and suchlike. I've passed it all on to the Child Safeguarding Unit.'

*Only fifteen abusers. Fifteen too fucking many!* But that was the tip of the iceberg from what Williams was saying. These were only the ones with some sort of physical identifier that they found. Nikki nodded. 'Good work – you've been here all night. Maybe Springer will let you go home after the main briefing for a couple of hours' sleep. You're no good to anyone at half energy.'

'Yeah, yeah I will. It's just ...' He shuffled again and still wouldn't meet Nikki's eye.

'Spit it out, Williams.'

Words running together, Nikki had to focus to keep up. 'I

cropped some of the images of the kids and the abusers' identi-fying marks – you know so they wouldn't be distressing and, well' – he licked his lips, head bowed – 'DS Springer directed me to head over to your mum's and Anika's before I catch some sleep. See if they can identify any of them.'

Nikki exhaled. She saw the logic of Springer's proposal. It was what she'd expect to happen with any of the Gaynor Street residents from that time. She'd just hoped that she'd be the one to take her mum and Anika through them. Springer was right, though. Nikki had to distance herself from procedure, but that didn't excuse her not giving Nikki a heads-up. Williams was a pleasant, reassuring presence and he'd be sensi-tive with them; still a puddle of acid settled in her stomach at the thought of possibly raking up old wounds for her sister and mum.

'I've specifically used images that give no indication of the context. I've been really careful, Nikki, honest, I have.'

Nikki nodded. 'Okay, Williams. I know you will take care to avoid any distress, even if we weren't talking about my mum and sis. Look, I need to look at them too – see if I can identify any of them.'

Williams' eyes widened. It was as if he'd forgotten that Nikki, his boss, was the daughter of one of these abusers. He stammered. 'Yes, of course.'

'I'll look at them in Archie's office.' She hesitated. 'Williams?'

Calmer now, Williams risked a smile. 'Yes, boss?'

Nikki moved closer. 'I have some mental blocks from my childhood.' Sweat pooled under her armpits. 'I don't remember everything – defence mechanism possibly. Did you ...?'

Williams' face flushed and he lowered his tone. 'Boss, I didn't identify *any* images of you or your sister – none.' He looked right into her eyes. 'And I promise you that if I do – I'll bring them direct to you. I've still got a few files to go through – but like I say ...' His words trailed away.

288

Placing her hand on his arm, Nikki squeezed lightly. 'Thanks, Williams. It's appreciated.'

'Oh, what's this then, Parekh? You thinking of ditching me and partnering with Williams here?'

Nikki spun round. Sajid stood, hands folded across his chest and Nikki snorted. 'Soon as Williams gets a Jag you're toast, Malik.'

# Chapter 60

Bradford sucks. What a dump! In broad daylight, it looks even worse than it does at night and that's saying something. I've got bits and pieces to do today. Got to get up to speed on where my next targets are. Before I go for the last two, I need to make sure I've got number four sorted – not that I expect any problems with this one, but I do need to start planning for the next. I'm leaving the best till last – my big finale!

It's funny though, I thought when I started out on all of this, that it was just necessity that drove me. Now, I'm not so sure. The word finale seems so – well – final. Truth is, I'm not sure how I'll feel when I'm done. When I was forced to take action, I had a clear agenda – a definite reason. Self-preservation is a powerful inciter. Now as I'm past the halfway stage, I realise what I've been missing all these years. All the time I directed my energies towards my little hobby, I was missing out on the real prize.

Power. That five-letter word has such meaning, for, without it, you can have no control. It's taken a while, but I've finally realised that power is what's been missing from my life. The *ultimate* control. Okay, my hobby kept me going, gave me some degree of power – but not the surging adrenaline force that pulses through me, at that moment when life becomes death. A definitive, all-encompassing, supreme, almost godlike strength. At that moment, I am undefeatable, immortal, the greatest – or worst, depending on your viewpoint – adversary. The finest superhero villain, the most feared serial killer, the most devious planner. What more control can there be than that? All my life I've been striving for it. Trying to work out what sets me apart. Why I am different. I always stand on the edge looking in. Unloved, disrespected – even when I make the ultimate sacrifices, it isn't enough.

I suppose I have Liam to thank for all of this. If he hadn't found out "the secret" none of this would have happened. I'd still be cowering in silence, making the best of things. I owe him a debt of gratitude for freeing me. His sacrifice was a worthy one – although I don't suppose he'd agree.

Which brings me back round to where I am right now. What will I do when the big finale is complete? It's a conundrum. The only definite is that, now I've got a taste for it, there's no stopping. All I have to do I suppose, is direct my energies to a new project. There will be plenty out there, I'm sure. Maybe I'll take that break abroad – satiate my needs for a while in an anonymous country and then come back rejuvenated, with a new project to work on. They'll never suss it out. The break between kills will flummox them. I've read all about that – seen it on *CSI*.

I feel a little more optimistic as I enter City Library. No point in hanging around when I can spend the day researching, before scoping out my target this evening.

# Chapter 61

Lalita hadn't felt this degree of fear for years, as she waited to hear word from the person she'd phoned. Occasionally over the years, she'd bumped into Downey's friend Jimbo. They tended to skirt round each other, neither keen to discuss their shared relationship with Downey, yet neither unwilling to ignore the other. Jimbo hadn't been Downey's typical thuggish mate. He'd always been respectful to Lalita, and although he hadn't helped her in any way, she hadn't held him accountable for Downey's actions. She was only too well aware of how painful the wrath of Freddie Downey could be.

It had been easy to get a number for Jimbo as he ran his plumbing business from his home. Being more or less a one-man band, the number she got from his rudimentary website, as expected, was answered by the man himself.

For a moment, she had the chance to hang up and forget her plan. She was tempted. Sweat made her palms slick as she gripped her phone to her ear, Jimbo's voice repeating his earlier greeting. 'Hallo, hallo, Spring-A-Leak plumbing services, how can I help?'

'It's Layla.' Speaking the name she'd decided years ago never to use again was hard. It was like she was raking it all up again

– but it wasn't her who was raking it up – it was Downey's presence. The minute she uttered the name, she wanted to wash her mouth out with carbolic soap – scrub and scrub until her tongue was raw. Even to her own ears her voice sounded weak and for a second she thought he hadn't heard her as her words were met by silence.

Then: 'Layla?'

She swallowed, no going back now. 'He's back, isn't he?'

To give him his due, Jimbo didn't prevaricate. 'Yes, Layla. Yes, he is.'

Having it corroborated was like a gut punch. Of course, she'd known he was back, but still, hearing it made it real. Brought his evil presence into the home she'd worked so hard to make her sanctuary. For long seconds the only sound was of Jimbo's breathing as he waited for her to speak. When she thought her voice was steady enough, Lalita made her request.

An hour later, her phone rang and she was plummeted back into her past as the familiar voice she'd hoped never to hear again came down the line.

# Chapter 62

The main briefing had been just that – brief – and mostly uneventful.

Updates from the child protection team had identified more victims and they were able to match some of them to the nauseating invoices that catalogued what the children had suffered. This should hopefully make it easier to track them down and get them any support they needed and also the justice that had been denied them for so long. This part of the investigation had been taken over by the child protection team, who were better equipped to investigate historic abuse cases. Nikki suspected that, as happened with the Jimmy Savile historic abuse case, more victims would come forward once proceedings were in place and the police had released the details of Hudson's crimes. For now, though, her team, led by DS Springer, was focusing on the three murders.

Archie and the big boss were hosting a media briefing at lunchtime where they would appeal for information from residents of Gaynor Street from the Eighties and Nineties and they would also reveal that Gerry Hudson was an organised paedophile and that the emphasis was now on making sure that Hudson's victims receive any counselling and support they needed, but also to identify and prosecute the other paedophiles who were part of his circle.

As Springer sent officers off to continue trawling CCTV footage, Nikki's experience of looking at CCTV footage for prolonged periods was ingrained in her mind. It was one of those jobs that often seemed pointless and the longer you watched the screens the more likely you were to miss something. Nikki had suggested they rotate the officers scrutinising the screens in two-hourly shifts with instructions to get up and walk round the room every twenty minutes or so. To give her her due, Springer had come on board with the suggestion, although the look she'd directed at Nikki had been less than friendly.

Some of the more "set in their ways" officers had made comments about the uniforms of the day not having the grit and stamina of the old dogs, but Saj jumped in with a: 'Yeah and we don't send our kids up chimneys now either' which resulted in a burst of laughter.

Despite officers being dispatched to question many of Downey's known acquaintances in the area, nothing had been forthcoming. Either they were wrong and Downey wasn't in Bradford at all, or, and Nikki suspected this was more likely, no one was prepared to be a snitch. Downey had always had a reputation as being quick to use his fists and it was unlikely he'd changed much over the years.

Archie allowed Nikki the use of his office to go over the images that Williams had prepared. With the blinds closed and free from prying eyes, Nikki massaged her aching temples. The envelopes containing Williams' cropped images lay on the desk, taunting her. She had no desire to open them, no desire to go through them, but she had to. No way could she expect Anika and her mum to look at them if she hadn't already done so.

When she'd first discovered that her ex-husband Khalid hadn't left her and Charlie, she'd been relieved. It had been difficult for her to relive that part of her past, but those memories, aside from the time when she thought he'd left her had been, on the whole, happy ones. The past she was being forced to delve into now was the one she kept locked up in that cubbyhole right at the back of her mind and she had no desire to unlock that now. However, she had no choice. There were victims out there who she, as a child back then, couldn't save, but, as the adult she now was, she was duty bound to find them justice, help, resolution. Who knows what they'd find, but if Nikki understood anything about trauma, it was that facing it could be as difficult as going through it.

She unscrewed the lid off a bottle of chilled water Saj had given her and took a long drink, savouring its coldness as it wet her dry throat. Wiping the few drips from her mouth, she pulled the first envelope towards her. Williams had written in his small spidery scrawl: *Cropped perps.* The use of the Americanism *perp* brought a small smile to her lips. Williams was addicted to US cop shows and on occasion it showed.

Pulling the seal apart with shaking hands, Nikki took the photos out. They were face down in her hand, which gave her another moment to calm herself. Then, using the philosophy her mum had always used with plasters – ripping them off fast and in one movement – Nikki flipped them over. There weren't many. Not every man would have an identifying mark on the parts of the body caught by the photographer, but these six had.

Williams had labelled each image with a number and Nikki discovered that he'd managed to zoom in on a few identifiers from different angles. Nikki focused on these marks: a tattoo of the Yorkshire Rose on a bicep, a large and detailed Celtic pattern on a back, a long scar on a thigh … it went on.

Looking at the images, Nikki felt divorced from them – as if she was on a cloud looking down at them – a sort of out-of-body experience. She didn't mind it – not right now, not whilst she was doing this, although when she'd experienced this detachment at other times, it had left her feeling disengaged and uninvolved

296

with her family or Marcus. She usually treated it as a sign to slow down, reset her batteries and recuperate. Trouble was, right now that wasn't an option. She was deep in the middle of this and she needed to get on top of it.

After she'd studied each of the marks, she broadened her gaze – checking that Williams had achieved what he'd promised and produced images that wouldn't upset the people looking at them. They were tastefully – *is that the right word for such monstrosities?* – cropped. If she hadn't already known what these men were doing, these pictures would not be distressing. However, Nikki was all too aware that, to someone who *could* identify the bearers of these scars and tattoos, the experience would be most horribly upsetting.

She picked up one more – the one with the Celtic design on a man's back. Williams had allocated that number five. She pushed the other images back in their envelope and pulled a second image also labelled number five. This one was of a Lion Rampant holding a Scottish flag with the words *Scotland Till I Die* underneath which had been tattooed onto a white male's hairy forearm. She didn't recognise the Celtic design, but Williams had clearly seen these two tattoos on the same man. The Lion Rampant one was familiar – all too familiar to her. Her mother would be able to confirm about the Celtic design, but she was certain that the other one was to be found on Freddie Downey's forearm. Without warning, her stomach flipped and she reached over, grabbed Archie's bin just in time and vomited.

When her stomach was empty she leaned back, beads of sweat dappling her brow and rinsed her mouth out with the last of the bottled water. The acrid smell of her stomach contents filled the room and the throbbing in her temple had increased its tempo. She couldn't look at the rest of the images with that smell in her nostrils, but on the other hand, she wasn't one hundred per cent sure she wouldn't need the bin again. Dragging herself to her feet, she went over and peeked through the blinds, checking who was in the incident room beyond. Saj was tapping away on his PC, so she jabbed out a text to him.

Nikki: *Been sick in Archie's bin – clear the room so I can dispose of it – also can I borrow some of your oh dee toilet?*

She watched through the blinds as Saj read her text. Saw him shake his head and then look over at the office before walking over and opening the door.

'Fuck's sake, that stinks.'

'I know … I just.' She shrugged.

'I know, Nik, it's hard.' He walked over, took the bin and left the room with it. Nikki watched him march through the incident room, dodging officers as he went. Seconds later he was back with the bin, spraying some sickly sweet air freshener in Archie's office.

The interlude had calmed Nikki and now she smiled. 'That's nice – new perfume, Saj? Much nicer than your usual.'

'This one's Eau de Trafalgar House men's loos. Not wasting my hundred-quid-a-bottle stuff on Archie's gaff.'

Settling behind the desk again, she looked at Saj. 'I owe you one, Saj. Really do.'

He nodded to the envelopes. 'Want me to stay? I can hold the vomit bucket for you.'

About to shake her head, Nikki changed her mind. Saj would have to view the images anyway, so why not look at them together.

'I'm just moving on to the kids now.' She pushed the men's envelope towards him and then pointed to the two loose images. 'We'll need to double-check with my mum, but I remember Freddie Downey with that arm tatt.'

She waited till Saj had sifted through the photos before opening the other envelope. 'If I recognise anyone, can you take a note of the image number and write down what I remember?'

Saj pulled a chair next to Nikki, positioned a pad of paper and pen in front of him and said, 'Right, let's go for it.'

Again, Williams had done a good job. He'd put various images of the same child together and Nikki was relieved to see that once more, he'd managed to avoid any explicit images. She studied each group of photos, taking her time – casting her mind back to the other kids in the street – kids from her class or Anika's class at school. There were six groups of photos. Only a fraction of abused children, from the hundreds that were catalogued. It wasn't enough, but along with the Child Protection Unit's work, it was a start.

Tapping her finger on the group labelled number six, Nikki said, 'I recognise him – can't think of his name – he was in the year below me, or maybe even in Anika's class at middle school – but at least we know he was local at that time.'

As Saj documented her thoughts, she picked the image up. The boy's round face looked terrified. He wore glasses, but they were lopsided on his nose, his mouth open in a scream. When she looked really closely, Nikki could identify fingertips in his hair – as if his head was being yanked backwards. Piling the photos together, Nikki sniffed and with an effort focused on the next familiar group of images.

This one was of a girl a bit older than the previous boy – maybe around 13. In the first image she was sitting demurely on a chair her head tilted down, her eyes on the camera – posing. That was the photo Nikki recognised her from. The others were of the same girl, but her eyes had lost their cheeky, teasing expression in those. Nikki assumed they'd been taken later. And in the final one, her eyes were closed, a tear rolling down her cheek as if she'd just given up. In a neutral voice, Nikki filled Sajid in. 'This girl lived down the road from us. Her dad had an ice-cream van – and her name was Georgia. Mum might remember more.

'These are the only children I recognise, but it was all so long ago and I was only a kid.'

'You've done well, Nik. None of this can be easy for you.' He put the photos back in the envelope as Nikki slipped into memories that had dark shadows.

'Shall I tell them to come in?' He indicated the door where Williams and the rest of the team were waiting.

'Give me a moment, Saj. Let me collect myself.'

As Saj left, a picture of a snowy night flashed into Nikki's mind. She was unsure whether something in the photos had prompted it, but it was there clear as day for a few moments. She and Anika on their own, petrified – police outside and – Dexy? She hadn't thought of, nor heard that name in a long, long time. She couldn't remember much about him. He'd been around the house a lot – Peggy had also stayed there too sometimes – when she wasn't high on drugs. Were there other kids too? Frustrated, Nikki shook her head. She was certain she was missing something crucial, but for now, that was all she could remember.

# Chapter 63

In the end it had been easy to shake off Ali's men. Nikki had agreed that while Lalita was at work, she was safe because she was in a public place, so Lalita took advantage of that. She spoke to the two men watching the back of her house and they agreed to escort her to her work and pick her up again at shift's end. Despite her pounding heart and the overwhelming guilt, Lalita was sure she was doing the right thing. She'd relied on Nikita for too long and now, if she was ever to shake off the curse that Downey had trapped her in, she had to take matters into her own hands. It was risky – of course it was. It was a do-or-die situation. But, regardless of how much she longed to stay in the safety of Listerhills, that just wasn't an option anymore.

Today she was determined; she would put an end to this once and for all. So, before leaving the house, she went through it all once more in her mind – all the insurances she'd put in place. She didn't intend to face him blindly and she was relying heavily on the hope that he would be unable to see past the weak girl she'd once been. Her chances were slim, but her careful planning might be enough to save her … She went over to the small Mundir – the Hindu shrine she kept in the corner of the living room, lit the incense and placed her offerings of fruit, before praying as never before to the Lord Ganesha – the remover of obstacles.

Ali's men followed her small car to Tyersal Library, watched her park up and then waved to her as she entered the building, carrying a slightly larger bag than usual. As they drove off, Lalita looked at their receding silhouette. That was her backup disposed of – now she really was on her own. She waited ten minutes before exiting the library through the front of the building and skirting round to the bus stop as arranged. Within seconds a vehicle drew up beside her. Heart hammering, Lalita, gripping her bag tightly in both hands, raised her eyes and for the first time in over twenty years faced the animal who had fathered her children sitting in the back seat, one of his thugs driving.

She had tried to prepare herself for this, but his cruel grin still took her breath away. *Will I be able to do this?* He was older now and fatter. The baseball cap seemed to cover a bald pate, but whether by design or old age, Lalita wasn't sure. His eyes were as cold and mesmerising as they had been when she first met him. The flattered flutter of a young girl's heart when praised and pursued by an older man was replaced by fear and the realisation of the enormity of her plan. So many variables, so many things could go wrong.

'Pleased to see me, Layla?'

His voice was hard, mocking and made her shiver. She looked down and shrugged. How could she respond to that?

The driver leaned back and flicked the back door open as Downey said, 'Get in, sweetheart. We're going to take you for a little ride.'

After walking round the vehicle, Lalita got in and attempted to slip her bag onto the floor unnoticed. No such luck.

'Bag.' Downey held out his hand, his grin mocking her as her hands fluttered up to her chest. Still avoiding looking directly into his eyes, she picked the bag up and passed it over. Downey took his time sifting through it, chortling to himself as he did so. 'Well, well, well. Looks like little old Layla's acquired a bit of a spine. Look what we've got.' One by one he took the items from the bag and lined them up on the seat between them. First the pepper spray, followed by the kitchen knife, followed by the Taser.

'Really, Layla. You didn't think I'd check for weapons? You're still as stupid as you always were. But, I'll have to make you pay for that little act of disobedience. You remember how I used to punish you, Layla?'

Head bowed, subservient, Lalita nodded, sniffing, and mumbled, 'I'm sorry. So sorry. I was scared.'

But her pleas were in vain and as Downey's fist slammed into the side of her head, Layla wondered why she'd thought she could ever beat this monster.

Downey's phone rang and he answered it, not even sparing a glance towards Layla, who lay in a crumpled, sobbing heap beside him. Smiling, he hung up after listening for a couple of minutes. 'Looks like we're on. My spies have come up with the goods – let's drive.'

# Chapter 64

Anwar jumped up from her seat and punched the air before doing a little dance. Nikki and Saj exchanged a surprised look. Anwar was not usually given to outward shows of emotion like this and the fact that she'd allowed herself to jump around showed that whatever she'd discovered was something that might progress their investigation. Used to being in charge, Nikki got up, intending to go over to Anwar's desk and find out what her excitement was all about, but was beaten to it by Springer's voice peeling out over the room. 'I hope that your performance means you've found something useful, DC Anwar.'

Nikki was aware how stressful this investigation must be for Springer; even so, she wanted to take the judgemental tone the SIO had used and thrust it down the woman's throat. Anwar, for her part, had stopped abruptly, the joyful smile faltering on her face as her cheeks reddened. 'Yes, boss. I think I might have found something useful.'

Not content with draining all joy from whatever the junior officer had discovered, Springer snapped. 'Well, get on with it and stop the melodrama. What have you got?'

Anwar's lips tightened, but she inhaled before replying and when she spoke, her tone was steady, reflecting none of the anger that flashed in her eyes. 'I've been going through the Liam Flynn files sent up from Cambridge, checking for anything that might shed some light on the link, other than the obvious cause of death and weapon, between the Flynn murder and the Dyson and Hudson ones.'

The hairs on the back of Nikki's neck began to rise. Judging from Anwar's expression she'd found something good – something that the Cambridge police had missed – and this might be just the breakthrough they needed. She edged closer, all senses focused on the other officer.

'I found an email from Flynn to a Fred.Downs63 at a yahoo email address.'

'Shit.' The word was out of Nikki's mouth before she could stop it. Sometimes, out of the blue, something previously cast aside as irrelevant or unimportant became the key to a case. Ignoring Springer's position and SIO, Nikki moved over to Anwar. 'Show me!'

Anwar pointed to her computer screen and there it was – two innocuous emails from the 1st of July that Cambridge police had overlooked, because they had no reason to imbue them with any importance. It was only when they came to Anwar's attention, with her knowledge of Dyson and Hudson's links to Freddie Downey that they took on an altogether more sinister meaning.

The first was to a Giuseppe Moretti:

*Dear Mr Moretti*

*I am sorry to contact you out of the blue, but your name was given to me by a past acquaintance of yours, a Margaret Downey, who, I believe, was your neighbour over twenty years ago in Bradford. I am keen to speak with you and would appreciate if you would call me at your earliest convenience on this number …*

*Yours sincerely*

*Liam Flynn*

The second was to a Mr Downs.

*Dear Mr Downs*
*I am sorry to contact you out of the blue, but your name*
*was given to me by a past acquaintance of yours, a Margaret*
*Downey, who is, I believe, your ex-wife. I am keen to speak*
*with you and would appreciate if you would call me at your*
*earliest convenience on this number ...*
*Yours sincerely*
*Liam Flynn*

This was a fantastic breakthrough for the investigation in that it linked the three cases and it also implicated Freddie Downey. Moretti had been her mother's neighbour and the link to Downey was obvious.

'Did he reply?' Springer's voice carried all the tension that was in the room, but when Anwar shook her head, Springer tapped her fingers on the desk. 'No other emails from Flynn to that email address?'

Again, although expected, Anwar's headshake was disappointing. Still, the young officer had done good work. Such a small detail could easily have been overlooked and she deserved the credit. Nikki squeezed her shoulder, smiling widely. 'Good work, Anwar, I ...'

Nikki's praise was cut off by Springer, who edged her out of the way, speaking over her as she did so. 'Yes, well done. The next move is to firstly find out if Downey contacted Flynn. You have Flynn's phone records?'

When Anwar nodded, Springer continued. 'And secondly, get the techies to check out that email address of Downey's. That's not the one that he used on his laptop, so we may find some useful stuff on that email. Get on with it, pronto.'

As Springer hovered, waiting for Anwar to access Flynn's phone records, Nikki fumed in silence. She had to admit she'd forgotten she was persona non grata and had let her excitement get the better of her. Still, Springer had been a cow, talking to Anwar in public like that.

'Got them,' Anwar said and Springer, Nikki and Sajid crowded round the screen again.

Saj's aftershave tickled Nikki's nostrils as she leaned in trying to see something notable, but all there was, was a list of phone numbers and call durations. Cambridge police had matched some numbers with names or nicknames, but a few were blank – probably cold calls. As they watched, all of them on tenterhooks, Anwar scrolled down to July and enlarged the screen, so they could look more easily.

Eyes screwed up, Saj said, 'I reckon we're looking for either a pay-as-you-go phone or one attributed to a nickname that might not be completely obvious at first glance as belonging to Downey. I get the impression that young Liam Flynn was keen to keep his communications with Downey low-key.'

Four pairs of eyes scanned down the page. Nikki, fingers crossed, hoped that they'd discover something to go on. When Saj found it, his yell almost deafened Nikki. 'There – it's there, look. FD – that's got to be it – got to!'

Convinced her partner was right, Nikki high-fived him. 'Let's get that checked out and nail this bastard once and for all.'

Springer turned to Nikki, her eyes flashing. 'DS Parekh, I hope I won't have to remind you again that I am leading this investigation, not you. Any actions will be activated through me. You understand?'

Nikki gave a taut nod and moved back to her own desk. She wasn't going to get into a pissing contest with Springer – not today. Not when they'd maybe just got the first real lead to link Downey to the murders. That didn't stop her temple from throbbing again, nor her shoulders from tensing.

Certain that if she remained in the office with the woman for even a second more, she'd explode, Nikki exhaled. Leaning over, she spoke in Saj's ear. 'I'm off to Lazy Bites for a break before I actually do break something over someone's head.'

It had taken a brisk jog down the stairs at Trafalgar House and a smart walk along to the Lazy Bites café, before Nikki's annoyance with Felicity Springer was even halfway exorcised. Why did the woman have to be such a bitch? If she was more like her partner, Stevie, then Nikki wouldn't have a problem with her, but the way she'd spoken to Anwar was inexcusable. Archie should send Springer on a few "getting the best from your colleagues" courses – the ones he kept threatening to send her on. Seeing Isaac so much in his element in his chef's whites made her feel marginally better. After the incident with the bullies the other day, Nikki had found out where they lived and had alerted the local beat bobbies to exert a little pressure on them. She doubted they'd bother Isaac again, but still she double-checked with Isaac's boss that the louts hadn't been back and then ordered a huge scone and a cappuccino.

Sliding into her favourite booth at the back of the café, Nikki pondered on the email from Liam Flynn to Fred Downs. There was no doubt in her mind that Downs was Downey – to think otherwise would be a coincidence too far. Downey hadn't replied to the email and it remained to be seen whether the techies could retrieve any more information from that email address. Springer was working on a warrant right now. The phone calls too could be a source of information. Ten calls in total dating from the 6th of July until Flynn's death. Most, after the first call from Downey, were made by Flynn. Maybe if they'd texted each other there would be some record somewhere in the ether.

Lost in thought, her coffee in front of her, scone eaten, Nikki jumped when someone slid into the booth opposite her. 'Anybody sitting here?'

What was this idiot playing at? The café was nearly empty. Why choose her booth to sit in? 'Yeah, I'm waiting for someone. There's loads of other places you can sit.'

'Ah, but Nikita, I wanted to sit at your table specifically.'

Nikki's head shot up, her eyes gliding across the muscular forearms with the all too familiar tattoo, which rested on the table, and on, up to his face. The face was more jowly than she remembered, but his eyes were the same – cold as ice and sharp as knives as they bore into her, stripping her naked, seeking out the darkest most secret parts of her soul. His lips twitched into a taunting smile, as he winked at her.

For a moment, Nikki was frozen in time – her eyes latched on to his, unblinking whilst the rest of her body seemed to cave in on her. Her heart, lungs, even her skin, withered before his toxic appraisal. She wasn't ready for this. Wasn't ready to face her worst nightmare and as the thought pulsed through her, she realised that this was the reason he'd chosen to confront her here.

Her hand lashed out to grab her phone from the tabletop, but he was quicker. As her fingers gripped it, his larger, stronger hand gripped her wrist, on top of her bandage, his fingers gouging into the already fragile wounds. He shook her wrist, until her phone clattered onto the table, his eyes never once leaving hers, the smile never budging. It took all of Nikki's inner reserves not to cry out in pain, but she wouldn't give him that. Not now … not ever again. She broke eye contact and glanced towards the kitchen area, where Isaac and Grayson worked, but his grip on her arm tightened. 'Don't even think about it, sweetheart.' And he inclined his head towards the window of the café.

Following his gaze, Nikki's heart took up an erratic beat inside her chest. Parked on the opposite side of the road was a car with a man in the driver's side and the small, haunted face of her mother peering through the window, in the back seat. Her mother mouthed the words. 'I'm sorry.'

Even from this distance, her mother's battered face was obvious. Her lip swollen and bloody, her hair dishevelled, her eyes bruised. Rage surged through Nikki, but she could do nothing with it. If she directed it towards the man in front of her, the only person to suffer would be her mum. She wrenched her enclosed wrist from his grip, uncaring of the pain it caused. His grip tightened for a second and then he laughed and released her. Grim amusement sparked in his eyes, as she began to slide from the booth.

'I wouldn't do that, if I were you … not if you want to see the lovely Layla again.'

Nikki stared through the pane at her mum, as the car drove off leaving another man, in a baseball cap, smoking a roll-up on the kerb. How the hell had this happened? Where were Ali's men? How the hell had this monster got her mum?

'What do you want?' Nikki's voice trembled a little, although her eyes betrayed no fear.

But Downey wanted to toy with her – just like he'd always done. Instead of replying, he smiled as Elaine came and placed a coffee on the table in front of him. 'Nice little caff, this and right near your place of work. I'll need to come back when I've got more time.'

Despite knowing it would only amuse him, Nikki was unable to stop the retort from spilling from her lips. 'The only place you'll be visiting won't have nice little caffs.'

'Oh, don't be like that, Nikita, my sweetheart.' He leaned

towards her, his stale fag breath mixing with the pleasant smells of baking. 'Surely you're pleased to see your old man after all this time – haven't you missed me?'

'You won't get away with this, you know. If you harm one hair on her head, I will come after you and I *will* kill you!'

Downey threw back his head and released a guffaw that echoed through the café, drawing eyes from the nearby table towards them. Nikki wished they'd pick up on the evil that was this man, but had the sense to realise that her wish was futile. To the onlookers, they were probably nothing more sinister than a father and daughter sharing a coffee.

'You're not hearing me, Nikita. You *should* listen to your old man. Show him some respect. Surely you didn't think I'd be stupid enough to come in here without a backup plan? I've got mates watching your dozy little cow of a sister.' He paused, sipped his coffee and smacked his lips together. 'Good cup of coffee, that. Anyone ever told you your two daughters are gorgeous – ripe for the picking, if you get my drift.' He winked at her and took another sip of his drink.

The colour drained from Nikki's face as a wave of uncontrollable anger made her legs shake. She clenched her fists under the table wanting nothing more than to drive them into this man's face, but that would be counter-productive. That's exactly what he was aiming for. He wanted to goad her, just like he had when she was a child. But this time, Nikki wasn't a child. She was an adult and, pulling her shoulders back, despite every bone in her body telling her to deck him, she inhaled and met his amused gaze and then glanced away with a dismissive shrug. 'That the best you got, Downey?'

A flicker near his eye was all that revealed that her taunt had caught him off-guard. He'd expected to encounter the child Nikki. He hadn't expected her to have grown tougher over the years and Nikki was prepared to use that against him if she could.

His smile deepened, but there was a forced quality to it that pleased her. Despite her hammering heart, despite all the odds being stacked against her, she *could* exert a little control over the situation. All her training kicked in. Her knowledge from years of experience dealing with men just like this, told her that the one ace she had up her sleeve was her ability to goad him by showing no fear. That was what would make him talk and the more he talked, the more time she had to think, the more likely he was to give something away.

'You've always been a little stirring slapper. Always causing problems, always sticking up for the other runt. Lot of good it did you.' His smile widened and he reached out with his index finger extended and ran it along the scar that marked Nikki's neck. 'Thought you'd have got rid of that monstrosity – or at least cover it up. What? Did the plastic surgeons think you were too fucking ugly to bother?'

Recoiling at his touch, Nikki forced her facial muscles not to react. No matter how badly his presence affected her, she had to play the game. She snorted and in a voice dripping with sarcasm, she said, 'Give me a break. I kept this to remind me that you weren't man enough to finish the job. How does it feel, *Daddy*, to have a kid beat you?'

As Downey swallowed, his Adam's apple spasmed, betraying his anger and for a second, Nikki wondered if she'd gone too far. Then, he flung back his head and again released that awful guffaw. 'Good try, bitch. But maybe you should show a little more respect, eh? After all, I've got sweet, juicy Layla and I have to say she's looking gooood and my bed's been cold without her all these years.'

'She's a big girl now, Downey. Not my responsibility anymore.' Uttering the words was like a huge betrayal, but she had no choice. She *had* to manipulate Downey. She'd no reason to disbelieve that Downey was capable of carrying out his threat. He was a sick fucker, but he wasn't stupid. No way would he come in here without having all his bases covered. Without an agenda.

312

'What do you want? After all these years you turn up. Was it just to kill off Peggy and Hudson, or is there more?'

'Tut, tut, tut.' He shook his head, with a mocking woeful expression. 'You haven't worked it all out yet. I thought the great DS Parekh would have been able to work it out from all the little clues I sent.'

'Oh yes – I've worked it all out. You killed Hudson to stop him from incriminating you in historic sexual abuse cases.'

'Oh Nikki, Nikki, Nikki. I thought you were smarter than that – thought you took after me – a chip off the old block, like. Looks like you haven't even considered the implications of those diaries. Some detective you are.'

Nikki thought she was going to vomit. She yearned to ram her fists, with force, down his smarmy throat. 'If you've got something to say, get it said.'

'Look, that's what I'm trying to tell you. I might have done the other things you say, who knows, I suppose Hudson kept evidence – he was stupid enough to. But I didn't kill him. I warned him. Same as I warned you. It's not my fault you're too thick to put the pieces together. But FYI, getting reacquainted with Layla is only a bonus – my real reason for coming back was to give you all a heads-up – but you've not managed to suss it out. Look, call it for old times' sake, or whatever. I'll give you one last clue.'

He fumbled in his pocket for a moment and then threw a small package on the table. 'You need to make the link with the lad in Cambridge.'

Glancing at his watch, he smiled before standing up. 'Nice seeing you again, sweetheart – I'll pass on your love to your mum.' He clutched his groin, his meaning all too clear, before reaching over and lifting Nikki's phone. 'You'll get this back later, but I don't want you leaving here for the next twenty minutes.' He nodded to his mate outside. The thug was built like a mountain – all muscle and brawn. 'He'll keep an eye out. Any activity from Trafalgar House before the time's up and your mum'll suffer.

Don't forget, I got her away from those thugs you hired – I doubt your kids will be any harder to snatch.'

He smiled, his teeth, what there was left of them, nicotine-stained. 'That's a good girl, Nikki. See you later.' And he walked out of the café, tossed her phone over the road, to the man who caught it deftly in both hands and then raising his hand to touch the tip of his baseball cap in a mock salute, he strolled off down the road.

# Chapter 66

Downey could hardly believe his luck. First Layla lands in his lap like a plump chicken ready for the slaughter and then he gets the opportunity to see first-hand what the wonderful Detective Sergeant Nikita Parekh had become.

It had given him a buzz to see that scar still there on her neck. No matter what the bitch said, he relished the fact that every time she looked in the mirror it was there – a constant reminder of him – a reminder that he was in charge. A reminder that no matter where he was, he'd disfigured her – scarred her for life.

He laughed as he walked. Things had gone so well. Daughter dear wasn't aware that her slut of a mother had contacted him – begging for forgiveness, begging to come back to him. Okay, she might have been prompted by a desire to save the rest of her dysfunctional little family from his wrath, but it had still felt so good to have her grovelling at his feet. What was disappointing though was that Nikki had failed to make the link between the three deaths. Call herself a copper – bloody gormless piece of crap – that's what she was. Couldn't investigate her way out of a paper bag, that one – had clearly inherited her mother's brains.

He chuckled. Maybe he'd have to send her an address – a birth certificate – yes, that's what he'd do. No more diary excerpts.

They were clearly too subtle for her to work out – but official documentation – now that might be a different story altogether. Good job, he had the foresight to deposit all his paperwork with his solicitor before he got banged up. Not that he'd imagined all those years ago that he'd have a use for those stupid diaries the kid had left behind. Not that he could have predicted that any grandson of his could be in a position to blow up that particular hornet's nest. He laughed again. God that was a juicy bit of information he'd been given – too juicy not to savour.

He had intended to sit on it for a while, consider his various options. Never in a million years had he considered that the chain of events that led him back to Bradford would be activated. At first he was shocked … then his plan had begun to form. He could capitalise on this, no doubt about it and of course, so far, things had progressed in his favour.

He got into the car that was waiting for him, and phoned the guy he'd planted outside Lazy Bites. 'She still there?'

'Yep, eyes on the clock or on me – but she's behaving herself, so far. I'll let you know when she's on the move.'

He laughed. Images of his wayward daughter sitting on her hands, letting him escape into the ether, whilst her precious mother was in his safekeeping, was exhilarating. Her frustration would be killing her and he revelled in that thought. She deserved all the shit that was coming for her, that one.

# Chapter 67

Lalita could hardly believe it when Downey got out of the car near Trafalgar House, but she had an uneasy feeling about it. If there was one thing she'd learned during her time with Downey, it was that he never did anything for no reason. She had a sinking feeling that his reason this time was to do with her and Nikita and, not for the first time since she'd entered the car, she wondered if she was up to pulling this off. With tender fingers, she prodded her temple. The lump was sore to touch, but he hadn't broken skin – not with that punch.

Her fingers moved to her swollen lip. Whilst they'd been driving, he'd taken the opportunity to punish her and in the confines of the back seat Lalita had had no option but to give in to him. She wiped the blood away and then cradled her twisted left arm gingerly. She'd screeched when he broke her finger, but he'd only laughed, his eyes flashing and her only respite from the series of jabs and punches came when he got out of the car.

But that hadn't been the worst of it. Minutes after he left, his driver started up the car again, and stopped just opposite the Lazy Bites café. Inside, Nikita, her precious daughter, was sitting opposite Downey. Lalita's unhurt hand reached out to touch the window, her lips parted and a groan left them. No, not Nikita – not my baby.

The tortured look on Nikita's face was ingrained in Lalita's mind. The last thing she'd wanted when she started all of this, was for her daughter to see her, beaten and subservient – she'd seen her that way too many times in the past. When the driver had started up the engine and driven away again, Lalita had been unable to stop the tears streaming down her cheeks. Every thought was with her daughter. And she prayed once more to Lord Ganesha to keep Nikita safe.

Hardly aware of her surroundings, Lalita was surprised when the car eventually pulled into a potholed yard with a few cars parked outside a building. She thought she might be in Barkerend, but wasn't entirely sure. There was a sign proclaiming the cavernous metal building to be a garage. The driver, maintaining the same silence he had all day so far, helped her out of the vehicle and showing more care than she'd experienced all day, helped her inside. Apart from a car, bonnet open, an oily rag hanging from its bumper, the room contained a range of mechanical stuff. Chairs were positioned in a semi-circle as if some sort of meeting had been held there. Two were occupied by the sort of thugs Lalita had come to associate with Downey and strewn over the floor were empty crisp packets and squashed soft drink cans. From behind a cloud of smoke, the two men nodded at the driver and continued playing on their phones as he escorted her past them to a partitioned-off room towards the back of the garage.

He opened the door and pushed her through. 'Make yourself comfy.'

He left her standing there, staring into the room, only to return seconds later with an empty bucket and a plastic bag containing a few chocolate bars, crisps and some drinks.

'In case you need to go,' he said, placing the bucket in the corner of the room. Then, darting a glance to the men outside, he slipped something into her hand before walking out and slamming the door behind him.

The sound of a padlock being engaged and his footsteps fading brought Lalita to life. She sighed and then looked down at the square box he'd placed in her good hand. Ibuprofen. All at once Lalita didn't feel quite so alone.

# Chapter 68

As soon as Downey was out the door, Nikki picked up the package Downey had left on the table and peered inside. She tipped the contents onto the table with a frown. A box of children's playing cards – what the hell was he playing at? Then she read the title: *Happy Families*. What message was he trying to send her? She couldn't think about that now, so she slipped the packet of cards in her pocket and Nikki spent the next twenty minutes trying to pretend that nothing was up. The last thing she needed was for the spy on the opposite side of the road to think she was somehow contravening Downey's orders. He'd managed to get through Ali's men to her mother and Nikki wasn't about to risk him getting to her kids.

She tried to summon up the calming breathing techniques her psychiatrist had taught her, but her nerves were too jangled. Her mother's pale, anguished face kept swimming into focus in front of her and she dreaded to think what exactly she might be enduring whilst Nikki waited for the minute hand to reach the twenty-minute target. For a nanosecond she was tempted to signal to Grayson – but a quick glance round the café told her that she didn't know the clients. Any one of them could be one of Downey's men and the stakes were too high for Nikki to risk anything. The time passed with frustrating slowness, whilst Nikki's mind worked at breakneck speed. Her imagination knew no bounds, because she was more than aware of what Freddie Downey was capable of. She alternated between fingering her scar and twanging the elastic band on her wrist, but none of that made time speed up.

The clock on the Lazy Bites wall had no sooner signalled that the twenty minutes specified was up than Downey's thug held up Nikki's phone so she could see it. He then placed it on the small knee-high wall that divided the pavement from the grass verge on the opposite side of the road. Nikki jumped to her feet and hared from the café, determined to give it her best shot to catch him, but as the door jangled shut behind her, a black car drew up next to the thug. Before Nikki could launch herself across the road, he'd got in and it had driven off, leaving Nikki kicking the wall in frustration as she realised the car had no visible number plates. Fucking Downey.

Breath catching in her chest, frustrated tears threatening, Nikki snatched her phone up and taking to her heels, she ran back to Trafalgar House, speed-dialling Sajid as she went. There was no time to be lost – they'd already lost too much. Panting as she ran up the steps, pausing only to use her ID to open the doors, Nikki updated her partner. Seconds later, she burst through the incident room doors and saw that Saj already had Springer, Williams, Archie and Anwar lined up. She held up a finger and waited for the call she was making to be answered. 'Charlie, that you? Are you okay? Where are you?'

'Chill, Mum. The Rubster and I are waiting for Marcy to collect us. What's up?'

'No time to talk now, just tell Marcus to bring you, Sunni, Ruby and Haqib to Trafalgar House. It's not safe at home.'

If she hadn't been so stressed, Nikki might have taken a moment to tell Charlie how proud she was of the way she just stood up to the mark and agreed to pass the message on to Marcus without fussing. Her little girl was growing up. A glance at Sajid

321

told her he was speaking to Anika on the phone. He flicked it to speaker so she could hear.

'Of course Ali's men are still out front. Where else would they be when *Lady* Nikita has ordered them to be there?' Anika's tone was bored – uninterested.

Saj rolled his eyes, but betrayed none of his frustration when he replied. 'Ani, your mum's been abducted by Downey. I need you to get Ali's men to bring you here, right now.'

'But … I don't wa …'

Sajid's reply was razor-sharp. 'I don't give a flying canary about what you want, Anika. Just get into the car with Ali's men and get your arse down here. NOW!' and he hung up.

Archie stepped toward Nikki. 'Aw no, Parekh. Cannae believe he's got your maw. I'd have bet my proverbials on Ali's men keeping you safe, until we manage to get official surveillance set up.'

Nikki shrugged; no time for guilt or apologies. 'Here's what I know …'

For the next ten minutes she filled her bosses in on Downey's appearance at the café and her mother being in the car with one of Downey's thugs. 'We need the CCTV from the surrounding area. I need to know where that bastard has gone. We need to get him before it's too late.'

Springer looked ready to step in, but Archie threw her a look. 'Let Parekh deal with this her way. She knows what needs doing.'

As her team swung into action, Nikki yelled instructions. 'Get officers back out to re-question Downey's acquaintances. Tell them to press hard this time. Some of them know where he's holed up.'

Williams ran over, his flushed face telling her he'd got something for her.

'Go on, quick. Tell us.'

Williams dived right in. 'Two of Ali's men took her to her work. They waited to see her go inside before driving off. They'd arranged to pick her up at five o'clock, but here's the thing. Her manager says that your mum never started her shift. She says she was seen leaving the library through the front entrance.'

Nikki's forehead furrowed as she tried to work out what that meant. Her mum had voluntarily left the safety of the library and that made no sense. She knew better than anyone just what Downey was capable of. Then it dawned on her – of course! She should have considered this before. Her mum had taken it upon herself to meet with Downey. Downey hadn't snatched her; Nikki's mum had gone willingly. Nikki could think of only one reason for that – one that would end in tears. Her mother had no experience of these things, so if she hoped to get the better of Downey, she was delusional. 'She must have contacted him through someone she knew from back then.'

Pacing the floor Nikki racked her brain. There was someone. Who was it? Someone her mum had seen. It had upset her mum so much she'd told Nikki about it. It was a plumber – he'd come to the house when she had a leaky cistern and her mum had been shocked to recognise the man. Then they'd bumped into each other a few times since. Nikki remembered now. 'Jimbo something or other. He's a plumber – he knows where Downey is – locate him now.'

# Chapter 69

With sirens screeching, they converged on the Spring-A-Leak offices in Wibsey – three marked police cars, Sajid's Jag, Archie's Land Rover and a SWAT team bringing up the rear. Saj had barely pulled to a stop when Nikki was out the car and running for the gate that led into the premises. Truth was, it was a side gate leading to a shed at the back of a domestic bungalow where Jimbo Lane conducted his plumbing business.

He was dressed in dungarees, and as soon as he saw Nikki flanked by uniformed officers and detectives, he splayed his arms in front of him. Before Nikki had a chance to be persuasive, he spoke. 'This about Downey?'

The wind was bashed from Nikki's sails. She'd expected silence, and had geared herself up to pressurise him in any way she could. She'd assumed, that like Downey's other contacts, he would be resistant, then Nikki caught sight of a couple of Baby-gros and a baby blanket on the washing line and she got it. Jimbo had turned straight – settled down.

'Look, I don't want any trouble with your lot. I knew Freddie years ago and I got into trouble myself back then, but I'm clean now. I've got a legitimate business, a wife, kids. No way I want to fuck that up for the likes of Downey.'

He glanced at Nikki. 'Besides, I like your mum – she didn't deserve to be treated the way Freddie treated her.'

Nikki's brief nod acknowledged his words. 'All we want from you is his whereabouts.'

Jimbo shook his head. 'I think he's been staying in folks' spare rooms and in a hotel since he's been back. Got a load of money, he has, and he's been splashing it about a bit.'

If Sajid hadn't stepped forward, Nikki would have taken Jimbo by the arms and shaken him till he spat out an address.

'All we want, Mr Lane, is an address for Downey. That's all.'

Lane's eyes clouded and he bit his lip. Clearly the thought of dobbing in his friend to the coppers was a hard one to make and although Nikki sympathised, they just didn't have time right now. Who knew what her mother was suffering at Downey's hands?

'He's got my mum, Jimbo. You got to tell us, if you know.'

Running his fingers over his head, Lane's cursed. 'Well, it's only rumour like, but, last I heard, he'd beaten up a lad who owns a garage over Barkerend way. Seems like he's taken it over as a sort of headquarters.'

Nikki nearly snarled from over Saj's shoulder. She didn't want a bloody tale – she only needed an address. 'Address, for God's sake.'

Jimbo, startled by her venom, took a step back and then shrugged. 'No address, but you could google it. Garage is called Clive's Body Work. I always remember it because Clive's such a wanker na …'

But he was talking to thin air as Nikki spun on her heel, phone out already googling the address on the way back to the vehicles.

# Chapter 70

It had been even harder to see Downey than she'd expected. She'd thought her fear would resurface and she'd collapse into a jabbering wreck, but that hadn't happened. It would have been easier for her in some ways if it had. Instead, she had to pretend to be in awe of him – petrified – still the weak little girl he'd beaten and pimped and abused. She was still scared – who wouldn't be? The man was a monster, but whilst he hadn't changed – not really – she had and that's what made the difference.

Her lip where he'd punched her was swollen and bruised, her entire face throbbed as did her finger, despite the four Ibuprofen tablets she'd taken earlier. Somehow the pain made her feel stronger. She'd survived a lot worse at his hands. However, if her plan worked out, this time she might be lucky enough to walk away with only a busted-up face and a broken finger – that was what she was hoping for anyway. That's what she had prayed for.

For now, she was alone. After he'd returned from his conversation with Nikita, he'd glared at her through the dim light, but he hadn't bothered to tie her up and he hadn't said anything. She'd blubbered and blabbered like a baby, demeaning herself, begging him not to hurt her and all the time he'd laughed –

getting off on her distress – but that was what she'd planned for. It was shadowy and the room had the oily smell of a garage. There was nothing in there except for a bundle of rags in the corner and bottles of oil and polish and stuff on a metal shelving unit along the long wall. The window had been boarded up from the inside, and a yellowy bulb that gave off barely a circle of light hung in the middle of the ceiling.

She'd hung on as long as she could before using the bucket, but then decided she was better to use it before Downey came back in. She could hear them talking outside the room. Downey laughing, other men joining in. She tried to count the different voices – three men and Downey. The odds were not in her favour. There was nothing in the room she could use as a weapon – no metal wrenches or knives or anything and of course, the bastard had taken the weapons he'd found in her bag.

Lalita smiled and shrugged. She'd just have to make do then. After what seemed like a long time, she heard the outer door of the garage open and shut. From beyond her cell all she could hear was silence. Had they all gone?

Lalita sat on the single chair beside a rickety desk and waited, her breath held. The telltale rattle of a key being inserted in a lock told her she wasn't alone and her heartbeat accelerated. This might be the opportunity she needed – Downey was coming to exact the revenge he'd waited years for.

With the door open, he stood there, a monster silhouetted against the light. Lalita was sure he could hear her heart pounding, as she waited for him to make his move. He was so much bigger than her – bigger than she remembered, now he was standing before her. What could she do against such strength?

'Time to even the score, whore.' His tone was conversational and sent a chill right to Lalita's marrow as she licked her lips, dreading what was coming next. He stepped forward, crowding her, accentuating the difference in their sizes. 'You'll regret ever arranging this meeting. Did you *really* think you could strike a deal? Did you really think that hurting you was going to be enough for me? How naive.'

He reached out and traced his finger down her mascara-stained cheek. 'I'm going to make you a promise. As soon as I'm done with you, I'm going for your daughters and then, your grandkids. You should have known better than to betray me. This time, my revenge will be sweet.'

Lalita wasn't ready for his fist when it launched at her stomach. It hit her low and hard, winding her so she stumbled backwards, bent double, gasping for air. He stepped back in and grabbing her hair, yanked her head upwards, but Lalita thrust her hand inside her bra retrieving the pepper spray she'd concealed there. Downey had been so convinced by her little-girl-lost act that he'd assumed her only weapons were those in her bag. She'd relied on that. Now, it was time to see if her plan would work. The lid was off, so she sprayed, long and hard, enjoying his yelp, as he began clawing his eyes. Then the backsplash of spray hit her own eyes, stinging her, as tears rolled, unbidden down her cheeks. She hadn't got the full blast like Downey had, but it was enough to blind her.

Stumbling, she tried to get past, but he stuck out his leg, kicking her legs away from her. She fell on top of him. He was breathing fast and groaning, but he grabbed her neck with one large hand and began to squeeze. Lalita struggled beneath his pincer grip. With one hand she tried to prise his fingers from her neck, as the other tried to reach the knife she'd stuffed down her sock, but he was too strong. She tried to cry out, but she was losing breath fast. Her eyes were blurring, waves of dizziness incapacitating her. What did it matter now anyway? No one would hear her. Visions of her daughters and her grandchildren shimmered in the half-light. Tears rolled down Lalita's cheeks as her useless hand fluttered to her side and she faded away to nothingness ...

# Chapter 71

'Can't you go any faster?' Nikki was aware that Saj was driving as fast as he could, but she couldn't stop herself from urging him on.

But they were nearly there now and despite the adrenaline flooding her body, Nikki's chest felt about to explode. She dreaded whatever they'd find when they arrived. If Downey had had his way, her mother would be dead. A flash of his sneering, taunting face made Nikki gasp out loud. Remorseless, he would take pleasure from reducing her beautiful mother to a pulp and celebrate the thought that Nikki would be the one to find her. 'Come on, Saj. Come on.'

Saj soared through an amber light, pushing the boundaries, foot pressed to the floor. 'We'll get there Nik. We'll get there.'

Nikki noted he didn't use the platitude "in time" and she knew why. Saj was no more certain than she was that they'd get there in time. Archie had sent out a call for any police units in the area to head to Clive's garage, but she couldn't rely on that. She closed her eyes, trying to calm herself, but all she could see was her mother's battered face staring at her from Downey's car. She cursed herself. She shouldn't have played Downey's game. What she should have done was yell to Grayson to phone for backup and then she should have run out of the café to her mum, leaving Downey sitting there.

Her tortured thoughts and useless "what ifs" persisted as Saj screeched into Barkerend Road and within seconds they were pulling into the lane that housed Clive's garage.

Heart pounding, Nikki barely noticed her surroundings as she freed herself from her seatbelt and stumbled from the still-moving vehicle, before running across to the corrugated metal door. Behind her, Sajid matched her speed and Archie's yells of 'Wait, Parekh. Let the SWAT team in first,' fell on deaf ears. Her mother was inside there and she was going in – no one could prevent her, no one.

She rattled the handle, but the door was locked. Behind her, a thunder of feet approached and as she half turned, a deep voice yelled its warning. 'Get out the way!' She'd no sooner jumped to the side than the battering ram burst the door open.

Before anyone else could react, Nikki was through and into the dark space behind. Glancing round, she peered through the grey shadows, looking for her mother. Her senses were on high alert as she took in the evidence of Downey's presence: food wrappers, chairs in a semi-circle, the heavy smell of fresh smoke and male sweat … and then she saw it.

At the far end of the cavernous space was another door – this one was slightly ajar, a dull yellow glow emanating from it. Despite the heavy weight of guilt pressing down on her, Nikki forced herself to action. She ran to the door and pushed it open, eyes raking the space within, but almost immediately they found the inert figure lying on the concrete floor, face bruised, and swollen, blue-tinged lips, open as if in a final scream and blood pooling all around.

# Chapter 72

A door banging roused her and voices drifted to her ears. Lalita didn't know if they were friend or foe, but it didn't matter – not now. Not at the last minute. They were too late. But she wouldn't go down without one final burst. Her hand fluttered to her waistband, all strength nearly gone. Then she thought she heard Nikita's voice in the distance, far off – urging her on, so she pulled and with her last ounce of strength before she choked to death. She aimed her hidden Taser at Downey and fired. His grip loosened, just enough for Lalita to drag in a lifesaving breath, then the Taser did its job, one of its prongs connecting with his arm. His hands spasmed, tightening round her neck once more, before falling away.

'You bitch … you little whore.' Downey's voice rasped as he tried ineffectually to grab her. Although the Taser hadn't hit him full on, it was enough for Lalita to crawl out of his reach. With cold determination, tears almost blinding her, Lalita reached down, the movement giving her so much pain she almost vomited. With effort, she pulled her trouser leg up and after a couple of tries managed to pull out the knife she'd concealed in her sock.

Downey was on his knees now, and this was her only chance – her last chance – to end it – once and for all. Forcing herself to grip the knife in both hands, despite the agony from her broken finger, she pulled herself to her feet and standing over Downey, steely-eyed, she spoke, in small spurts, each word punctuated by a pause. 'This … ends … today.'

Using the last of her strength, she thrust the knife between his shoulder blades. Then as he groaned and tried to roll onto his side, she yanked it out and thrust once more into his side. But, as she went to drag it from the wound once more, the effects of the mild Taser shot he'd received faded and he kicked out at her. Weak, Lalita fell to the floor as Downey yanked the knife from his own wound. His face ghastly white, he still managed to sneer at her. 'You're right, Layla. Today is the day it ends for you.'

And, as his men entered, clearly alerted by the noise, he lifted the knife high and stabbed her again … and again … and again, until they heard the sirens in the distance.

As the lifeblood drained from Lalita Parekh, Downey, bleeding and clutching his side, was helped from the room by his friends. Seconds later as she drifted into oblivion, Lalita heard the sound of a car starting up and driving away. She'd lost.

# Chapter 73

The paramedics arrived soon after and took her mum to the hospital. She was seriously hurt. The paramedic, whom she knew well from previous incidents, was sympathetic but matter-of-fact. 'This doesn't look good, Nikki. She's lost a lot of blood. Has suffered severe trauma to her throat and may have been deprived of oxygen for some time. She may have internal bleeding from the repeated stab wounds and …' she put her hand on Nikki's shoulder, uttering the words Nikki did not want to hear '… it's unlikely she will make it.'

Unable to speak, Nikki nodded her acknowledgement and walked away. Her priority now was finding Downey. Her mother was in the best hands she could be and Nikki was driven by a rage that threatened to immobilise her if she didn't keep moving, keep thinking. Like an automaton, she phoned Marcus. Her voice emotionless and factual, she relayed what had happened and then left it for him to bear the brunt of the news.

'Nikki, Nikki …?'

She heard Saj calling her name, but it was dreamlike – not quite real. When he touched her arm, she turned.

'Nikki, you need to get changed and then go to the hospital. Come on, I'll take you.'

She looked down at her hands, they were sticky with blood – her mum's blood. Her jeans and T-shirt were drenched. For the first time, she noticed her T-shirt was on inside out and frowned. She'd worn it that way all day and only noticed now, when it was drenched with her mother's blood.

Her mind flew back to the scene in that garage – when she'd seen her mother lying there, lifeless. She hadn't cared about the blood, she'd just run right over, knelt beside her mother and checked for vitals. Her heart had stopped beating, but Nikki wouldn't give in. She started pumping her mother's chest, willing her heart to kick in. 'Come on, Mum, come on. You can't let that bastard win now.'

She'd still been doing compressions, Saj blowing air into her mother's lips, when the paramedics arrived.

Thrusting the memory aside, her lip quivered, so she bit down hard on it. She couldn't lose it. Not now. She had to find Downey.

'Thanks, Saj, I'd like to get changed, but then we're going after Downey. Marcus will look after everyone. My job is to find Downey.'

Saj looked like he wanted to argue, but as Nikki walked over to his Jag, he shrugged, moved over to tell Archie what the score was and then drove Nikki home to change.

The shower was too hot – but at the same time not hot enough. Head bowed, Nikki let the scalding water pummel her, watching the blood turn pink as it circled the plughole before disappearing. When it finally ran clear, she switched it off, dried herself and pulled her hair into a damp ponytail, before dressing in jeans and T-shirt and heading downstairs.

Predictably, Saj had made tea – sugary tea – and despite herself, she smiled and took the cup. After one sip that landed in her stomach like a rock, she shuddered and placed it back on the table. 'Any sightings? Anything? CCTV?'

'Not a damn dickey bird. It's like he's disappeared off the face of the earth. Who knows if he's even still in Bradford?'

'I saw cameras on the garage premises.'

'Yep – disabled – I wonder why. We got nothing, Nik. We don't even know what car he left in. Springer sent the heavies to pressurise his known contacts again, but so far – zilch.' He paused. 'I've even got Ali on the case. If there's anything to be found, we can rely on him to find it. He feels guilty as shit over what happened to your mum.'

Nikki brushed that last statement away. She'd no time for other people's guilt – not until they'd caught him. Picking up her jacket, she headed for the door, avoiding Saj's eyes when she asked, 'Any word from the hospital?'

'No change, Nikki. They're operating on your mum now.'

Until his response, Nikki hadn't been aware she'd been holding her breath. Now, she released it before saying, 'Let's go find Downey.'

# Chapter 74

Turns out Flower Hill is some sort of place for folk past their sell-by date. Lots of white bungalows dotted around with trees and flowers and all sorts. It's fenced off from the main street, with a long drive, winding round, but I find an entrance near the top – a shortcut for those strong enough to walk up to the row of shops at the top. I see a few doddering old fools strolling up the hill, probably using their last breath to take them up there, but I can't go into the complex – not while it's light. I'd stand out like a sore thumb. So, I've no option but to wait till it's dark.

I head off down the road. There's a park at the bottom, so I can always sit on a bench and have a bevvy before going back up the hill. I nip into the off-licence on the way down and buy a few cans and a meal deal. Then, I head down to the park. Lister Park, it's called. Looks nice – quite a busy little place, but I find a bench near the top where it's quieter and eat my sandwich, washing it down with a few beers. I need to find out exactly which of those white pebble-dashed houses belongs to my target, so I can make my plans. I finish the last dregs of my fourth can and pack the other two in my rucksack for later and then I wander over to some bushes and have a piss. Trust my luck though, some stupid Paki lady with a horde of kids sees me and mouths off. I nearly let her have it, but just in time, I draw back. Can't risk drawing any more attention to myself than I've done already. Should've checked to make sure I was alone before relieving myself – rookie mistake, but I won't make that again.

It's getting dark now and the streetlights come on, casting a nice little glow into the park. It's time for me to head back up the hill and scope out the old man. I hoist my rucksack onto my back, and, enjoying the slight buzz as the alcohol fizzes through me, I set off. By the time I reach Flower Hill, most of the houses have their curtains drawn, lights casting silhouettes behind them. I hesitate by the top gate, looking around for activity in the complex, but it's dead. The only sounds are the creaking of bird feeders moving in the slight breeze and the rustle of leaves in the trees. I edge down the path, eyes darting from side to side. I try to make sense of the door numbers. They're all higgledy-piggledy and it takes me ages to find the one I want, but finally I do and I'm in luck. The old bloke's house is in the centre of the hill with a few houses around it, but what's good about that location is the huge chestnut tree that has branches reaching as far as his small walled-off bin area. Perfect for me to keep watch.

It looks like this is the back of the house, because although there's a light on, it seems to be coming from down a corridor. Should I risk peering in the window? Sod it! Why not? I deposit my rucksack under the chestnut tree and take out my weapon – best to be prepared. There's no one around; the whole place feels like a graveyard, so I creep forward. Excitement and antici-pation send tingles up my spine as I get closer and closer. *Oh, this is such a good feeling.*

I'm nearly there at his back door when the outdoor light flicks on. I stand still as I hear the lock disengaging and then … he's there. Right in front of me, a rubbish bag in his hands. This is too damn good to be true. He's not looking at me – his attention is focused on the job in hand. A shiver goes up my spine. *Dare I?* I grin. Course I do – I'm the man, after all.

I creep forward, glad I brought my weapon. Pays to be prepared – and I'm nothing if not prepared. He doesn't notice a damn thing till I'm almost right in front of him. He looks up startled, his eyes behind his milk-bottle specs, huge and owly. I raise my arm, screwdriver ready but, as it descends, the old man turns to the side and I end up nicking his arm. Still, I push onwards, using my body weight to force him backwards and into his kitchen. As he falls to the floor, I grin, raise my arm again, enjoying the anticipation. One more stab and he'll be pliant. This one gets him in the belly. I turn, ready to slam the door shut, but there's a figure blocking it. Panic makes me take a step back and then, barely registering that this figure, like me, is hooded, I slam the screwdriver towards him too, but I miss as he sidesteps. *Bastard!* I see his fists rise and I barrel my way past him. Taking to my heels, I run like the wind, pissed off and furious that my plans are scuppered. *Who the fuck was that?*

Getting my breath back, I call Elvis Taxis – Elvis? Who the hell calls their taxi firm after a dead hamburger-addicted singer? As I wait far enough away so as not to be conspicuous, I ponder on the presence of the other hooded stranger. A burglar? Probably. In fact, quite likely. Everyone knows those old folks stash their life savings under their beds, don't they? As I get into the taxi, the sirens approach and I wonder who found Mr Moretti and, more importantly, if he'll bleed out before the paramedics arrive.

# Chapter 75

Nikki had to keep moving. If she stopped, she'd collapse into the darkness of grief and there was no time for that – not till she had Downey. Not till he was no longer a worry for them. They were driving towards Eccleshill, when her phone rang. Nikki was glaring out the window, scrutinising everyone they passed, hoping that by some fluke she might spot Downey in the sea of unfamiliar faces. Desperate for information; a sighting of Downey – anything that brought them closer to the man who had injured her mum so badly. With a quick glance at Saj, she grabbed her phone from the Jag's dashboard, trying to still the rush of hope that tumbled inside her belly. The number was unfamiliar to her, and she was on the point of sending it to voicemail, suspecting it was one of the cold calls she'd been plagued by recently, when she reconsidered. It could be one of Downey's mates, calling back – reconsidering their stance on giving the coppers info on their mate.

Switching to speakerphone she answered. 'Hallo, DS Parekh here.'

The voice on the phone was vaguely familiar, but very hesitant and Nikki crossed her fingers, hoping this was their big break – that this person would take them a step closer to Downey. That all the hours of pounding the streets had finally paid off.

'You said to phone you. Anytime day or night, if I had any information.'

Nikki exhaled quietly, and bit her lip. The caller sounded ready to hang up and Nikki had to be careful. She needed to bring this person on board. Despite her impatience – her anguish – Nikki pasted a smile on her face and hoped it shone down the line. 'Of course, I'm always available for information. Can I ask who's speaking and what information you have?'

'It's Daniel. Daniel Lammie ...' His voice trailed off. A slight hitch in the last word told Nikki the man was near to tears.

She frowned. Lammie. Who the hell was that? Saj touched her arm and mouthed: 'Liam Flynn's partner.'

Shit, how could she have forgotten? So caught up in the quest to locate Downey, she'd put the rest of the investigation to the back of her mind. However, right at that precise moment, the last thing Nikki wanted was to be distracted by a distraught and grieving partner, who might have nothing important for her. Before she could fob him off with a call back later or by redirecting him to Springer, an image of his face as he sobbed for the tragic loss of his boyfriend came to her. Swallowing her impatience, Nikki said, 'How can I help you Daniel?'

'Can I come to see you? Tomorrow? I'm in Manchester – I came for Liam's funeral and I'm spending a few days visiting the places he spoke to me about. Places we visited together before ...' Again his words trailed away.

Nikki gave him a few moments before prompting him. 'Daniel?'

Sniffling, Daniel seemed to collect himself. Nikki imagined him straightening his spine and willing himself to be brave. Her heart went out to him. She knew all too well how he felt.

'I drove Liam's car ... and ... well, I found something. You said if I found anything that could help or was strange, to contact you ... so I am.'

'What have you found?' Nikki suspected that whatever he'd

found, it would be useless to the investigation, but the lad needed to feel he was helping to avenge his lover's death.

'He'd hidden it under the carpet covering in the boot – you know the bit that covers the spare tyre. It was bumpy – that's how I noticed. It's a file, with all sorts of weird stuff in it. Can I bring it to you tomorrow? Bradford's not far.'

Wishing she could palm the boy off on another officer, Nikki shook her head, but against her better judgement agreed that she could give him a half-hour the next day.

'Wonder what Liam Flynn was hiding in the boot of his car?' Saj said trying to engage Nikki in a conversation that didn't revolve around Downey, but Nikki shrugged and continued her perusal of passing faces until they got to their next port of call.

# Chapter 76

The day had passed in a blur of activity for Nikki. With Saj as her chauffeur, beside her every step of the way, Nikki had pounded the streets, following up on all the interviews previously done with Downey's colleagues and the little glimmers of information that Ali and his men had been able to extract from their sources. All to no avail. Downey had disappeared. Nikki had been unable to identify either the driver of the car that her mother had been in, or the man who'd held onto her phone whilst Downey made his escape. Neither of them showed up on Downey's ex contacts list and Nikki began to wonder if he'd brought them from another city. Whatever the case, he'd left no fingerprints, so even a trace on those wasn't an option.

Finally, she'd succumbed to Saj's suggestion that she go and be with her family at her mother's bedside. Lalita was out of surgery, on a ventilator, in an induced coma and although holding her own for now, her prognosis was uncertain. Nikki didn't want to see her mother like that. The memory of her lifeless body was bad enough, but to see her immobilised and on death's door at Bradford Royal Infirmary ICU was just too much for her to bear. However, she was aware that her kids needed to see their mum … and Marcus.

Walking through the corridors, accompanied by Sajid, like a faithful retriever, she felt grateful for his unwavering friendship. Not once had he railed against the ever-increasingly obscure leads that Nikki had insisted they follow up on. Not once had he flinched, when she got a little too heavy handed with some of Downey's colleagues. Instead he'd followed her lead, supplying drinks that remained undrunk, and food that remained uneaten while they were driving from place to place.

The ICU nurse took her straight to her mum. Lalita, hair loose and spread out over a pillow like a halo, was still and silent. The only sound came from the machines that kept her alive. The whooshing of air through the ventilator, the heart monitor beeping and the gentle movements of the nurse who stood guard over her. Nikki hesitated by the door, her gaze taking in the frailty of the mother who today had demonstrated her true strength. In that moment, Nikki's heart broke. Without approaching the bed or touching her mother, she turned and left the room.

Taking a few moments to compose herself, Nikki stood in the corridor, hating the antiseptic smell that pervaded the entire unit – it smelled like death to Nikki – it was death. With a final twang of her wrist band, she opened the door and walked into the waiting room. Her entire family was there. The kids, heads down on their phones, Marcus cupping a coffee, one leg bent over the other, his own phone in one hand, and Anika, pacing the room, wringing her hands.

For a long moment Nikki stood there, drinking in the scene. Taking strength from the proximity of those she loved most. Then Anika saw her. For a moment their eyes met across the room and then Anika lunged at Nikki, her hands stretched out, screeching at the top of her lungs, 'You bitch! This is all your fault. Saint fucking Nikki! Are you satisfied now?'

Haqib and Marcus both jumped to their feet to pull Anika away from Nikki, but they were too late to stop her making contact with her older sister.

Nikki didn't flinch as Anika's fingernails raked down her cheek. Instead, she mumbled, 'I'm sorry.'

Turning, shoulders slumped, Nikki stumbled from the room. *I shouldn't be here; I should be out catching Downey. I was wrong to come.*

Halfway along the corridor, Nikki heard the waiting-room door open behind her and moments later she was engulfed by her children. Turning, tears in her eyes, she breathed in their familiar smell and then looked over their shoulders at Marcus, who stood, a forlorn smile on his lips. She kissed the top of each child's head and then went into Marcus's arms.

'She's a bitch, Mum.' An involuntary smile tugged at Nikki's lips. The Rubster was nothing if not direct.

Sunni, not wanting to be outdone, repeated his sister's words, whilst wrapping his arms round Nikki's waist. 'Auntie Anika's a real bitchbag cowface.'

Charlie moved closer to Nikki and got to the heart of the matter. 'This isn't your fault, Mum. None of it is. The *only* person responsible is Downey.'

Nikki looked at them. 'You know, you four are my rocks. Truly you are.'

Marcus stepped forward and kissed her forehead. 'Take the kids home, Nik. You've done enough for one day and they need to sleep. I'll stay here with your mum and Anika and I'll let you know as soon as there's any change.'

# Chapter 77

The taxi drops me off near City Park, but I'm not sure what to do. *What happened back there? Where did that other bloke come from?* I should have stuck to the plan. That's why it all went wrong, because I thought I could forget the plan and act on instinct. I sit down on one of the benches near the mirror pool. The fountains aren't working right now – thank God. The sound of the water would make me want to piss.

I shouldn't have had those beers. Should have kept a clear mind. Shit! I shouldn't have phoned a taxi either. At least that call was on my burner, and the bloke was probably not paying much attention to me. Still, that was a bloody mistake. Two mistakes in one night. *Come on. Get a grip! You're better than this. Stick to the plan and you'll get it all done.* There was no point in rushing things. I should never have done that. Tonight was to scope out the area – not to kill the target.

I groan as the repercussions sink in. The old bastard Moretti will probably be in hospital now and fuck knows how long he'll be there. I open my rucksack and grab one of the cans from earlier. All my plans messed up and it's all my own fault. *Stupid, stupid, stupid!* Hudson and my dad were right about that. Who was I kidding that I could be smart? I reconsider opening the can. The Wetherspoons is still open and I could do with a stiff drink. It's been a traumatic night and I need a treat.

I head over there and order myself two doubles. As long as I keep my dark hoodie zipped up, no one will notice the blood that's seeped through it onto my T-shirt. Besides, it's too damn busy. I manage to find myself a stool near the bar – handy as I can just keep them coming till I decide what to do next.

Hunched over, I stare into my vodka and think. Okay, so Moretti has to be put on hold for now. I can move on to stage two. That's the logical thing to do. All is not lost. I'm still in control. God, even the best of us killers have made mistakes. This was just a blip. Tomorrow I'll regroup and move on with the rest of the targets. Then another thought comes to me. Who says all's lost? Moretti might well be dead. It might all work out for the best. He's an old geezer, after all. Must have a dicky heart or something to be living in that old folk's complex. I grin – maybe there's cause to celebrate after all. I shouldn't really – booze always makes me maudlin. What the hell. I raise two fingers with a twenty between them and signal for another two doubles.

Thursday 24th September

# Chapter 78

By the time the kids had settled down – Isaac sleeping on the bottom bunk in Sunni's room, the girls huddled up in the double bed in Charlie's room, as if seeking comfort from each other – Nikki collapsed in her own room. She'd barely been able to find the energy to undo the laces on her DMs and kick them into the corner of the room, let alone take her clothes off. The bed felt too big without Marcus's reassuring presence, so she grabbed his pillow and held it to her chest, her face buried into it, calming her as she inhaled his scent. At last, the tears that she'd held at bay all day were released, muffled by the pillow.

When her phone rang at 3 a.m., she had no recollection of drifting into sleep. Her eyes were gritty and swollen, yet she was alert and reaching for her phone before the third ring. 'Yes.'

She hadn't taken time to look at the caller ID and was surprised when the voice didn't belong to Marcus. She'd assumed something had happened to her mum, but that wasn't it ... that wasn't it at all.

'DS Parekh, we've got your nephew down here in the cells. Drunk as a skunk and arrested for vandalism in the city centre.'

Nikki ran her fingers through her hair as she flung the covers back. *Fuck, fuck fuck. What the hell is Haqib playing at?* 'I'm on my way.'

Stopping briefly before leaving to tell Charlie where she was going and why, Nikki raged internally at Haqib. As if they didn't have enough on their plates right now. What the hell was he thinking? He wasn't usually a drinker. Then, just as quickly, her anger left her. Contrite now, she acknowledged that the lad had been pushed to breaking point over the last few months. Perhaps what had happened to his Ajima was the last straw for the lad. Whatever his reasons, she'd have to sober him up before they talked about it.

Tiredness like she'd never felt before flooded her as she parked up and walked into Trafalgar House. If she could, she would curl up into a ball – a little cocoon – and wake up when it was all over. When her mum was well again, cooking in her kitchen, Isaac helping, and Nikki and the kids scoffing … but the reality was that that wasn't going to happen anytime soon. The thought "or maybe not at all" niggled at the back of her mind, but she dismissed it. That wouldn't happen.

The officer who'd phoned walked with her down to the cells and filled her in on where they'd found her nephew. Nikki was glad they didn't ask about her mum. She wasn't sure she could deal with Haqib and talk about her mum in the same half-hour.

However, when she got to the cells, she frowned as the man locked behind the metal bars jumped to his feet, stumbling a little, grinning stupidly and headed towards her, slurring his words. 'Well, well, well, if it isn't my lovely little auntie. Auntie DS Nikita Parekh come to bail me out.'

Close up, the blood smeared down the T-shirt he wore under a dark hoodie and across his cheek was obvious. Stinking of booze and sweat, he made an attempt to grip the iron bars, missed and slumped to a heap on the concrete floor, before vomiting.

As the odour of sour regurgitated alcohol hit her, Nikki turned to the officer. 'That's *not* my nephew, but I know who he is. Get him cleaned up, sobered up and keep him locked up till tomorrow. I'll deal with this then.'

As the echoes of scan regurgitated alcohol filled the cabin, Nikki sighed in the cabin. 'That's not my nephew, but I know why he's here. Get him some clothes, sober him up and tell him to deal with it tomorrow. I'll deal with this then.'

# Chapter 79

On auto drive, Nikki headed back to Listerhills wondering why the hell Johnny Flynn had got rat-arsed in Bradford, vandalised a couple of benches in City Park, got banged up and then told the beat officers she was his auntie. There was something definitely iffy about it all and she suspected that if exhaustion wasn't making her head fuzzy, she might be able to make some sense of it all. Blinking her eyes hard, to keep her alert, she pulled into her street and parked up. The Johnny Flynn thing was yet another thing she had to deal with the next day – another thing keeping her away from finding Freddie Downey.

Slumped behind the wheel, contemplating just sleeping there, Nikki picked up her phone from the passenger's seat and speed-dialled. Marcus answered straight away, the hint of gravel in his voice telling her she'd disturbed his sleep. The momentary pang of guilt was soon replaced by a sense of calm when he spoke to her. 'How's my favourite DS?'

She smiled, allowing his voice to soothe her. 'Fine. How's Mum?'

'No change yet. Anika's with her. Haqib and I are trying to catch an hour's sleep in the waiting room. Why are you up? Couldn't sleep?'

Nikki told him why she was up and where she'd been. Like her, Marcus was too knackered to make sense of it. Saying goodbye, Nikki forced herself out of the car and went back inside, nodding to Ali's men who were now positioned outside her house. She and Ali had spoken earlier and Nikki had been quick to reassure him that his men were in no way responsible for what had happened. Her mum had tricked them. No one had expected that.

Using the banister to drag her heavy limbs back upstairs, Nikki wanted nothing more than to settle into bed. She had a couple of hours before she needed to be up. But, within an hour, her phone rang again. This time she took a moment to check the caller ID – Williams!

'Boss, didn't know in the circumstances whether to tell you or not, but thought it best – you know, keep you updated like …'

Sensing that Williams was about to go into one of his long-winded explanations, Nikki cut through his excited chatter. 'You got Downey?'

Sounding deflated as if realising that his news wasn't the news his boss wanted most, he said, 'Eh, no. No word yet on Downey. Springer has extended the search and one of the uniforms is now checking ferries and airports.'

As if realising that the news he was giving wasn't reassuring for Nikki who wanted to get her hands on Downey in this country, he moved on. 'Actually, it's not Downey I'm ringing about. I was checking through the nightly incident reports – I've got into the habit, since Hudson's death, of checking through them – seeing if anything sprung out. Thought maybe our killer might target someone else and I wanted to catch anything odd …'

Nikki couldn't keep the weariness from her voice. 'Williams.'

'Ah, right. Well, Mr Moretti was attacked – stabbed at his home tonight by a hooded intruder – he's in ICU.'

Moretti? Images of a cheery Italian man with an ice-cream van, handing her a cone with multicoloured sprinkles flooded her mind. Then it went to his daughter – an older girl who went to her school. 'Shit, Williams. One of the girls on those photo packs you made was Mr Moretti's daughter. I felt the face was familiar, but I couldn't place her until now. My mum said Mr Moretti helped her and Peggy numerous times when Downey was beating her. It's likely that he was the killer's next target and, despite his denials, Downey is still in the picture for that and he has every reason to want revenge on Moretti. Maybe Downey hasn't flown Bradford just yet. I'm on my way.'

All the way over to the hospital, something played on Nikki's mind. Something just out of reach. Something she'd noticed earlier, but she was damned if she could bring it into focus.

By coincidence, Mr Moretti was in the next ICU room to Nikki's mum, so after finding out that his injuries – two stab wounds – were similar enough to the other victims', Nikki added him to the list of debts that Freddie Downey had to pay for. Mr Moretti had aged and, even allowing for the effects of being in an ICU bed with machines towering over him, he looked shrivelled and worn out. His hair, once so black, had turned grey and his cheeks were sunken. Beside him, his daughter Georgia sat. When Nikki placed a hand on her shoulder the face of the little girl in the photo pack looked up at her and anger exploded deep within Nikki. Not only would this woman, a couple of years older than Nikki, have to deal with the likely death of her father, but her childhood past would be dragged up whether she liked it or not. Unsure whether or not Georgia recognised her, Nikki introduced herself, saying they'd been to school together. For now, she would leave this woman to tend her father, but soon, she – like so many of the girls exploited by Hudson, Downey and faceless other men – would be confronted by the demons from their past.

After the Savile case, many victims had been relieved to have the abuse brought to light, to have their claims ratified and in some cases to get the help they needed to move on with their lives. Others had suffered more by the thought that Savile had got off lightly and some had been overcome, all over again, by the entire process. Nikki wondered how all of this would affect the woman before her.

Whilst Anika was dozing in the waiting room, Nikki stole a moment or so with her mum, Marcus by her side. 'Don't you give up, Mum. Don't you bloody let that bastard get the better of you. Not after all this time.'

Gently she pushed her mother's hair back from her face, careful not to touch the multiple bruises that covered it. The machines whooshed and beeped, but Lalita Parekh was still and silent. The only thing keeping her heart beating was the ventilator. Where there were no bruises, Lalita's skin was translucent, like all her blood had drained from her body, and in that moment Nikki knew she'd lost her mother. Nikki and Anika had both ignored the early indications shared by the doctors that her mother's brain function would be impaired even if she managed to survive the internal injuries caused by the stabbing. Now, looking at her mother, Nikki knew that she was kidding herself. Downey had done what he set out to do. He'd destroyed her mum.

She placed her hand over her mother's, bent over and kissed her, tears dripping onto her mother's face. 'You can let go now, Mum. We've got you.'

As she stepped back, her mother's heart machine beeped louder, nurses ran in from all over intensive care and as Marcus pulled her away from the bed, Nikita watched as they pummelled her mother's frail chest until finally, unable to stop herself, Nikki cried out. 'No more … no more. Let her go.'

As the doctors and nurses drew back from the bed, Nikki moved close, held her mother's hand and watched her die.

# Chapter 80

Brushing aside all attempts by her colleagues to offer condolences, Nikki focused on the two investigations. This was the only thing that could keep her sane during this time. Springer had insisted she take a leave of absence, that she wasn't fit to be at work, but Archie had overruled her. Anika still blamed Nikki for what had happened to their mother and Nikki had agreed to let Marcus liaise with her aunts and uncles. Her mum had wanted a traditional Hindu cremation and, although not religious herself, Nikki had spent a tense few hours arguing against Anika's desire to have a non-religious funeral. Naturally this had widened the already massive chasm between the sisters, which had prompted Nikki to bow out from the rest of the arrangements. Sometimes she wondered if it was cowardice that prompted her decision to back off, but deep down she knew that her conscience was clear – it was her need to limit the damaged relationship between her and Anika that had prompted her decision.

She'd spoken to her kids too and although overcome with grief, they'd all three of them been adamant that Nikki should – in Sunni's words, 'Find the bastard that did this to Ajima.'

Neither Nikki nor Marcus had had the desire to admonish him for his language and, as always, in his way, Sunni had brought their little unit closer. Nikki had kissed them and left with strict instructions that if they needed her, she was on the end of the phone and would come to them no matter what.

Isaac was a different matter. It was hard for him not to take the blame for Lally Mum's death. In his mind, Lally Mum had been punished because he'd broken his pinkie promise. He was inconsolable and the only one who could distract him was Sunni – so yet another binge fest of *Dr Who* was the remedy.

Instead of making funeral arrangements, Nikki was working. Blotting out the memory of her mum reduced to a bundle of bruised skin and bones, treated by dedicated nurses intent on keeping alive a woman who had sacrificed everything for her children … The fact that it had been to no avail was something Nikki would never let lie. She *would* hunt down Freddie Downey no matter where in the world he was, and early indications pointed to him having flown to Amsterdam under an assumed name and no doubt onwards from Schiphol to one of the many destinations available from there – and he *would* pay.

Sajid kept a watchful eye on her, but never intruded. He too knew Nikki well enough to realise that this was her coping strategy. 'Daniel Lammie's here, Nik. You ready?'

Nikki glanced round. If Springer knew she was talking to Lammie, there would be trouble, but Saj had agreed to lead their chat and get it on tape that Lammie insisted on Nikki's presence. Lammie was happy to do this, so it was all systems go. Having decided to give Johnny Flynn a little more time to dwell on his presence in the cells, Nikki had taken the opportunity to get the officers to offer him a change of clothes. The previous night she'd been niggled by the blood on his T-shirt and now she wanted to double-check that it was Johnny's own blood. They were awaiting the results, but the more she thought about it, the more she was convinced that the blood would match with Mr Moretti's.

Saj had shown Daniel into one of the more comfortable inter-view rooms. Instead of a bare table with handcuff hooks and hard chairs, this room was reserved for children and victims and was decked out like a living room. Daniel perched on the edge of the sofa, a folder on the coffee table in front of him. When the officers entered, he jumped to his feet, nervous energy making his actions stilted and overeffusive. 'You've got to look at this. I don't know what it all means but it must be something important. Why else would Liam hide it?'

Nikki gestured for him to sit down, and she and Saj sat opposite. Saj began to question Daniel about how he'd come to find the folder, whilst Nikki put on gloves before opening it and sifting through.

The first document was a copy of a death certificate for a William Flynn dated October 1992. It looked authentic enough, and Nikki was puzzled. Why would Liam have a death certificate in his father's name? There must be umpteen William Flynns who died over the years. Nikki looked at it more closely. The date of birth was January 1976. So this William Flynn would have been almost 16 when he died.

Putting this document to the back of the pile, she studied the next one with rather more surprise. This was a copy of a birth certificate for William Downey dated November 1976 and parents registered as Frederick Downey and Margaret Dyson. This was Dexy – Peggy's son's, and her half-brother's birth certificate, but why did Liam Flynn have a copy of it? Spine tingling, Nikki swept on to the next document: a birth certificate for Candice Downey dated January 1978 and with the same parents registered. She barely remembered Candice – a skinny girl who never had time for her and Anika – she seemed sad most of the time and then one day, according to Nikki's mum, Candice and Dexy were gone.

This put an entirely new perspective on things. No longer was the link between Peggy Dyson's death and Liam Flynn's so tenuous. Liam Flynn had been researching Peggy and possibly Freddie for whatever reason. Moving Candice's birth certificate to the back, Nikki saw a typed letter.

*Hi Dannie,*

*If you find this, then it probably means I'm dead. Nobody seems too keen on me raking all this up – but hell – I can't just sit on it. Ever wondered why Josie has a heart condition, like my parents? Or why Tommy's like he is? Well, now I know and it's all going to come out. You've gotta make sure it does, right?*

*First up – watch out for Johnny. He's really mad with me. Spitting mad. Threatened to kill me – threatened to make me pay – but I can't keep a lid on this. It all needs to come out. Everything needs to come out about my parents' past – about Johnny's dad – about my mum and dad. I'm still putting this file together, Dannie, but I know you'll do what's right. I know you will. I love you so much.*

*Love Liam xxx*

Wordlessly, Nikki handed it to Saj, giving him a chance to rifle through the documents before saying, 'Can we ask you to stay here for a little bit longer, Daniel?'

# Chapter 81

'Boss, we've got a report in about a man booking a taxi from just down the road from Flower Hill – that's the retirement complex where Mr Moretti resides. Says he heard about the attack on the news last night and says he picked up a weird, sweaty dude around the time he heard the sirens heading to Flower Hill – around ten-ish.'

Although Anwar's words had been directed at Nikki, Springer stepped in. 'Thanks, Anwar. You and I will go and interview this taxi driver. Did he come in?'

Nikki was pleased that Springer was elsewhere, because she intended to go over the other woman's head, straight to Archie. She didn't want Springer anywhere near this interview, yet she was also aware that she couldn't be the one to speak with Johnny Flynn. Sajid and Archie would make a good team.

Looking into the interview room at Flynn from the observation room, Nikki noticed how nervous he was. Perhaps the repercussions from his actions had finally dawned on him. Three, possibly four, murders were enough to keep him inside for a large part of his life. It was only natural he was worried. Even wearing a mismatched blend of ill-fitting clothes, Johnny looked very different from the truculent lad they'd interviewed in Manchester.

The frown, which she'd assumed was a permanent fixture on the lad's face, was gone. He looked to have lost weight although it was only a few days since they'd last seen him.

Archie had settled into the chair opposite, his weight, although reduced over the past few months, was still enough to elicit an ominous creak. For this interview they'd decided to go in hard, so Johnny Flynn was in Room 2. The worst of all the rooms because it stank, was cold even in summer and was small and therefore claustrophobic. Saj settled in next to Archie, the two so dissimilar as to be almost amusing. Nikki knew from experience that any amusement at the disparity in weight and dress sense, would vanish when the duo got to work. Saj dropped the folder of documents copied from Liam Flynn's original onto the table and followed that up by slapping the palm of his hand on top of it. The sudden noise made Flynn jump.

Flynn looked at the folder, then raised his eyes first to Archie and then to Saj. 'Where's Nikita? I need to talk to her.'

Archie, settling into role, responded by shaking his head and exhaling woefully. 'That's DS Parekh to you and och no, laddie, that's no how it's going to go.'

Saj stepped in, pressed play on the recorder and formalised the interview by reading Johnny Flynn his rights and introducing those present. 'Want a lawyer, Mr Flynn?'

Johnny frowned and shook his head, 'Why would I need a lawyer? I'm here voluntarily to tell my aunt something she should know. I know who killed Liam and I think I know why.'

The silence in the room lasted for long seconds. Nikki, watching, frowned. This was a turn-up for the books. They'd expected to have to push the lad, but here he was willing to share information. Saj recovered first. 'The first thing we need to know is, why is Mr Gianno Moretti's blood all over your T-shirt?'

Flynn had frowned when Saj began to speak, clearly expecting a difficult question, but by the time Saj had finished, he splayed his hands, smiling. 'That's what I'm trying to tell you. I was following him. I knew it was him. Knew he was up to no good, and when he stabbed that old bloke, I knew for sure. I frightened him and he ran off, but I tried to help the old guy and phoned 999. That's why I've got blood on me. It went right through my hoodie.'

Saj and Archie exchanged glances. This was not what any of them had expected. They'd expected Flynn to confess to killing his brother and the others, not to point a finger at someone else.

Doing exactly what Nikki would have done under the circumstances, Saj leaned back and spoke in a friendly tone. 'Do you think you could clarify, Mr Flynn? Who attacked Mr Moretti?'

'William Flynn, although his real name is …'

But Nikki had burst through the door. Everything made sense to her, why Johnny called her auntie, Liam's letter to Daniel, the birth certificates, everything. '… Dexy Downey, my half-brother and your dad.'

Saj and Archie stared at her and at another time, Nikki would have laughed out loud at their stunned expressions. Coming to his senses, Saj said, 'Interview suspended at 11:05,' and clicked the tape off just before Flynn continued and everything was now off the record … They'd have to sort that all out later. Johnny shook his head. 'No, you got that wrong. William Flynn's not my dad. Not sure if that's a blessing or a curse – nowt to choose between the pair of them I reckon.'

Nikki hadn't expected that. She was sure she had it all worked out. 'The pair of them? Who is your dad, Johnny?'

With a rueful shrug, Johnny exhaled. 'Gerry Hudson is. Bastard raped my mum. That's why William hates me. Glad he's dead – Gerry that is. I'm just the poor relative in that household. No, William is Liam, Josie, Maria and Tommy's dad though.'

All three officers took a moment to let this information sink in. Then Nikki, sure she'd worked it out this time, but wanting to be sure, moved closer. 'Why did he do it, Johnny? Why now?'

'Liam did some DNA tests without us knowing – some study

he was doing, He figured it all out – said that because William was doing Candice – his sister – that's why Josie and Tommy were like they were. He said he'd spoken to Peggy Dyson and Hudson and was going to go to the police. William flipped ...'

'And William? He's really Dexy Downey, isn't he? DD in the diary extracts.'

With a sniff, Johnny nodded. Having the confirmation at last made Nikki's heart hammer in her chest. It was so hard to equate this hardened killer with the young lad who'd helped his sister escape the foul paedophiles.

'And your mum?'

Johnny shrugged. 'What could she do? He controlled her – always has – nothing she could do.'

'Where is he, Johnny?' Archie stood up, ready to leave. 'We need to catch him before it's too late.'

And Johnny told them.

# Chapter 82

Jumping to action, the team organised surveillance of the Vespa hotel and Nikki, agitation making her antsy, wanted them to drive straight over there and tarp the bastard, but Archie and Saj's common sense had prevailed. Instead, they'd spoken to the manager and learned that Graham Crabtree, AKA Dexy Downey/ William Flynn was currently sleeping off what, according to the night manager who'd witnessed him staggering in around half one in the morning, would be a massive hangover. Eager to avoid too much scrutiny on their *rent rooms for an hour* policy, the manager had already sent their CCTV recordings over and both Saj and Nikki confirmed that the man now sleeping it off in room 325 was indeed Dexy Downey. The phrase "like father like son" kept echoing round Nikki's head and she couldn't shake it. Dexy shared Downey's genes – but so did she. Her previous conversation with Saj hadn't fully put the worry of nature versus nurture to bed for Nikki. Especially when she'd had twelve years of nurture at the hands of her genetic maker. The odds were stacked against her, no matter what Saj or Marcus said.

In Archie's indomitable way, he'd side-lined Springer, making decisions that he would have left to Nikki had she been in charge. Springer's face was a perpetual crimson as decision after decision was taken out of her hands, until finally, she just sank to a chair behind a computer and did as Archie had told her to do – scrutinise the CCTV for sightings of Dexy Downey around Flower Hill, her anger clear in every click of her mouse.

'Right, we need to get all our proverbials in a line. Make this airtight before we grab him. We've got time – he's under surveillance and I've doubled up the numbers. No way can he go anywhere without us knowing. We'll get him. But let's get tying up some of those loose ends, so we can trip him up during interview.' He looked at Sajid. 'Get this Sarah/Candice woman over here pronto. Enlist the Manchester coppers to get her using the blues and twos. I want her side of the story, not just Johnny's.' He stroked his stubble. 'Oh and while I'm at it, Parekh, you can watch Saj interviewing the woman, but by heck if you storm the room like you did earlier, I'll have you banged up for weeks.'

Despite realising it was an empty threat, Archie's expression brooked no argument and Nikki was sensible enough to realise that this was her last chance, and that Archie was giving her a huge concession even allowing her to observe.

Still, all she wanted to do was get on with it and arrest Dexy. Instead, she decided to head back home to cuddle her kids, breathe in some of Marcus's strength. She'd be back in time for the interview with Candice/Sarah and if anything kicked off, Saj would contact her.

# Chapter 83

If anything, Sarah Flynn looked skinnier and more bedraggled than she had on the day Sajid had found her and William hiding upstairs. Her hair was greasy and for the life of her, Nikki couldn't recognise her as the sullen girl from her childhood – her half-sister. It was all surreal and Nikki was glad she'd taken the time to recoup with her family. The respite had given her the chance to recharge her batteries, although lack of sleep still fuzzed the edges of her brain, making her sluggish. Swallowing a couple of caffeine tablets with a bottle of water, she focused.

Saj walked in all smiles and gentleness. He would work his Saj magic, Nikki was sure. They'd decided to stick to only one interviewer so as not to rattle the already fragile woman any more than was necessary, which left Archie in the observation suite with Nikki and Springer. Nikki found his presence oddly reassuring. Gruff though Archie was, his heart was in the right place.

After the requisite introductions and formalities, Saj began. 'First, I want to stress that at this point you are in no trouble whatsoever. If you feel at any point that you are incriminating yourself, you can ask for a lawyer – indeed, you can ask for one at any time. Is that clear?'

Sobbing, Sarah nodded and, as Saj fumbled in his pocket before producing one of his posh hankies, Nikki smiled. Predictable, but effective.

'We have a witness who says that your real name is Candice Downey and that you only took up the name Sarah Flynn after escaping from your abusive father's clutches with your brother Dexy, William Flynn. Is that right?'

'Yes.' Her voice was low, but she looked straight at Saj. 'Yes, that's right. I was pregnant with Johnny and Dexy took me away from all of that.'

'Can I ask who Johnny's father is?'

Sarah's head came up, eyes flashing. 'It was that bastard Hudson what made me pregnant. My mum was off her face most of the time and so she didn't stop that bastard Downey from sending me over to Hudson. I were only a kid.'

Nikki's heart contracted. She and Anika would have faced the same fate if her mum hadn't managed to find the courage to dob Downey in and escape.

Saj pushed a CCTV image from the Vespa hotel across the table. 'Do you recognise this man?'

They'd already had confirmation from Johnny that this was William Flynn, but another independent corroboration would help in court.

'Yes, that's William – Dexy – whatever you want to call him. He pissed off after Liam's funeral. Haven't seen him since.'

Saj took out another piece of paper and placed it on the table between them. 'You recognise this?'

With shaking fingers, Sarah lifted it, almost reverently. She took her time, reading it, savouring it, then, 'Yes, it's from my diary from before we escaped. I kept one for years but Downey found them and confiscated them – punishing me for saying I didn't want to go near Hudson anymore.'

'So, to the best of your knowledge, Freddie Downey had your childhood diaries.'

'S'pose so. Unless he gave them to someone else, but why

would he?' She replaced the extract on the table. 'Thing is, Downey kept all sorts of stuff. Socks from little girls he'd abused, little trinkets – bobbles from their hair, Y-fronts from the lads – anything that took his fancy. He was a real sick bastard.'

'We'll talk about Freddie Downey more later, but can we focus on Dexy, or William, for now?'

'Call him Dexy – he wasn't such a bastard when he was Dexy.'

'Okay, shall I call you Sarah or Candice?'

'Oh, I left Candice behind a long time ago, but I'm not Sarah either. Sarah was the name he, Dexy, gave me ...' For the first time a flicker of a smile flitted across her lips and Nikki realised just how attractive this woman could be. 'Maybe you should just call me Jane ... like Jane Doe?' She laughed. 'After all of this is over, I'm gonna change my name to Jane.'

Saj smiled. 'I wish I could, but I need to use one of the two names you already go by.'

She shrugged. 'Okay, Candice – at least Candice had the guts to escape – Sarah didn't.'

'Can you tell me how Dexy and you escaped?'

'Dexy swiped some money from Downey, and we just hoofed it down to the Interchange and took a train to Manchester. We thought it was the ends of the earth; that we'd never be found. Soon found out it wasn't though – but we still weren't found. Dexy had mates and they helped him forge his birth certificate. Told him to go to the newer cemeteries and find a gravestone belonging to someone born around the same time as him. That's where William Flynn came from. He got all the stuff from that and that's where we've been ever since.

'Thing is, we'd no money to get me a new identity so I couldn't work, couldn't do anything – couldn't leave the country, learn to drive, apply for a course – nothing. But that's how Dexy liked it. It kept me at home at his beck and call.

'He wanted me to get rid of Johnny, but no matter how he came to be conceived, there was no way I could get rid of him

– not when I saw him for that first time. And he's a good lad. He could've left home like the others but instead, he put up with all of Dexy's crap, tried to protect me when Dexy got violent. He's a good lad.'

The observers remained silent, as Candice Downey catalogued the abuse she'd faced as a teenager at the hands of Gerry Hudson – with the approval of her own father: Freddie Downey. Nikki sank into a chair when Candice, stoic and brave despite everything that happened, confirmed everything her son said about Dexy. Never once did Candice look at Saj, hesitating only occasionally to wipe her eyes. The mere thought of being able to escape her life of abuse from her brother cum lover had opened the flood-gates.

Finally, she looked up at Saj. 'I don't regret having my kids. I know it's wrong. I know that because Dexy and I both have heart conditions that Josie inherited hers and I know that that's why Tommy's like he is.' She sniffed. 'But I don't regret it. I don't think I could have survived without them. And look at Liam – he was so clever – cleverer than any of us.' She collapsed then, her words coming through a torrent of anguished tears. 'I didn't want to believe he'd killed him – I couldn't believe it and he told me he hadn't. But it was him, wasn't it? It was Dexy who killed my baby.'

# Chapter 84

When they raided the Vespa hotel on Thornton Road, Nikki was told to stay outside. Being there, albeit outside, was the only concession Archie would give her. Springer, on the other hand, wanted Nikki banished to Trafalgar House, but Archie once more overruled her. 'Seeing Parekh outside the hotel might be just the shock the bastard needs to loosen his tongue.'

Saj stayed with Nikki in the car park and she suspected he'd been positioned with her to ensure she didn't spring for Dexy. Nikki wouldn't. Although he was a bad bastard by all accounts, he had tried to save his sister from Downey and Hudson's perversions. Still scared of him, Candice refused to say he raped her, insisting it was always consensual, but they had enough evidence to put Dexy away for a long, long time. Candice, although grateful for her freedom and pleased that Johnny was around to look after her, still worried about a time after Dexy had served his sentence and was released. Nikki was sure Johnny would deal with that issue if and when it came to it.

Yelling and cursing preceded Dexy Downey's exit from the Vespa hotel. Half-dressed and still half-drunk from the previous night, his bloodshot eyes narrowed when he saw Nikki leaning against Saj's Jag. He strained against Williams and Anwar, who were positioned at either side of him.

'You bitch. You'd do this to your own brother?'

With a further lunge, Dexy broke free of the two officers and got right up in Nikki's face, his handcuffed hands raised before him. Before they descended, Nikki twisted to the side and his fists landed on her shoulder. Exhaustion replaced by adrenaline, Nikki swung round, raised her leg and kicked him right in his balls. He fell to his knees, trying to cup his injured parts with his cuffed hands, but Anwar and Williams were already on him, dragging him to his feet.

Going right up to his face, Nikki – sotto voce – said, 'Too damn right I would. You deserve every piece of shit that's coming to you for what you put Candice through. You're no brother of mine.'

Feet dragging as the two officers escorted him to the waiting police car, Dexy yelled, speckles of spit flying from his mouth. 'You're a bitch, Parekh. Your mother was next on my list – she better watch out, because she'll be my first port of call when I get out.'

Ignoring the reference to her mum, Nikki waited till Williams had slammed the door shut behind Dexy and the vehicle set off, before winking at him and Anwar. 'Shame you weren't holding him tighter.'

Grinning, Anwar nodded. 'Yes, such a shame … but lesson learned, yeah.'

*God, my team are good!*

A yell from the hotel entrance had Nikki looking up. An officer, smiling widely, held up a rucksack. 'Reckon we got enough here to send him down for a long, long time, boss. Got the weapon and a list with names on – some crossed out.' Williams hesitated. 'Your mum's and Freddie Downey's were the last two names on it after Mr Moretti's.'

# Chapter 85

One bite from the bacon butty Saj had insisted she eat was enough for Nikki. Her stomach roiled at even the smell of it and she had to rush to the loos to puke. Never in all her life had a single case reduced her to so much vomit. The result of grief, exhaustion, caffeine pills combined with too much coffee was kicking in and Nikki was aware that if she didn't give in to it all soon and go home, she might fall asleep at her desk – which of course was something she would never live down – something Saj would not allow her to live down.

Hours after Dexy's arrest, Nikki wanted to be here as the evidence against him filtered in. Langley had been happy to pull a late shift and, with Mr Moretti's death allowing him access to his body, he confirmed that the large, long-handled flat screwdriver found in Dexy's rucksack matched both Mr Moretti's wounds, but also each of the other victims' wounds. Poor Mr Moretti. His only link to all of this was his desire to protect the women Freddie Downey kept in his home and his anger at his own daughter being one of their victims. And reports from Cambridge came through that they had found a blood-covered van abandoned in a golf course between Cambridge and Manchester. The blood type matched Liam Flynn's and what was even luckier was that one of the houses backing onto the golf course car park had cameras that covered the dark corner where Dexy had parked up. They'd caught rare footage of him without his baseball cap on. Cambridge had agreed that, with most of the deaths occurring in Bradford, they'd be happy to allow Bradford to prosecute Dexy Downey.

Archie had got a warrant to search Candice and Dexy's home in Ashton, and Manchester police had secured more evidence than expected. Apart from his blood-soaked clothes, which Nikki was sure would match up to some if not all of Dexy's victims, they'd uncovered a raft of child pornographic images on a laptop hidden under his bed. Early reports linked the images to current investigations ... The evidence was stacking up even more strongly than Nikki could have hoped for.

Now, all she wanted was for Freddie Downey to be located. No matter where he was, she'd get there and make him pay. More and more evidence was also coming through about Downey and his criminal career in Scotland. Apparently, rather than the sad ex-con Nikki had assumed him to be, Downey had used his prison time to great benefit – making contacts with influential criminals. He now headed up a county lines operation that brought in most of the drugs from England and flooded the larger Scottish cities with misery and degradation. He'd been on the drug team's peripheral vision in Scotland for a long time, but he was clever and managed to keep his nose clean, by using a range of acquaintances – mainly new and/or illegal immigrants – to do the dirty work.

He'd made sure not to flaunt his wealth and Nikki was sure that whatever he'd accumulated would more than finance a life of luxury in some far-off country with no extradition treaty with the UK.

In terms of the boxes taken from Gerry Hudson's house, more and more of the victims were being identified. Georgia Moretti had agreed to make a statement and Nikki applauded the woman's bravery. Still grieving for her father, Georgia was determined to help in whatever way she could and with her help, they had located more victims.

It had taken all of Nikki's inner strength to remain strong for Georgia whilst the woman recounted everything she could remember about being abused by Downey and Hudson. Under the woman's long sleeves, Nikki saw the telltale scars of self-harm and a bitterness that so many victims had gone unsupported for so long. No more though. No more. Every one of their victims would get the help they needed. At the end of the interview, Georgia – her face pale – smiled at Nikki and exhaled. 'That was one of the hardest things I've had to do, but I'm so glad I've done it. Now maybe I can start to heal.'

Archie had made the decision to use the media in an attempt to locate more, and the investigation, although not getting the celebrity profile of the Savile case, was getting enough publicity to keep the hotline busy.

Forensics experts had identified many of the abusers involved in the Downey/Hudson circle and Nikki was glad that more and more evidence was coming through implicating Downey.

Finally, a hand on her shoulder wakened her and Nikki looked up into Marcus's worried eyes. 'You've done enough now, Nik. It's time for me to take you home to us.'

Nikki stretched and smiled. Despite her grief, the thought of heading home made her heart sing. She stood up, stumbled a little and then turned to Saj, who spoke before she could. 'Yeah, yeah, yeah. Any word on Downey and I'll ring.'

'No matter the time?'

With an exaggerated sigh, Saj nodded. 'Yeah, no matter the time. Now take her home, Marcus – she's making me feel sleepy just watching her.'

Wednesday 30th September

# Chapter 86

For the first time ever, Nikki was happy to wear a sari. She and Charlie stood next to each other in front of the mirror wearing identical turquoise and yellow saris – one of the many her mum had brought from India for her earlier in the year. Despite Hindu tradition for muted colours to be worn as funeral attire, Nikki and Anika had agreed that their mum had been too colourful to be sent off to heaven by people wearing pale insipid colours. Instead they'd instructed that everyone attending the crematorium must wear bright clothes.

Nikki had opted not to participate in the ritual washing and dressing of Lalita's body, but Charlie had surprised her by saying she would accompany Anika and their aunties to do this. It had been, so Charlie said, the last opportunity to show her love for her Ajima and Nikki had hugged her for that. Nikki had surprised herself by gaining some comfort from the daily Poojas in honour of her mum and the constant influx of visitors coming to pay their respects. Wisely, they'd set up the shrine with the lighted Diva in Lalita's own house, which had allowed the immediate family breathing space. Nikki had taken her turn at keeping the candle lit. The portrait of her mum, with a garland draped round it and a red chandlo on her brow, far from filling her with sadness, had instead made her smile.

She and Anika had spent a long night talking over everything, crying, venting, yelling and eventually falling into each other's arms and falling asleep, much as they had when they were Raphael and Donatello, in a locked room in Gaynor Street.

'It's time, Nik.' Marcus's voice came up the stairs and, with a final hand squeeze, Nikki went through to Ruby's room to collect her and Sunni. Both had opted to wear the Indian suits chosen by their Ajima and were ready. Marcus too wore an Indian suit gifted by Lalita and as they left the house to walk the few doors to Lalita's house where the Brahman would conduct the funeral service before they transported Lalita to the crematorium, Nikki's heart missed a beat. The reality of never seeing her mother again pierced right through to her soul. Anika and Haqib joined Nikki's family, and holding hands the sisters looked around overwhelmed by the support.

The street was lined with their neighbours, both Muslim and Hindu, their work colleagues, Lalita's library friends, and Nikki's huge extended family. Never had she felt so supported – so loved – as they walked into the house where her mother waited for one last time, the visitors following on to also pay their respects. It didn't matter that Nikki herself wasn't religious, her mum had been and this, her final day, was all about Lalita Parekh.

# Epilogue

## October

The two figures sat in a battered old Zafira, windscreen wipers on at full speed, still ineffective against the deluge that pounded the car.

'Think it's an omen – the rain?'

With a shrug, Nikki watched the rain bouncing on the ground. 'Dunno. Not sure I believe in that stuff, but I suppose it might be.'

'You don't want me to go in, do you?'

Not wanting to be caught out in a lie her sister would see straight through, Nikki grinned. 'You got me. Course I don't. But it's your decision and if you do, then I'm here for you.'

They were parked down the road from Wakefield prison and, as Nikki had promised her nephew –Haqib, not Johnny, – she couldn't quite get her head round having an extended half-family – she was accompanying Anika to see Haqib's dad.

'Wonder how Isaac is. You heard from him?' Anika was changing the subject, her anxiety making her chatter on like she always did when she was nervous.

Nikki had wanted Isaac to live with them, but Isaac and his

social worker had both expressed the opinion that he needed to have some independence. So, they'd helped him move back into the shared accommodation that was near to his work and he'd settled in, made some friends and was happy.

Nikki had pulled in a few more favours to ensure that her colleagues in uniform kept an eye out for him and they'd put the word out on the street that the people in the home were off limits. So far it had worked. 'He's fine. More than fine. I think Elaine from the café is his girlfriend, you know? Charlie pops in regularly and he comes over for tea. He's great.'

Anika looked out the side window and Nikki suspected that whatever she was about to say was going to be difficult. 'We're done with Downey, aren't we, Nik? I mean he can't come back. He's had his revenge and forgotten all about us now, yeah?'

Damn! Nikki hadn't expected her sister to bring this up – not right then. She fingered the postcard that was in her jacket pocket beside the packet of playing cards Downey had taunted her with – Happy Families indeed. She'd been meaning to talk to Anika about it later, but now she hesitated. Did she really want to burden her anxious sister with the news that Freddie Downey had sent her a postcard from Venezuela, one of the few places that did not extradite to the UK? She really did not want to have Anika petrified, locking herself in and jumping at every shadow for the rest of her life, especially if she read the message written on the card: *I'll be back. Your choice – Who's next, you or your sister?*

The words tumbled from her mouth and she was committed to her answer. 'No, he's gone, Anika. We've no need to worry about him ever again.'

Anika nodded, then turned and, grinning, handed Nikki something. Nikki took it. It was a crumpled-up, melted sweet in a familiar wrapper.

'I love you enough to give you my last Rolo.'

Nikki grinned, glad to have her sister back and began to pick

380

the gold foil from the sticky sweet. 'Trust you to melt it, Ani. Just like old times.'

Anika inhaled, glanced out the window and pointed through the rain that had slowed to a slight drizzle. 'Look, a rainbow.'

She turned to Nikki. 'Let's go home, Nik. I don't need to see Yousaf to know what a tool he is.'

**Gripped by *Dark Memories?* Sign up to the Liz Mistry newsletter to receive exclusive content and be the first to hear about the next book in the Detective Nikki Parekh series. tinyurl.com/LizMistrySignUp**

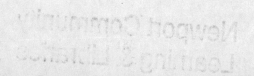

# Acknowledgements

Creating a novel takes a team and I am so lucky to have a special team here at HQ Stories. My editor Belinda Toor is exceptional and truly dedicated to getting the best she can from me, and it is with huge credit to her that *Dark Memories* is much improved now she's helped me mould it into shape. So, thanks, Belinda, for all your efforts. My copy editor Helena Newton has done an excellent job catching all my errors and again her insight has been welcomed at every point.

My trusty team of Beta readers have worked their socks of, held me to account, made me laugh and supported me all the way – thanks to Toria Forsyth-Moser, Anita Waller, Dee Groocock, Carrie Wakelin, Emma Truelove and Maureen Webb for being on hand to sort me out. My ARC readers have also been brilliant and although there are too many of you to mention, your comments and thoughts, as always, make a difference.

As always, a special thanks must go to my brilliant family who keep the coffee and food coming, help me when I'm down and celebrate with me when I'm on point.

Rachel Gilbey from Rachel's Random Resources created an

amazing blog tour for *Dark Memories* and I am hugely grateful to her. Thanks, Rachel!

Lastly, huge thanks to all of the bloggers, reviewers, book groups and readers who take the time to read, talk about, spread the word and generally share the book love. You are all STARS!

# Keep reading for an excerpt from
## *Last Request ...*

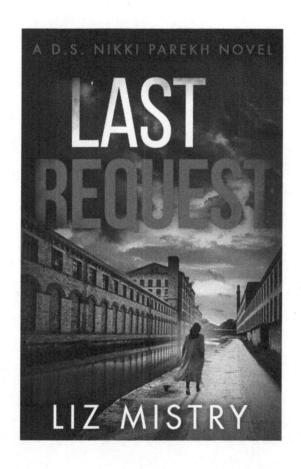

Keep reading for an excerpt from

*Last Request* ...

# Prologue

## 1983

Her hand, scaly and trembling, reaches out. The flash of shocking-pink nail varnish that I'd applied with painstaking care whilst she'd been sleeping is incongruous against her yellowy skin. The stench of death hangs heavy around her, as if she's rotting from the inside out. I take her hand, careful not to grip too tightly. Every worm-like sinew, every frail tendon, every arid vein a braille pattern against my palm. Still, she flinches, the pain flashing in her milky eyes. A sheen of sweat dapples her forehead. Her nightdress is soaked with perspiration that mingles with fetid pus and piss, creating a cacophony of odours that make me want to retch. Her pink scalp shines through matted hair. Her cheekbones, jutting against paper-thin skin, bear raw scabs.

The room is dire – stinking and filthy. I should clean it, but I don't know how. That was never one of *my* jobs – cleaning up, keeping things neat, tidy. That had always been her job. Her eyes look heavy. Soon, once the morphine kicks in, she'll doze off. The dim light from the bedside lamp illuminates the layer of dust that covers the cabinet top. We don't use the main light anymore. It hurts her eyes. With the curtains drawn against the outside world, we are cocooned in this hell hole together … slowly disintegrating … decomposing like two worthless corpses thrown on an unlit pyre.

The carpet's gross. I've spilled more piss on there than has made it into the bedpan and that's not mentioning the stains where she's thrown up. No matter how much Dettol I use the overwhelming stink of vomit still hangs in the air.

When she drifts off into an uneasy sleep, I switch the television on. Casting anxious glances her way, I wait. Today's the day. The court hearing. It's like the entire country is on tenterhooks waiting for the verdict. I've tried telling myself I'm imagining things – the looks, the surreptitious glances, the whispers every time I go to the shops – each one a piqueristic experience of both pleasure and pain. Each one grounding me in the reality of what *he's* done to us. Deep down I know that everyone – the postman, Mr Anand at the corner shop, Mrs Roberts two doors down – everyone in the entire fucking world is waiting, holding on to their bated breath, with the heightened anticipation of an illicit orgasm.

They barely noticed me before this. Now it's as if, in the absence of my mother's presence, I've been thrust into minor celebrity status, my every move scrutinised. At least the paparazzi have slung their hooks, for now. Not before Mum had to face them though. When the story first hit the news, she was forced to run the gauntlet, her head hung in shame, her eyes swollen and red, her gait unsteady. It took its toll. Well, that and the shit that he'd infected her with. It all combined to drag her down, drain her.

The recording I've seen so many times, the standard one they played on endless repeat when the shit first hit the fan, flits across the screen. He looks so suave, sophisticated. All spruced up in his suit, beard trimmed, sleazy smile playing around his lips. Like he'd done nothing. Like none of this was *his* fault.

I daren't put the volume up so I flick to subtitles …

*'Three more students under the care of Professor Graham Earnshaw have come forward, with accusations of rape. This brings*

388

*the total number of victims to fifteen. Professor Earnshaw's solicitor still maintains his client is not guilty and as the trial enters its fifth day, the court heard how Professor Earnshaw is alleged to have infected not only his wife, but four of his victims, three male and one female, with the HIV virus. It looks like this case could run into its second week, if not longer.'*

The camera flicks to the front of Leeds Court and after a quick glance to make sure Mum is still asleep, I pull forward to hear what the Dean of Social Sciences is about to say about my father.

*'... and the department has responded to student concerns as quickly as possible. We are doing our best to support our ...'*

A groan from the bed and I press the remote. The screen goes dark and I look round. She's holding her hand up in front of her, a slight smile tugs her thin lips into a toothless grimace. 'Thank you. I like pink, always have.'

I lean over, tuck the sheets around her emaciated frame, ignoring the wafts of decay that hit my nostrils. Her frail hand grips my arm and I pause, turning my head towards her. 'What, Mum? What is it?'

Her smile widens, and I try not to flinch at the bloody cracks at the corner of her mouth and the gaps inside. She nods once and swallows. I go to lift the half-filled glass from the bedside table but she shakes her head – a painful movement that pulls a frown across her forehead. When she speaks her voice is low and raw. 'Promise me.'

I lean closer, hardly able to hear her words.

'My last request – you've *got* to promise that you'll do it. Live your dream. Do *everything* you always planned to do before this.'

Her hand gestures towards the TV. She saw it. I haven't been quick enough.

I bow my head and promise her. I'd promise her anything right now, but still, I keep my fingers crossed. I curse my carelessness but there's no point, for when I glance back her eyes are closed. She is on her final journey and, as if on cue, my entire body responds to the smash of a train hurtling through my core, pummelling me to the ground and, as she gasps her last breath, I cower on the floor hugging my knees tight to my chest. My heart shatters into a jigsaw of fragments that can't ever reconnect; a sense of relief coddles me like a woollen blanket and guilt and anger swamp me.

Days pass with those whose slurs had previously scorched us, now offering platitudes. Each false word drips like acid, as I take in the detritus that is my life from here on in, and all the time her last request plays in my mind like an annoying jingle.

There's nothing else for it. I'll have to do something about that.

Monday 15th October

2018

# Chapter 1

Dour rain pummelled the cobbles that ran between the two rows of houses on Willowfield Terrace, making them sleek and dangerous underfoot. Except for the oppressive, grey clouds that promised more of the same, the alleyway was deserted. The air hung heavy, waiting to embrace the latest drama involving the Parekh women as Detective Sergeant Nikita Parekh flung open the back door and stormed out. Anger emanating from her every pore, she flew down the steps into the yard and out the gate, followed by her daughter. Leather jacket flying loose, she ignored the spatter of mucky water that her trainers kicked up the back of her jeans. With a plastic bag looped over one wrist, she raked her waist-length hair back into a ponytail and slipped a scrunchie round it. She was on a mission and nothing would deter her.

'Mum ... Mum! Wait up.' Charlie, a foot taller than her mum, ran behind, hitching her schoolbag onto her shoulder. Unlike her mum, she tried to avoid the puddles created by the worn cobbles.

But Nikki was already pushing open the back gate of the neighbouring house and striding up the steps. Using her fist, she brayed briefly on the door before turning the handle and pushing it open, not waiting for a reply. Entering the kitchen, she glanced at the hijabed woman cooking a fry-up in a huge frying pan on the cooker. 'Where's Haqib?'

The woman puffed her cheeks out in a 'what's he done now?' expression and, shaking her head, pointed her spatula towards the kitchen door. 'Front room.'

Stopping only to grab a bite from a piece of buttered toast on a plate on the worksurface, Nikki marched out of the kitchen, through the small hallway and into the living room. The room was in semi-darkness, with just the light from an Ikea tabletop lamp and the TV illuminating the area. She went straight over to the large bay window and swished the curtains open, allowing the scant light from outside to penetrate.

'Oi!' All angles, acne and attitude, Haqib, slouched on a bright red leather sofa, TV blaring, remote control in his hand, bare feet balanced on top of a glass-topped coffee table. 'What d'ya think you're doin'? Can't see the telly, can I?'

Nikki turned with her hands on hips, and glared at him, the spark in her eyes forcing him to back down.

Charlie panted into the room, the knot on the top of her head wobbling as if it might fall off, her cheeks spattered with raindrops. 'Mum, if you'd just hang on a minute.'

Nikki extended her hand, one index finger raised to her daughter, just like her own mother had always done, '*Chup kar.*' She rounded the bulky couch and positioned herself right in front of the TV.

Charlie folded her arms under her boobs, one hip extended towards her mum, pure sulk dripping from her pursed lips.

Haqib bobbed his head, first to one side and then to the other, trying to see the TV, his tone a little less confrontational this time. 'Can't see.'

Nikki bent over and swiped his feet off the table.

'Hey.' He glanced from his aunt to his cousin, his hands splayed before him. 'What's up? What've I done now? You can't just come in and do that, you know?'

Nikki snorted before tipping the contents of the plastic bag she was carrying onto the table where Haqib's feet had been. Haqib stopped, mouth open. If Nikki had been in a better mood she'd have laughed, but right now she was fuming. Really fuming. Haqib's eyes moved from his aunt's stern face to the bags filled with multicoloured pills, then up to Charlie. The pills with their smiley faces, love hearts and winky eyes incensed Nikki. Over the past few months she'd seen umpteen cases of kids in the city taking E and landing themselves in Bradford Royal Infirmary. This new batch was potent – three deaths and a brain damaged kid testified to that. It made Nikki's piss boil. She snatched the remote from her nephew and switched off the racket that boomed from the speakers. 'Spill!'

Haqib clipped his mouth shut, then opened it, before once more closing it like a minnow about to get swallowed by a shark. That analogy appealed to Nikki. All she wanted to do was to swallow the lad up, chew him till he squealed and spit him out.

'I ... erm, I ...' He looked at Charlie as if expecting her to bail him out.

Nikki moved closer, breathing heavily, her anger exuding from every pore. 'You selling MDMA to my 14-year-old, are you? Got a death wish, have you?' Another step and Haqib was trying to mould his body into the leather couch.

'You all right in there?' Nikki's sister, Anika, called from the kitchen.

Nikki glowered at Haqib. 'You'd better start spilling before your mum comes through.'

'For God's sake, Mum.' Charlie, her face perfectly made up, eyeliner on point and her school skirt too damn short, flounced forward and flung herself onto the sofa beside Haqib, sliding her schoolbag round till it rested on her lap. 'If you'd give me half a chance to explain. Haqib didn't *sell* me it.'

Nikki glared at the lad, eyebrows raised. 'You *gave* them to her? You *gave* your 14-year-old cousin E? That's no better. In fact, that's bloody worse.'

He ran the back of his hand across his nose and glanced at Charlie. 'I didn't. I wouldn't – she …' He glanced at Charlie and shrugged.

Charlie elbowed him in the ribs. 'Tell her then – you might as well …'

Head bowed, looking like a 2-year-old in trouble for stealing the Easter eggs, he mumbled something.

'What?' Nikki's voice was sharp. She'd thought Haqib knew better than to bring drugs of any sort near her family, near her home or even onto the damn estate. What the hell had he been thinking?

Clearing his throat, Haqib tried again. 'She' – he jerked his thumb towards Charlie – 'confiscated it.'

'You *what*?' Nikki looked at her eldest daughter who was all sulky indignation and 'I told you so'.

'What? So, you thought I'd *buy* Es? I'm not a loser, you know!'

Nikki grinned and scooped the bags up. Charlie wasn't a loser. Definitely not. Nearing the sofa, she leaned over and kissed the top of her daughter's top-knot head. 'No, *you're* not.' She leaned over further and cuffed Haqib's head. 'You, on the other hand, will be, if you don't stop with the damn drugs. Now I've got to bail you out, yet again. Not good enough, Haqib – not fucking good enough.'

She could just about put up with the weed that was rife on the estate – turn a blind eye and all that – but *this*? Once this shit got a grip on the estate it'd spread like wildfire bringing with it crime and violence and despair. She'd seen it all before on other Bradford estates and she was buggered if she'd allow it on hers. But what was she to do about Haqib? She was tempted to turn the little scrote in – let him see what it would be like – but deep down she knew she couldn't do that to her family or to this runt of a boy.

Haqib rubbed his head. 'I don't take them, Auntie. It's just …' He sighed.

Charlie broke in. 'What he's trying to say is that Deano's back.'

A talon curled its way round Nikki's heart and squeezed, hard and sudden. If Deano was back, then that meant his drug lord boss Franco was too … and he was an evil sod. 'I'll deal with this.' She hung the bag back over her wrist and chucked the remote control at Haqib, making sure it whacked his head. 'Don't be late for school, you two.'

When she re-entered the kitchen, Anika handed her a mug of steaming coffee. 'Weed? Again?'

Nikki sighed. Anika took a pragmatic approach to her son's weed consumption. Personally, Nikki would rather he didn't smoke the stuff, but then she knew how many alternatives there were out there, so she let it pass. She could tell her sister the truth, but what purpose would that serve? Anika would wail and moan and threaten to ground him and Haqib would do what he always did and ignore her.

She'd deal with it and they'd move on with her keeping a closer eye on the little turd. 'Yeah, summat like that.' She shrugged. 'Deano's back … and Franco. Don't worry, I'll sort it though.'

Anika nodded and went back to the fry-up she was cooking. 'He's trouble, that lad, but I've heard Franco's worse. Sort it before it gets out of hand – like last time.'

Nikki munched the remains of the toast she'd started on her way in. She enjoyed spending time in her sister's kitchen. It was homely. Filled with clutter and love. Kids' schoolbags by the back door, shoes kicked off in a huddle next to them, well-tended plants on the windowsill, a series of sentimental 'There's No Place Like Home' plaques and cutesy pictures of cats. Her own kids were always telling her to get some plants and put some pictures on the walls. Truth was, Nikki was as green-fingered as weed killer and the only plant that had been able to flourish in her home was the cactus Charlie had given her three Christmases ago. As for the sentimental crap? Well, that was *so* not Nikki. She liked things streamlined – no clutter. That way she knew if her space had been infiltrated. That way she felt safe and in control. As she watched her sister, something niggled at her. Something was different. When she realised what it was, she smiled but her heart sank. Why did Anika have to be so needy? 'You can't have it both ways, Anki.'

Anika frowned. 'What you on about?'

Taking a sip of coffee, Nikki pointed at her sister's head. 'You can't wear the hijab on one hand and fry bloody bacon and sausages on the other, now can you?'

Anika's face broke into a grin. She flung her head back, laughter bubbling out of her like warm fuzzies on a winter's day. 'Just as well I'm not wearing it on my hand then, innit?'

Covering her sigh with a smile, Nikki nursed her coffee, observing the warm flush across her sister's cheeks. Anika was happy ... for now. 'Take it *Yousaf's* back an all.'

'Aw don't be like that. I love him. Maybe he'll stay this time.'

Nikki wanted to shake her. Make her wise up. 'You know he'll never leave his Pakistani family. 'Specially now he's a "councillor".' Nikki made air quotes round the last word and crossed her eyes for effect, pleased that her silly actions seemed to have taken the sting out of her words when Anika laughed.

'He loves me and he loves Haqib.'

Nikki groaned and stuffed more toast into her mouth, chewed, swallowed and then spoke. 'Come on! When's the last time he bought Haqib owt – or you for that matter? Yousaf's a loser. You keep taking him back every time he turns up for a booty call and he'll get you up the duff again and leave you. The likes of us – working-class, dual heritage and Hindu to boot – are *not* good enough for well-off businessmen-cum-councillors and especially not for married ones. He won't leave her.'

Anika's eyes welled up and Nikki could have kicked herself. Maybe sometimes she should just learn to shut her big mouth.

She jumped to her feet and moved round to put her arms round her sister, hugging her tight. 'I'm sorry. I know I'm bitter and twisted, but I just don't want you getting hurt again.'

'Not everyone's like you know who, Nikki.'

Nikki sighed. Anika was right. Just because she'd had a bad experience didn't mean Anika would. But the truth was Yousaf just was not good enough for her sister. She only had to convince Anika of that fact. The sisters hugged until, smelling something beginning to burn, Nikki wheeled round, turned off the cooker and yelled through the house, 'Breakfast's ready.'

Haqib and Charlie appeared from the living room as Nikki knocked on the wall that adjoined her house and yelled. 'You two, Auntie Anika's got breakfast ready. Shift it.'

Faint yells of, 'I'm starving' and 'Hope it's a fry-up' filtered through the walls and within seconds, Nikita's younger two children, dressed in school uniforms, faces all rosy and clean, ran into the kitchen and plonked themselves down at the table, grabbing their cutlery and looking like they'd never been fed in their lives. As Nikki grabbed another slice of toast, she felt her phone vibrate in her pocket. Pulling it out, she saw it was a text from her boss, DCI Archie Hegley. She circled the table to drop kisses on each of the kids' heads in turn. 'Work. Gotta run. Be good and, Charlie, change into trousers. Your skirt's too damn short.'

Driving down Legram's Lane in her clapped-out Zafira, windscreen wipers going like the clappers, Nikki wondered if she had transferred her wellies from the pool car back to her own. She had a sinking feeling she hadn't. Every so often a drop of water landed on her head and Nikki cursed. She really needed to get a new car, but the kids seemed to have an endless stream of requests for stuff that was never free. The car would have to wait. A new drip splatted on her head, rolled down her forehead and landed on her nose. She wiped it off with her sleeve. Maybe after she'd done her Inspector's exam and got a promotion, she could treat herself to a car that didn't leak – or maybe she'd have to repair the leaky tap in the bathroom and the thermostat on the central heating and double-glaze the kitchen window before its old wooden frame rotted and released the pane.

After taking a right at Thornton Road, Nikki joined the trail of commuters. A few hundred yards and she could already see the telltale police vehicles and crime scene vans. She abruptly took advantage of a gap in the traffic and bounced her car onto the opposite kerb. Ignoring the hoots from cars travelling in the opposite direction, she got out and turned her collar up against the rain. Typical! Weeks without a suspicious death and then you choose the day when it's pissing down to reveal yourself. She jogged the last few hundred yards, hoping the crime scene tent would be up and she could get some shelter.

Dear Reader,

You are the most important people in this entire process because it is you who invests so much time into the characters and stories I dredge up from the darkest reaches of my mind. *Dark Memories*, although the third in the DS Nikki Parekh series, was always meant to be. I always knew that when I created Nikki I owed it to the readers to reveal some of her backstory and in *Dark Memories*, I do that.

Nikki is a special character to me. I saw many Nikki's during my time teaching in inner-city Bradford and that's why I wanted her to live in the inner city. I wanted Nikki to be strong but vulnerable – I hope you find her so.

In the writing of *Dark Memories* I found myself creating a character called Isaac. Isaac, for me, is the light in the darkness. I loved bringing him to life and making him part of Nikki's family. Isaac kept me grounded and offered me light relief when I was writing what turned out to be a very dark novel (maybe that was the Covid impact).

*Dark Memories* is all about families; from the dysfunctional ones to the blended ones to the work place ones and more. In this novel Nikki is forced to consider her past and how that impacts on her as a person and, as in each novel, Nikki evolves a little bit.

I hope you enjoy *Dark Memories* and joining Nikki on this leg of her journey. If you did, the best gift you could give me is to shout about Nikki and her team and family to anyone who'll listen, recommend her to your friends or leave a review – it needn't be a long one, but I read every one and would love to see your feedback.

Till the next Nikki adventure,
Stay safe and Best Wishes

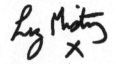

Dear Reader,

We hope you enjoyed reading this book. If you did, we'd be so appreciative if you left a review. It really helps us and the author to bring more books like this to you.

Here at HQ Digital we are dedicated to publishing fiction that will keep you turning the pages into the early hours. Don't want to miss a thing? To find out more about our books, promotions, discover exclusive content and enter competitions you can keep in touch in the following ways:

### JOIN OUR COMMUNITY:
Sign up to our new email newsletter: hyperurl.co/hqnewsletter
Read our new blog www.hqstories.co.uk
🐦 : https://twitter.com/HQStories
📘 : www.facebook.com/HQStories

### BUDDING WRITER?
We're also looking for authors to join the HQ Digital family!
Find out more here:
https://www.hqstories.co.uk/want-to-write-for-us/
Thanks for reading, from the HQ Digital team

ONE PLACE. MANY STORIES

If you enjoyed *Dark Memories*,
then why not try another gripping
thriller from HQ Digital?

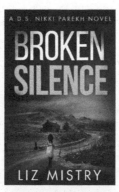

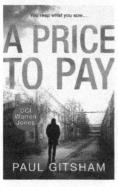